M000273726

PRIESTESS

of

PARACAS

BOOK 4

THE ANLON CULLY CHRONICLES

K. PATRICK DONOGHUE

Published by Leaping Leopard Enterprises, LLC

This book is a work of fiction. All the characters, incidents and dialogue are drawn from the author's imagination or are used fictitiously. Any resemblance to actual locations, events or persons, living or dead, is entirely coincidental.

PRIESTESS OF PARACAS
Copyright © 2019 Kevin Patrick Donoghue
All rights reserved.
eISBN: 978-0-9997614-8-9
Paperback ISBN: 978-0-9997614-7-2
Hardcover ISBN: 978-0-9997614-9-6

Published by Leaping Leopard Enterprises, LLC
www.leapingleopard.com

No part of this book may be reproduced or transmitted in any form or by any means, electronic or mechanical, including photocopying, recording or by any information storage and retrieval system, without prior permission in writing from the publisher.

First edition: December 2019

Cover art and design by Asha Hossain Design, LLC

Print edition interior design by Amber Colleran

DEDICATION

During the writing of Priestess of Paracas,
my extended family lost four loved ones.
In remembrance of the light and love
they shared with family and friends,
I dedicate this book to my sister-in-law Susan Patton,
my aunt Kathleen Woodland, my uncle Harry Donoghue
and my cousin Maureen Coulter.
May the stars light their way until we meet under the same sky.

CONTENTS

ACKNOWLEDGMENTS

I received a great deal of support in crafting *Priestess of Paracas*, and I would like to acknowledge the special people who helped me.

To developmental editors Dustin Portia and Katherine Pickett, thank you for helping me refine the plot and improve the quality of the story. To my copyeditor, Annie Jenkinson of just-copyeditors.com, and my proofreader, Cheryl Hollenbeck, thank you for your thorough scrubbing of the draft manuscript under the pressure of a tight deadline.

I would also like to extend my thanks to the cadre of readers who reviewed the prerelease draft of *Priestess of Paracas*, including Paulette Jones, Jeff Baker, Lisa Weinberg, Tom Voss and Carol Voss. Your comments, suggestions and edits helped me further polish the story.

Speaking of polishing the story, a special note of thanks goes to my wife, Bryson Donoghue, who also reviewed the prerelease draft and provided me with invaluable feedback throughout the writing and editing process.

Next, I would like to recognize my designer, Asha Hossein, for her creative blending of images from the story into the book's cover art. Thanks also goes to designer Amber Colleran for creating a fresh layout of the print edition interior.

To cap off the acknowledgments, I would like to thank my web designers, James Lee and Kevin Maines, for continually improving my author website as I add more titles.

NOTES TO READERS

Greetings, friends, fans and new readers! Thank you in advance for choosing to read *Priestess of Paracas*, Book 4 in my archaeology-based mystery series, the Anlon Cully Chronicles.

Unlike the previous stories in the series, *Priestess of Paracas* is a stand-alone mystery, meaning it is not a continuation of the same storyline explored in the previous three books. It is an all new mystery. That said, the *Priestess of Paracas* storyline does draw upon events in the previous books in the series, but I have incorporated all the necessary background from Books 1-3 into the new story. Therefore, whether you have just finished reading Books 1-3, or you have not read them in a while, or you are new to the series, you will be able to fully enjoy the story told in *Priestess of Paracas*.

I have also tried to limit the use of Munuorian terms in *Priestess of Paracas*, as I realize it might be challenging to recall their meanings if you have not read Books 1-3 recently. For those Munuorian terms that do appear in the story, I have included an appendix with a glossary, complete with definitions and a pronunciation guide. I hope you will find it a helpful resource.

Separately, there are a couple of nuances to note about the timeline in *Priestess of Paracas*. First, for those of you who have read the other books in the series, *Priestess of Paracas* begins roughly a year after the climax events in Book 3, *Curse of the Painted Lady*.

Second, if you have read the books in my other series, a sci-fi thriller series called the Rorschach Explorer Missions, you know that Anlon, Pebbles and a few other characters from the Anlon Cully series make cameo appearances in the first two books of the Rorschach series, *Skywave* and *Magwave*. From a timeline perspective, *Priestess of Paracas* begins shortly after Anlon and Pebbles' cameo in *Skywave* and concludes before their appearances in *Magwave*.

As to the story itself, *Priestess of Paracas* is similar to the past books in the series in that it is an exploration of archaeological mysteries. It includes a mix of historical facts, real archaeological artifacts and perplexing ancient riddles that I have blended together with some speculative answers to the riddles and a fair bit of fantasy.

On the flipside, *Priestess of Paracas* is different from the other stories in the series in that it is also an exploration of psychological mysteries, specifically the crossroads linking brain injuries, memories, dreams and the supernatural. Much like the archaeology portion of the story, I have blended scientific facts and real psychological phenomena with fantasy and some additional speculation on my part.

I hope you enjoy these additional story elements, as well as the new character introduced in the story, Dr. Sanjay Varma.

PROLOGUE

Quick! Into the bushes. Into the bushes. Hurry! Don't look back. Keep running. Run! Run! They're right behind. I can hear them! Keep going. Get to the river. The river. Faster! Faster!

She slipped on slick mud and fell, her shoulders and hips banging against roots as she slid across the forest floor. Vines and branches raked across her bare arms and legs. Though she managed to stifle a cry of pain, she could not suppress the cracking of branches or the swish of fronds marking her trail.

Scrambling to her feet, she turned to look back. Through gaps of foliage, she could see light from their torches. They were closing in. She reached for the bag slung over her shoulder and rummaged inside. The contents were intact. Staring upward, she thanked the stars.

With a firm tug, she cinched the bag closed and took off running again. In the faint glow of moonlight penetrating the canopy of trees, it was impossible to avoid bumping and scraping bushes and saplings. She tripped again and fell face-down into a puddle. The bag, clutched tightly in her hand, bobbed on the puddle's surface.

Get up! Get up! Run!

Tunic torn away from her shoulder during the fall, she crawled out of the puddle. As she stumbled forward, mud slid down her forehead and covered her eyes. She dug the muck away and squinted. In the distance, she could see moonlight through the maze of tree trunks.

Yes! So close. Keep going!

The slash of blades cutting through the underbrush echoed all around her. Looking left and right as she raced for the river, she spied a second set of torches making their way along the riverbank.

Run! Run!

She never saw the broken branch that felled her. Tilted up like a spike, the sharp point of the branch gouged through her foot. This time, there was no hiding her agony. The earsplitting scream shook alive the wildlife hunkered down for the night. Birds and rodents scattered. Howling monkeys traded warnings from treetop to treetop.

Grasping at her foot, she felt a sharp piece of wood poking through and ripped it out. Another scream. With frantic sweeps of her arms, she felt around for the bag.

Where is it? Where is it!

The back of her hand swiped over the bag's furry surface.

Get up! Run!

She dragged her body up and limped on. Daggers of pain assaulted her with each step. There was no need to look behind now; she could hear their labored breaths and their torchlight illuminated the area around her. Eyes riveted ahead, she huffed and groaned her way through the final stand of trees and emerged at the riverbank.

An arrow whizzed by her face. Another thudded into her thigh. She twirled around and fell into the river. Under the water, she heard the sound of other bodies plunging into the river. The bag in her hand floated up. She tried to pull it down, but the buoyant animal skin fought its way to the surface. Hands grabbed at her shoulders and ankles.

No! No! Get away! Stop!

Another hand wrestled with her for the bag. With the last of her energy, she kicked with her feet and flailed her arms, yanking the bag away for a brief moment before letting it go into the current. As it was swept away, she heard more splashes in the black water around her. Hands grabbed at her from every direction, ripped away what was left of her clothes, and hauled her to the surface.

With her arms pinned behind her back and legs clamped together at the ankles, a powerful hand wrapped around her neck and shoved her face into the muddy bank. She writhed her body and head like a fish caught on a line.

She cried for mercy...the hand tightened...she gasped for air and squirmed...the hand buried her face deeper into mud...

Pebbles McCarver flashed awake, her face pressed into her pillow. Legs kicking and arms swinging, she fought to breathe in between muffled screams. "Stop! Stop! Let go!"

Drenched in sweat, she hopped up on her hands and knees. With head bent low, she drew in deep gulps of air, wheezing with each breath. As her respiration began to steady, she rolled over and collapsed on the jumbled mass of soaked sheets and pillows.

In a dark corner of the bedroom, Anlon Cully looked at the glowing numbers on the alarm clock and marked the time. For the twelfth night of the last fifteen, Pebbles' nightmare reached its peak at 4:46 a.m. As he moved toward the bed to comfort her, Anlon wondered whether the dream was another repeat or a new visage of terror.

CHAPTER 1

HOUSE CALL

The drive from Flagstaff to Sedona would have been enjoyable under most circumstances, but Anlon was too immersed in thought to pay attention to the stunning scenery around him...or the road. As he rounded yet another twisting mountain pass, he crossed the center line and almost clipped an oncoming car. After jerking the car back into his lane, Anlon turned to his passenger, Griffin Taylor. "Sorry. My bad."

"Eyes on the road, bro!"

Anlon returned his gaze out the front window and slammed on the brakes. A hundred yards ahead, a group of hikers dashed across the pavement. While Anlon stopped in plenty of time, the squeal of tires drew angry glares from the hikers as they scrambled down an embankment to reach the safety of a creek that ran beside the road.

Heart racing, Anlon took in a few deep breaths and waved an apology to the hikers. Just as he started to drive again, he heard the frantic beeping of a car horn. Looking up at the rearview mirror, he spied two cars bearing down upon him at high speed. "Oh crap!"

Anlon floored the gas pedal and the car lurched forward. Behind him, he heard the two cars come to screeching halts. As Anlon fought to keep the car in his lane, Griffin said, "Bro, you may be a world-class scientist and all, but you suck at driving. Pull over on the shoulder and let me take it the rest of the way."

"What shoulder?" Anlon said.

To his right, the base of a towering red mountain hugged the road. On the other side of the two-lane road were the embankment and creek.

"See that patch of gravel up ahead?"

"I see gravel, but it ain't no patch."

"Start signaling. Slow down and pull over on it."

"Griffin, there's no way this car can fit on that."

"It'll fit. Just get over and let these buttheads go by."

Griffin's comment was directed at the two cars lustily honking as they once again motored up from behind. Anlon followed Griffin's instructions and gingerly pulled onto the sliver of a shoulder beside the mountain. As the cars raced by, the occupants shouted obscenities and flashed middle-finger salutes. Once they disappeared around the next bend, Anlon turned to Griffin. "Friendly people around here."

"Probably locals fed up with tourists. They're always doing stupid shit like those yahoos back there who ran across the road to get to the creek," Griffin said. "Now get in the back. I'll take it from here."

"The back? How?" Anlon pointed out the driver-side window. "If another car comes along, it'll slice the door off and take me with it."

"Just climb between the seats and I'll scoot over once you're through. Don't worry about kicking me. I'll survive."

"You're joking."

"Look, you want to help Pebbles, right?"

"Yeah."

"Well, to do that, we have to stay alive long enough to get her help. Now back you go."

After a grunt-filled minute of contortions, Anlon settled in the back seat. Griffin then clambered over the center console, took the wheel and they resumed their journey. For the first several miles, there was no conversation until Anlon broke the ice. "I don't suck at driving, by the way."

He saw Griffin look at him via the rearview mirror. "You do when your mind's somewhere else. What were you all zoned out about, anyway? I know you're big-time worried about Pebbles — we all are — but you were gone, man. In another universe."

Anlon stared out the side window at the rocky basin of Oak Creek. "I was thinking about how to start the conversation with Sanjay. Honestly, I don't know where to begin."

"Well, relax. I already gave him a sneak preview. Didn't faze him at all. You gotta remember, Sanjay's into a lot of mystical shit."

"Not like this, he isn't," mumbled Anlon.

As they continued down the road, Anlon imagined how Griffin's conversation with Sanjay must have gone. On one end of the dialogue, Griffin, the lead-guitarist for the 1990s-era heavy metal band Ice Zombies, and on the other end, Dr. Sanjay Varma, psychologist and existential guru. In Anlon's vision, the two men sat around a campfire, trading a doobie back and forth while staring at the flames.

Griffin: "Gotta favor to ask of you, bro."

Sanjay: "Hit me with it, man. What kind of favor?"

Griffin: "I got this friend who's been having some trippy dreams. They're really messing her up."

Sanjay: "Yeah? Like what kind of dreams, man?"

Griffin: "Strange shit. People chasing her and stuff. People trying to catch her, take shit from her. Kill her. You know, boogeyman kind of shit."

Sanjay: "Sounds like she's high, man. She on something?"

Griffin: "Nah, it's not like that. She's not a junkie. Some serious shit happened to her, and she can't get it out of her head."

Sanjay: "Yeah? What kind of shit are we talking about?"

Griffin: "Dude, some freaky bitch sucked my friend's mind out of her body and zapped it into a stone."

Sanjay: "No way. You're shitting me."

Griffin: "Nah, bro. For real."

Sanjay: "Her mind is in a stone?"

Griffin: "Nah, it's out now. Some other dude zapped it back into her body. But ever since, she's been flipping out. Weird dreams and shit. What do you say, man? Can you help her?"

Sanjay: "Sure, bro. Anything for you."

It was an unfair characterization, Anlon realized. While he was sure Griffin partook of mind-altering substances on occasion, he was not a stoner. In fact, the goateed, gray-haired rocker was a health nut.

Anlon's portrayal of Sanjay was also unjustified. While it was true Sanjay had de-emphasized his traditional psychology practice to study the mystical attributes of the human mind, and while it was widely known his explorations involved dabbling with hallucinogenic drugs, Anlon knew Sanjay was also a highly respected psychologist — a psychologist who specialized in helping people who suffered from the aftereffects of traumatic events.

A comment from Griffin roused Anlon from his thoughts. "Uh oh. Take a deep breath. This is going to be a grind."

Looking up, Anlon saw a long line of stopped vehicles ahead. The cause of the gridlock, Griffin explained, was a combination of clogged roundabouts and pedestrian crosswalks in Sedona's art district. By the time they cleared the last of the roundabouts, Anlon realized they had spent nearly as much time crawling through the art district as they had during the twenty-five-mile drive from Flagstaff to reach Sedona.

Free of traffic, they headed south, passing the iconic Cathedral Rock and Bell Rock on their way to the town of Oak Creek…where they ran into another glut of backed-up roundabouts. But traffic around these moved more quickly and soon they were headed down a side road that led to Sanjay's home. A few miles in, they passed the last neighborhood and the asphalt surface of the street gave way to a rutted dirt road with scrubland on both sides. A few miles after that, they finally arrived at their intended destination…almost.

Though Griffin had been to Sanjay's home before, it had been several years since his last visit. Therefore, he completely missed the hidden entrance to Sanjay's driveway and they dead-ended in the parking area of a hiking trailhead. Chagrined by his error and tired of driving, Griffin suggested they park and walk back to the secluded home. Anlon readily agreed.

He grabbed his backpack from the trunk and followed Griffin. The rocker seemed completely in his element to Anlon. With his flip-flops left behind in the car, Griffin padded along the dirt road in bare feet. In his sleeveless T-shirt and cut-off jeans, he looked like a hippie in search of a music festival.

Anlon was in the midst of examining his own attire — golf shirt, jeans and hiking boots — when he heard the sound of windchimes and caught the aroma of incense. At the same time, Griffin announced, "There it is. There's the driveway."

Turning to follow the direction of Griffin's pointing finger, Anlon finally caught a glimpse of what appeared to be a one-level, adobe-style ranch house hidden behind shrubs and the leaves of several gangly-looking trees.

He could also see a floppy-eared bulldog galloping toward him, its drool-flinging tongue slapping the air as it ran. Anlon halted in place, bent his knees and braced for impact. The dog never barked or growled as it launched itself at him. Raising up on its hind legs, its front paws collided with Anlon's thighs, streaking his jeans with the reddish dust of the road. The blow from the beefy dog staggered Anlon. "Whoa there, champ. I give up. You win."

He extended his hand and the dog's tongue completely coated it with goo in a matter of seconds. It then turned its attention to Griffin, hopping up and down as if greeting a long-lost friend. As Griffin petted the dog's wrinkled head, Anlon heard a voice call to the dog. "Come, Happy. Show our guests the way before you drown them in slobber."

Anlon spied Dr. Sanjay Varma standing beneath a pergola attached to the far side of the ranch house. Dressed in an untucked, white, short-sleeved dress shirt and khaki shorts, the barefooted psychologist waved. As Anlon waved back, the dog ran circles around Griffin before it turned and took off in the direction of the house.

On the way, the dog stopped every ten feet or so to exhort Anlon and Griffin to pick up their pace. When they finally arrived at the pergola, Sanjay nodded with his palms pressed together, fingers touching just below his chin. "Namaste."

Anlon followed Griffin's lead and returned the greeting. Then Griffin and Sanjay shared a hearty hug that seemed to Anlon more befitting of friends than therapist and former patient. But Anlon guessed that was to be expected given how long Griffin said Sanjay had treated him for post-traumatic stress. The impetus, Griffin had shared with Anlon, was a rock concert stampede early in the Ice Zombies' rise to fame. Several teens had been trampled to death near the stage and Griffin had tended to one of the dying victims. He said the memories of the stampede and dying teen-ager had haunted him for many years.

When the two broke from the embrace, Sanjay reached for a towel on the patio table beside him and presented it to Anlon. "Sorry about your hand. Happy gets excited when we have visitors."

"Not a problem. After all, what's a little saliva between friends?" Anlon smiled at Happy as he wiped his hand. With its tongue hanging out, the dog panted and wagged its stub of a tail.

With the cleansing completed, Sanjay led them to patio chairs overlooking a valley of desert scrubland ringed by Sedona's red mountains in the distance. As he invited them to sit, Sanjay asked, "Where is your car?"

"Up the road at the trailhead." As Anlon spoke, Happy sniffed the backpack he'd placed on an unoccupied chair next to him.

"It's my fault," said Griffin. "It's been a while since I've been out here. I forgot about the creek bed and we ended up missing the driveway."

"No worries. Everyone misses it," Sanjay said with a smile. "I'm just glad you found your way back."

For the next ten minutes, Sanjay and Griffin updated each other on developments in their lives while Anlon sat quietly and listened to their conversation. He was pleased to discover Sanjay was enthusiastic about Griffin's relationship with Jennifer Stevens, a close friend of Anlon's, and even more pleased to see Griffin light up when he talked about her.

The dialogue also gave Anlon a chance to study Sanjay. He appeared to be in his late forties, a little older than Anlon, but a bit younger than Griffin. With thinning black hair and spectacles, Sanjay looked more like a research scientist than he did a mystic. Anlon felt the urge to blurt out, "Where are your beads, man? And the tie-dyed robe?" but he managed to contain himself.

When Griffin and Sanjay finished their respective recaps, Sanjay then turned his attention to Anlon. "Thank you for indulging us while we caught up, Dr. Cully."

"No problem. I enjoyed listening to you get reacquainted. And, please, if you would, I'm not much on formality. Anlon is just fine."

"Very well, Anlon. First name basis it is."

"Deal."

"Excellent. Now, before we get into the heart of our conversation, can I interest either of you in some refreshments?" Sanjay asked.

"Hell, yeah, I'm starving," Griffin said. After Sanjay disappeared through the patio door leading into the house, Griffin leaned toward Anlon. "Dude makes these amazing little curried chicken sandwiches."

A short while later, Sanjay emerged from the house carrying a pitcher of fresh-brewed iced tea and a tray laden with finger sandwiches. Griffin relieved him of the sandwich tray and scooped up four sandwiches before passing the tray on to Anlon. While the three men snacked, Sanjay said, "So, Griffin told me you are living on a boat?"

"Boat? Nah, man. I said it's a freakin' superyacht," said Griffin. "Over a hundred foot long, four levels, crew of nine. It's a mansion on the water."

"My apologies," Sanjay said, bowing to Anlon. "Griffin tells me you are living on a mansion on the water these days."

"Yeah, I guess it is a little over the top. It's unusual for me. I don't like to flash my wealth, I'm pretty much a jeans-and-sweatshirt kind of guy. But we'd planned to take a trip around the world, and I worried something smaller wouldn't fare well in open ocean."

"*Had* planned? You have cancelled your trip?" Sanjay asked.

"It's been put on hold for the time being. The situation with Pebbles kinda threw a monkey wrench into the whole around-the-world thing."

"Ah, I see," Sanjay said. "I am curious. Where did the idea originate? Living on a boat, that is."

Anlon finished sipping iced tea and placed his glass on the patio table. "It's hard to fully answer that without discussing Pebbles and what she's been going through, but the short version is we thought a change of scenery — shaking our routine up, getting away from it all — would help with her nightmares. But it didn't. If anything, it made the situation worse."

"Hmm…I am sorry to hear that, Anlon. In theory, the idea was a good one," Sanjay said. "A change in environment can often disrupt a cycle of nightmares."

"Yeah, that's what we both thought, what we hoped for. But it kinda backfired. Before we even got out of the dock in San Diego, she started having random daymares in addition to the nightmares. You'd probably call them flashbacks, but I call them hallucinations."

Anlon watched Sanjay sit back and stare at the smoke swirling up from the incense pot. After a short stretch, Sanjay said, "Many people confuse the two. To the untrained eye, a flashback can look like a hallucination. The person experiencing the flashback is literally acting out, reliving, an event from the past. To the person watching, it appears as if they are seeing someone tripping out."

"I understand the distinction between the two, Sanjay, but, in this case, the line between flashback and hallucination is so thin, it's hard to know which side of the line Pebbles is on from one moment to the next."

"Why do you suppose that is?"

"Because it's hard to fathom what's going on in her mind," Anlon said. "You have to understand, Sanjay. I respect the hell out of this woman. Everything about her. She's smart as a whip and tougher than nails. She's genuine, grounded. And she usually has good instincts. Really good instincts. But I can't help feeling she's wrong about what's going on. And I'm worried she's going to hurt herself — or worse — if she is wrong."

There. I said it. That's what's really bothering me...why I can't figure out where to begin. I'm worried she's going to off herself, intentionally or in some hallucinogenic fit. Her freaking brain was damaged. She's not in her right mind. It's affecting her judgment. Why can't she see it?

"You love her," Sanjay said.

"I do."

"I am sure it has been difficult to see her going through the nightmares Griffin described to me. Her struggles must be weighing on you too."

"I'd be lying if I said they weren't."

Sanjay nodded as he lit a new stick of incense and slid it into the vase at the center of the table. "I understand. You want to see an end to her suffering. Just like her, you want the bad dreams to stop."

"That I do. She's been through a lot."

"Yes, from what I read online about her kidnapping, she certainly has," said Sanjay. He leaned over and petted Happy on the head. "I understand from Griffin that Pebbles is reluctant to consult a therapist."

"That's right. There are some...unusual aspects about what happened to her that make it hard for her to talk about. She doesn't think any therapist will take her seriously."

Sanjay locked his gaze on Anlon's eyes. "You agree with her."

Anlon sighed. "Yes, and no. Yes, in the sense I understand why she feels that way. No, in the sense I want to believe there are therapists with open enough minds to take her seriously. Griffin seemed to think you might be such a therapist."

"Well, it is certainly true that I am more open-minded than most. I find the human mind a never-ending source of mystery and I enjoy delving into those mysteries."

"Then I'd say Griffin led me to the right man."

"We shall see." Sanjay rose from his chair. "Let us go for a walk and continue our discussion."

With Happy tagging along, Sanjay led Anlon and Griffin back onto the dirt road. As they walked toward the trailhead where Anlon's rental car was parked, Sanjay said, "Anlon, I think it is important to start by saying that I cannot directly assist Pebbles without her consent. We can talk about her situation in general terms and I am happy to answer your questions as best I can, but you should not consider my answers diagnostic or therapeutic. She is not my patient, and I am not her therapist. Do we understand each other?"

"Yes, of course."

"Good. Now, if, after we have talked, it seems like I might be of direct assistance to Pebbles, and you would like me to meet with her to discuss a possible consultation, I am open to do so."

"Okay, got it. Appreciate you keeping the door open."

"Now that we have that out of the way, let us first talk about the traumas Pebbles experienced. From the articles I read online, she was kidnapped from your home and assaulted, the latter resulting in a coma. Is that correct?"

"There was a lot more to her ordeal than that, but, yeah, that's the gist of what happened."

"And from what Griffin shared, when she awoke from the coma, she reported having an out-of-body experience."

Anlon turned and stared at Griffin. "An out-of-body experience? That's how you described it to him?"

Griffin shrugged. "It seemed like a good way to describe what went down. I figured you could do a better job of describing the nitty gritty than I could."

"Am I to take it she did not have an out-of-body experience?" Sanjay asked.

With his eyes still latched on Griffin, Anlon said, "Oh, she had an out-of-body experience all right. Just not the kind you're thinking of. She didn't see a bright light at the end of a tunnel. She didn't float up and see herself. She didn't enter the Pearly Gates."

"Okay, then what happened?"

Here we go. He's gonna freak. Or laugh. Or both.

"You said you had an open mind, right?"

"Yes."

"Like, a little open or a lot open?"

Sanjay stopped walking and turned toward Anlon, bringing the full hiking party to a halt just shy of the trailhead. As Happy circled Anlon's boots, Sanjay said, "You have nothing to fear, Anlon. I am not here to judge, only to learn."

"Okay, Sanjay, I'll take you at your word." Anlon tightened the straps of his backpack, nudging it higher toward his shoulders. He then took a deep breath and said, "If you've read articles about her kidnapping, you know Pebbles was strangled to the point of unconsciousness. What you don't know, what the articles don't mention, is that the woman who strangled Pebbles then transferred her mind from her brain into a stone tablet. Thankfully, with some help, we were able to find the stone and transfer her mind back into her brain."

Sanjay's expression did not change. He did not blink. He did not twitch. Anlon was not even sure he drew in a breath. He just stared at Anlon for a moment and then turned his gaze to take in the vista of the valley. After a short spell, Sanjay resurfaced from his thoughts and scratched at his thinning crop of black hair. "Well, that's a first."

Griffin interceded. "Look, Sanjay, I get it. It's a hard story to believe. But I know Anlon well enough to know he's on the up and up. And if you meet Pebbles, you'll see she is too. What Anlon just told you *did* happen. Now, I wasn't there when it went down, but I've seen these stones. He's not bullshitting you."

"I don't doubt your sincerity, Griffin. It's just—"

Anlon interjected to finish Sanjay's sentence. "It's just that it isn't possible, extracting someone's mind and downloading it into a stone."

"I would have chosen different words, but it does come across as, um, fantastical."

Griffin leaned toward Sanjay. "If you think that's fantastical, wait until he fills you in about the ten-thousand-year-old woman who strangled Pebbles. Or the ten-thousand-year-old dude who put her mind back in her body."

As Anlon slid off his backpack, he saw a deep frown form on Sanjay's face. Meanwhile, Griffin fought to keep Sanjay from tuning out.

"Oh, come on, Sanjay. You've heard crazier shit than this...and *believed* it. I know you have. Like the dude you told me about who would get high on LSD and enter a fourth dimension. Or that hippie from Nevada you said can read people's minds. Hell, you've even shared your Pearl Harbor story with me. Your 'past life' experience. If you can believe all that mumbo jumbo, you shouldn't have any trouble believing Anlon."

"I did not say I did not believe him, Griffin. I said it was fantastical. There is a difference."

Anlon opened his bag and pulled out a squarish black stone. It was about the size of a dinner plate and etched on both sides. Handing the stone to Sanjay, he smiled. "From one PhD to another, nothing makes a scientist happier than proof. Am I right?"

"Proof of what?"

Withdrawing another stone from the bag, this one grayish and shaped like a hockey puck, Anlon scanned the area near the trailhead. "We need you to lie down for this. What's your preference? We could try the backseat of my car over there or find a nice smooth rock. Or we could head back to your house."

"I do not understand. Lie down for what purpose?"

"Uh...a demonstration."

Griffin nudged Sanjay in the ribs. "You're gonna dig this, bro. I shit you not."

CHAPTER 2

IN THE DARK

ABOARD THE SUPERYACHT *SOL SEAKER*
KONA KAI MARINA, SAN DIEGO, CALIFORNIA
SEPTEMBER 18

The match ignited with one stroke. Jennifer Stevens cupped her hand around the flickering flame and guided it to the candle. As she held it near the wax-encased wick, her eyes danced between the wick and the fire moving up the matchstick toward her fingers. Behind her, she heard Pebbles McCarver huffing. "Would you *please* hurry up? I can't hold this position much longer."

Just as the flame licked at Jennifer's fingertips, the wick caught fire. She whisked the charred match away and blew it out. "Chill out. The whole purpose of yoga is to relax you."

"How can I relax like this? I'm straining every muscle just to stop from keeling over."

Jennifer turned and spied Pebbles' half-hearted attempt to maintain the downward-dog pose. Clad in a tank top and yoga pants, Pebbles was bent over in the shape of an upside-down V with her hands pressing against the floor on one end of the V and her feet gripping the floor on the other. As Pebbles' arms and legs wobbled, Jennifer said, "Get your butt in the air. Higher. Higher."

"I'm trying, I'm trying," Pebbles grumbled. "Who does yoga on a boat anyway? It's hard enough balancing on land."

Jennifer knelt down on a mat beside Pebbles. Before assuming the same pose, she slapped Pebbles on the butt. "Higher."

"Hey!"

"Shh…close your eyes and breathe. Listen to the seagulls and breathe. Relax your neck."

"This is too hard. Can't we start with something easier?"

"You'll loosen up, just be patient. Once your body heats up and stretches out a little, you'll feel better."

"If I live that long. My hamstrings are killing me."

"Try this," Jennifer said. She lifted her foot off the floor and pulled her knee up under the arch of the upside-down V. Then she slowly straightened out the leg as she pressed it backward in the air before returning it to the ground. With the movement completed, she repeated the motion with the other leg. "Come on, try it. It feels good."

"It'll only feel good if I get to kick you on the way back."

Before Jennifer responded, she heard the sound of Pebbles crumpling to the floor and turned to see her friend lying on her back and staring at the ceiling. "That's it. I'm done."

"Hey! Hold on there," Jennifer said. "We just started!"

"No. *You* just started. *I'm* heading to the galley for a smoothie." The barefoot Pebbles slapped Jennifer on the rear as she walked toward the cabin door. "Have fun twisting yourself into a pretzel. Scream if you need a rescue."

Pebbles emerged from the portside gym cabin and into the center hallway of *Sol Seaker's* lower deck. A short walk later, she hustled up the spiral steps amidships and arrived on the main deck. A quick saunter aft brought her to the galley on the yacht's starboard side. Before pushing through the swinging door, she peered through its porthole and spotted chief stewardess Cindy Tanner restocking provisions in the refrigerator. With a fist pump, Pebbles whispered, "Yes!"

Not only was Cindy the best margarita-concocter on board, she was also *numero uno* when it came to smoothies…better even than the former bartender, Pebbles. She pushed through the door and greeted Cindy. "Hey! Good morning there, matey."

Decked out in white from her freshly pressed, button-down shirt to her pleated shorts and squeaky-clean sneakers, the dirty-blond, deep-tanned Cindy turned from the refrigerator and smiled at Pebbles. "Good morning, Miss McCarver. Is it smoothie time?"

"You know it, but I can whip one up myself if you're busy."

Tanner closed the refrigerator and pushed the box of supplies back on the counter. "It's no trouble at all. What'll it be today? Strawberry-banana or something new? We have fresh passion fruit."

"Ooh, passion fruit. That sounds good. How about mixing it with strawberry?"

"Very well. Where should I serve you?"

"Nah, don't worry about that. I'll just hang out here 'til it's ready."

"As you wish, miss."

Pebbles found it awkward to converse with the formal Cindy, but no matter how many times she begged the stewardess to call her Pebbles instead of Miss McCarver or engage with her in casual banter, Cindy maintained a distant, professional air about her. In fact, all of *Sol Seaker*'s crew interacted with Pebbles with the same formality.

It was her least favorite aspect of living on Anlon's superyacht. Pebbles would have preferred to live on a ship full of pirates, people she could call swabbies who would in turn call her a sea dog as they guzzled rum and swapped stories about their respective tattoos. A crew with whom she could sing ditties in between trading tales of hidden treasures and visiting far-off lands.

But Anlon's selection of the über-disciplined Isak Hansen as ship's captain squelched any possibility of rubbing elbows with the crew. The Norwegian skipper was as buttoned-down as they came. And while it meant *Sol Seaker* operated with incredible efficiency, it also meant living amid an aristocratic, upstairs-downstairs kind of vibe. Not exactly Pebbles' style. Nor Anlon's.

As she stood silently watching Cindy cut up fruit, Pebbles recalled discussing her misgivings with Anlon during their first journey, a few-days jaunt around the islands near San Diego. It was intended as a "shakeout" trip in which Hansen tested out the ship's systems and trained the crew.

"It's like living in a museum. Every time I turn around, someone's cleaning up after me or bowing. It's uncomfortable," Pebbles had said.

"Look, I know it's not what we're used to, how we normally live, but give it some time. I think the crew will loosen up a bit and we'll get more used to being around each other."

"I don't think I'll ever get used to this."

"I hear you, but let's give it a try for a while. If you feel the same way in a month, we can tell Hansen to lighten up a bit. But I think we ought to give him time to establish his way of doing things with the crew."

Anlon had then explained Hansen's logic in maintaining the formal atmosphere. They would be at sea for the better part of a year, save for periodic stops at various ports of call as they traversed the planet's oceans. The former cruise ship captain knew from experience that discipline had a tendency to wane during long voyages, which he viewed as undesirable when confronting difficult sea conditions or issues with the ship when far from assistance.

"I get all that," Pebbles had said. "But would it kill them to loosen the top button on their collars? Or fist bump instead of bow? Maybe sit down and hang out every now and then?"

Anlon had responded by reminding her that Hansen had a zero fraternization policy. "He said fraternization leads to intrigue, and intrigue leads to trouble."

With that last thought percolating in her mind, Pebbles watched Cindy drizzle honey into the blender atop the awaiting fruit and yogurt. Seconds later, the machine whirred until the red, white and gold mixture turned orangish-pink.

"Looks yummy," Pebbles said above the blender's whine.

Cindy smiled and retrieved a chilled Pilsner glass from the freezer. She stopped the blender on two occasions to test the drink's consistency by lightly stirring a spoon in the smoothie. When satisfied with the blend, Cindy poured the contents into the glass, wedged a strawberry onto the Pilsner's lip and retrieved a straw from a cabinet.

As Cindy put the finishing touches on the drink, Pebbles gazed at the stewardess and wondered what the woman thought of her. Did she get that Pebbles was in a committed relationship with Anlon? Or did she look at Pebbles' purple fade-cut hair, tattoos and plethora of facial piercings and figure she was nothing more than Anlon's young plaything? Did

Cindy know Pebbles was a former attorney? Or that she ran a foundation to preserve archaeological relics? *Probably not,* thought Pebbles. *After all the trouble I've caused the last few nights, she probably thinks I'm just a junkie or a whack-job who might flip out at any moment.*

Cindy bowed and presented the smoothie atop a folded linen napkin. Pebbles thanked her and took a sip. "Mmm…perfect as always."

With hands clasped behind her back, Cindy bowed again. "Thank you, Miss McCarver. Can I get you anything else? A breakfast bar, perhaps?"

"Nah, I'm good, but thanks." Pebbles raised her hand to coax a high-five from the thirty-year-old stewardess, a woman only a year older than Pebbles. "Up high!"

The request obviously caused conflict within Cindy, for Pebbles saw her eyes twitch and her arms flinch as she debated an appropriate response.

"Come on," Pebbles urged, "don't leave me hangin'."

With her eyes looking away from Pebbles, Cindy snuck her arm from behind her back and held up an open palm. A big smile formed on Pebbles' face as she slapped Tanner's hand. "Yeah…that's what I'm talkin' 'bout."

Small victory achieved, Pebbles turned and left the galley with her pilsner raised like a trophy.

Cindy had barely finished cleaning out the blender when she heard the sound of breaking glass followed by a heavy thud. She tossed aside a dish towel and took off for the galley door. Under her breath, she mumbled, "Jesus, what now?"

Pushing into the center hallway, she looked around. Directly aft of the galley was the ship's dining room. She took a few steps into the room and looked around. Seeing nothing out of place, she returned to the hallway and gazed in the direction of the central spiral staircase. Pebbles often enjoyed drinking her smoothie while lounging on the upper deck's aft patio. Had she fallen on her way up? As Cindy started for the staircase, she heard the thumping of running feet above and the sound of someone growling. Cindy dashed up the stairs, whispering, "Shit! Shit! Shit!"

Cresting into the upper deck's cabin, Cindy looked forward toward the ship's bridge, then aft. Through the cabin's bar and lounge area, she spied two deckhands on the patio outside. They were kneeling next to Pebbles. She was on all fours, head lowered.

Clipped to Cindy's belt was a walkie talkie. She yanked it loose as she ran toward the patio. "Brody, come in."

"Yeah, Cindy, I'm here. Whatcha need?"

"Find Miss Stevens. I think she's in the gym. Miss McCarver's having an attack on the upper deck patio."

"Okay. On it."

Cindy pushed open the cabin door and told the two deckhands to back away from Pebbles. "Just make sure she doesn't try to jump again."

The memory of the incident two nights ago flashed through Cindy's mind. Pebbles had awakened everybody aboard with bloodcurdling screams. Before Cindy had made it out of her cabin to investigate, she heard one of the other crew shout, "Guest overboard." It took three of the crew to haul Pebbles back aboard. All the while, Pebbles kicked and screamed at them, waking up boaters on other yachts anchored in the marina. Cindy had wanted to slap Pebbles after they finally settled her down. That urge rose again as she watched her crawl around the patio.

The two deckhands took positions on the starboard and port sides of the patio where teak walkways ran along the outside of the deck's cabin. Cindy tiptoed around the chanting, growling Pebbles and crouched down in front of the sectional sofa that abutted the aft railing of the patio.

Her eyes vacant, her face contorted into a panicked sneer, Pebbles came within inches of broken glass from the smoothie Pilsner. Cindy reached behind for a cushion from the patio sofa. Tucking it under one arm, she ducked low to avoid getting clocked in the head by Pebbles' flailing arms. As she crawled toward Pebbles, Cindy tossed the cushion over the broken glass and the spilled smoothie. Just then, Cindy saw Pebbles' shadow move. She looked up to see the ranting woman dashing for the aft railing with one arm aloft.

Out of the corner of her eye, she caught a blur of motion and then Jennifer came into Cindy's view. Jennifer tackled Pebbles on the sofa and wrapped the writhing woman in her arms.

Under a crescent moon, the woman crouched down and listened. Up this high, the wind masked most sounds but not the tumbling of rocks down the steep slope.

There. There it is again! They have slowed down. Good. Good.

She quietly turned around on the narrow path and felt around for loose stones. When she found ones of manageable size, she slowly stacked them in the center of the trail, careful to avoid dislodging any that might slip over the edge and start a chain reaction. Below, far down the mountain, she could see the lights of the village and the glint of the moon on the river, but she saw no signs of movement on the switchbacks. However, she did hear the echo of more rocks sliding down into the ravine. She smiled.

There are too many of them. They are too clumsy.

She finished stacking her booby trap and then resumed her trek up the maze of switchbacks. Looking up ahead, she spied the ridgeline silhouetted by the star-filled sky.

You must be quick. As soon as they see the glow, they will light their torches.

As she crept toward the summit, chilly gusts pummeled her bare legs. She bent down lower to cover the exposed limbs underneath her poncho but there was nothing she could do to protect her feet. If she lowered any closer to the ground, she risked the wind whipping the poncho's braided tassels against loose rocks. She gritted her teeth.

Just a little farther. Keep going.

Reaching the safety of a nook in the last outcrop, she slid off the pack slung over her back. First, she fished out a torch and unwrapped it from its wool sheath. After laying the torch on the stone floor of the nook, she stowed the wool back in the bag and pulled out two sharp rocks and a wad of spongy tree fungus. Before striking the rocks against each other, she took in several deep breaths.

You must be quick.

As she hovered over the torch with her finger pressing the fungus to one of the rocks, she hit the two stones together. The sound of the collision reverberated in the nook. She grimaced and struck them again. Sparks leapt out but not enough to light the fungus. In scraping blows, she hit the two rocks again and again. In between, she heard the shouts of her pursuers. She pleaded with the stones.

Light! Light! Hurry!

A small glow formed on the edge of the fungus, the pungent aroma of its smoke swirling in the nook. She dropped the stones and cradled her hand around the fungus as she guided it to the torch. When the torch caught fire, she tossed aside the spongy kindling, shoved her fire-starting stones in the bag and grabbed the torch.

Go! Go! Go!

Stumbling out of the nook, she held out the torch and gazed down. The wind buffeted the flame, but it remained lit. Several switchbacks below, she saw angry faces looking up at her. Some of them began to run while others desperately tried to light their own torches. She turned and scampered over the ridgeline, plunging her pursuers back into darkness. With the torchlight leading her way, she dashed down the first leg of the backside's series of switchbacks.

Run! Run faster!

Curling around a sharp bend, she stopped to look up. There were no signs of other torches or moving figures above. She did not look up again until the fourth turn in the switchback. Here there was a junction. One that veered off to the left and another that continued down the switchbacks to the right. Before sprinting down the trail to the left, she gazed up again. Still no sign of followers.

As she ran, she could see the end of the trail in the distance — the sheer face of the mountain…or so it would seem to those chasing her. Lungs burning, she raced onward until she neared the apparent dead-end. Within a few strides of the wall, the path ended, revealing a hidden gap of jagged stones that looked like a staircase that wound down into a canyon.

Panting heavily, she lowered the torch to the ground and descended the first few of the narrow steps while bracing her arms against the canyon wall. With only her head left above the path, she reached up and gathered the torch. Before continuing on, she swept the torch over the side of the stairs and stared down at the inky water below. Retraining the torch and her gaze on the stairs in front of her, she proceeded lower until she reached a thin ledge that sliced its way underneath the span of a wide overhang. At the far end overhang, she saw the ledge widen into more of a balcony. There, cut into the canyon wall, she saw the black holes leading into the caves.

Go! Go! Hurry! Get inside quick! Before they reach the stairs!

Leaning her back against the wall, she slid her feet along the ledge until she reached the balcony. She knelt down, tugged off her bag, retrieved the wool cloth and used it to extinguish the torch. In the instant darkness, bright splotches clouded her vision.

Get inside! Now!

Three steps into the cave, she felt a tug from behind and a hand covered her mouth.

Pebbles sat on the bed in the master bedroom cabin she shared with Anlon. A blanket was wrapped around her shoulders and across her curled knees. In the low light afforded by slivers of sun peeking through the cabin's wooden Venetian blinds, Pebbles jotted down more notes in her dream journal.

Seated at the foot of the bed, Jennifer watched her friend's furious scribbles. When Pebbles finished writing, she tossed the pen down and looked up at Jennifer. "How bad was it?"

Jennifer waved her head from side to side. "Not as bad as the last one."

"How's your nose?"

During Jennifer's struggle to hold onto Pebbles on the patio, Pebbles had worked an arm free and caught Jennifer in the nose with her elbow.

"I'll be fine. There's no break. It's just a little tender."

"Again, I'm super sorry."

Jennifer dismissively waved her hand. "I know. Just let it go. It's okay."

"I guess I just freaked when you put your hand over my mouth."

"Excuse me?" said Jennifer. "I didn't touch your mouth."

"Well, I know what I felt. Someone put their hand over my mouth," Pebbles paused then said, "Word to the wise — that pisses me off. I'd advise against *ever* doing that."

Jennifer nodded. "Duly noted." She pointed at the dream journal and asked, "Which dream was it this time?"

"The cave one."

"Any different than last time?"

Pebbles shrugged and then tightened the blanket around her shoulders. "A little. I'll have to go back and reread my notes from the last time it happened, but I'm pretty sure there were some new details this time."

"Like what?"

"Apparently, I know how to start fires with fungus and two rocks."

"Interesting." Jennifer smiled. "Let's try not doing that while we're on a boat with a lot of teakwood."

Pebbles laughed for a moment and then stretched out on the bed. "What is going on with me, Jen? I just don't understand why these dreams keep happening."

Jennifer crawled across the bed and lay down next to Pebbles. As both stared up at the beamed ceiling, Jennifer said, "I wish I knew."

"Am I going crazy?"

"No, definitely not. Don't say it, don't think it."

"It's hard not to think it," Pebbles said. She rolled over and faced Jennifer. "They're getting worse, happening more frequently. And there doesn't seem to be a rhyme or reason as to when they start or stop. I mean, one moment I'm sipping on a smoothie, minding my own business, enjoying the sunshine and then the next thing I know, I'm being held down like I'm having some kind of seizure."

Jennifer ran her fingers through Pebbles' hair. "It's gotta have something to do with what Muran did to you, don't you think?"

A tear trickled from Pebbles' eye, slid across her nose and dripped onto the bed. "I haven't been the same since."

Jennifer leaned her forehead against Pebbles' and smiled. "You're still the same mouthy, know-it-all jitterbug to me."

Pebbles smiled as another tear fell over the bridge of her nose, this one landing on Jennifer's cheek. She reached the blanket up and wiped the tear away and then poked her blanket-covered hand against Jennifer's shoulder. "I'm the know-it-all? What about you, yoga torture-master?"

They traded several more playful barbs before Pebbles' eyes closed and she nuzzled the blanket under her chin. Jennifer resumed stroking her friend's hair until Pebbles fell asleep. Then, as carefully and quietly as she could, she backed away and slid off the bed.

After rearranging the blanket to cover the sleeping Pebbles, Jennifer picked up the open journal and closed it around the pen Pebbles had used to record her memories of the latest dream. Retreating to an easy chair in the corner of the cabin, she edged the Venetian blinds a fraction of an inch wider to let in more sunlight and then cracked open the journal labeled *Vol. # 3 of ?*

CHAPTER 3

COLLECTED WISDOM

RESIDENCE OF DR. SANJAY VARMA
SEDONA, ARIZONA
SEPTEMBER 18

Sanjay opted to return to the house where they settled in his living room. Sanjay sat on a couch with Happy curled up next to him. Anlon and Griffin took seats on armchairs opposing the sofa. On the coffee table in between, Anlon placed the two stones he had pulled from his backpack earlier.

Anlon kicked off the conversation. "Well over ten thousand years ago, there was a race of people who called themselves Munuorians, pronounced *moon-war-E-uns*. They were seafarers and they were unique, physiologically-speaking, compared to other humans living at that time. They possessed an ability to detect and interact with the Earth's magnetic field, sort of a sixth sense just as palpable to them as our other senses are to us today. You following me so far?"

With a nod, Sanjay said, "Yes. I am with you."

"Okay, good. Now, over time, they learned to use that extra sense to build tools that allowed them to manipulate magnetism, kind of like how we've built tools that allow us to manipulate water and air. Windmills that help generate power, water wheels that help generate motion, those kinds of things. In the case of the Munuorians, the tools they built were made of stone...stones with unusual — and powerful — properties." Anlon hovered his hand over the table. "Like these, right here."

Anlon continued his description of the stones by telling Sanjay the Munuorians created the tools for a variety of purposes: to build, farm, heal, communicate, travel and defend themselves, among other applications. He told him the stones were forged into various shapes and sizes, but all had similar components — olivine basalt, kimberlite, diamonds and gold. Some of the tools, Anlon explained, could be used as stand-alone devices, but most applications required simultaneous use of at least two different stone types.

"The most remarkable of those tools allowed them to store important cultural memories." Anlon lifted the black stone. Sanjay studied the designs etched into its surface. "It was the Munuorians' way of solving an age-old problem: how does one ensure a civilization's collective knowledge and wisdom are preserved and passed from generation to generation without loss?

"Oral traditions become altered as they are passed from one person to another. Some details are left out while new ones are added, different words are used, meanings change and so on. Written traditions face different challenges but the same basic problem. Paper disintegrates, paint and ink fade, stone surfaces erode. Even in our modern world, photographs, audio recordings and videos degrade over time, regardless of the medium used to store the memories. It's impossible to escape the decay of time, or the impact of natural disasters—"

Griffin interrupted. "Or wars. Conquerors have wiped out plenty of monuments and libraries over time."

"Sad, but true," said Anlon. He lowered the black stone to his lap.

The Munuorians' solution to this problem, Anlon told Sanjay, was to create a memory storage device embedded inside a stone — an ancient flash drive the Munuorians called an *Aromaegh*. Only instead of storing bytes of data, *Aromaeghs* stored fully constituted human memories, including not just the factual recording of events or traditions, but the sensory elements of memories as well.

Sanjay had been content with Anlon's descriptions thus far, but this last statement caused him to bristle. "When you say sensory elements, what do you mean?"

"I mean sights, smells, sounds. Sensations of touch and taste. Emotions. Every component of a memory that we file away in our brains, they figured out how to extract and store on their memory stones."

Anlon must have noticed the frown forming on Sanjay's face because he immediately launched into an example. "Let's say you accessed one of their *Aromaeghs* that housed a tutorial on how to spearfish. You don't see an instruction manual, you know, words with illustrations. No, you experience a vision *way* beyond the most sophisticated virtual reality simulation you could find today. You're inside the memory of the student receiving the tutorial. You are standing in the surf. You can feel the cold of the water on your legs, the shifting sands move over your feet. You can feel the weight of the spear in your hand. You see the fish swimming beneath the surface of the water in full color. You hear the crash of waves on the beach, smell the salty air. An instructor stands beside you, speaks to you and guides you on how to use the spear. You feel yourself thrust it, the vibrations from the fish as it wriggles to escape. You sense the student's exhilaration as a result of his success.

"It's stunning how realistic it is. There's no ambiguity to the memory, no information lost in translation. And because it includes so many different memory cues, it sticks with you in a way that words or illustrations never could."

"It's true, Sanjay," Griffin said. "I've experienced the memory stones. They're wicked cool."

The two men spoke with such conviction in their voices, Sanjay found it hard not to believe them. Yet the entire notion of extracting human memories and implanting them in any kind of device, stone or otherwise, seemed impossible. But then again...

Whether by physical or sensory interactions, Sanjay had witnessed supposed "telepaths" communicate with other humans. And at its core, telepathy was the transfer of thoughts or ideas from one person to another. While Sanjay knew there was considerable scientific skepticism about telepathy, he also was aware of the growing body of research projects aimed at examining the possibilities of brain-to-brain communication. And some of those projects had proven rudimentary success in transferring thoughts between humans.

On the other hand, transferring a thought like "hello" or "move" is dramatically different than transferring a fully formed memory. The brain does not store all the components of a memory in one spot. No, the various sensory inputs of a memory are housed in different locations in the brain. It is a complex process that requires a gatekeeper-cataloger-retriever to capture the memory, break apart and code all the sensory inputs, send the coded inputs to their assigned storage locations, maintain a map where all the inputs are stored and then when called upon to retrieve the memory, summon and reassemble the various inputs back into a person's consciousness. In humans, this gatekeeper-cataloger-retriever is a structure in the brain called the *hippocampus*.

To accomplish what Anlon described about the memory stones, the Munuorians would have not only had to construct a storage device, but also a hippocampus-like controller. That seemed impossible to Sanjay and he said as much to Anlon.

"Memory is too complex for such a feat to be possible."

Anlon smiled and nodded. "I know. You're right. But as you'll see for yourself in a few minutes, the Munuorians did indeed accomplish that feat and a lot more. They also found a way to embed a human's consciousness along with their memories."

He held up the black stone once again. "This here stone is a special type of *Aromaegh* the Munuorians called a *Sinethal*. Unlike other *Aromaeghs*, it doesn't just house a tutorial. It houses a person's full memories *and* consciousness. By that I mean, you can interact with the mind of that person just as if he or she were sitting here talking with us. You can ask questions, and so can the mind of the person embedded in the stone. They can show you mental visions, you can share visions back. The Munuorians created *Sinethals* to store the minds of the most knowledgeable, the most revered, members of their society so that future generations could directly tap these venerable minds for wisdom and knowledge. This one houses the memories and consciousness of a woman named Malinyah. Her mind has been inside the stone for over ten thousand years."

The urge to laugh bubbled up within Sanjay. While he was able to suppress the sound, his mouth widened into a "yeah, right" smile — a smile that quickly faded as he exchanged looks with Griffin.

"I'm telling you, Sanjay, he's not bullshitting you," Griffin said. "I've met her. She asked me to play one of my songs for her. I'm like…what? She says…play a song. I'm like…I don't have my guitar, my instrument.

She's like…hold my hands and imagine playing a song. I'm like…okay. And bam…I'm sitting next to her under some big-ass tree with pink leaves playing "Under the Waterfall" from our *Frozen Dreams* album on my favorite acoustic guitar. Dude, I could feel wind on my face. I could hear the leaves of the trees flapping around. There were all these butterflies floating by. It was grade-A crazy shit."

Arms crossed, Sanjay said, "You cannot be serious."

"Actually," Anlon said. "Griffin had a bit of an unusual experience with Malinyah. He was able to understand her language, speak with her and vice versa. There are only two other people I know of who can do that, Pebbles being one of them. When most people visit with her, including me, there are a lot of hand gestures required in order to communicate. She's made an effort to learn some English and French, so you may be able to communicate basics, but I can't promise you that you'll understand what she says when she speaks to you."

Dumbfounded, Sanjay stared at the two men. His stupor was interrupted when Anlon said, "You don't have to believe us. Just lie back and see for yourself."

Lying on the sofa, Sanjay watched Anlon kneel on the floor next to him. The black tablet and gray hockey-puck-like stones were in his hands. Anlon placed the puck on the sofa cushion near Sanjay's hip and flipped over the black stone so Sanjay could see the three depressions cut into the back side.

Sanjay studied the depressions. Two were half-circles carved on the left and right sides of the stone. In the center was a circular cut. Anlon slid his fingers into the side-cuts and said, "These are fingerholds. You slide your fingers inside the cuts. When the visitation starts, you'll feel a tingling in your fingertips, somewhat like low-level static electricity. It won't hurt, but you'll definitely notice it."

He handed the stone to Sanjay, who edged his fingers into the slots as Anlon instructed. The surface of the stone was coarse, but Sanjay felt no other sensation. He looked at Anlon. "Am I holding it wrong? I do not feel any tingling."

"No, you won't. Not yet. First, we have to insert the key, so to speak." Anlon held up the puck-shaped stone. "The Munuorians call this stone a *Naetir*. For all intents, it's an ignition key. It activates the *Sinethal*. As soon as I insert the *Naetir* in the center cut on the back of the *Sinethal*, that's when your fingers will start tingling and, within a few seconds, you'll be in Malinyah's presence."

Sanjay looked over at Griffin. "Why do I feel like this is a prank of some sort?"

"It ain't no prank, bro. I wouldn't do that to you."

"Uh huh. Better not be." Turning his attention back to Anlon, Sanjay asked, "How long will this so-called 'visitation' last?"

Anlon shrugged. "Depends. If you freak out, it'll be real quick. Seconds. If you can keep your emotions in check, stay calm, it could last for hours if you and Malinyah wanted it to go on that long."

Sanjay shook his head from side to side while staring at the ceiling. "This is bizarre."

"Hey, it's no worse than tripping on peyote, and I know you've done your fair share of that!" Griffin said.

Before Sanjay could retort, Anlon said, "Now, I visited with Malinyah when I went to borrow her *Sinethal*. Told her—"

"Excuse me? What do you mean you *borrowed* her *Sinethal*?"

"Oh, uh, we'll talk about that later. Anyway, as I was saying, I visited with her and let her know she would be meeting with you. So, she's expecting you. And she knows why we've come to you. She knows what happened to Pebbles and she wants to help. Pebbles won't accept her help directly, so we'll—"

"Hold up. Why won't Pebbles accept her help?" Sanjay interjected.

"It's a long story. She's angry at Malinyah," Anlon said. "She feels Malinyah wasn't truthful about some things. Plus, she's not willing to get anywhere near any of the Munuorian stones after what happened to her. Brings up bad memories. She feels contact with the stones will only make her nightmares worse."

Confused by the cryptic explanation, Sanjay stared at Anlon. Meanwhile, Anlon edged the *Naetir* closer toward the *Sinethal.* "Just relax and close your eyes. You'll hear a loud slap when the *Naetir* locks into place."

The clap of the two stones bonding together sounded like a gun firing. Sanjay was so startled he nearly dropped the *Sinethal.* At first, he still felt nothing in his fingertips but the scratchy surface of fingerhold cutouts. But then, just as Anlon had indicated, he started to feel small shocks of electricity. Well, not really shocks, more like a sizzling sensation. They did not burn, but Sanjay could feel the vibrations of the electrical current begin to slowly snake up his forearms. Then, like a bolt of lightning, the vibration shot upward. He felt a prick inside his head, right between his eyes, and then the darkness behind his closed eyelids began to lighten.

The cloudy vista grew brighter and soon he could detect blob-like shapes swaying back and forth against the grayscale backdrop. Sanjay flinched when he heard the sound of rustling leaves. He tried to suppress the sensation, believing it to be nothing more than the power of suggestion from Griffin's earlier description.

But an avalanche of sensations followed and overwhelmed Sanjay's effort to fight off the sound of the leaves. Colors began to fill the splotches of gray. More sounds infiltrated his mind. Crashing waves, creaking branches and the strangest of all — a woman's voice humming the tune of the Ice Zombies' "Under the Waterfall". Aromas mixed with the other senses — the smell of saltwater, the fragrance of flowers and the earthy odor of moist soil. He felt wind upon his face that was strong enough to lift strands of hair. He could sense them tickling his forehead as they moved.

All the while, his vision continued to sharpen until there was a flash… and then he could sense everything in vivid detail. Ahead of him was a white-barked tree with massive roots that spread atop the red clay surrounding it. Its leaves — just as Griffin had described them — were pink, though as Sanjay stared at them, he noticed the undersides were a darker shade than the tops of the leaves. And perched on one of the roots was a tanned, blond woman in a sleeveless cream-colored tunic. Several butterflies rested on her bare shoulders. To Sanjay, it seemed as if they were listening to her hum. Beyond the tree was a cliff and beyond that was a tropical-blue ocean.

Out of the corner of his eye, he sensed movement. The woman on the root stood and ceased humming. She smiled, holding out both hands toward him. She spoke. "Sahndge-yay?"

Sanjay staggered backward, his heels depressing the soft clay. He looked down and saw the impressions of his bare feet in the soil. "This is impossible."

A butterfly floated in front of his face as another sound from behind invaded his ears. Sanjay wheeled around to see a sloping hill leading down to a wide cove. The hill was covered in flowers of a deep-blue hue Sanjay had never seen in his life. Running among the flowers were the sources of the sounds. Children. Several of them frolicked in the field of blue, their white-blond hair jostled by the wind, as they pursued a formation of darting and weaving butterflies.

As his mind grappled with the scene, he felt a touch on his shoulder. He looked around to see the woman standing next to him. Her blue eyes seemed to sparkle as she once again said, "Sahndge-yay?"

He could see the weave of her tunic, smell the floral scent of her perfume, feel her fingers on his shoulder. "Yes, I am Sanjay."

"Malinyah," she said, patting her chest.

"Hello, Malinyah."

She reached for his hand and squeezed. "Will you please help Pebbles?"

Sanjay dropped the *Sinethal* on his lap and his hands began to tremble. Eyes riveted on the ceiling, he tried to speak but could only muster a few mumbled words. The *Naetir* separated from the *Sinethal* and rolled off the sofa. Anlon caught it before it hit the floor. Recalling his own stupor after meeting Malinyah for the first time, Anlon said, "Just take it easy, Sanjay. Concentrate on your breathing. Slow and steady...that's it...nice and easy...big breath in...long exhale out...there you go...that's it. Keep it going. We've got some water for you if you want some."

The psychologist closed his eyes and nodded his head. Anlon patted him on the shoulder. "Pretty impressive, Sanjay. You lasted a little over two minutes. That's about twice as long as I made it during my first visit with Malinyah."

Three glassfuls of water later, Sanjay was finally capable of speaking. He opened his eyes and looked at his two guests. "I am speechless."

"Told ya it wasn't a prank," Griffin said, a wide smile on his face.

"Yes, you did. And still I did not believe you."

"But you do now?"

"How could I not?" Sanjay shook his head as if to clear cobwebs from his mind. Fluttering his eyelids open and shut, he said, "I can still hear the ocean in my ears, the warmth of her fingers on my hands. I close my eyes and I see pink leaves. It is surreal."

"Beats peyote by a long shot, doesn't it?"

"Wow, does it!" Sanjay turned from Griffin to look at Anlon. "She asked me to help Pebbles."

"Yeah, she has a soft spot for Pebbles. Malinyah says Pebbles reminds her of her daughter, Alynioria."

"One of the children in the meadow."

Anlon and Griffin shared a smile. Anlon said, "That's right."

Sanjay propped himself up on his elbows and directed his gaze at the *Sinethal* now resting on Anlon's lap. "And you say Pebbles' mind was transferred into one of those."

"Yes. Obviously not this one, but one like it."

"How?"

"The short explanation? They use electromagnetism to stimulate the hippocampus to 'download' a person's mind," Anlon said. "There are several of their stone devices involved to make it happen, and I couldn't begin to explain what triggers the hippocampus to comply. The best analogy I've come up with is that it's like tuning a radio to a certain frequency. Adjust the electromagnetic stimulation just right and the hippocampus starts downloading your memories."

Sanjay sniffed the air. "My God, I can still smell her perfume."

"It takes a little while for your senses to let go of what they experience," Griffin said. "For me, the feeling of wet clay between my toes lasted a couple of days."

"A couple of days?" exclaimed Sanjay.

"Yeah," said Anlon. "Like I said earlier, the Munuorians included the sensory elements of their memories to make them stickier, so to speak. I guarantee the next time you hear ocean waves, the memory of meeting Malinyah will come back into your mind so vividly, it'll feel like you're with her all over again."

Sanjay sat up and asked Anlon to hand him the *Sinethal*. As he slowly examined it from all sides, he whispered, "Incredible." After a stretch of quiet reflection, he looked back at Anlon. "Was the process to move Pebbles' mind back into her brain the same, but in reverse? Tuning the hippocampus to upload instead of download?"

"From what I understand, yes."

"Though I am struggling to accept this as real...a *ten-thousand-year-old* woman's mind inside this slab...I am beginning to see how Pebbles' brain might have been injured during the transfer of memories. For example, I find it impossible to believe that a flood of a person's memories uploaded en masse could be handled by the hippocampus without repercussions."

"Agreed," said Anlon. "I can't imagine the hippocampus is capable of processing a deluge of memories in the same way it would with a normal inflow. At a minimum, it seems hard to believe the pieces of each reloaded memory would end up getting coded the same as they were when originally stored. As a result, I would think a lot of Pebbles' memories are stored in different locations than they were before."

"One would also think there was potential for lost or incomplete memories. Or pieces of memories that were mixed up with pieces of unrelated memories," Sanjay said.

"Right," Anlon said. "Then lump on to those possibilities the certainty that the coma damaged some of her brain tissue. Even if her hippocampus was able to accept the stream of returning memories without a problem, the coma-damaged tissues would have forced it to dump certain memories or scramble to find new storage locations."

After placing the *Sinethal* beside him on the couch, Sanjay sipped some more water. To Anlon, the look on Sanjay's face implied he'd fully regained his composure and now his mind was working out the puzzle. Griffin must have felt the same way about Sanjay, for when Anlon looked his way, the rocker gave him a thumbs-up. Finally, Sanjay turned to Anlon and asked, "Other than the dreams, have you noticed anything else unusual about Pebbles? Does she seem forgetful? Does she have troubling speaking? Any personality differences? Unusual mood swings? New behaviors?"

"Well, there are certainly differences," Anlon said, "She definitely has more highs and lows, but I would expect that given what she endured. I wouldn't say she's forgetful…she doesn't seem to me to struggle recalling things. She's more distant than she used to be, but that comes and goes in spurts. The only behavior that's notably different, aside from her dreams, is her ability to draw."

Sanjay perked up. "Oh?"

"Yeah, you should see her pictures," Griffin said. "They're not run-of-the-mill sketches, no stick figures or doodles, but full-on, museum-quality, works of art."

Sanjay pressed Anlon for a more thorough explanation. "Are you saying that she has always drawn, but suddenly her skill level has risen? Or are you saying she never was much of an artist, but now is?"

"I've only known her for a few years," Anlon said, "but in that time she's never picked up a pencil or pen to draw, not that I recall. But now? Holy crap, she's freaking Van Gogh."

Sanjay stood. "Ah! Now we are talking!"

"You're thinking savant syndrome?" Anlon asked.

"Yes, it is quite possible." Sanjay began to pace. "Her hippocampus, it has opened new pathways in her brain to compensate for the damage inflicted by the coma."

"Or…to handle the flood of memories going out and then back into her brain," Anlon added.

"Or both," Griffin said.

"Almost assuredly both," said Sanjay with a nod. He continued to pace. "How fascinating."

Within the first few days of Pebbles' newfound artistic abilities, Anlon had suspected *savant syndrome,* a rare condition which can occur in people who have suffered brain injuries. Out of the blue, these people develop stunning new abilities. Some master music simply by listening to it. Others suddenly possess the ability to solve complex math equations in seconds or memorize entire volumes of texts with instant recall of every word. And some become exceptional artists, à la Pebbles.

In the midst of his ruminations, Anlon was stirred back to the conversation by comments from the pacing Sanjay. "So, we have multiple clues pointing to an injury to Pebbles' brain, most likely the hippocampus. And given she has developed a savant behavior, the temporal lobe must also have been affected."

Anlon concurred. Through his research on savant syndrome, he had discovered that brain scans of savants often revealed damage to the anterior temporal lobe...a part of the brain that sits directly atop the hippocampus...and a part of the brain that plays a pivotal role in storing memories.

"Given she is also experiencing PTSD-like dreams," Sanjay said, "it is likely her amygdala was injured as well."

This also rang true to Anlon. The *amygdala*, another brain structure that physically touches the hippocampus, is widely believed to be the place in the brain where emotional elements of memories are stored. Further, it is believed to be the part of the brain that governs the fight-or-flight response in humans...a key feature of Pebbles' dreams. Sanjay's back-of-the-envelope injury analysis created the perfect segue for Anlon to introduce an alternative theory for both Pebbles' dreams and her savant artistry.

"Sanjay, I agree with you that some combination of Pebbles' hippocampus, amygdala and temporal lobe were likely affected by what happened to her, but I wonder if *injury* is the right word to describe what's happened?"

Anlon's comment drew a puzzled look from Sanjay. He ceased pacing and sat down on the sofa. "What do you mean?"

"Well, there's another explanation for her dreams, her drawing ability, that we've been considering. It's a stretch, to be sure, but it feels to us like it is within the realm of possibilities." Anlon paused and tapped Malinyah's *Sinethal*. "We're wondering if there was more than one mind stored on the *Sinethal* used to store Pebbles' memories."

"What? Why would you think that?" Sanjay first looked at Anlon and then turned to Griffin.

"It has to do with her dreams," Griffin said. "They're more like trippy flashbacks than they are dreams."

Sanjay waved his hand dismissively. "That means nothing. Flashbacks are very common in PTSD patients."

"We know," said Anlon, "but these flashbacks are unusual, Sanjay. They aren't replays of anything that's ever happened to Pebbles. In fact, they come across as someone else's memories entirely."

CHAPTER 4

FRACTURED MIND

ABOARD *SOL SEAKER*
KONA KAI MARINA, SAN DIEGO, CALIFORNIA
SEPTEMBER 18

As Jennifer reviewed Pebbles' entry of her latest "cave" dream, she noticed a new detail — the mention of a poncho. To be certain she had not overlooked that in Pebbles' previous recordings of cave-dream memories, Jennifer retrieved the other two journal volumes from the built-in bookcase beside the chair and scanned all six other cave-dream entries. The poncho did not appear in any of them. Jennifer's further comparison of the entries yielded another new detail — the fungus used as kindling to light the torch.

Jennifer made a mental note to discuss those two features with Pebbles when she woke from her nap. Turning her attention back to the collection of cave-dream entries, Jennifer found it curious there was no mention of a hand covering Pebbles' mouth. Jennifer knew for a fact that no one had touched Pebbles' face or mouth while they'd been trying to prevent her from jumping over the upper deck railing, but Pebbles had been adamant that someone had.

It seemed obvious to Jennifer that it must have occurred during the dream, but the lack of a reference to it in the entries suggested Pebbles did not believe it had happened in the dream. It was another topic Jennifer intended to explore with her once she awoke.

The collaborative process, whether Pebbles discussed the dreams with Anlon or Jennifer or both of them, always produced new insights and, from what Jennifer could observe, the chat sessions also appeared to soothe Pebbles. In fact, on more than one occasion over the last three months, Pebbles had referred to the chats as her dream therapy.

The weird part to Jennifer was that Pebbles' entries were devoid of non-sensical scenes one typically experienced in dreams. Instead, Pebbles' recollections of her dreams were coherent recitations that followed the same serial pattern every time. In this way, the entries struck Jennifer as retellings of memories rather than dreams. Jennifer recalled her first conversation with Anlon about this peculiarity.

"I could understand it if she was reliving what happened to her in Tahoe or Mexico, but these dreams have no connection with getting shot or beaten or strangled."

"We don't know that, Jen. They could be her brain's way of coming to grips with what happened to her."

"Yeah, I hear you. But I'm telling you, the police detective in me sees these dreams differently. When I read the entries, when I hear her verbally walk through them, they feel like witness statements to me."

Anlon had not bought into Jennifer's theory, but as the chats continued, Jennifer began to subtly introduce questioning techniques she had used as a detective to stimulate recall of crime scene details from eyewitnesses.

In some questions, Jennifer focused on sensations rather than events. Questions like: Is the water cold or warm? How heavy is your bag? What color is it? Do you hear anything in the trees around you? Does the cave have a musty odor?

A separate technique Jennifer employed involved asking Pebbles to begin reciting her memories of the dreams at different points in the dreams. For the cave dream, Jennifer had in the past asked Pebbles to start the story at the point she lit the torch, or as she descended beneath the rocky overhang.

On other occasions, she would ask Pebbles to imagine herself as one of the pursuers and recount the dreams from the pursuer's perspective.

Sometimes Jennifer would plant false cues to elicit new details. For example, in one dream, Pebbles was being chased through the halls of a temple. As Pebbles recounted a portion of the tale where she dashed down a stone staircase, Jennifer had interrupted to ask her why she ran down the stairs instead of taking the door to her right.

"There's no door to the right. It's a stone wall with a huge mural on it."

"What's the mural of?"

"A naval battle."

"Are we talking modern ships?"

"No…dudes with spears and arrows."

While these methods did not produce "aha" breakthroughs in interpreting the dreams, they did produce a litany of new details to add to Pebbles' journal entries. And each time they discussed the new details gleaned from the questioning, fresh nuances began to appear in future iterations of the dreams, which seemed to spark further details from Pebbles in her next entries.

Such was the case with the poncho. In a previous retelling of the cave dream, Jennifer had asked Pebbles what she was wearing in the dream.

"I don't know."

"It's nighttime, right?"

"Uh huh."

"And you're going up a mountain."

"That's right. There's a series of switchbacks."

"And there are guys chasing you."

"Well, I'd say they're more following me than chasing me. They're being real quiet, kind of slinking along."

"You mean like they don't want you to know they're following you?"

"Yes. Exactly."

"So how can you tell where they are?"

"I can hear them above the wind. They keep knocking rocks over the edge."

"Ah. So, there's a lot of wind?"

"Yep."

"Must be pretty cold. Mountaintops usually are, especially at night. Especially when it's windy."

"You're not kidding. In the dream, my legs are freezing."

"You remember that?"

"Uh huh. I remember bending down to warm them up."

The Q&A had produced no further insights on that occasion, but Pebbles had noted in today's entry that she was wearing a poncho. Within a sentence of mentioning the garment, Pebbles revealed the use of fungus to light the torch. One new detail had led to another.

As more details emerged through their chats, Pebbles began to amend her journal entries. Whether in the form of new text scribbled in the margins, crossed-out sections in the body of the entries, or new paragraphs appended to the end of each recording, the books began to take on the appearance of heavily edited manuscripts rather than volumes of a diary. And each successive volume contained more edits.

Then, out of nowhere, Pebbles began to doodle in the journals. She couldn't explain why or what had precipitated the new additions. She claimed she had never been much of an artist, or the type to express herself through drawing. But one would never have known that by looking at her illustrations in the three journals.

As Jennifer flipped through the pages of volume three, she was amazed at how elaborate Pebbles' illustrations had become. And much like her edits, the drawings increased in number with each new volume.

In fact, Pebbles now had two separate sketchbooks in which she drew pictures too large to fit on the pages of her composition-book-sized journals. Drawn with colored pencils, the sketchbooks were filled with stunning images. There were depictions of trees, birds and animals as well as various landscape scenes, some of mountains, others of forests, a few with deserts or rivers and even a couple of caverns or caves. There were also pages and pages of architectural structures that ranged from stone temples to fortresses to mud huts.

The most bizarre aspect to Jennifer? If you asked Pebbles to draw something, like a boat in the marina or a seagull perched on the pier, she could not do it. If you directly asked her to illustrate something she had experienced in one of her dreams, she was similarly incapable of rendering a coherent image.

But let her stretch out on the sofa on *Sol Seaker*'s upper deck patio, smoothie by her side, pencil in her hand and sketch pad on her lap, and she morphed into Van Gogh.

It seemed obvious to Jennifer and Anlon — as well as Pebbles — that the drawings were depictions of elements from Pebbles' dreams, but they did *not* depict the dreams themselves. For instance, one could not point to her sketch of a snake coiled on a mountain trail and ask Pebbles how it fit into her recurring dream of hiking up a mountain in the dark while shadowy figures below pursued her. In fact, she would tell you she could not recall the snake ever appearing in the dream.

And while the drawings contained fanciful styling and colors similar to that found in paintings created by Van Gogh, they did not contain fanciful content. In other words, there were not any pictures of pink unicorns flying over rainbows while cherubs followed behind on Harleys with cigars hanging out of their mouths. Pebbles' drawings were of ordinary objects and landscapes, yet they looked anything but ordinary.

Jennifer closed the journal and peeked through the blinds at the seagulls floating over the marina. She was convinced Pebbles' drawings were clues as important as the words written in her journals. It was as if there was a part of Pebbles' subconscious that was not satisfied with her written recollections and was either trying to supplement her journal entries or call Pebbles' attention to details she'd overlooked.

SANJAY'S RESIDENCE
SEDONA, ARIZONA

Anlon devoted nearly thirty minutes to describing Pebbles' recurring dreams. During the overview, Sanjay took copious notes, stopping Anlon on several occasions to ask questions. When Anlon finished, Sanjay summarized the overview.

"So, you say she has a half-dozen different dreams that repeat at random. Most of them involve fleeing from other people, but there are a couple in which she is not pursued by others. In the dreams where she is chased, she carries a bag with something inside. You say Pebbles believes the woman is protecting the bag from those pursuing her. But in the other dreams, the ones in which she is not pursued by others, she desperately searches for something. The bag is present in these visions, but it is empty.

"In all of the dreams, her pursuers are never clearly seen, the objects of her search and protection never revealed. The dreams occur in specific locations: two in a jungle, another in a temple, the others on a mountain, in the desert and on a river. These dreams sometimes occur at night when she is asleep, but other times they occur during the day, while she is awake. When the daytime dreams happen, she goes into a trance. Over the past few weeks, the frequency of the daytime dreams has increased a noticeable amount."

Anlon nodded. "That's a pretty good recap, but you left out something I said at the beginning. For the first two months after her mind was reunited with her body, she had nightmares that were literal flashbacks of things that happened during her kidnapping. She wouldn't talk about them and they eventually faded. Everything seemed fine for another six months."

"Right," Sanjay interjected. "Then, about three months ago, you said the new dreams started surfacing, but only at night. The daydreams began within the last month, and they are the most concerning to you because when she goes into these trances, she gets physical. She fights and tries to run. You are worried she is going to hurt herself."

"Correct," Anlon said. "I had hoped the new dreams would fade like the ones she had right after her coma, but the situation has gone in the opposite direction."

"I am sure that is very troubling, to you *and* Pebbles." Sanjay set down his notepad and sat back, apparently collecting his thoughts. After a stretch of silence, he said, "As you suggested, Anlon, there are many curiosities about Pebbles' dreams. Some elements are very common among PTSD patients and suggest a brain injury, but there are other aspects which are unusual. For example, in some ways, Pebbles' trances sound like the type of behavior we see in patients who experience flashbacks."

Sanjay gave the example of a combat veteran with post-traumatic stress disorder who is walking down a city street when a car backfires. The sound of the backfire might sound like gunfire, causing the soldier to dive behind a car, crawl along the sidewalk, scream out to take cover. While in the flashback, the soldier is completely disconnected from the reality of what is happening around him. He truly believes he is in a high-stress combat situation and acts accordingly.

"That sounds just like what happens to Pebbles," Griffin said. "She definitely seems to be acting out whatever is happening in the dream when she's in one of her trances."

"Right, but the content of her dreams during the trances appears to be symbolic in nature. The content is very different from the type of content one would find in flashbacks," Sanjay said. "Now, not all people with PTSD experience flashbacks. Many do have symbolic dreams, but you don't find people who experience flashback-like trances where the content is symbolic."

"Are you certain her dreams are symbolic?" Anlon asked. "Couldn't she be reliving actual experiences? Experiences that have been jumbled by the injury to her brain?"

Sanjay nodded. "Yes, it is certainly possible but the symbolism in her dreams is very prominent, Anlon."

He went on to explain his point. The fleeing woman, Sanjay told them, was a symbol that suggested Pebbles was running away from something she was afraid to confront in her waking life, such as memories of the abuse she endured during her kidnapping or feelings she suppressed during or after her ordeal.

Moving on to the searching woman, Sanjay theorized it was a symbol implying Pebbles had lost something during her ordeals and was afraid she could not get it back. In Sanjay's opinion, the empty bag reinforced the notion that Pebbles felt something was missing — her self-esteem, her sense of safety or trust, or something along those lines. He finished his back-of-the-envelope dream analysis by saying, "The fact that the bag is also present in the fleeing dreams, and the fact that in those dreams there is something inside the bag that the woman acts to protect, suggests a connection between whatever Pebbles feels she lost and whatever she is suppressing."

The analysis made sense to Anlon. He knew Pebbles was adamant about not returning to their home in Lake Tahoe, the place where she had been beaten, shot and then kidnapped. The sanctity of the home had been violated, she had told him. There would be no way she could ever again walk into the kitchen or living room or front hall and not think of what had happened to her there. Truth be told, Anlon felt the same way. He had seen the crime scene before it was sanitized. Perhaps her subconscious was rebelling against her efforts to suppress those memories. Anlon shared the thought with Sanjay.

"It could very well be," Sanjay said. "Most PTSD patients feel an unrecoverable loss as a result of their trauma. It is as if a piece of their personality or spirit was broken or taken and no amount of therapy or reflection can recapture it. It is a palpable loss…like a loved one has died. The feeling may dull over time, but it never goes away."

This commentary also resonated with Anlon. There were days when Pebbles exuded the effervescent, glowing spirit he had fallen in love with, and other days where she was uncharacteristically downtrodden and withdrawn. While he understood it would take time for her to recover physically, mentally and emotionally, her recent regression was troubling. He mentioned his concern to Sanjay.

"Anlon, PTSD surfaces on its own time schedule, and proceeds at its own pace," Sanjay said. "And setbacks are common. Just like no two people are the same, no two people react to trauma in the same way or at the same time. Even people who experience multiple traumas can react to each instance in different manners."

Sanjay's last comment reminded Anlon of an important point he should have mentioned at the outset of their discussion. "Sanjay, I must apologize. I forgot to share something with you that's important to know about Pebbles."

"Pebbles had a fiancé before she met me. They were taken with each other and she thought they were going to spend the rest of their lives together. Then there was this car accident. He died, Sanjay. Pebbles harbored tremendous guilt about his death because she felt partly to blame for the accident. She attempted suicide on more than one occasion."

"Hmm…that does cast a different light on the situation," said Sanjay. "Has she exhibited any recent suicidal behavior? Made any troubling comments?"

"No. Absolutely not."

"Is she taking any medication? For anxiety or depression? To sleep?"

"For sleep…but they haven't helped much. No to the others," Anlon said. "You're scaring me a little, Sanjay. Should I be more concerned about that risk?"

"My apologies, Anlon. I do not mean to alarm you, but there are a couple of aspects of the dreams that concern me more now I know of her previous struggles."

"Well, don't hold back. Please elaborate," Anlon said. "If there's a heightened risk, I need to make sure I'm tuned into any warning signs."

Sanjay did not sugarcoat his answer. "The cycling of different settings in the dreams concerns me. It implies Pebbles subconsciously believes no matter where she goes, she cannot escape the thoughts and emotions she is suppressing. A sense of hopelessness that she cannot escape them may well be what is behind the recent escalation in the frequency of the dreams, and why she seems to be physically acting them out. Together, these factors suggest her internal conflict is coming to a head."

Anlon let Sanjay's comments sink in before he responded. There was no doubt in his mind that Sanjay was right about it coming to a head. Anlon felt that way and so did Pebbles. But she did not seem depressed about it. Yes, she wanted the dreams to stop and wanted to understand why she was having them, but her mindset was one of a puzzle-solver rather than one on the verge of giving up. He said as much to Sanjay.

"Unfortunately, Anlon, sometimes there is no warning, no overt sign that a person is contemplating extreme measures to end their suffering. And sometimes people bury their feelings so deep inside, their suffering is not even apparent until they have acted upon the desire to end it," Sanjay said. "But we are getting *way* ahead of ourselves. It is impossible to make a judgment of Pebbles' mindset without more information, without interacting with her. I just think it is prudent, given her past history, given what you have described about her dreams, for us to pay closer attention to potential warning signs."

"Us? Should I take that to mean you're open to helping her?" Anlon asked.

"If she is willing to meet and talk with me, then yes," Sanjay said. "After all, how could I say no to Malinyah? She will haunt my mind for years if I don't help."

"You're probably right." Anlon laughed. Turning serious, he asked, "How long will it take you to pack? I'd suggest bringing a week's worth of clothes."

"Um…I do not mean to be rude, Anlon, but I cannot just snap my fingers and take off for a week. I have other commitments."

"Didn't you just say that you thought the situation was coming to a head?"

"Yes, but—"

"Look, Sanjay, I *really* need your help. Pebbles really needs your help. I'll pay you whatever you want, reimburse you for any inconvenience, any lost business. We can help reschedule all your appointments."

After a short pause, Sanjay said, "I need to make arrangements for someone to watch Happy."

"Bring Happy along. Does he like boats?"

"I don't think he's ever been on one."

"Well, we'll take good care of both of you."

CHAPTER 5

A FLOCK OF FLICKERS

DRIVING ON ROUTE 89A
NORTH OF SEDONA, ARIZONA
SEPTEMBER 18

O n the way to the Flagstaff airport, Happy sat next to Griffin in the back seat of the rental car while Sanjay joined Anlon up front. During the drive, Sanjay asked Anlon about his earlier comment about Pebbles approaching her dreams as puzzles to be solved.

"I take it she has an analytical mind," Sanjay said.

"You know it," Anlon said. "She's determined to understand why she's having the dreams and what they signify. So, she's been keeping track of them in a journal. It's a technique she learned when she was in therapy after her suicide attempts.

"And then there are the drawings I mentioned earlier. That's not a technique from her previous therapy, of course, but something Pebbles considers part of the puzzle. We all do. So, we talk about them after she draws them, just like we do after each new journal entry."

"This is wonderful, Anlon. Extremely valuable. You should encourage her to continue with the journal," Sanjay said. "If I could make a suggestion; before going to bed each night, I would recommend that she revisit the journal and look for details that are murky in her memory. By concentrating on those details while she is awake, right before she goes to sleep, she may find her subconscious delivers greater detail in future dreams."

"You'll get to make that recommendation yourself...assuming she doesn't kick us both off the boat."

"What do you mean?"

"She's not exactly aware I came to see you."

ABOARD *SOL SEAKER*
KONA KAI MARINA, SAN DIEGO, CALIFORNIA

Pebbles was still asleep when Jennifer edged open the cabin door to peek inside. Phone pressed against her ear, she stepped back and closed the door as quietly as she could. On the other end of the line was Anlon. He had sent a group text to Pebbles and Jennifer to let them know he and Griffin were inflight to San Diego. Jennifer had texted back a private message to acknowledge receiving his, and to let him know that Pebbles had had another trance-dream. Within a minute of sending the message, Jennifer received a call from Anlon. Retreating to the ship's central staircase, Jennifer whispered into her cell phone, "She's still out."

"Okay, thanks for checking. How long has she been asleep?"

"About an hour." Jennifer sat down on the steps and rested her elbows on her knees. "It was the cave dream again. She tried to jump off the upper deck, but we stopped her."

Jennifer ran through the incident, providing her own observations and a recap of the observations by the crew who had arrived on the upper deck before her. She then relayed a synopsis of Pebbles' journal entry, including the new details about the poncho and fungus, as well as the omission of the hand-over-mouth that led to Jennifer getting socked in the nose.

"Ouch. How is your nose?" Anlon asked.

"It's a little swollen, that's all. Nothing to worry about. I'm used to it. You'd be surprised how often I've been hit in the nose, both in the Army and on the police force. Is Griffin with you?"

"Yep, he's sitting next to Dr. Varma, petting the good doctor's dog, Happy. You want to talk with him?"

"His dog?"

"No, Griffin."

"No, I mean, Dr. Varma brought his dog?"

"Yeah, you'll get a kick out of him. He's a hoot. Slobbers a lot though." Jennifer heard Anlon's muffled voice say, "Sorry, Sanjay, no offense."

She also heard Sanjay's response. "None taken. He does slobber a lot."

When Anlon returned to the line, he said, "So, do you want to talk with Griff?"

"In a few," she said. "Given that Dr. Varma *and* his dog are with you, I take it the meeting went well?"

"Yes, I'd say so."

"You told him about the stones?"

"I did…and…he met Malinyah."

"Really? How did he take it? Did he freak?"

"Nah. Actually, he handled it better than I thought he would."

"That's great to hear. Do you think he can help her?"

"Yeah, I do."

"So how do you plan to introduce him to Pebbles?"

A voice from behind Jennifer said, "Introduce who? Who are you talking with?"

Jennifer turned to see Pebbles standing a few feet away. She had the blanket draped over her shoulders like a cape, one hand clutching it closed beneath her neck. Jennifer's face involuntarily flushed red. She held out the phone, "Uh…it's Anlon. He called to check on you."

Pebbles snaked her free hand from beneath the blanket-cape and took the phone. Before speaking to Anlon, she asked Jennifer, "You told him about the cave-dream this morning?"

"I did, yeah," Jennifer said.

"Okay, good." Pebbles raised the phone to her ear and said hello to Anlon.

When Anlon heard Pebbles' voice on the other end of the line, he excused himself from the others and disappeared to the rear of the chartered plane. As he slunk into the last seat in the cabin, he said, "Hey, love. How are you feeling?"

"I've been better."

"You want to talk about it?" Over the phone, Anlon heard muffled voices, presumably a conversation between Pebbles and Jennifer, and then the sound of a door shutting. "Pebbles?"

"I'm still here. Just wanted a little privacy. Jennifer said you're on your way back?"

"Yes, indeed. We should arrive at the marina before dinner."

"So, what was Jen talking about? I heard her say something about you introducing me to someone."

Anlon took a deep breath, then said, "Um, I'm bringing a couple of guests."

There was a long pause on the other end of the line and then Pebbles let out a long sigh. "You went and did it, didn't you? Even though I told you I didn't want to see anyone."

Anlon winced. "I did."

Pebbles snapped back in a raised voice, "We had a deal! No shrinks."

"I know. And I tried real hard to honor your wishes, but we need help to sort—"

"I don't *want* that kind of help. I thought you understood that!"

"I do understand."

"Bullshit! If you understood, you wouldn't have gone behind my back."

Well, this is going great, thought Anlon. He reached out his hand as he spoke, somehow expecting for Pebbles to notice the beseeching gesture. "Look, I'm sorry I didn't talk to you about it beforehand, but please hear me out."

"Is it the guy Griffin told us about?"

"Yes. His name is Sanjay Varma."

"Great. So, Jen and Griffin are in on this too," said Pebbles between huffs.

"We're all just trying to help, Pebbles. Swear to God." Anlon placed a hand on his heart.

"You don't get it, do you?" she said. "He's gonna get inside my head. Make me think about things I don't want to think about. Bring up stuff that hurts. Stuff that makes me angry. I don't need that shit in my life right now. I just want to stop the effing dreams…and I want to do it in *my* own way in *my* own time."

Anlon stood and began to pace. "You don't have to bare your soul to him. He knows you're not interested in therapy."

"Then why are you bringing him?"

"With your permission, I'd like to show him your journals and sketches. You know, see if he spots something we've overlooked. Maybe offer a few suggestions."

Another sigh through the phone.

"He'll only be with us for a week," Anlon said.

"A *week*?"

"I'll make sure it's totally casual. We'll take *Sol Seeker* out, do some snorkeling, eat too much, drink too much, shoot the shit. Get to know him, let him get to know us. Talk about the journals here and there. You don't have to meet with him privately, just be cool with him hanging out with us. He seems like a good dude. I like him. I think you'll like him too."

"It sounds like a plot to trick me into talking to him," Pebbles said, her voice punctuated with sniffles.

"Heavens no," Anlon said. As he began to offer further assurances, Happy appeared in the aisle and began to bark at Anlon. Sanjay popped out of his seat and mouthed an apology while he corralled the dog.

"What's going on, Anlon? Is that a dog I hear?"

Happy broke free from Sanjay's hold. He ran to Anlon and began to jump up and down, his front paws pounding against Anlon's thighs. Over lusty barks, Anlon said, "Uh…yeah. Sanjay brought his bulldog with him. Couldn't find a sitter on short notice. His name is Happy."

"You're joking. A shrink with a dog named Happy? Does he have a cat named Tranquility? Or maybe two goldfish called Peace and Harmony?"

While her words were thick with sarcasm, there was a teasing quality to her voice that Anlon interpreted as a slight ebbing of her anger. He tried a little humor. "No, just a comfort Tarantula named Cuddles."

Anlon heard the teeniest of snickers, then Pebbles said, "Hmm…why do I feel Happy is part of your plot?"

As Sanjay finally snagged the bulldog and led him up front, Anlon took advantage of the apparent détente to say, "Please give Sanjay a chance, Pebbles. He thinks he can help. I do too."

After pulling Happy away from Anlon, Sanjay led the dog toward the front of the plane and commanded him to lie down by Sanjay's seat. The obedient Happy lowered to the floor, his eyes beseeching forgiveness. Sanjay petted him and then turned his attention to his open laptop. On the screen was an unfinished entry in the journal Sanjay maintained for recording details from patient visits. While Pebbles was not officially a patient, yet, Sanjay wanted to capture his thoughts from the meeting with Anlon and Griffin before meeting Pebbles. Picking up where he left off, Sanjay finished the entry by musing about his interaction with Malinyah:

When it comes to unusual psychological phenomena, I try to maintain an open mind, but I also find it important to maintain scientific discipline. Could there be a supernatural explanation for Pebbles' nightmares as Anlon suggests? It seems impossible to me, but I have no proof to invalidate the notion and have seen stranger phenomena turn out to have real, albeit supernatural, bases.

Anlon has earned a point in his favor by introducing me to Malinyah, thereby proving the possibility of storing a person's mind on a stone tablet. I have to say I am still shaken by the experience. It was as real to me as if I had been standing in my own home talking to her. The most remarkable part of the experience was the range of emotions that flowed through my body when Malinyah squeezed my hands and pleaded with me to help Pebbles. I not only felt the weight of her words in the tone of her voice, but also in the sincerity of her soul and the depth of her concern. When I say that, I mean I felt as if her emotions became my emotions, like they were literally passed from her brain to mine.

So, I ask myself, is it that crazy to consider the possibility that the residue of someone else's mind was on the same stone Pebbles' mind had been stored on? The scientist in me says no way. The Malinyah in me says otherwise.

The first sign of Anlon's imminent arrival was a ping on her phone that Pebbles ignored. Then she heard the sound of scurrying footsteps outside the master bedroom cabin as the crew took their positions for the boarding. This was followed shortly thereafter by a high-pitched whistle signaling the shore party was coming aboard.

Pebbles closed the sketchbook she had been leafing through and rose from the bed. On her way out of the cabin, she sighed. The next week was going to be miserable but the sooner it started, the sooner it would end.

When she entered the living room cabin, Pebbles spied Happy on top of one of the sofas, barking at a seagull cleaning its wings on the deck railing outside. His owner sat on the couch near the dog and tried to settle the dog by petting him while he listened to Griffin.

Happy was the first to notice Pebbles' entrance. He whirled his panting head around, slinging a rope of slobber at Sanjay's face. The psychologist grimaced as he wiped away the goo with his hand. *I like this dog already,* Pebbles thought.

The feeling must have been mutual, for Happy leapt off the couch and dashed toward Pebbles, his haunches whacking Sanjay in the back of the head on his descent. As she knelt to greet the oncoming dog, the others looked her way. Pebbles heard Anlon call out, "Careful, he's pretty powerful."

So am I, thought Pebbles.

Happy stopped short of toppling her. Instead, he opted to raise up on his hind legs and plant his front legs on her shoulders. He sniffed at her face and then slathered her chin with licks. Pebbles rubbed his head and neck. She looked up at Sanjay and smiled. "Cute dog."

Sanjay bowed slightly. "Namaste, Pebbles."

She returned her eyes to Happy while she continued to pet the dog. "You got the wrong person with the *namaste* stuff. Jen, there, is the yogi, not me."

"I see," said Sanjay. "Well, then, hello."

"Hi ya," she said, standing up and wiping her saliva-streaked hands on her yoga pants. "Wasn't really intending to entertain visitors, so sorry for my appearance. I know I must look like shit."

Before Sanjay could reply, Pebbles looked toward Griffin. "Traitor."

As Griffin darted a look across the room at Jennifer, Pebbles turned toward Sanjay. "So, what do you know about woodpeckers?"

The question seemed to startle the psychologist. He backed up a step and adjusted his glasses. *Good,* thought Pebbles, *you came to ruffle my feathers, how's it feel to have yours ruffled first?*

"I am afraid I know nothing at all about woodpeckers."

"You mean to tell me there's no namaste psycho-babble meaning about woodpeckers in dreams? Who would have guessed?"

Pebbles felt a hand on her shoulder as Anlon spoke, "Hey, take it easy."

"No, I won't." She tugged her shoulder away from Anlon's hand while maintaining her gaze at Sanjay. "If you don't know squat about woodpeckers, you can't help me. Like I said, cute dog, though."

She spun around and stomped away.

"Do you hear them or see them in your dreams?" Sanjay asked.

"Neither." Pebbles slammed open the living room door. Without looking back, she raised a hand and waved. *"Hasta la vista."*

Anlon rubbed the back of his neck and apologized to Sanjay. "I'm sorry. I thought she would be more cordial."

"Do not apologize, Anlon. It is all right. She is just testing me."

"Oh, that wasn't a test," Anlon said. "Trust me. That was a definite 'get the eff out of here' kiss-off."

"Maybe," said Sanjay. "How quickly can you take us out on the ocean?"

"Excuse me?"

"Do you need to file some kind of 'flight plan' with the marina operators for a ship this big or can you just unmoor and go out to sea?"

"Uh…pretty sure we can just go, but the captain's not aboard right now. I don't think he'd be happy stranding him ashore."

"Pity." Sanjay knelt down to pet Happy. "Guess we're not going to get to swim in the ocean after all, buddy."

The door to the living room slammed again. Anlon wheeled to see a red-faced Pebbles heading straight for Sanjay. In her hands, she carried her journals and sketch pads. By the time she reached the therapist, he was standing. With jaw clenched, she glared at Sanjay. For a brief second, Anlon thought she was about to wallop him in the face. Instead, she reached out for his hand and said, "Follow me. You too, Happy."

"Lead the way," said Sanjay, taking hold of Pebbles' hand.

Anlon watched them exit the far end of the living room cabin and emerge onto the covered, outdoor bar. Through the living room's window, he saw Pebbles slap down the books on the round table in the center of the bar and point Sanjay toward a chair. She then pointed to another chair and Happy hopped up from out of view.

"What's she doing?" Jennifer asked as she sidled up beside Anlon.

"Beats me."

They watched her flip open one of the sketchbooks. Standing over Sanjay, she pointed at the page, then flipped to another. Then, a third. As Sanjay leaned forward to study the page more closely, Pebbles turned around and glared at Anlon, Jennifer and Griffin. In a swooping motion, she whipped her arm through the air several times with a "get your asses out here" look on her face.

"Guess we're being summoned," Griffin said.

"Looks that way," said Anlon. "Tell you what, you guys go ahead. I'll be out in a couple of minutes. I'm gonna go to the bridge and convince Popeye to take us out into the bay."

Popeye, the ship's first officer whose real name was Matthew Ellis, was so nicknamed by the crew for his stocky build, his weather-beaten face and his penchant for mumbling dissatisfaction with many of the captain's orders when out of earshot.

Griffin laughed. "Oh, he'll lap that up!"

"That's what I'm counting on."

With one hand petting Happy, Pebbles tapped her other hand on the second sketchbook and spoke to Sanjay. "Look in this one. You'll see more of them."

The creak of the forward living room door caused her to look around. As Jennifer and Griffin stepped through the opening, Pebbles said, "Took you long enough. Pull up some chairs."

"What are you up to, Pebbles?" asked Jennifer.

"I'm starting a bird-watching club. What do you think I'm doing? I'm showing Sanjay, here, all the woodpeckers I've drawn."

Jennifer came up on Sanjay's righthand side. "What are you talking about? What woodpeckers?"

Pebbles pointed at the bird on the upper right quadrant of the page of drawings. In the picture, it was sitting on a tree branch, minding its own business. "Okay…they don't exactly look like woodpeckers, but they are. They're called flickers. Same bird family, just look different, behave different. I looked them up online. That one right there is a northern flicker."

Griffin, leaning over Sanjay's left side, gazed at the picture. "That's a woodpecker?"

Sanjay removed his glasses and turned to look up at Pebbles. "And you say you have never seen one of these before?"

"Nope. Never. Nada. Wouldn't know one if it walked across the table."

"The detail is exquisite," he said. "You are quite sure it is a northern flicker?"

"I am. I can show you one on my tablet later." She tapped the drawing. "What I want to know is — why do I keep drawing them? Different flickers. Like, go back two pages…yeah…there, right there. See that one? That's an Andean flicker.

"There are other ones in both books. Some in the journals, too. Campo flickers, gilded flickers. None of these birds are in my dreams, and like I said, I've never seen one in real life that I know of, but somehow I know exactly what they look—"

Pebbles stopped in midsentence as one of the ship's crew came hustling down the forward stairway to the right side of the bar. It was Cindy Tanner. She entered the bar area and announced the ship was imminently shoving off. Pebbles thanked her for the heads-up and turned back to the sketch pad. "Now, where were we…?"

The choppy water was barely noticeable as *Sol Seaker* moved out of the harbor and into the bay. The same was not true of the wind. Gusts curled into the outdoor bar and whipped the pages of the journals and sketchbooks to and fro, so the group retreated back into the living room where they were joined by Anlon.

With Happy stretched out next to Pebbles on the sofa beneath the cabin's portside picture windows, Sanjay sat in a catty-cornered easy chair and continued his review of the second of the dream journals. On the opposing starboard-side sofa, Griffin examined Pebbles' most recent entry in journal number three while Jennifer sat beside him and compared images of flickers on her smart tablet with those in Pebbles' sketchbook. There was a frown on her face.

As Anlon approached Pebbles, she looked up and smiled. Arriving at her side, he leaned over and kissed her. She patted the small sliver of couch next to her. Anlon slid on it while aiming a fisheye at the sleeping Happy occupying the majority of the sofa on the other side of Pebbles.

"Looks like I missed a lot," Anlon whispered.

"No, not that much."

"Catch me up. What did you mean about woodpeckers?"

Pebbles held a finger to her lips. "Shh…let's wait 'til Sanjay finishes reading."

"Okay," he mouthed. Leaning close to Pebbles' ear, he asked, "How are you feeling?"

She reached for his hand and squeezed it. "Better."

"Good. That's the goal."

Pebbles smiled and kissed him on the cheek. "Sorry I was such a bitch."

A gasp from Jennifer caused everyone to look up. She slammed her fist on the sofa. "That's it! Son of a gun, that's it!"

She put down the sketchbook and tablet, hopped off the couch and headed for the living room's aft door. The sudden exclamation and activity woke Happy. He rolled onto his feet and barked at Jennifer.

"Hey, where are you going?" Griffin asked.

"Be back in a few. I need to make a phone call."

Pebbles rose to her feet. "What's going on, Jen?"

Jennifer stopped and turned around. She pushed her blond hair back into a long tail behind her neck and twisted a hairband around it. "I don't know why it didn't hit me earlier. I've looked at your sketches at least a hundred times. I should have made the connection right away."

"Connection to what?" Pebbles asked. She looked at Jennifer's tablet. "You noticed something about the flickers."

Jennifer nodded and smiled, then turned around to continue toward the door.

"Whoa, whoa, whoa! Get back here. Tell us what you found," Pebbles demanded.

"Just hold your horses, I'll be back in a jiff."

She pushed through the door. Pebbles started after her. "At least tell us who you're calling."

As the door slid closed, Jennifer spun around and called back. "Cesar Perez."

With Pebbles standing dumbfounded in the middle of the room, Griffin picked up the sketchbook Jennifer had been looking at and compared the page to the image on her tablet. "Well, I'll be damned. Would you look at that!"

He held up both for the others to see. On the tablet was a stone-carved image of a bird on a branch. The sculpture had at one time been painted, for flecks of color still adhered to crannies here and there. On the sketch pad, a fully painted version of the exact same bird and branch occupied the upper right-hand side of the page.

Pebbles squinted at the tablet image as she approached Griffin. "What website is that?"

Griffin pulled down the tablet and examined the web page. "Archaeology site."

When Pebbles came alongside him, he handed her the tablet. As her eyes rapidly scanned the web page, her face reddened. "Oh, my God."

Then her pupils rolled back behind her eyelids and she collapsed on the couch next to Griffin. Anlon and Sanjay were up in a flash. Griffin looked to them and said, "Uh oh. Here we go again."

CHAPTER 6

BONFIRE OF THE MEMORIES

ABOARD *SOL SEAKER*
CRUISING IN SAN DIEGO BAY
SEPTEMBER 18

ll is lost. There is no escape.

She turned from the roaring bonfire and looked at the villagers standing before her. There were hundreds of them, both men and women. Bare-chested, they raised spears and chanted. Their faces and torsos were painted with gold designs that glittered in the firelight.

A loud explosion quieted the chanting as she and the others turned to see flaming shards whistle above the forest canopy. She darted her eyes to the villagers.

It is too late. There are not enough. It will end here. I have failed.

Among the villagers was a commotion. A burly male warrior barked out commands and a slew of the villagers took off toward the forest. Within seconds, they disappeared beyond the glow of the bonfire, but she could hear their whoops and hollers for several seconds before they, too, faded away.

Out of the corner of her eye, she spied the male warrior grab hold of a teenaged girl and lead her toward the bonfire. He called for others to surround the teen, while he dispatched others back to their huts. Another explosion in the forest was followed by the sounds of screams.

"Run!" she implored the villagers. *"Save yourselves! Flee!"*

She watched in horror as the burly man shouted down her command.

"*They will die!*" she yelled to him.

He did not answer. Instead, he turned and stripped off the teen's loin-cloth and ordered others to bathe the girl's face and torso. While the teen pleaded with the man, he turned away and pointed a group of other villagers toward the bonfire…and then he leveled his finger at *her* and barked out more commands.

As the villagers advanced toward her, she looked at the sobbing teen behind the mob and called out to the burly man, "*No! It will never work! I forbid it!*"

Before she could protest further, hands were upon her. She fought them as they relieved her of her headdress while other hands wrestled her tunic up and over her head. They tried to take her necklace too, but she declared it forbidden to touch.

The bonfire's flames licked at her bare backside as she continued to struggle against the hands disrobing her. An elderly man stepped forward and dipped two fingers in a small pot of gold liquid. He murmured incantations as he pulled the fingers out and began to paint designs on her body. She began to cry, begging the villagers to let her go. Looking past the elderly man, she saw the burly warrior order the teen to don the tunic and headdress. "*No! She does not deserve this! I am the one who has failed!*"

Two more explosions echoed through the night air. They were closer, and this time there were no screams that followed. The burly man ordered another small group of villagers toward the forest and yelled at the others to hasten their ministrations to the two women. The crack of splintering wood at the tree line signaled time was up. He commanded the elderly man to finish his painting and ordered the remaining villagers to make for the river.

She fought them as they dragged her away with them. Over her shoulder, she watched the burly man march the teen to the bonfire. He ordered the teen to kneel, then kissed her forehead.

Savages broke through gaps in the foliage and advanced. The teen bowed her head and sobbed. The man stood with his back to her and raised his spear toward the savages.

Pebbles awoke with a scream. Pinned to the floor by Anlon, Griffin and Sanjay, she looked around at them, her eyes as wild as a trapped animal's. She yelled at them in a foreign tongue and struggled for release. Happy began to bark. Pebbles' head snapped in his direction and her eyes fluttered. She darted her eyes back to the men holding her down and her body went limp. Breathing heavily, she closed her eyes and mumbled, "She forgot the bag."

Jennifer reentered the living room with her phone pressed to her ear. She froze in place when she saw Pebbles laid out on the sofa with a washcloth layered on her forehead. Anlon and Griffin were across the room, huddled in conversation. Sanjay, sitting beside Pebbles, was listening to her speak.

Covering the phone with her other hand, Jennifer caught Griffin's attention and whispered, "What happened?"

"Another daymare."

As she was about to ask another question, she heard a click on her phone. "Miss Stevens, are you still there?"

"Yes, I'm here."

"I am a colleague of Señor Perez. He is on an expedition in Guatemala. Have you tried his cell phone?"

"I have. Several times. I left a voicemail."

"The cell reception at the dig site is not very good but he usually checks his phone messages when he gets back to the hotel in the evening. I can leave a message for him at the hotel if you'd like."

"Um...yeah, sure. That would be great. Thanks. It's pretty important."

After the archaeology professor on the other end of the line rang off, Jennifer pocketed her phone and joined Anlon and Griffin.

"Is she okay?" Jennifer asked Anlon.

"I think so. She's shaken up, but Sanjay seems to be helping her settle down." He cocked his head toward the outdoor bar. "Why don't we go outside and give them some space."

Outside, the wind was still whipping around the open-air bar, so they climbed the forward stairs to reach the upper deck cabin. On their way to the dining room, they passed by the bridge. First Officer "Popeye" Ellis stepped out and asked to speak with Anlon.

"Captain Hansen just called from the dock. He's mighty put out. Wants me to turn about and return to the marina. I don't know why it's such a fuss, taking the boat out without him, but he really gave me an earful about it."

"Okay, that's fine. Let's head back. I'll sort it out with him later."

The first officer grumbled something unintelligible and then disappeared back onto the bridge. Anlon and the others continued on to the dining room. Once there, Anlon and Griffin took turns filling Jennifer in on what had happened to Pebbles and then Anlon asked Jennifer about the bird carving displayed on her smart tablet.

"How did you make the connection between her drawing and Muran's art collection?"

"The snake tipped me off."

"Snake? What snake?"

"The one on the mountain trail."

Jennifer explained that as she flipped through the pages of one of the sketchbooks, she came to a page with one of Pebbles' bird drawings. Her eyes drifted down the page and she spied the drawing of the snake blocking the trail. She told them she had not examined the snake in detail before, concentrating more on the whole scene rather than the snake itself.

"But the longer I looked at it, I realized she'd drawn the snake with feathers, not scales, or at least it seemed that way to me. It's hard to tell unless you look real close. Anyway, the feathers reminded me of an artifact I'd seen somewhere. I just couldn't remember where."

"*La Venta*," Anlon said.

"Yes, that's what I thought at first."

"La what?" asked Griffin.

Jennifer explained that two years prior, she had traveled to the La Venta Park Museum in Mexico in search of information about a statuette in the art collection of Anlon's deceased uncle, Devlin Wilson. The museum, she told Griffin, housed ancient Olmec artworks, including a vast collection of stone sculptures.

"There are definitely feathered serpents in their collection, but I went online and didn't find any that looked like the one Pebbles drew, so I broadened my search phrase and, boom, there it was on the first screen of images. I clicked on it and up popped a news article about the battle over Aja Jones' estate, including her art collection. And in the same article was a picture of the bird carving."

"Who is Aja Jones?" Griffin asked.

"The last of the aliases used by Muran, the woman who strangled Pebbles into a coma," said Anlon. "The one who transferred her mind onto the stone."

"Do you think I'm losing it?" Pebbles asked, wiping a tear from her cheek.

"No, not at all," Sanjay said.

She studied his almond-colored eyes. They seemed to reflect the same sincerity evident in his voice. "Well, I sure feel like I'm losing it."

"I understand. You want the dreams to stop, but they keep occurring. It is frustrating."

"You can say that again. Especially because they're getting worse, not better."

Out of the corner of her eye, she saw Happy's head rise into view. The dog placed his front paws on the sofa next to her shoulder and stared at her, his eyes beseeching her to pet him. Pebbles lifted her head from the throw pillow and complied.

"When you say they are getting worse, do you mean the events that happen in the dreams are becoming more upsetting?"

"No. I mean they're happening more frequently. Not so much at night when I'm asleep, more so when I'm awake, like the one I just had."

"It is interesting you mention that."

She paused petting Happy and looked up at Sanjay. "You think that means something."

"I do."

"Is it something bad?"

"I will give you the politically correct answer first. I do not know enough to say."

Pebbles frowned. "That's not much help."

"Well, I do have a theoretical answer, but it comes with disclaimers."

"All right, let's hear 'em."

"Very well. You are not my patient and I am not your therapist. You and I have only just started to get to know one another. We have yet to talk about your dreams in any depth or discuss the events that seem to have precipitated them. I have only been through your journals and sketches once, and I would not say it was an exhaustive review. I know very little about your past traumas, only the small amount Anlon shared. And though he also mentioned you have had a full battery of brain scans, I have not reviewed them, nor have I talked to the doctors who analyzed the test results."

"You sound like a pharmaceutical ad on TV. Are you going to start listing the horrible side effects of my dreams now?"

She was pleased when he smiled and said, "No."

"All right...so what's the *real* scoop? I won't hold you to it."

"Hold on, now that I think of it, I do have a few other disclaimers."

Pebbles laid back on the pillow and clenched her eyelids shut. "Oh, God, here they come."

"Relax. These are about me, not you." As she squinted through one eye, Sanjay continued. "I have counseled many people who have experienced a wide range of traumatic events, but I have never counseled someone who has experienced the kind of event that led to your coma.

"I do not doubt that it happened as Anlon described, but the idea of having your memories and consciousness extracted from your brain and then later replaced raises the possibility that something physiological occurred during one transfer or both. They might have literally changed how your brain works.

"So, while I have a gut feeling for what may be going on, it is only that... a gut feeling. And since I am *not* your therapist, you should treat it as one man's barely informed opinion, *not* a professional diagnosis."

Pebbles opened both eyes fully. "Got it. Buyer beware. So, what's your barely informed opinion?"

"Setting aside something physiological…"

"Yeah, yeah…"

"Your daytime subconscious mind is frustrated that your conscious mind is not paying close enough attention to what your nighttime unconscious dreams are trying to communicate."

Pebbles propped up on her elbows. "Come again?"

"The daydreams are acts of your subconscious mind, and so are your drawing skills. Both are triggered by stimuli in your conscious environment. In the most recent instance, it appears your daydream was brought on by the photograph of the stone bird carving. It was probably brewing anyway given our discussion about flickers, and reviewing your drawings, but seeing the photograph seems to have been the catalyst for the dream to start."

"Okay, that makes sense. But, Sanjay, there was no bird in the dream. Why would seeing the carving of a bird make me dream about something completely unrelated?"

She watched Sanjay remove his glasses and rest them atop his knee. He then reached into his back pocket, withdrew a handkerchief and used it to clean the glasses. "Just because the bird does not appear in the dream does not necessarily mean it is unrelated. Those who interpret dreams might say the bird symbolizes flight, and, in your dream, you are fleeing."

Pebbles sat all the way up so that she was eye to eye with Sanjay. "I've given that a lot of thought, the fleeing part. When I'm in the dreams, I always seem to run away at some point. I always feel panic, like I'm frightened of being caught. That whoever is chasing me is going to hurt me. In some of the dreams, they *do* catch me and *do* hurt me."

Sanjay finished cleaning his glasses and placed them back on. As he folded the handkerchief, he said, "Yes, I noticed that in your journal entries. I also noticed you are very protective of the bag in your dreams, the bag you seem to always be carrying."

Pebbles curled her legs up to move around Sanjay. He must have divined her purpose, for he scooted farther down the sofa so she could angle into a sitting position next to him. Careful not to clip the now sleeping Happy in the face, Pebbles lowered her feet to the living room carpet.

"Yes, that's right. In some of the dreams, I put my hand inside the bag to make sure nothing has fallen out. I can feel things inside, but I can't see them. And I definitely feel protective about what's inside. But in other dreams, I reach inside and pull out ordinary things I need at the moment, like a rock or a torch, but I don't feel protective about them. In fact, I expect them to be in the bag, as if I know exactly what's inside. It's weird."

"I find it interesting that your first comment when you came out of the bonfire dream was about the bag. You said, 'she forgot the bag.'"

"Did I?"

Sanjay nodded.

Pebbles closed her eyes and massaged her temples as she tried to recall the dream. "I don't remember the bag being in the dream."

"Yes, that is another interesting observation I took note of when you described the dream right after you woke up," Sanjay said.

"What do you think it means?"

Sanjay shrugged. "Metaphorically? The bag and its contents might symbolize the thoughts or emotions your conscious mind is suppressing. You know, you keep them in the bag and protect them from other people. That may be why you cannot figure out what is inside. They may be amorphous physical objects that represent your emotions or thoughts."

"Hmm…but how does that square with other dreams where I'm pulling out random stuff I use in the dreams?"

"Perhaps your subconscious is trying to tell you that what you are trying to protect is special, not an everyday kind of item. Then again, there could be a much simpler explanation. Maybe the bag is in the dream, but you just do not remember it. From all the edits in your journals, it is clear you remember new details of your dreams some period of time after you set down your initial memories of them. Maybe you will recall more about the bag later tonight or tomorrow…or the next time you have the same dream…assuming it is like the others and repeats."

Pebbles stared out the window. "Or maybe there's a reason it wasn't in the dream. Like, maybe I'm not worried about what's inside anymore. But that doesn't make any sense. I had a different dream this morning and the bag was definitely in it."

"Do you have a photocopy machine aboard the ship?" Sanjay asked.

The odd request stirred Pebbles' attention back on Sanjay. "Excuse me?"

"A copier. I have an idea that might help us analyze your journal entries."

"Oh," said Pebbles. "Um…let me think…Anlon has a printer in his office that copies. I'm pretty sure there's another one on the bridge."

"Good. We should get started right away."

"Started doing what?"

He pointed at the three open journals spread on the opposing sofa. "Your entries are chronological, which is to be expected since it is a diary, but I think the ordering may be hindering the ability to analyze the entries. I think we should photocopy every page and then reorganize the copies to group together the pages associated with each distinctive repeating dream."

"Okay. We can do that," Pebbles said. "Let's go."

On their way to Anlon's office, Pebbles, Sanjay and Happy encountered Anlon, Jennifer and Griffin at the central staircase. During the hallway exchange, Jennifer told Pebbles about the source of the picture.

"Who is Aja Jones?" asked Sanjay.

"Long story," Anlon said. "Come with me and I'll fill you in."

"Hold up, A.C. You can give him a history lesson later," said Pebbles. "We're working on something else right now. Come on, Sanjay, let's go."

As they started to walk away, Anlon said, "Pebbles, I haven't provided Sanjay a full download on everything that happened. If he's going to help us, he needs to know about Muran. Especially now, since we've got a connection between your dream and a piece in her collection."

"Okay, fine." Pebbles turned and crooked a finger at Jennifer and Griffin. "Come on, you two, we have work to do."

CHAPTER 7

TOUCHY SUBJECTS

KONA KAI MARINA
SAN DIEGO, CALIFORNIA
SEPTEMBER 18

Finding a quiet spot for the conversation about Muran proved harder than Anlon expected. He had intended to meet with Sanjay in his office but discovered Pebbles needed it for the photocopy project. *No problem,* Anlon thought. *I'll just use the living room.* But Pebbles nixed that idea too. The living room, she informed him, would be her assembly area for grouping the photocopied pages.

So, Anlon led Sanjay and Happy to the dining room, only to discover stewards setting up the room for dinner. He briefly considered using one of the ship's four outdoor deck areas but was concerned about the possibility they might be overheard by the crew.

Sanjay suggested they take Happy for a walk through the marina, accomplishing two objectives at once, a bio-break for the dog and privacy for their conversation. So, with Happy on a leash, the two men disembarked *Sol Seeker* and headed for a small park abutting the marina.

When they were out of earshot of the ship, Anlon began the tutorial.

"Aja Jones was an alias for Muran, the woman who orchestrated Pebbles' kidnapping, the one who strangled her, the one who transferred Pebbles' mind into a *Sinethal.* She was a Munuorian, like Malinyah."

"The ten-thousand-year-old woman Griffin mentioned," said Sanjay.

"Yes. It's misleading to say she was that old in a physical sense, because she changed bodies many times during that span. Only her mind was ten thousand years old."

Anlon explained that Muran had used the Munuorians' mind transfer technology for a different purpose than the Munuorians had intended. Instead of using the tech to permanently store her mind on a *Sinethal*, she used it to *temporarily* park her mind for the sole purpose of then transferring her parked mind into the body of another person. It was a forbidden practice among the Munuorians, he told Sanjay, because to accomplish the feat, one had to first erase the memories and consciousness of the person whose body would be occupied.

"To do what Muran did was murder, plain and simple. But she didn't really care about the lives she took. It was all about her."

"She did this to achieve eternal life?"

"Not at first," Anlon said. "The first time she killed, it was about revenge. After that, yeah, I think she used mind transfers as a way to extend her life and improve her circumstances. Well, *escape her circumstances* is probably a better way to put it. She had a knack for making enemies."

The conversation paused as they passed the docking berth of another yacht. Happy had stopped to sniff the mooring bollards and it took Sanjay a moment to tug him away. After they resumed walking, Sanjay said, "You realize this sounds like a fairy tale."

"Oh, yes I do. And, truthfully, I wish it had been. But it wasn't."

"At the moment, I have no choice but to take you at your word," Sanjay said. After stopping yet again to let Happy investigate the briny smells of the wood-planked dock, Sanjay posed a question. "So, tell me, what led this Muran to take an interest in Pebbles?"

"That's an even longer story. The short version — Muran thought I had some artifacts of hers, some artifacts that she believed my uncle Devlin stole from her. She sent a lackey to take them from me, but I wasn't home when he broke into the house. Pebbles was. He shot her when she tried to escape and then beat the hell out of her when she told him the artifacts weren't in the house. Thank God he didn't kill her. But he did take Pebbles to Muran, who decided to ransom Pebbles in exchange for the artifacts."

"Wait a second. If Muran intended to exchange Pebbles for the artifacts, why did she transfer Pebbles' mind into one of the memory stones?"

"Muran said it was a precaution in case we didn't produce the artifacts she wanted, though Pebbles says Muran made it clear to her before the mind transfer that she intended to take her body. Thankfully, she never got the chance to follow through on that part."

"What happened?"

"Craziness on a scale you wouldn't believe. Imagine a battle on the steps of an ancient Mayan temple in the middle of a Mexican jungle in the wee hours of the morning. If it hadn't been for Mereau, Muran would have prevailed."

"Mereau? Who is Mereau?"

"The ten-thousand-year-old 'dude' that Griffin mentioned in Sedona. The one who transferred Pebbles' mind back into her body."

Anlon's answer coincided with their arrival at the park. Sanjay led Happy a discreet distance from the park walkway and Happy wasted no time taking care of business. As Sanjay slid a bag from his pocket to clean up the mess, he said, "You confuse me, Anlon. You say to me this Muran violated the laws of her people by transferring her mind into other bodies, but then you tell me another of her contemporaries is the one who saved Pebbles. This would only be possible if Mereau, too, violated the Munuorian laws."

"I hate to keep saying it, but that's another long story. The best way to put it is this — Mereau and Muran were as far apart on the evil scale as you could possibly imagine. Muran lived scores of wicked lives over ten thousand years, Mereau lived only one valiant life."

Sanjay deposited the poop bag in a park trash can and joined Anlon on a nearby bench and gazed at the cityscape of San Diego. As there was no one else in the fenced-in park, Sanjay let Happy off the leash and let him roam.

"Are you saying Mereau's body lasted for ten thousand years?" Sanjay asked.

"No. His mind was stored on a *Sinethal* for nearly all that time. A man named Jacques Foucault discovered Mereau's tomb and his *Sinethal*. Foucault figured out how to activate the *Sinethal* and he formed a long friendship with Mereau. Ultimately, Foucault willingly gave up his body, his life, so that Mereau could vanquish Muran."

"And Mereau succeeded."

"Spectacularly. And after we found the *Sinethal* Muran used to store Pebbles' mind, Mereau helped us reunite her mind with her body."

Tears formed in Anlon's eyes as he recalled the moment when he first heard Pebbles speak after the reunification was complete.

"This has been a trauma for more than just Pebbles," said Sanjay.

"Yeah, it has." Anlon swept away some more tears and cleared his throat. "Which brings us to Muran and Aja Jones."

"Ah, yes."

"The FBI was involved in helping us find and rescue Pebbles after she was kidnapped, and they discovered evidence linking Muran with a woman named Aja Jones. They ended up raiding Aja Jones' home on New Caledonia, looking for evidence related to Pebbles' kidnapping, and found a trove of ancient artifacts. Thousands of pieces she'd accumulated and hidden, over ten millennia. The collection is supposedly worth billions, but its true worth is impossible to value. There are hundreds of pieces that have no connection with any known cultures."

"Is the bird carving one of those mystery pieces?"

"I don't know. It's the reason Jen put in a call to Cesar Perez. He's an archaeologist and a friend of ours. He was called in to help the FBI catalog the collection before the New Caledonians kicked them out."

"Kicked them out? Why?"

"Well, I guess the New Caledonians felt the FBI was overstepping its bounds. Plus, they discovered Aja Jones died without a will and no heirs. Under New Caledonian law, that made her estate the property of the government. And once they found out how much the estate was worth, they booted out the FBI and seized the collection."

As Anlon spoke, Happy trotted over to the bench and began to whimper. Anlon patted the dog and asked, "What's the matter, buddy? Run out of things to sniff?"

"No. He is telling us he's hungry."

"Ah. I guess it is dinner time, isn't it, Happy?" said Anlon. The dog barked loudly. Anlon turned to Sanjay. "I see he knows the word *dinner*."

"He knows our words for any kind of meal."

On the way back to *Sol Seaker*, Sanjay asked Anlon if Pebbles was familiar with Muran's collection. "By that I mean, has she seen it in person
or seen photographs of some or all of the pieces?"

"As far as I know, she's not seen anything from the collection. You have
to understand, Sanjay. Muran is a very touchy subject with Pebbles. She
doesn't like to talk about her, think about her or come into contact with
anything to do with her. It's been that way ever since Mereau reunited her
mind and body."

"I see. We'll have to broach the subject more carefully, then."

Dinner turned out to be more of a work session for Sanjay than a social
occasion. Pebbles, Jennifer and Griffin had finished grouping the journal entries and Pebbles was eager for Sanjay to review the dream-packs.

So, in between bites, Sanjay read through one of the packs. When he
finished, he asked for another. After reviewing a third pack, he looked up
at Anlon and said, "You know, reviewing the entries in this way, I can
better appreciate why you suspect the dreams may be memories. They are
so alike. They follow the same timeline. There is never an alternative ending or disjointed scenes. While the entries do not always include the same
details, and here and there Pebbles has added new details after the fact,
there is tremendous consistency from entry to entry."

"Yeah, but there's one problem with that theory. They aren't my memories," Pebbles said.

"That may not be true. You may be experiencing amnesia."

"Amnesia? Look, I don't mean to be disrespectful, Sanjay, but I'm one
hundred percent certain I've never been chased through woods or
through a temple. I've never had an animal skin bag in my life or been in
a village with a bonfire. None of that stuff."

"I do not doubt you."

"Then how can you suggest I have amnesia?"

"Just because you have never experienced the events in your dreams
does not mean they are not memories."

With a quick shake of her head, Pebbles turned to Anlon. "Is he making sense to you?"

Before Anlon could answer, Sanjay said, "You might have read a book about similar adventures earlier in your life. Or seen a movie or television program. Someone may have told you a story. Your mind may be treating the memories of one or more of such stories as your own memories."

"Hmm…I think I'd remember if I saw a movie with any of the stuff in my dreams."

"You experienced a coma, Pebbles. Regardless of what caused the coma, your brain was injured, and it is quite possible your memory was affected."

"But I haven't lost any of my memories." Pebbles once again turned to Anlon. "Have I?"

"Not that I'm aware of."

She turned to Jennifer and Griffin. "I haven't forgotten who you guys are or my name or anything like that, have I?"

"If you have, I haven't noticed," said Jennifer.

"Me neither," Griffin said.

Pebbles directed her attention back to Sanjay. "See."

"Amnesia can affect older memories—"

Her voice turning gruff, Pebbles cut Sanjay off. "Look, I don't have amnesia. Okay?"

Sanjay sat back. For several seconds, he stared off into space. When he spoke, his voice was level, almost melodic in tone. "I apologize. I did not mean to upset you. I merely meant to present a possible explanation for the flashback-like qualities of your dreams."

"Well, you're barking up—"

"Hold on, Pebbles," Anlon said. "Let's hear him out."

"Why? I don't have amnesia."

"Your coma occurred roughly eleven months ago, correct?" Sanjay asked.

"Yeah, so what?"

"And for a period of time afterward, you experienced flashbacks about your kidnapping. From what Anlon shared, they eventually faded and for a stretch of six months or so, you had no nightmares. Then, all of a sudden, these new dreams began to occur. They, too, seem like flashbacks even though you do not consider them memories. Better stated, you do not consider them *your* memories."

"Yes, all that's true. Again, what are you driving at?"

"Amnesia occurs when a brain injury damages areas where memories are stored. Sometimes the damage is significant enough that a person never recovers certain memories, but in most people, the brain eventually establishes new connections, and lost memories are at least partially restored.

"For example, you may always have remembered a birthday party based on your memory of a favorite gift you received. But as a result of your injury, the area storing the memory of the gift may have been damaged, causing you to forget about the party because you don't recall the gift. But, later, as the brain links together new pathways with other memories of the party, you find you can recall the party again. However, instead of the memory of the gift being the cue that triggers the memory, it might be the taste of a cake or the sound of children singing Happy Birthday. Depending on the severity of the brain injury involved, the process to build new links to lost memories can take weeks, months or years.

"The time gap between when your early flashbacks ended and your most recent dreams began suggests your brain has been in the process of building new links to certain memories lost as a result of your coma. The emergence of your drawing ability supports this conclusion."

"My drawing ability? What does that have to do with amnesia?"

Anlon interjected. "I think what Sanjay means to say is that your sudden artistry is an additional indication that your brain is in the process of establishing new connections."

"Correct," said Sanjay. "As Anlon and I discussed in Sedona, brain scans of people who develop savant behaviors after brain injuries often show damage to the temporal lobe, a part of the brain heavily involved in memory management. Damage to the same lobe is also prevalent among people who suffer from amnesia *and* PTSD."

"Look, I'm not disputing a connection between my dreams and the drawings," Pebbles said. "They both started around the same time, so I get that they're related, even though a lot of my drawings have nothing to do with my dreams — like today with the bird carving. What I am disputing is that I have amnesia. These dreams, if they are memories, aren't *my* memories."

"I would not be so sure. They could be bits of disparate memories that your brain has linked together to create a unified memory. That's what dreams are at their core," Sanjay said. "I can give you an example in my own life. I am fifty-six. I was born in Kavali, India, though I remember nothing of living there."

Griffin piped up. "I've heard this intro before. You're going to tell your spooky Pearl Harbor story, aren't you?"

"Your memory serves you well, my friend."

"What can I say? I'm good at remembering spooky stories."

Sanjay smiled and returned his attention to Pebbles. "As I was saying, I was born in India. When I was a small boy, my father moved our family to Vancouver. I lived there with my family until I went to college in the United States in the early 1980s. Somewhere during my life, I do not know when or where, I must have read or seen a graphic depiction about the Pearl Harbor attack, an account I do not remember. Whether it came from a history book, or we talked about it in a class or I saw a move, I just do not recall.

"But one day in the mid-1990s, I was in Fiji on vacation, and I woke up and took a walk on the beach. And there was something about the color of the sky, the puffy clouds hovering over the water, the humidity in the air, or all of it, that triggered the most intense vision I have ever experienced.

"I swear to God I was there. At Pearl Harbor. Just as the attack began. I can close my eyes right now and hear the whine of the Zeros, the ocean breeze rustling the palm trees. I can see the black spots coming over the mountains toward the base, growing into planes as they drew near. I can remember taking cover when the first explosions occurred. The smell, the acrid smell of burning fuel, is so strong in my memory, I can detect it in my nose right now."

Sanjay's eyes opened. "Pearl Harbor happened seventeen years before I was born. And before that vision I had never been to Oahu. But after the dozenth time I recalled the vision, I went there. I stood at the very spot where my vision takes place. I ask you — how is this possible?

"Did I read an account of the battle that was so vivid it lodged into my mind as my own memory? Was I half asleep during a television program that recounted a survivor's tale? Was it a reenactment I saw in a documentary or movie? I cannot say. I have researched every resource imaginable, but I have never been able to find any book or movie with a depiction of what I experienced during the vision. But, if the wind blows a certain way, or I hear the whine of a vintage airplane over Sedona, or the sun peeks through the clouds and colors the sky just right, the vision sometimes pops into my mind as clearly as if I were standing on the base again.

"Is it a figment of my imagination? Most likely. But it is so vivid, I cannot believe such a vision could be manufactured in mind without reference points. Therefore, it must be a memory of some kind, but it cannot be *my* memory because *I* was not there."

Griffin interrupted again. "Reincarnation, dude. That's the answer."

"As we have discussed before, Griffin, my mind is open to the concept of reincarnation, but I think there is a more rational explanation for my Pearl Harbor vision. My mind has concocted a false memory about the attack based on bits and pieces of information my mind has accumulated over the years. The vision feels like *my* memory, though it is not. It cannot be. By the same token, it also cannot be someone else's memory."

Sanjay touched Pebbles' hand. "Look, I do not know for certain if you have amnesia. I freely admit I am theorizing. But the more I read your entries, the more they seem like flashbacks, and the harder it is to ignore the possibility of amnesia."

"Let me play devil's advocate," said Jennifer. "Let's say you're wrong. Not about Pebbles' brain making new connections, not about the dreams being flashbacks, but about amnesia. I know we keep harping on it, but what if Pebbles picked up bits and pieces of someone else's memories when her mind was transferred into the *Sinethal*? And those pieces tagged along when her mind was transferred back into her body. Couldn't the dreams be Pebbles' mind's way of trying to fit those foreign pieces into her own memories?"

"My mind is open to that possibility, Jennifer. But amnesia strikes me as a more likely explanation."

"So, where does that leave us? Leave me?" Pebbles asked. "Are you saying I have no choice but to let the dreams continue until my brain sorts everything out?"

"No. There are some things we can try to alleviate the frequency and intensity of the dreams."

"I'm not taking any drugs."

"I am not suggesting you do."

"Then what are you suggesting?"

"Let us start with the daydreams. If we can pinpoint the stimuli that seem to be triggering them, we may be able to reduce the frequency with which they are happening by avoiding the stimuli or employing strategies to condition your mind to react differently to them."

Oh, that's not gonna go over well, thought Anlon. He winced, waiting for Pebbles to erupt at the suggestion that Sanjay "condition" her mind. To his surprise, Pebbles said, "At this point, I'll try anything to make them stop. What kind of conditioning are we talking about?"

"There are several approaches we can try but we should first focus on identifying the triggers."

"Like the bird carving," Jennifer said.

"Yes, that clearly seems to be one of them, or flickers, woodpeckers, in general."

"And how are we going to do that?" Pebbles asked. "I mean, how are we going to find other triggers?"

"Your drawings seem like a good place to start to me," Sanjay said.

The suggestion made sense to Anlon. Pebbles had recognized the preponderance of flickers in her sketch pads and journals. And the discussion about them, or seeing the stone carving, had prompted her latest dream. Perhaps there were other clues hidden in her drawings.

"What about comparing them to Muran's art collection?" Jennifer asked. "Maybe there are other artifacts that look like some of your drawings?

Or maybe seeing pictures of the artifacts will trigger visions? When Cesar calls me back, I'll ask if there's a way we can tap into pictures of the rest of the collection. Who knows, maybe he has a set?"

"Good idea," Anlon said. "When do you expect him to call back?"

"Given the time now, and the fact he's ahead a few time zones, I'm guessing I won't hear back from him until tomorrow."

Anlon saw Pebbles sigh as she turned back to Sanjay. "What else can we do?"

"Hmm…you said you had a vision earlier this morning. Do you remember what you were doing right before it happened? Were you drawing? Thinking about your dreams?"

"No. None of that. I had just escaped Jen and her attempt to get me into yoga. I went to the kitchen for a smoothie. I took it up to the patio on the upper deck. I was just going to enjoy the sunshine and then *boom*… the next thing I knew, I was wrestling with Jen on the sofa up there."

"Maybe there was a flicker around," Griffin suggested.

"At the marina?" Pebbles said.

"You never know, there's lots of wood. Maybe you heard one of them pecking. You said they were woodpeckers, right?"

"I did. But the flickers in my drawings don't peck wood. I looked it up. They peck the ground, trying to snag worms and bugs and such."

"Hold on, Pebbles," Sanjay said. "Griffin may be on to something there. Do you know what a flicker sounds like?"

"Yeah. I listened to some recordings online when I researched them."

"Maybe you heard a bird make a similar sound, whether it was a flicker or not. The triggers do not have to be visual. They can be sounds, tastes, smells or all of the above."

"Okay, I'll give it some more thought, but I don't remember hearing any birds. Then again, I can't say I was paying attention to any particular sounds when I went up top."

"That is another reality we will face," said Sanjay. "Some of the triggers will not be obvious. You may not consciously notice them."

In listening to the conversation, Anlon became concerned that the discussion of triggers was focused solely on Pebbles' daydreams. He asked Sanjay how Pebbles could identify triggers of her nightmares.

"That is more difficult, since nighttime dreams often lag the stimuli that trigger them significantly. For nightmares, I typically recommend evaluating sleep hygiene as a first step. Much like Pebbles is keeping a dream journal, that means starting up a sleep journal where she records her nighttime routine for the few hours leading up to sleep each night. Oftentimes, we find clues to triggers in those routines, everything from variances in what time people go to sleep each night to what they watch or read before turning out the lights. We look at conversations they have before bed, foods or drinks they consumed, those sorts of things."

"I can totally start doing that," Pebbles said, "but is there anything we can do to get ahead of a nightmare? Like something I can do tonight?"

"Yes, as a matter of fact, we can. We could try a therapeutic technique called imagery rehearsal therapy, or IRT. It is a common treatment for PTSD-related nightmares, particularly repeating nightmares. Have you heard of it?"

"No."

"You and I would pick one of your nightmares, one that is comparatively less disturbing than your most frightening dream. We would discuss the nightmare and then imagine alternative aspects we could insert into the dream, including an alternative ending. We would write down the alternative scenario and then have you mentally and verbally rehearse it before you go to bed. It is not a technique that can be counted on to produce immediate results, as repetition of the therapy over a number of days is typically needed to produce an effect, but it is a proactive step you can take tonight to start trying to manage your nightmares. I have used IRT with many of my PTSD patients in the past and I have found it effective in reducing the frequency and severity of repeating nightmares for most of them. Would you agree, Griffin?"

"You took the words right out of my mouth, Sanjay. He's right, Pebbles. IRT really helped me out. I think it's worth a try."

"All right. Let's get to it," Pebbles said. "I know just the dream to start with."

CHAPTER 8

DESERT OASIS

ABOARD *SOL SEAKER*
KONA KAI MARINA, SAN DIEGO, CALIFORNIA
SEPTEMBER 19

W*ho are you and why are you inside my head?*

Pebbles had not really expected an answer, but she waited for one anyway. When nothing but black silence filled her mind, she prodded the interloper some more.

I know you're there. I feel your presence. Why won't you talk to me?

Rolling on her side, Pebbles pulled the top sheet over her head and curled her body into a ball.

If you would just talk to me, it would make things better for both of us. The dreams, the drawings, they're too hard for me to understand. I can't make sense of them. I mean, I can tell you're scared but I don't know why. I know you're trying to protect something, but I don't know what.

More silence. Pebbles inhaled deeply through her nose and exhaled slowly through her mouth. In and out, she repeated the rhythm several times.

Just relax…everything is okay…you don't have to be scared.

The sound of water lapping up against the boat was soothing, almost hypnotic. Pebbles adjusted the rhythm of her breathing to match the rise and fall of the sounds.

See how I'm relaxing? Now you do the same, okay? That way, when the dream starts, we'll both be in a better place. You can show me more and

I'll be able to notice more. We both won't be so scared, and we can help each other. Now, come on, breathe with me...in...out...in...out.

A sensation of relief passed through Pebbles just as she fell asleep.

The sand singed the soles of her feet. Above, the sun pounded down upon her head with so much intensity, her hair seemed afire. No wind to cool her, no trees for shade, she trudged on across the lifeless wasteland.

Do not fear them. They will not dare follow in daylight.

Her tunic stained with the salt from her sweat, her lips cracked and blistered, she pressed forward, her eyes locked on the shadow stretched out ahead of her. She could not believe how thin the shadow made her arms and legs.

It must be a trick. The desert is trying to trick me into giving up. It says to me: you are too weak, you are unworthy. Just lie down and die. There is no use in going on. You will never make it. It is too far. There are too many of them. Even if you make it to the river, they will catch you. They will take what they want. They will cut you into pieces and send your head back in a pot.

She sneered at the thought as she grasped the strap of the bag slung over her shoulder.

Never. They are too fat, too slow, too stupid to catch me. I will not fail.

The rocky debris beneath her feet began to cut into her skin. It was as if the desert had teeth and was biting her, trying to halt her crossing. She staggered and fell to the ground. The thin layer of sand coating the hardpan puffed up into the air as she landed, while her arms and legs scraped across the coarse surface. Rolling onto her hands and knees, she began to crawl.

You cannot stop me. I will not give up.

The desert howled with laughter...evil cackles that sounded like a thousand vultures gathering to feast. She lowered her head, sweat dripping from her nose, and kept crawling. The desert continued to mock her until a gust of cool wind flowed over her. It seemed to choke the desert, for the cackles quickly sputtered into silence. Another gust, this one even cooler. She craned her neck to look up. A cloud had passed in front of the sun. She closed her eyes and offered thanks. A voice responded. It was soothing.

"Relax...breathe in, breathe out."

Her eyes snapped open. She looked around but saw no one. Just endless miles of shimmering desert in every direction.

"Close your eyes again," the voice implored.

"You do not fool me, desert," she shouted. *"Try your tricks elsewhere and leave me be!"*

Suddenly, the sounds of birds filled her ears. They were chirping happily...and splashing. She looked up again and saw a stand of trees and a pond in the distance. Flowers and fruit dotted the branches of the lush foliage. Birds swam across the surface of the water, their paths marked by tiny wakes. She closed her eyes to shake the mirage from her mind.

"It's not a mirage," the voice said. *"Open your eyes, cool yourself in the water. I won't let the desert hurt you."*

Eyes clamped shut, she felt water dapple over her fingers and toes.

"Come on in," the voice said.

She gasped as she opened her eyes. In the center of the clear-water pond was a pale-skinned, naked woman. Her hair was shaved on one side and it was purple. Her shoulder and neck were painted with images. The woman smiled and said, *"Lose the bag, take off your tunic and jump in. We'll swim, we'll talk. You'll feel better, I promise. We both will."*

The pounding was so loud, so sudden, Sanjay jolted up from the bed with his fists balled, ready to fight. As his eyes adjusted to the dark room, he looked around. Over the pounding rose a weeping voice.

"Wake up! Can you hear me, Sanjay? Get your ass up!"

It was Pebbles. Of that, Sanjay was sure. He felt around for his robe at the foot of the bed and called back. "Just a moment. Is everything all right? Are you okay, Pebbles?"

The locked door's handle rattled. "Just open the effing door!"

Sanjay gave up searching for the robe and groped his way from the bed to the door. Standing in his boxer shorts and T-shirt, he unlocked and cracked open the door. In the nightlight-illuminated corridor, he saw Pebbles, similarly clad, tears streaming down her face. Behind her was the disheveled duo of Anlon and Jennifer.

Pebbles pushed open the door and collided with Sanjay. Wrapping her arms around him, she squeezed him tight. "You're amazing."

"I…uh…"

She kissed him on the cheek. "It worked! It freakin' worked! Come on, I've got something to show you."

Grabbing him by the arm, she pulled him through the door. Sanjay darted looks at Anlon and Jennifer. Also in their underclothes, they looked as confused as he felt. But all three followed Pebbles as she scurried down the hallway and raced up the staircase.

On the way up the stairs, a steward appeared and asked Anlon if everything was okay. Anlon said he wasn't sure and told the steward to join them. They tracked Pebbles to the living room, where they found her kneeling next to the coffee table, sketch pad open and furiously drawing. She stopped to look up and wipe tears from her cheeks. "I know her name! I know what she looks like! I know what's in the freakin' bag!"

She hopped up and hugged Sanjay again. He staggered backward, nearly tipping them both over on the sofa behind him. In a voice thick with happiness, Pebbles whispered, "Thank you."

Sanjay lightly patted her on the back while he looked toward Anlon. "I am so happy for you, Pebbles. Tell us about the dream."

Pulling back from Sanjay, Pebbles turned and hugged Anlon and then Jennifer. Her voice cracking, she said, "I'm *not* going crazy. I don't know how she got in my head, but she's real. She's freakin' real!"

As Pebbles returned to the coffee table to snatch the sketch pad, Anlon took a quick look at the nautical-style clock on the wall. It was 4:24 a.m. Anlon excused the steward and then lowered onto the sofa next to Pebbles. Jennifer and Sanjay sat on the opposing sofa. All of them gazed at the sketch pad. It was not one of her savant works of art. In fact, it was not even close. The pad showed three stick-figure-like drawings. One looked to Anlon like an arrowhead, another looked to be a clam shell and the last was either a spider or a chair.

Pebbles pointed her pencil at the three doodles. "Okay, so these are what she's carrying in the bag. I'll bet they're in Muran's collection."

"Um, Pebbles?" Jennifer raised her hand. "I know you're excited, but can we take a step back? It may be because I'm half asleep, but I feel like I just walked in on the end of a story instead of the beginning. What dream was it?"

"Sorry. Guess I kinda did skip ahead. It was the desert one."

As Pebbles began to describe the dream, Jennifer interrupted again. "Not to be a prig, but shouldn't we talk about this dream the same way we've talked about the others? You know, you write down what you remember in the journal and then have you walk us through it."

"Ugh, do you always have to go by the book?"

Jennifer shrugged. "Sorry, the cop in me likes to be methodical."

"Yeah? Well, not this morning, sister. I don't have the patience to write it down right now. I'll do it later."

Rising from the sofa, Jennifer said, "In that case, give me thirty seconds before you start."

"Where are you going?"

"If you're not going to write it down now, then I will," Jennifer said. Before she reached the cabin door, she turned back to Anlon. "While I'm getting my notepad, any chance we can get someone to whip up some coffee?"

"Good suggestion. I'll take care of it," Anlon said. He leaned over to kiss Pebbles on the cheek. "Be right back."

On his way out of the room, Anlon heard Sanjay say to Pebbles, "If we are going to take a quick break, I am going to get my robe. It is a bit chilly."

Pebbles' retort caused Anlon to smile. "Geez, Louise! What's wrong with you people?"

As Anlon approached the galley, he was surprised to detect the aroma of brewing coffee. Before opening the door, he peeked through the porthole and spotted Cindy Tanner, already attired in her pressed uniform, preparing a tray with coffee mugs. He slid open the door and said, "Hey there, Cindy. Whatcha doin' up so early?"

"Good morning, Dr. Cully." Tanner smoothed her hands over her uniform as if preparing for a military inspection. "Um, there's a storm coming our way. Captain Hansen and First Officer Ellis have been up for a while tracking it. I was making some coffee for them."

"Oh. Okay. When you get finished with theirs, we could use some coffee in the living room. Four mugs, please."

"Yes, Dr. Cully. If you wish, I can take care of yours first."

"No, that's not necessary. Captains keeping eyes on storms take precedence over passengers up early."

When Anlon returned to the living room, he received a second surprise. Jennifer had returned and so had Sanjay, but they were not seated on the sofa. Instead, they stood behind Pebbles whispering to each other. Anlon looked more closely at Pebbles and saw she was in the midst of drawing again.

Jennifer turned and looked at Anlon as he began to walk toward them. She broke from the conversation with Sanjay and intercepted Anlon halfway across the room. Now dressed in sweatpants and a sweatshirt, she whispered, "She's in a trance. Van Gogh's returned."

The robed Sanjay joined them. In a low voice, he said, "It is fascinating to watch her work. There is no hesitation in her strokes, no stopping to ponder what she is incorporating in the scene. It is almost as if she is copying a photograph."

"Or a memory," Jennifer said.

Sanjay nodded. "Or a memory."

"What's she drawing? The items in the bag?"

Jennifer bit her lower lip and shook her head. "It's a bit racier than that. Matter of fact, Sanjay and I should probably step out before she comes out of the trance. If she isn't aware of what she's drawing, she'll probably be embarrassed to know we've seen it."

"I agree," said Sanjay. "We will just tell her we have not seen the picture. If she chooses to show it to us later, then it will be her choice."

"What the hell is she drawing?" Anlon asked.

Jennifer nodded in Pebbles' direction. "Go see for yourself. Call us when she's ready to talk."

After the two left the living room, Anlon quietly walked up behind Pebbles and peered over her shoulder. Her drawing showed a pond surrounded by palm trees and flowering bushes. Without her colored pencils, the scene was produced in shades of gray, but the details were still beyond belief. Whether one focused on the birds perched on the treetops, the clouds reflected on the surface of the water or fruits dangling from drooping branches, the drawing had an eerie three-dimensional feel to it.

In the center of the sketch, resting on a grassy patch behind the pond, were two women, both sans clothing, engaged in conversation. As Anlon gazed upon them, he thought Pebbles would likely be proud of how accurately she had drawn the tattoos on her body…not so much for how explicit she had been with certain other anatomical features. For though she was beautiful from head to toe, Pebbles was not the type to put it all out there.

As his eyes lingered on Pebbles, Anlon found it ironic she had incorporated such detail about her own body when the true focal point of the drawing was the other woman. Not because of her appearance but because of her commanding presence.

In contrast to Pebbles who lay stretched out on her side in a relaxed pose, the other woman squatted like a baseball catcher, one hand resting on her knee, the other pointing toward the water's edge. In the image, the woman was speaking to Pebbles, her facial expression animated as if trying to drive a point home. Pebbles was listening, lips slightly parted, as if absorbing the woman's words.

Where Pebbles had depicted her own body as small-breasted and willowy-thin, she had drawn the other woman with more cleavage, sinewy limbs and a chiseled abdomen. While Pebbles was light-skinned in the drawing, the other woman was darker-toned. Her distinctly Anglo facial features seemed to imply she was a tanned Caucasian, but without further clarification from Pebbles, it was just a guess on Anlon's part.

Interestingly, Pebbles had drawn her own hair as long and wavy instead of her current style, a short-cut fade. She'd also depicted herself with dark hair instead of approximating its present soft lavender color by using a thin layer of gray shading.

The other woman's hair was long and straight, save for elaborate braiding that circled the crown of her head. Pebbles' exclusion of any shading for the woman's hair seemed to suggest it was white or very light blond. This assumption was reinforced by Pebbles' unmistakable depiction of darker hair further south on the woman.

Returning his gaze to the woman's head, there was one oddity Anlon could not reconcile when compared to the rest of the picture. The back of her head was elongated, stretching upward at a steep angle. If Pebbles had included other abstract elements in the sketch, Anlon might have concluded the odd-looking skull was intended as symbolism, or just a vagary one experienced in dreams. But in every other respect, the objects in the drawing were of normal proportions.

Besides, it was clear Pebbles had drawn the woman's hair to fit the elongated head. On a man, the woman's hairline would have been considered receding because it began so far up the skull. But it was an illusion. For, from the beginning of the hairline back, the woman had a full head of hair with tresses dangling down from the braided crown circling the bulbous peak of her head.

As Anlon watched Pebbles insert a distinctive-looking necklace onto the other woman, he couldn't help but think of the necklace as another contrast between the two women. I'm delicate, you're strong. I have questions, you have answers. You talk, I'll listen. I'm lost, you point the way. I'm just the peasant, you're the queen with the necklace.

With the last stroke completed, the kneeling Pebbles gently set the pencil down and sat back, resting her buttocks on her heels. She lifted her head and stared forward with a vacant expression, her mouth hanging open.

Anlon spoke to her in a soft voice. "Hey there. You okay?"

She did not seem to notice, she just kept staring at nothing.

"Pebbles?" Anlon said, his voice now a tick louder. "Pebbles, it's Anlon. Time to wake up."

She closed her eyes and lowered her head, her body swaying slightly. Thinking she was about to slump to the floor, Anlon reached out to catch her. But the swaying stopped, and her eyes opened. In slow motion, she reached for the pencil, leaned her torso over the picture, inserted an additional feature and then collapsed. Anlon grabbed hold of her before her head hit the edge of the coffee table and eased her the rest of the way to the floor.

He wiggled the pencil from her grip as he pondered whether to lift her onto the sofa or let her sleep where she was. Not knowing whether she was truly asleep or now in the midst of another dream, Anlon decided to leave her where she was. He snatched a pillow from the sofa and carefully placed it under her head, then retrieved a throw blanket from a storage chest across the room. After laying the blanket atop her sleeping body, Anlon picked up the sketchbook and examined Pebbles' last-second addition. Squinting at the page, he mumbled, "Now what the heck is that?"

While Pebbles slept, Anlon stepped out briefly to have one of the stewards bring back Jennifer and Sanjay. When they returned, both were fully dressed. Sanjay in Bermuda shorts and button-down shirt, Jennifer in yoga pants and a long-sleeved T-shirt. She carried a coffee mug which she handed to Anlon as she looked over his shoulder at Pebbles. "She's asleep again? Did she finish the drawing?"

"Yeah, she did." Anlon took a quick sip of the coffee and nodded his head in the direction of the storage chest. "Sketchbook is over there. Go take a look. You should see it, too, Sanjay."

"In a second," Sanjay said.

While Jennifer headed for the chest, Sanjay bent down next to Pebbles and studied her face.

"Is there a problem?" Anlon asked.

"No, just looking for rapid eye movement. Most dreams happen during REM cycles." Sanjay looked up at Anlon. "How long has she been asleep?"

"Five, maybe ten minutes." Anlon described how Pebbles seemingly finished the drawing but then picked up her pencil and added onto the picture before she conked out. "She inserted a symbol. I'm not sure what it is. Hopefully, when she wakes up, she'll be able to tell us. She also added a necklace on the other woman."

As they turned to join Jennifer, Sanjay asked, "What did you make of her rendition of the other woman?"

"Her head, you mean?"

"All of her."

"Looks like the kind of woman you wouldn't want to cross, with or without the alien-looking conehead."

They arrived at the chest. Standing alongside Jennifer, Sanjay peered down at the completed drawing, "Yes, that's very telling, don't you think?"

"What's telling?" Jennifer asked.

"We were talking about the other woman," Sanjay said. "If one ignores the idyllic oasis-setting, the full-frontal nudity, she looks like a field general outlining a battle plan."

"She definitely doesn't come across as a wallflower, that's for sure." Jennifer turned to look at Anlon. "Which is weird, because Pebbles isn't a wallflower either, but she totally drew herself like one."

"Yes, that's what I mean when I say the depiction of the other woman, of both women, is telling," Sanjay said. "We have journals full of Pebbles' dreams portraying this other woman fleeing in fear, yet she exhibits no fear in this picture. Quite the opposite. On the other hand, we have Pebbles, whom you have both described to me as being a scrapper, a fighter, and she is very passive in the drawing. It is a complete role reversal."

"I noticed the same thing." Anlon waved his hand over the drawing. "Is it possible we're misinterpreting the picture?"

"How so?" Sanjay asked.

"Maybe it's a reflection, a reverse image." Anlon paused, then said, "When I first looked at it, before the inconsistencies began to bother me, I saw it as Pebbles seeking guidance from the other woman. But the more I study it, I wonder if it's the opposite. I wonder if Pebbles drew this picture, not for us but for the other woman."

"Say what?" Jennifer frowned.

"You are thinking of the symbol Pebbles added," Sanjay said.

Anlon nodded. "Exactly. I think she may have created the picture to say to the woman—"

"Oh, my God. That's it," said Jennifer. "Pebbles used the picture to tell her to buck up...to get her shit together."

"Something like that." Anlon smiled.

"It is an interesting theory, but I am not sure I agree," Sanjay said. "When Pebbles and I discussed projecting a safe haven into her dream, the purpose was to coax the woman in her visions to reveal why she is frightened, why she is fleeing, what she is protecting. From what Pebbles said to us earlier, she seemed to believe she had all those answers...*before* she drew this picture."

"What picture?"

The three turned to find Pebbles standing behind them, the blanket wrapped around her shoulders. Through the gap between them, she spied the open sketchbook. Anlon stepped aside while Jennifer and Sanjay backed away. As Pebbles edged forward for a closer look, she said, "Oh, my."

CHAPTER 9

FLASHBACK FURY

Curled into the corner of the sofa, the blanket now resting over her legs, Pebbles watched Cindy Tanner enter the living room pushing a breakfast cart. As she approached the sitting area, Anlon closed the sketchbook.

"Thanks, A.C.," Pebbles said. She covered her blushing face. "I can't believe I drew *that*."

As Cindy began to pour out coffee into waiting cups on the tray, Sanjay asked, "You do not remember drawing the scene?"

"Nope."

"Well, I think it's beautiful," Jennifer said.

Pebbles accepted a saucer and cup from Cindy before answering Jennifer. "Would you feel the same if it was *your* privates on display?"

"Probably not."

"Uh huh. That's what I thought."

With the coffee distributed, the white-gloved Cindy readied a tray holding spoons, a cream dispenser and sugar bowl.

"To the best of your recollection, was the drawing an accurate depiction of your dream?" Sanjay asked.

"A little too accurate," Pebbles mumbled as she poured cream into her coffee.

"So, you were both naked in the dream?" Sanjay asked as a follow-up.

"Not at first. Well, I think I might have been from the get-go, but Citali wasn't."

"Sit-who?" Anlon asked.

"Citali, like Italy with a soft 'c' in front. That's her name," Pebbles said. She darted a look up at Cindy as she replaced the cream dispenser on the tray the stewardess held out. "Sorry we're subjecting you to more talk about my psycho visions."

"Hey, don't say stuff like that," Anlon said. He patted Pebbles' knee. "Neither you nor your visions are psycho."

The blushing Cindy moved quickly to the opposing sofa to offer the coffee add-ons to Sanjay. While he spooned in some sugar, he said, "You were saying that Citali was dressed when the dream began."

"Yeah, just like all the other times I've had the desert dream. She's in rough shape, kind of staggering across this huge rocky wasteland."

"When did the oasis come into the dream?" Anlon asked. "Before or after men start chasing her?"

"Before. Sanjay suggested inserting the oasis into the dream before the stress part of the vision."

"What was she wearing in the dream?" Sanjay asked.

"Same tunic-dress she has on in most of them. But in this one, it's nasty. All stained and torn. She reeks pretty bad too."

Jennifer sat up and placed her cup on the coffee table. "You've never mentioned the tunic was stained before, or anything about her being stinky. See, this is why we need to set this all down in your dream journal before you forget stuff."

Pebbles rolled her eyes. Sanjay pressed on. "So, when did she take the tunic off? And did she seem bothered by it? What I mean is, was she embarrassed to be naked in front of you?"

With a frown forming on her face, Pebbles said, "You seem pretty infatuated about her getting naked."

"It's a potent symbol in dreams. If she seemed upset by being seen without her clothes, it typically would mean she feels vulnerable. If she seemed comfortable, at ease, it is a sign that she feels confident."

Pebbles glanced at Cindy, who was now readying a basket of muffins on the cart, and then back at Sanjay. "So…I don't know how to say this without it sounding super weird, but…"

"But what?" Sanjay asked.

Pushing off the blanket, Pebbles uncurled her legs and scooted forward until she was perched on the edge of the sofa. She looked at each of her friends and said, "The moment the oasis formed, the dream stopped. The whole time we were together, the whole time we were talking, it felt real, like being with Malinyah. You've met her, Sanjay, you know what I mean."

"The experience of meeting Citali was different than what you experience in your dreams?"

"Exactly."

"In what way?" Jennifer asked.

Pebbles turned toward her. "Well, both feel real, but in the dreams, I don't ever feel part of them. You know? I'm someone else. I'm her. Everything that happens is about Citali. But, in the oasis, I was there. I was interacting with her." Pebbles redirected her gaze at Sanjay. "What I'm trying to say is that Citali, her consciousness, is inside my head. So, when you ask me how she felt about taking off her tunic like the answer is some kind of symbolism, I can't tell you. Because it wasn't a dream. It was a *real* interaction with a *real* person."

Sanjay listened, nodding at intervals. When Pebbles finished speaking, he said, "I think I understand what you are saying. In the dreams, you see and feel what she sees and feels. But in the oasis, you observed from your perspective, not hers. So, you do not have a sense of how she felt about removing her tunic."

Cindy began to cough and excused herself from the room. Pebbles could not be sure, but she thought she heard Cindy giggle before she started coughing. As she watched Cindy leave, she answered Sanjay. "Well, that's not entirely true. I could see her reaction when I suggested she take it off."

"Ah…so you encouraged her to remove it."

"Yeah. So what? She looked hot, dirty and tired. I thought she would feel better if she took it off and came in the water with me."

"Whoa. Wait. You were in the water? Your picture shows you two sitting by the pond, not in it," Jennifer said, her pen poised above her notepad.

"Well, first, we swam and talked for a while. I thought it would cool her off, make her feel better."

Jennifer turned to Sanjay. "Can we just start at the beginning and go through the dream…excuse me…the oasis meeting…from the top? We're missing important details jumping around like this."

"I agree with Jen," Anlon said. "I know you want to skip to the end, Pebbles, and talk about what was in her bag, but we could use some context."

With a huff, Pebbles said, "All right, all right. Just quiet down so I can concentrate."

She closed her eyes and took several deep breaths while she revisited meeting Citali.

The water was cool, refreshing, the scent of the flowers pungent. The chirps of the birds were melodic. Pebbles closed her eyes and treaded her legs in long, slow strokes. "I'm telling ya…you'll feel *so* much better if you just come in."

With her eyes shut, Pebbles could not see the white-haired woman standing at the pond's edge, but she could hear her labored breathing. She could feel the woman's aching muscles and weary mind. Pebbles' feet throbbed with the pain of the woman's swollen cuts, and her throat burned with thirst.

When the woman first came into view, her appearance had shocked Pebbles. Not because of her haggard condition — Pebbles already knew she was withering from the desert's cruelty —but because of her physical attributes. From her deformed head to her snow-white hair and its sharp contrast to her dark tan, to her MMA-fighter-toned body and glowing tiger-orange eyes, she looked like a circus freak.

Pebbles imagined a barker calling out, "*Come one, come all, you've seen the elephant man, the two-headed sisters, the bearded lady, but you've never seen an attraction like this! Is she an alien half-breed? A mutant from an experiment gone wrong? Or something more sinister — a demon among us mortals? You be the judge…*"

But Pebbles knew she was none of these things. She was just a woman, scared, tired and all alone.

Cupping her hand, Pebbles pooled water in her palm and sipped. The burning in her throat began to subside. She took another drink and opened her eyes. The white-haired woman fell to her knees and stabbed both hands in the water. Forming a bowl with them, she gulped and sloshed down several handfuls. After the last of them, she looked up at Pebbles.

"Tastes good, doesn't it?" Pebbles said.

The woman nodded. "Who are you? Where am I?"

"My name is Pebbles. What's yours?"

"Citali."

"That's a pretty name. Prettier than mine." Pebbles reached out her hand. "Won't you come swim with me, Citali?"

"Where are we? Where is this place?"

"I made it up in my mind. Do you like it?"

"You are a sorceress."

"No...I'm just me."

"You are marked like a sorceress." Citali pointed to Pebbles' neck and shoulder.

Gazing down at the Japanese symbol representing the word *strength* on her shoulder, Pebbles said, "Oh, those. They're just tattoos. I've got more." She held up both wrists. She floated onto her back and pointed to her pelvis and ankle. "Kind of like the gold paint you sometimes have on your body, only these don't wash off."

Citali rose up and stepped back. "How do you know I wear gold paint?"

"You've been in my dreams. Have I been in yours?" Pebbles lowered her legs and glided through the water toward Citali.

"Dreams? What dreams?"

The closer Pebbles got to Citali, the farther the woman backed away. Pebbles halted and treaded in place. "Dreams of you running away. Of people chasing you. They want what's in your bag." Pebbles pointed at the bag resting on Citali's hip. "What's in there, anyway? Why are people trying to take it from you?"

Citali pulled the bag up to her chest and clutched it. "I was right. You are a sorceress!"

She turned to flee. Pebbles cried out, "Please don't go! I want to help you."

"You cannot help me. It is too late."

A mist formed beyond the oasis, a mist into which Citali disappeared.

"Then stay and help me!" Pebbles shouted. She watched the mist grow thicker. "Please!"

She waded to the pond's edge and crawled on her hands and knees onto the sandy bank. Head lowered, she whispered, "Tell me why you're inside my brain. Tell me how you got there."

A thin voice whispered back. "It cannot be. I am dead."

Pebbles looked up. Though she could not see Citali through the mist, she could feel her presence. "I know, Citali. She put your mind on a stone. The same one she put my mind on. Our memories, our consciousnesses, got mixed up together."

"What do you speak of? She? Stone?"

"She suffocated you, didn't she? In the mudbank of the river." Pebbles collapsed onto the sand and rolled onto her back. Covering her eyes with her forearm, she said, "The bitch strangled me—"

Pebbles stopped her recitation of the oasis encounter in mid-sentence. Anlon reached out to touch her shoulder. "Pebbles? Are you all right?" Her body was afire and trembling. He looked up at Jennifer and Sanjay. "Something's wrong."

Sanjay was off the sofa and kneeling by her in an instant. As he felt her wrist for a pulse, he stared up at her lowered head. "Her eyes are flicking back and forth. I can see them move under her lids. She is in REM. She is dreaming."

Pebbles began to grunt. She flailed her arms, smacking Anlon in the face. Sanjay said, "Quickly, help me move the table out of the way."

With one hand covering his bleeding nose, Anlon grabbed hold of the table just as Jennifer began to drag it from between the two sofas. With the two men pushing and Jennifer pulling, they cleared the area just as Pebbles tumbled onto the floor. Head thrashing from side to side, she coughed and gasped.

"We need to wake her up…like, right now!" Anlon said.

"No…don't," said Sanjay. "Let it play out. She has suppressed it so long. It needs to come out."

In the candlelight, evil flickered on Muran's face. Woozy, Pebbles tried to speak but no words would form. She tried to move, but her arms and legs would not respond. Muran's hands slid underneath Pebbles' tunic and stroked her body. The woman nibbled on her neck and licked at her chin. She laughed as Pebbles whimpered.

"I wish you hadn't ruined your beautiful body with these horrid tattoos, but you'll do," Muran whispered in her ear. "Now, don't struggle, dove. Shh…be still."

Pebbles felt her tunic tear away and hands fondling her. As Muran kissed and licked her way around Pebbles' body, rage flared inside — a rage strong enough to heat her skin but too weak to move her drugged limbs. She pleaded for Muran to stop, but all that came out were bleats. Muran laughed and slid off the bed.

As she moved past the footboard to which Pebbles' legs were lashed, Muran removed her own tunic. She turned away from Pebbles and looked at the wall of tribal masks facing the bed. Pebbles lolled her head to the right to will her wrist to slip from the bind that gripped it, but the limp hand barely twitched.

She felt a weight upon her and turned her head to see the naked Muran above her. A smile on her face, Muran whispered, "Be still, my pet. Close your eyes."

Pebbles shook her head and grunted in protest as Muran cloaked her eyes. Seconds later, she felt Muran's hands traveling all over her body before they snaked upward and closed around her neck. Pebbles then felt the weight of Muran's body stretch out on top of her. Muran let out a moan and crushed her thumbs down on Pebbles' throat.

No! Stop! Help! Get off! Stop! I can't breathe! Stop! Please!

The writhing struggle was brief, for Muran was too practiced and Pebbles was too weak to stop her. As the darkness that covered her eyes also blanketed her mind, Muran's coos echoed in Pebbles' ears. "Yes, that's it, dove…go to sleep."

A hand touched Pebbles' shoulder. Startled, she turned to find herself sitting beside Citali at the edge of the pond. Citali said, "That was terrible. I'm so sorry. Are you dead too?"

Pebbles raised her hands to her throat and soothed the raw skin. "What? No. I'm still alive. God, I haven't thought about that night in a long time. I hope I never do again."

She closed her eyes and rolled back into the pond. As she disappeared into the cold depths, Pebbles heard a loud splash above her. Opening her eyes, she looked up to see Citali swimming toward her, the ribbons of her white mane flowing behind her naked body. Citali reached out a hand. Pebbles took hold of it and together they rose to the surface.

With their heads and shoulders bobbing above the water, Citali touched Pebbles' face. "I can feel you."

"Same here," Pebbles said. "It's strange, isn't it?"

Citali nodded. "You were right. The water feels good."

Pebbles smiled and enclosed Citali in her arms. "Thank you for coming back. I didn't want you to go. I need you."

"Why?" Citali asked.

"To find peace...for both of us."

When Pebbles opened her eyes, she saw Anlon, Sanjay and Jennifer leaning over her, concerned expressions on their faces. "Why am I lying down again?"

"You went into a trance," Anlon said. "A very intense trance."

"Why is your nose all swollen?"

"You clocked me in the face."

Pebbles propped up on her elbows. "I did? Oh, geez, I'm sorry, A.C. It looks like it hurts."

"It's okay, just a little tender. How are you? How do you feel?"

She laid her head back on the floor. "A bit dizzy. And sore. Especially my hands and feet."

"You were pounding them on the floor pretty hard," Jennifer said.

"Was I?" Pebbles flexed her hands and then rubbed them together.

Jennifer nodded. "Yeah. It was hard to watch. Really wanted to wake you up, but Sanjay thought it was best to let the dream…the memory… go to the end."

Pebbles looked at Sanjay. "Kinda wished you'd let them wake me. Didn't enjoy getting strangled all over again."

"I thought it would be more traumatic to interrupt the vision," Sanjay said. "Do you feel like talking about it?"

"Are you effing kidding me? N. O. Hell, no." Pebbles sat up. Her nose filled with the scent of the candle. She felt fingers stroking her breasts. Muran's laughs cackled in her ears. She glared at Sanjay, her face flushed. "Talking about it will just piss me off. God! It makes me so fucking angry! What she did to me…the way she laughed at me."

Tears welled in her eyes. Her voice quivered as she spoke to Anlon. "Give me that pillow. I need to punch something."

Anlon handed her the pillow. She tossed it on the floor and knelt over it. With her eyes closed, she conjured the cloying sounds of Muran's whispers. Her breathing quickened. She grit her teeth and began to cry.

"Let it out, Pebbles. We are here for you," Sanjay said.

She shook her head from side to side. "It hurts. It hurts to think about. It makes me so fucking angry!"

Pebbles slammed both fists on the pillow. Over and over again, she punched as hard as she could. Panting heavily, she spat expletives in between sobs. As she rained down blows, she imagined straddling the naked Muran and pounding her face into a bloody pulp. "*You* go to sleep, you bitch!"

The smile wouldn't leave Muran's face no matter how many times Pebbles imagined smashing her in the mouth, nor would her laughing cease. "Stop it! Stop laughing!"

She stopped flailing and squeezed the pillow so hard her arms trembled. At the top of her lungs, she screamed, "Die you bitch! Die! Stop laughing! Leave me alone! Get out of my head!"

With wild eyes, Pebbles cast aside the pillow and cursed Muran once more. Rolling over onto the floor, she curled into a ball, closed her eyes and summoned a vision of the oasis. Muran's cloying words and cackles began to fade from her mind. When they disappeared, she opened her eyes and peered up at Sanjay. "Happy now?"

"Are you?"

Rolling on her back, she spoke in between pants. "Getting there… a few thousand…more times…of doing that…would make me…feel much better."

"We'll get lots more pillows," Anlon said.

Pebbles laughed. "Sounds like…a good investment." She wiped tears from her cheeks. "It was so awful…she mocked me…she put her fingers inside me…licked me all over...talked to me…like I was her lover."

Rage spiked again. Pebbles reached for the pillow and squeezed it with all her might. "And then…she choked me…I couldn't see her…she put a mask over my face…but she was getting off on it…she was rubbing up against me…like she was having sex with me…moaning like she was turned on…whispering for me to go to sleep…I was pleading with her… please stop…fucking *bitch*!"

She winged the pillow across the room. "I'm so happy Mereau cut her in half…I only wish I'd been there to see it."

As her breathing subsided, she rolled onto all fours. "What time is it?"

"A little after nine," Jennifer said.

"Why is it so dark outside?"

"Storm coming," said Anlon.

Pebbles stood up and started to walk toward the cabin door. Anlon called out to her. "Hey, where are you going?"

"I'm gonna take a shower. Need to wash the bitch's ick off," she said. "I'll be back in, like, twenty minutes. Would you do me a favor?"

"Name it."

"I'm starving all of a sudden. I need something to eat before we finish up talking about Citali."

"Okay. I'll get Cindy to whip something up. You sure you don't want to take a break? Pick it up later today or put it off until tomorrow."

"Heck no. I don't want to waste any time. We've got to find out what happened to them."

"Excuse me? Them, who?"

"Not who. Them. The pieces she had in her bag. We need to find out what happened to them."

As soon as Jennifer saw Pebbles disappear from view, she turned to Sanjay. "That was supremely disturbing. I don't think I'll be sleeping tonight."

Sanjay reached down and picked up a pillow that had fallen from the couch while Anlon retrieved the one Pebbles had thrown across the room. "Watching someone relive a trauma is difficult."

"I know just what you mean," Jennifer said. "It's like taking a statement from a crime victim or a witness. You feel their pain, you want so badly to make it go away for them."

As Anlon crossed the room to join them, Sanjay said, "Yes, but it rarely goes away easily or quickly. And it will not for Pebbles. This was a beginning — a good beginning — but it is not the end."

"Guess I'd better order some more pillows quickly, then," Anlon said. He took the pillow from Sanjay and tossed both of them on the sofa. "In all seriousness, I'm relieved she finally opened up about that night…though I have to be honest with you, I'm really angry. If I had known all of that at Calakmul, Muran would never have made it four steps down the temple."

"Amen to that," Jennifer said. "I would have emptied my Glock on the bitch."

"So, what do we do from here, Sanjay?" Anlon asked. "How do we help her?"

"Listen to her. Be with her. But let her take the lead. More of her anger, her frustration, her other feelings about it will come out, but we have to let them come out when *she's* ready to talk about them. We cannot force it. And we must remember, the strangulation was not the only trauma she suffered. The next time she opens up, it may be about the shooting or something else."

"What do you think will happen with the dreams?" Jennifer asked. "I mean, we've all felt they were building up to something. Is this what they were leading to? Pebbles meeting Citali? Confronting what happened with Muran?"

Sanjay sat down. "I do not know. They definitely seem intertwined. I could easily see the dreams tapering off now that she has opened up about Muran. But if they do not, we have a couple of assets to work with now to help Pebbles."

"Citali," said Jennifer.

"Yes, she could be very helpful. More important, though, is that we learned Pebbles was able, through the power of suggestion, to interrupt and change the desert dream. If we can work together to develop different 'safe zones' within each of the repeating dreams, she may be able to reduce the stress-inducing elements of the other dreams or, if we are lucky, stop them from happening."

"What's your view of Citali?" Anlon asked. "Do you think she's real as Pebbles believes?"

"In all candor, Anlon, I do not know. If you had not introduced me to Malinyah, I would say Pebbles had created a personality to go with the woman in her dreams. Some of the contrasting imagery is so vivid, Citali strikes me as a cut-out, a proxy, for a part of Pebbles' personality."

"I thought the same as I listened to her talk about Citali and the oasis," Anlon said. "But, on the other hand, she was adamant that Citali is real."

"Except, from what Pebbles said, Citali didn't seem to recognize her description of the *Sinethal*, which suggests Citali didn't know anything about the Munuorian stones," Jennifer noted.

"Yeah, that's true," said Anlon, "but if you think back to Calakmul, Pebbles didn't know Muran moved her mind into the *Sinethal* until *after* we rescued her. If Muran incapacitated Citali in a similar fashion before transferring her mind, Citali may have no idea her mind went onto the stone."

"Good point," Jennifer said.

"Yet, the Munuorian stones do not appear in any of Pebbles' dreams," Sanjay said. "Might they be the items in the bag that Citali is protecting? Possibly. You have made it clear that Pebbles did not want to have anything to do with the stones after her mind was back in her body. It would stand to reason that the items in the bag are proxies for the stones. She does not see them in her dreams because her subconscious knows she does not want to see them."

"And there's no evil bitch in any of Pebbles' dreams," added Jennifer. "When she's being chased, she's being chased by men."

"Good point," Anlon said.

"In any event, let us hope Citali is a figment of her imagination," said Sanjay. "If not, we have a more substantial problem to deal with. If Citali's memories and her consciousness are indeed inside Pebbles' mind, how in heaven's name do we extract them?"

CHAPTER 10

A BAG OF SURPRISES

With Sanjay's comment hanging in the air, Anlon left the living room to find Cindy, partly to talk to her about preparing a more expansive breakfast and partly to talk to her about her sudden departure in the middle of serving coffee. On the way to the galley, he spied Griffin out the window. Bundled in a jacket, he was coming aboard with Happy walking alongside on a leash. Anlon stepped outside and said, "There you are. I wondered why you hadn't joined us."

Griffin told him Jennifer had urged him to go back to sleep when Pebbles came banging on their stateroom door. "I tried, but I couldn't get back to sleep. I got up, got dressed and was on my way to find you guys when I heard old Happy here whimpering. So, I figured, what the heck, I'll take him for a walk. Everything okay now?"

"Yeah, I guess. For the most part. Why don't you head up now? They're in the living room. Pebbles had a breakthrough. She's going to tell us more about it over breakfast."

Happy began to bark. Anlon laughed. "I guess you do know all our words for meals. Don't worry, buddy. I'll make sure they bring food for you too."

After Griffin and Happy departed, Anlon continued on to the galley where he found Cindy busy preparing the normal breakfast buffet served aboard each morning. When she saw him enter the room, her face turned red and she stopped her preparations. Without Anlon even uttering a word, Cindy said, "I am very sorry, Dr. Cully. It was very unprofessional of me. It won't happen again. I promise."

"Yeah, I don't want to make a mountain out of it, Cindy, but it was kind of out of character for you. But I get it. If I had been in your shoes, I probably would have had a similar reaction. Just do me a favor, would you? Let's not go there again."

"Yes, sir. I understand. Like I said, it won't happen again."

"Good. Look, I know Pebbles' nightmares have made your job more difficult. I'm sure the same is true for the rest of the crew. But you guys have pitched in and been a big help so far. I just need everybody to hang in there a little while longer. We're doing our best to help Pebbles sort things out and get things back to normal. It'll be easier to do if we can continue to count on everybody to be allies."

"You can count on me. You can count on all of us."

"Great. Enough said. I'm going up to talk with Captain Hansen about the storm. Do me one more favor?"

"Yes, Dr. Cully?"

"Can you add some of the breakfast burritos that Pebbles likes to the buffet, and maybe a few more for Happy? He looked pretty hungry when I saw him in the hallway."

After conferring with the captain, Anlon returned to the living room to discover Pebbles devouring a burrito with Happy at her feet doing the same. Jennifer was snacking on a protein bar while Griffin and Sanjay were dining on bowls of cut up fruit.

As he approached the diners, he heard Pebbles say, "She basically had one job. To protect what was in the bag."

"The three objects you sketched earlier," Jennifer said.

"Yeah. Only my sketches suck. What Citali showed me didn't look anything like what I drew." Pebbles noticed Anlon and smiled. He kissed her on the cheek as he sat down next to her.

"Feeling better?" he asked.

"Much. Want some of my burrito?"

"No thanks. I'm not all that hungry."

"'K. Suit yourself." Pebbles leaned over and said to Happy, "You hear that? More for us."

Happy barked and licked Pebbles' foot. She turned to Sanjay. "Breakfast burritos are okay for him, right?"

"They are not his usual fare, but when in Rome…"

Pebbles laughed and returned to her conversation with Jennifer. "Where were we?"

"Talking about the objects in Citali's bag."

"Oh, right. They looked like unfinished clay sculptures. I mean, they had basic shapes to them, but not a lot of detail. Maybe I'll be able to draw them better in one of my trances."

"Did she say why she was protecting them?" Griffin asked.

Pebbles nodded while she took another bite of her burrito. After a few chews, she held her hand over her mouth while she said, "She said a rival tribe invaded the place where she lived. They came to take the pieces… *and* Citali."

Anlon noticed Sanjay raise his hand to ask a question, only to be met by a raised hand back from Pebbles. "Let me finish eating." She popped the last of the burrito and quickly consumed it. "Okay, fire away."

"It is interesting what you say about the invaders wanting Citali in addition to the objects in the bag. Did she say why?"

"She said she's the only one who knows how to use them."

Pebbles' recitation of Citali's words echoed in Anlon's mind. *She's the only one who knows how to use them.* If the contents of the bag were Munuorian stones as Anlon suspected, Citali's comment made sense. He thought back to comments Pebbles had relayed from one of her early visitations with Malinyah. She had said the Munuorians avoided using their stones in the presence of foreigners, fearing the more primitive cultures would be disturbed by the display of their powers.

Had Citali been indiscreet in using the stones? Had the rival tribe seen what they could do? If so, Anlon could understand why they would view Citali's tribe as a threat…and why they would want to possess them. It also explained why they needed Citali. The stones were of no use without knowing how to wield them.

When Anlon finished expressing these thoughts to the others, Jennifer said, "I was thinking along a similar track, but from a different angle."

"How so?" Anlon asked.

"Well, in order for what you said to be true, someone had to have given the stones to Citali and then showed her how to use them. She's not Munuorian, right? I mean, she sure doesn't look like one of them. And Pebbles, you haven't said anything about her being one of them."

Anlon glanced over at Pebbles, who confirmed Jennifer's supposition with a nod of her head. Jennifer continued to describe her theory. "So, I'm wondering if Citali was one of the great flood survivors, or a descendent of one. We know the Munuorians dispersed after the flood to help foreigners start over. And, by then, they were very open in sharing their stones and their knowledge."

Sanjay interrupted. "Excuse me. You have lost me. Great flood?"

Jennifer provided Sanjay with a quick Munuorian history lesson. Ten thousand years ago, she told him, there had been a large asteroid that passed by Earth. Its magnetic pull on the planet was so intense it flipped Earth upside down, or nearly so. The sudden reorientation caused a massive tidal wave that circled the Earth multiple times before the wave's kinetic energy was spent. The asteroid's tug on Earth also ripped apart the land masses across the globe. New lands thrust up from the depths of the oceans while some lands collapsed under the sea.

The combined upheavals devastated the planet's plant and animal populations, including humans. Those humans that survived did so by sheer luck. Scattered in small bands, with little shelter and less food, the human race teetered on the brink of extinction.

The Munuorians, Jennifer told Sanjay, had known the asteroid was coming and had a sense of what it might unleash on the Earth. So, they prepared their own population and lands for the potential catastrophe but did nothing to warn or prepare foreigners with whom they had friendly relations.

Jennifer finished the history lesson by saying, "The effects of the asteroid went far beyond anything the Munuorians expected, devastating their lands and population too. And when it was all over and the dust settled, the Munuorians had two choices. They could either choose to rebuild their own culture and say screw it to everyone else left alive on Earth. Or they could take to the seas and help the foreigners they had turned their backs on before the asteroid."

Anlon supplemented Jennifer's description by telling Sanjay that many cultures around the globe had the great flood myths that described "fish-men" who came by sea bearing strange objects. With these objects, the fish-men helped the cultures learn how to build, farm and protect themselves.

"The mythical fish-men were the Munuorians. They spread out around the globe and assimilated into the survivor groups they encountered. For a time, they were treated as gods, but eventually the people they saved began to covet the stones. And as one might expect, that led to conflicts to possess them. The Munuorians, by and large, lost those conflicts and, as a result, their stones."

"Right," Jennifer said. "So, you see, if the objects in Citali's bag are Munuorian stones, she must have belonged to one of the cultures that re-volted against the Munuorians and took their stones. And then found herself defending the stones later on. Does that fit to you, Pebbles?"

When Pebbles did not blurt out a definitive yes or no, Anlon studied her face for clues to what her answer might be. Her expression was thoughtful, as if she was trying to reconcile Jennifer's theory with her dreams and interaction with Citali. Yet, there was a hint of skepticism communicated by her furrowed forehead and a twitch of her lips.

"I don't know, Jen. The objects in the bag don't look like any of the stones. There's no cone-like object, no bowl, no hockey pucks or tiles or cookie-shaped stones. Like I said before, they look more like half-made clay sculptures."

Jennifer turned to Sanjay. "Tell her what you were saying about the objects, how Pebbles' subconscious might be obscuring what they re-ally look like."

Pebbles cocked her head in Sanjay's direction. Anlon could not help but notice her cheeks begin to flush. "You still think I'm making all this up, don't you?"

The glare she pointed at Sanjay was effective. Anlon noticed him adjust his posture in a manner close to a squirm. "Not at all. I believe you are having these experiences, just as you say."

"But you don't believe the experiences are real. You think they're imaginary."

"They might be." Sanjay locked eyes with Pebbles. "They might not."

Anlon cringed as her face turned a deeper shade of red. *Uh oh, here we go!* But before she erupted, Sanjay said, "But my comment that Jennifer referenced was not questioning whether your experiences are real or imaginary. It had to do with the continued amorphous nature of the objects in Citali's bag.

"I was saying that *one* explanation for this might be your mind's unwillingness to think about the Munuorian stones. I have been told that ever since you awoke from your coma, you have made it clear you don't want to see or touch the stones. Even now, in this conversation, you look visibly uncomfortable discussing them. So, while your interaction with Citali *might* be real, your mind *may* be exhibiting the same discomfort with the stones that you have expressed consciously by obscuring how they appeared to you at the oasis."

The red began to fade on Pebbles' face. Anlon sighed in relief. The last thing they needed was for Pebbles to shut down.

"Okay, I get what you mean. I guess it's possible," she said. "If Citali's mind ended up on the same *Sinethal* mine was stored on, she obviously came in contact with the stones somewhere along the line. Muran or another Munuorian or…"

When Pebbles' voice faded, Anlon finished the sentence for her. "Or someone the Munuorians trained to use the stones."

"Yes. And if that's the case," Jennifer said, "there's another possible explanation that has nothing to do with Pebbles' subconscious."

"Such as?" Sanjay said.

Jennifer stood and began to pace the room. "Well, for starters, we don't know the time period in which Citali lived. Right? I mean, for all we know, she might have been introduced to the stones thousands of years after the great flood, after they'd been passed down through many generations. By then, her people might have developed their own names for them. She might not think of them as stones. They might not use them for the same purposes."

She stopped pacing and grabbed Pebbles' sketchbook. Flipping back to the crude sketches Pebbles had made of Citali's objects, she pointed at the one that looked like a clamshell. "See what I mean? This might be the stone the Munuorians called a *Breylofte*, the Sound Stone. We know it was bowl-shaped, but maybe that's not how Citali or her people viewed it. After all, Pebbles, Citali is showing you *her* memories."

Anlon followed Jennifer's eyes as she looked at Pebbles. Once again, Pebbles seemed deep in thought. However, this time, he did not observe signs of skepticism. When she finally spoke, her question was directed at Sanjay.

"Do you think it's possible to call her back?" Pebbles asked. "While we've been talking, I've been trying to visualize the oasis, hoping her consciousness would pop back into my mind, but no dice."

"We can try what we did last night. Relax you, plant some suggestions and see what happens."

"All right. Let's do it," Pebbles said. "Whether she's real or imaginary, we need answers."

As soon as Pebbles and Sanjay departed the living room, Anlon picked up the sketchbook and turned to Jennifer. "Come with me. I have an idea."

"Where are we going?"

"My office."

"What for?"

He flipped to the oasis drawing and stared at the squiggle symbol Pebbles had added after completing the main portion of the drawing. In a near whisper, he said, "It might be enough for Cesar to go on."

"I'm sorry, what did you say?" asked Jennifer.

"I'm thinking of emailing a picture of the oasis drawing to Cesar Perez, writing up a synopsis of Pebbles' meeting with her to go along with it."

"You sure about that? I don't think Pebbles will be real happy when she finds out you sent Cesar a naked picture of her."

"I'll redact the racy parts. I just want him to see the symbol and Citali's necklace."

"You think the necklace might be in Muran's collection?"

"It's worth a shot, don't you think? There's also Muran's manifesto. I know Cesar has a copy of it. He and Mereau have been trying to translate some of the passages. Maybe there's a mention of the name Citali, or a description of a tribe of people with deformed heads. Who knows, maybe Muran drew in her journal like Pebbles does. If so, maybe the squiggle's in there. The journal might help us pinpoint Citali's place in history."

"Presuming she's real, you mean. And presuming Muran has anything to do with Citali."

"Two big presumptions, I know. But Muran's art collection and manifesto are as good as any options we have right now of validating or disproving a connection between Muran and Citali. Wouldn't you agree?"

"Yeah, you've got a point there." Jennifer flipped one page back in the sketchbook to Pebbles' drawing of the items in Citali's bag. "Even though these are pretty nondescript. We should probably send him a picture of this page as well. Maybe he can make more sense out of them than we could."

Less than an hour later, Anlon received a text message from Cesar. "Got your email. VERY interesting. I have some additional research to do, but I can talk later this afternoon. Say 2 p.m. Pacific? Are you available then?"

Anlon replied immediately. "Great news! Yes. 2 p.m. Pacific is good. Talk to you then."

When Cesar's call arrived, Anlon and the others were back in the living room, eager to hear what the archaeologist had to say. Anlon put the phone on speaker, exchanged greetings with Cesar and introduced everybody on his end of the call.

"I'm so glad to hear back from you so fast," Anlon said. "We're actually on pins and needles here. Your text made it sound as if you found something of interest. We can't wait to hear about it."

"Yes, indeed. I discovered several things I think you will find of great interest. Beginning with Citali."

"Really?" Pebbles perked up.

"Yes. Based on what you provided me, she was one of the Paracas people. They lived in Peru. Their civilization flourished for a thousand to fifteen hundred years, depending on who you believe. As is often the case, the archaeological record is murky. Could have arisen as far back as 1000 BCE and could have died out as late as 500 CE, but most hold to a tighter range, somewhere between 800 BCE and 300 CE. But I believe your Citali almost assuredly lived closer to the end of their reign. Call it 200 to 300 CE. Right around the time the Nazca civilization began to arise."

"That's amazing, Cesar. Tell us how you pieced it together," Anlon said.

"It actually wasn't that hard. While Pebbles' squiggle isn't an exact reproduction, it looks somewhat like a famous geoglyph known as the Paracas Candelabra. I've sent you a photograph of it. It's a design cut out of petrified rock on the side of a hill in Paracas, Peru.

"I'm not sure I would have made the connection with the Candelabra, however, had it not been for Pebbles' depiction of Citali, specifically her elongated head. There are mummies that were discovered at a cemetery in Paracas with similar elongated heads. I've also sent you photographs of the mummies and some artists' recreations of what they looked like in real life."

Pebbles turned to Jennifer. "Where's your smart tablet?"

"In my room."

"Come on, let's go."

In one motion, Pebbles turned, grabbed Jennifer's hand and began to pull her toward the living room door.

"Hold on a sec, Cesar," Anlon said. He muted the phone and called out to Pebbles. "Hey, where are you two going?"

"To get Jen's tablet. I've gotta see these pictures," Pebbles said.

"Well, wait up, let's go down to my office and pull them up on my computer," Anlon said.

He then grabbed the phone from the coffee table and together with Sanjay and Griffin, followed after Pebbles and Jennifer. By the time Anlon arrived at his office cabin, Pebbles had already logged into the laptop and was waiting for Anlon's email app to download Cesar's message.

When the mummy images loaded, Pebbles inhaled sharply. "Oh, my God."

Anlon noticed her hand cupping the mouse was trembling. When she clicked on the image of the Candelabra, she pushed back from the desk and began to massage her wrists. Shaking her head, she said, "Oh, no..."

"What's the matter?" Anlon asked.

"Something's happening."

Her whole body began to violently shake. She slipped from the chair and slumped to the floor while the shaking continued.

"She's having a seizure," Jennifer said as she pushed the chair away from Pebbles. Kneeling beside her, she gently rolled Pebbles on her side.

"What are you doing?" Anlon asked.

"This will help her breathe."

As the spasms continued, Pebbles began to growl. With a blank stare, her mouth twisted into a snarl.

"Jesus," Anlon said. It was then he realized Cesar was still on hold. Un-clicking the mute icon, Anlon quickly told the archaeologist he would call him back later. He did not wait for Cesar to answer. He ended the call and knelt next to Jennifer. "What else should we do?"

"There's not much we can do. Just make sure she doesn't bang into something. Make sure she's breathing."

It was maddening to Anlon to just watch, but he trusted Jennifer's in-stincts. The former police officer's emergency medical training had come into play on more than one occasion in the past.

Though the seizure only persisted for another minute or so, it felt like an eternity to Anlon. Then, as if someone had flipped a switch, Pebbles yelled, "kill them," and passed out. Anlon's flesh prickled, his heart raced.

Jennifer felt for a pulse and did a quick visual examination. "She's still breathing. Look at her eyes. They're moving like crazy. She's dreaming."

CHAPTER 11

INVADERS IN THE TEMPLE

IN THE MIDST OF PEBBLES' VISION
ABOARD *SOL SEAKER*
KONA KAI MARINA, SAN DIEGO, CALIFORNIA
SEPTEMBER 19

The stone walls of the temple did little to protect against the chill. Citali tucked her body deeper under the blankets and nestled up against the warm body beside her. Peeking toward the window, she could see a faint glow.

I should have left already. If what they say about her is true, our defenses will not hold for long.

Through the window, Citali could hear the clanging of weapons and shields and the murmur of soldiers as they moved past the temple on the avenue below.

If I leave now, I can make it into the mountains before sunset. The people will not be happy, but they do not understand. There is nothing I can do to stop her.

She threw back the blankets and climbed from the bed of hay. Wrapping a serape around her bare body, she padded across the icy stones to reach the window. Citali edged the heavy drape to peer down at the city. She saw a procession of dark figures illuminated by thousands of torchlights. Some proceeded toward the northern trails, while others headed west toward the cove and the armada of waiting ships.

Raising her eyes, she could see a flotilla of six ships rowing out of the bay. Their sails still furled, they crept through the gray waters like a line of snakes stalking prey. Aboard the ships were sacks of gold and gems, tributes to appease the advancing conqueror.

It is futile. She will not be satisfied. She does not come to share. She comes to take. I must go before it is too late.

Citali crossed the room and began to gather her belongings. From the direction of the bed, she heard the rustling of hay followed by the voice of her attendant, *"Seer, it is cold. Come back to bed."*

"Quiet, child."

Alarm arose in the young woman's voice. *"You are packing? Are they close?"*

"Go to the larder and bring back a sack of provisions. Enough to last me a week."

"But, Seer, you cannot go—"

"Silence, girl. Do as you're told. Be quick about it…and quiet."

With the chastened attendant gone, Citali retrieved her necklace and fastened it in place. It was dangerous to wear it but if she was to garner the assistance of the dwellers, she would need to offer proof of her station.

They will not trust my word alone, even if I paint my body with the emblems.

Into her bag went the tools Citali had set aside the night before, tools that would be needed to make the first leg of the journey: a torch, flint stones and kindling. With plenty of room left in the bag for provisions, Citali donned a hooded poncho and slipped from her quarters. She moved quietly through the torchlit hallway until she reached the tower stairs. Before descending, she stopped to listen for sounds of activity below but heard nothing.

Where is that lazy girl? It should not take this long.

Careful to make no noise, Citali headed down the circular stairwell, pausing every so often to listen again. There were likely only a few worshipers in the temple nave given that most of the city's population had already fled south and east. Hopefully, their heads were bowed in prayer instead of watching the gallery, waiting for Citali to appear and bless them.

No one must know I have gone until I am far from the city. They will despair when they learn I've left, but they know not what is at stake and I cannot tell them.

When she reached the landing at the bottom of the tower stairs, she peered toward the balcony of the gallery and then quickly ducked into the unlit passageway that led to the vestry and larder. She had gone no more than four paces when she saw the girl's naked body sprawled on the floor ahead, the pool of blood surrounding her as black as ink in the darkened hall. Heart racing, Citali halted and crouched down.

What is this treachery?

At the end of the hall, the figure of a man appeared from the door to the larder. While Citali could tell little about his appearance, she could see the outline of a long blade clutched at his side.

Behind her, Citali heard movement. A shadow blocked the light filtering into the passage from the tower landing. She wheeled to see another man with a blade. Dressed in peasant's clothes, the man tapped the blade against the wall and smiled.

"Be still, freak, or end up like your pretty little bed warmer."

Citali swore under her breath. There was nowhere to hide...and nowhere to run. She reached for her bag and the knife inside. The men on both ends of the hall closed in.

"It would not be wise to fight, freak. There are more of us in the temple. You will not escape."

The crouched Citali rose up, knife in hand. The men froze in place. The one approaching from the tower vestibule gaped at the much larger Citali and whistled.

"Do you see this, Alamare? The tales are true."

Citali slid back the hood of her poncho. *Be gone, assassins! Or I shall eat your hearts."*

Concentrating her attention on the man blocking her ability to retreat to the vestibule, she advanced. Her eyes, having now adjusted to the low light, watched his face twist into a horrified expression as he stared at her elongated head.

"Get back, demon!"

The man slashed his blade wildly as he backed up, striking the walls each time he missed the dodging Citali.

"Stay your blade, Uhton!" called the man behind Citali, the one Uhton had called Alamare. *"The Lady wants her captured unsullied."*

"And let her run me through?" said Uhton, extending his trembling blade to keep Citali at a safe distance.

Unfortunately for him, Citali's arm was twice as long, her knife twice as sharp. With a chopping blow, she lopped the man's hand off, rendering him weaponless in the process. The sound of his blade hitting the floor was muted by his howling scream.

Citali did not bother to turn and challenge Alamare. She dashed for the vestibule, knife poised to defend herself against more of the assassins. Caught by surprise, the first two she encountered were too slow to react. She dispatched the short, pudgy men with thrusts into their chests.

She heard Alamare whisper a curt command as she raced down the vestibule's steps into the nave. There, she spied several more men, their blades at the ready.

How can there be so many? How did they get past the temple guards? Where are the guards? Did they not hear the man scream?

The sound of her pursuer's pounding feet grew louder. She dared not turn to look. Instead, Citali began to shout, *"Help! Intruders! Assassins! In the temple!"*

With so many soldiers outside the temple, surely one or more would hear her cries for assistance. There was a tug on her poncho. Stumbling forward, she beckoned for help again. A great weight collided into her and she splayed onto the stone floor, the bloody knife slipping from her hand. In seconds, she was surrounded by the other assassins.

She tried to scramble toward the knife but was tackled and pinned to the floor by two of the men. As she continued to call for aid, a hand slipped beneath her chin and pulled it up. She felt a blade press against her throat. In the distance, she heard the temple doors open and the growls of angry men pouring into the nave.

Alamare was one of the men on top of her. He called out, *"Stop or I will kill the freak!"* His blade dug into her skin as he whispered into her ear. *"If you care to save your sheep, Keeper, then tell them to lower their weapons. The Lady comes for you and what you keep, not your flock. Surrender to us and we shall send word to call off the attack."*

Citali yanked against the hand holding her chin so she could look toward the soldiers amassed inside the temple entrance. Bows loaded and drawn, spears and machetes poised, there was no fear in their eyes, only defiance. She returned their gazes. *Yes, brothers, it is better to die than surrender.*

"Kill them!" Citali commanded.

Before Alamare could react, arrows whistled through the air and struck him. Citali felt both of the men on top of her shudder each time they were hit, and she heard the groans of the other assassins as they were felled. Alamare's grip on her chin faltered. As he lay dying on her back, he whispered, *"She will burn everything, freak. You will be the Keeper of nothing but ashes."*

As if a curtain had been lowered over her eyes, all went black. Citali no longer felt the weight of the dead men on top of her, nor did she hear the sounds of their dying comrades lying nearby.

What is happening? Why can't I move? Where are the soldiers? I need to run.

The darkness began to fade into a gray haze. New sounds began to fill her ears. Birds again, and the fluttering of leaves, then the roar of distant waves mixed with the aroma of salty air. The gray took on color, a dark blue with white and pink at the center. The tendrils of pink swayed. As her vision sharpened, Citali found herself by a white tree with enormous roots that spread over the ground in all directions. Its leaves, a shade of pink Citali had never seen, danced in the wind. Beyond the tree was a cliff and beyond that a vast turquoise ocean.

A voice out of her field of vision said, *"It's okay, Citali. You're safe now."*

The voice was familiar. Citali turned and saw the emblem-painted woman from the oasis sitting on one of the tree's roots. Citali stepped back, her feet pressing into the wet red clay around the tree roots. Looking down, she saw she was dressed in a tan tunic piped with crimson and gold. She raised her gaze and pointed at the woman. *"You! Sorceress!"*

"I'm not a sorceress. I'm Pebbles, remember?"

Pebbles stood up and walked toward her. Citali backed away, her voice rising. *"Stay back, demon!"*

Arms outstretched, Pebbles slowly advanced. *"I'm not a demon. I just want to talk some more."*

"Come no closer or I will strike you down." Citali reached for her bag but it was gone. With panicked hands, she felt for her necklace. It was missing too. She snarled. *"What have you done with my things? My necklace, my knife. Where are they?"*

"Haven't a clue," Pebbles stopped and slowly spun around in a circle, her arms raised above her head. *"See? I don't have them."*

"You are clever, sorceress, but I am no fool. Give them back or I will kill you with my bare hands."

Citali crouched down and leaned forward, ready to charge. Pebbles took a few steps back. *"Whoa, now. There's no need for that. Like I said, I just want to talk."*

"Why? So you can trick me? Understand this, demon — no matter how sweetly you speak to me, I will not tell you anything. I did not tell the Lady. I will not tell you."

"I wish you would stop calling me a demon. I'm really not. I'm just a woman like you."

"Ha! You are nothing like me. You fill my mind with visions. You—"

"I fill your mind with visions?" Pebbles snapped back. *"Your freaking visions, or dreams, or memories, or whatever the hell they are, have been haunting me for months, sister! I got a deal for you — you stop showing me your visions, I'll stop showing you mine!"*

Pebbles began to stalk back and forth in front of Citali. *"It's so frustrating. You replay the same shit over and over. People chasing you through the temple, through villages, forests, over mountains, into the desert, across rivers. Your thoughts are always about running, hiding, protecting. Why run? Who are you trying to hide from? What is it you are protecting?"*

Citali relaxed her stance. *"Why do you care?"*

Pebbles tugged at her hair and shouted, *"Because you're inside my eff-ing head! Your visions, your memories, are inside of me! I can't get them out and don't understand them!*

"For instance, the craziness just now at the temple. What was that about? I mean, I get your people were preparing to defend the city. I under-stand they were trying to protect you…but I don't understand why. The girl in your room called you Seer. The man who attacked you called you Keeper. I don't understand what those titles mean. Were you some kind of priest-ess? Were you the ruler of the city? Who are the Dwellers? Who is the Lady?"

Citali's eyes followed the stalking Pebbles. *"It is done. It is all over. It matters not."*

"Oh, but it does matter…otherwise, you wouldn't be thinking about it con-stantly, now would you? Your mind wouldn't keep going back through the same stuff over and over. It matters to you a whole lot. The question is why?"

Citali turned without answering and walked to the edge of the cliff. Staring out at the sea, she weighed opening up to Pebbles. If she was an agent of the Lady, the consequences of answering her questions were dire.

"I am not an agent of the Lady," Pebbles said. *"I don't even know who the freakin' Lady is."*

Wheeling around, Citali said, *"You can hear my thoughts?"*

"Hello! You're inside my brain. Of course, I can hear what you're thinking," Pebbles said. She walked up to Citali and stared into her eyes. *"Is the Lady in your thoughts the one known as the Painted Lady, the one legends say would sacrifice young women, not by destroying their bodies, but by destroying their spirits, their minds? The one they say could then paint her mind into the soul-less, mindless bodies of the young women? She's the one who strangled me in the vision I showed you. She was going to do that to me. Wipe away my mind and take my body. Is that the Lady in your thoughts? She would have looked different to you, she would have been in a different body than the one in my vi-sion, but she would have been just as evil."*

"I know of no such legend."

"She would have had strange powers. The ability to shoot fire from a stone or throw boulders through the air like she was tossing blades of grass — just by humming on a stone. Things like that. Things that you or I couldn't do."

The description rattled Citali. She averted her eyes, choosing to gaze at the surroundings rather than at Pebbles. Farther along the coastline she could see a large volcano. Panning her vision inland, she saw a long slope running down to a cove. The slope was covered by deep-blue flowers. Thousands of butterflies danced over the swaying blossoms. In the distance, she could see a city made of stone.

"What is this place?"

"Nice try, Citali. I can feel you trying to suppress your thoughts. I'm right, aren't I? The Lady who came to destroy your city, the one who wanted you captured, had strange powers."

Citali sighed as she watched the butterflies frolic. *"She had many names. The Gold Queen, the Lady of the Mask People, the Blood Goddess, the Soul Taker."*

"I see. And she came to your city to take your soul."

With a shake of her head, Citali said, *"No. She wanted to see what I see. She wanted to take what I made. She wanted to have what I keep."*

Pebbles was still in the dream when Cindy Tanner appeared at the door to Anlon's office. Out of breath, she asked, "What happened?"

"We were looking at some pictures." Anlon pointed to his laptop. "And she had a seizure of some kind. Nothing like we've seen before. She felt it coming on beforehand, said she felt wrong. And then after a couple of minutes, she dropped into a dream. She appears to still be in it."

As Sanjay lifted Pebbles' eyelid to examine her eyes, Jennifer turned to Cindy. "Get some water and cold washcloths."

"Yes, miss."

Cindy disappeared from the doorway. Behind her, two other crewmembers stared into the room from the hall. Sanjay moved back from Pebbles and looked at Anlon. "Where does she keep her sleeping pills?"

"In our bathroom. Why?"

"Just considering all the possibilities."

As Cindy returned with bottled waters and washcloths, Anlon said, "You're thinking an overdose? No way. You were with us. She was fully alert before the seizure. The pictures triggered it, I'm sure of it. Jen, is that how you saw it?"

"Yeah, that's right. She wasn't groggy. No slurred speech. She didn't have the shakes. Nothing that suggests to me she'd taken any sleeping pills."

"And you are sure she does not have access to some other drug? A sedative, perhaps? Painkiller? Something recreational? Perhaps she appealed to one of the crew…"

Sanjay looked up at Cindy. Without hesitation, she said, "Out of the question."

"What about your first aid kits on board?" he asked. "Do you have opiates? Other narcotics?"

The suggestion stirred a twitch on Cindy's face. "We do. But they're under lock and key on the bridge."

"I would suggest taking an inventory, just to be sure."

Cindy looked to Anlon.

"Yeah, better go check."

She handed the bottles and washcloths to Jennifer and departed the room once more. Anlon dismissed the other stewards congregating in the hallway and then turned to Sanjay. "You really think she OD'd on something?"

"Like I said, I am just trying to consider all the possibilities. It could just be a psychogenic event. Seeing the picture might have created a strong enough surge of anxiety to trigger spasms. But, then again, it looked more like an epileptic seizure than a psychogenic one to me. That suggests either a reaction to medication or an electrical misfire in her brain. If you want my opinion, I would recommend taking her to a hospital, let the doctors run some tests, do a CT scan and an EEG."

"Not a chance," Pebbles said, her eyes fluttering open. "I don't need any doctors…present company excluded."

She propped her torso up with her elbows. Anlon, still kneeling beside her, helped her into a sitting position while Jennifer handed her a bottled water. After a sip, Pebbles looked at the collection of concerned faces. "We have to stop meeting like this."

"Are you all right?" Anlon asked.

"I kind of feel groggy and my head hurts a little, but other than that, I feel fine." Pebbles said.

"Yeah, well this trance was very different from the others. You were shaking so much, it was downright scary."

Pebbles rolled her eyes and turned her head to look at the laptop. "I'm fine. How fast can we get to Peru? To Paracas? I want to go there and see the Candelabra and the mummies."

"Uh…I don't know. But before we talk about going to Paracas, we need to get you checked out."

"I told you, I don't need—"

"My boat. My rules."

Pebbles glared at Anlon. "Pulling rank on me, eh?"

He glared back. "Aye."

Cindy returned to the room. She first looked at the now awake Pebbles and then at Anlon. "All good on the bridge."

"Okay, thanks, Cindy." Anlon turned back to Pebbles. "Well, what'll it be?"

"Fine, Blackbeard. You win. What's the closest hospital to Paracas?"

"Hold your horses. We're going somewhere here in San Diego, not Peru."

"We can call for an ambulance," Cindy said.

"Now, wait a minute," Pebbles said. "I don't need an ambulance."

"An ambulance won't be necessary, but we will need a ride," said Anlon. Cindy nodded and bolted away as Anlon refocused his gaze on Pebbles. "Come on. The faster we get you to the hospital, the quicker you get released."

Pebbles sighed. "All right, I'll make you a deal. I won't put up a fuss about seeing a doctor, if you book us on a flight to the closest airport to Paracas as soon as I'm released. Do we have a deal?"

Anlon hesitated long enough to exchange glances with Sanjay and Jennifer. "We have a deal…presuming the doctors give you the green light to fly."

"Fine. But as soon as the green light is given, we need to get going."

"I don't understand," Jennifer said. "What's the rush, Pebbles?"

"I finally got Citali to open up a little and I don't want to risk her clamming up before we get to Paracas."

"So, you had another chat with her?" Sanjay asked.

"Yeah, you're two for two, doc. I was able to interrupt a new version of the temple dream. Uh, scratch that. The temple *memory*," Pebbles said. "It's definitely a memory. In fact, it's where all Citali's troubles began."

CHAPTER 12

DRAWING CONCLUSIONS

MERCY HOSPITAL
SAN DIEGO, CALIFORNIA
SEPTEMBER 19

During the wait for Pebbles to return from a CT scan at the hospital, Anlon stepped outside the emergency room, found an unoccupied bench and called Cesar. After providing Cesar with an explanation of what had happened during their earlier call and an update on Pebbles' condition, the conversation gravitated toward Cesar's findings. They began with a discussion of the people of Paracas.

"We don't have a written record, unfortunately," Cesar said, "but there are multiple archaeological sites and plenty of artifacts that have been discovered in and around the Paracas necropolis…in addition to wonderfully preserved mummies. The air in Paracas is so dry, the mummies, their clothes, jewelry, all of it, are in incredible shape."

"I see what you mean. I pulled up a map of Paracas on my phone earlier. It looks like it's essentially surrounded by a desert."

"That's right, it's part of the Atacama, a desert that's spread over a thousand kilometers of the coastlines of Peru and Chile. But if you look closely at your map, you'll see patches of green around Paracas where rivers bring water down from the Andes. These patches were even more extensive two thousand years ago and the Paracas people settled along the riverbanks."

"So, is that what ended their civilization? The rivers ran dry? Or did something else happen? You mentioned something about the Nazca people in our call earlier."

"No one knows for certain, Anlon. There is definitely a commingling of Paracas and Nazca artifacts in Nazca-area strata, with the Nazca-created artifacts more prevalent in quantity and more recent in dating. It suggests the two cultures merged, but who knows? Maybe Paracas became uninhabitable and they moved to Nazca. Or it's possible Paracas weakened as a society and Nazca conquered it. There are as many theories about what happened to the Paracas people as there are about the Nazca lines."

Anlon had planned to raise the subject of the Nazca lines, so he was glad Cesar had touched upon them first. Famed for their elaborate animal shapes visible only from high altitudes, the Nazca lines had long been the subject of controversy. Some considered them massive landmarks created to attract ancient aliens, while others considered them landmarks of religious significance or simply elaborate works of art.

"Cesar, since you brought it up, is there a connection between the Nazca lines and the Paracas Candelabra you sent us a picture of? I know they look very different, style-wise, but I was thinking of their construction. You know, the fact they both used rocks and trenches to create designs in desert hardpan."

"For some people, there may be — ancient alien believers and the like — but not for me. They were created hundreds of years apart and are over a hundred miles away from each other. Plus, as you say, the designs are very different. The only real connections, so far as I can see, is that we don't know the purpose of either and both have withstood the passage of time better than other geoglyphs of similar vintage. The dry air again, I suppose."

Cesar's latter point resonated with Anlon. As he looked at a picture of the Candelabra on his phone, he could not help but think it looked like something a person could easily wipe away with the stroke of a hand. How had winds not destroyed it? Especially when one considered its location. The Candelabra was carved into the slope of a hill that abutted the Pacific Ocean.

It was a curious location to place the monument in Anlon's opinion, for the hill upon which it was carved formed the outer lip of a cove. Facing north, the Candelabra had no protection from the elements. Why had the builders chosen this spot? Wouldn't it have made more sense to construct it in a more hospitable area? Anlon posed these questions to Cesar.

"You have hit upon questions that have confounded many an archaeologist," Cesar said with a laugh. "Since no one knows who built it or why, we are left to guess its purpose and the logic employed to choose its placement. The most practical theory that's been proposed suggests the Candelabra served as a beacon to ships sailing for the Paracas cove. Since the Peruvian coastline is mostly desert, the theory suggests it would have been challenging for ships to pick out the cove among the desert backdrop unless there was a distinguishable landmark."

"Sounds compelling to me," Anlon said. "Is that where the idea of calling it a Candelabra came from? You know, a beacon lighting the way?"

"Most likely, but, between you and me, I don't think the designs on the prongs look like lighted candles," Cesar said. "And a lot of other archaeologists agree with me. If they were lighted candles, wouldn't they have been designed to look the same?"

Anlon squinted at the image on his phone. Using his fingers to zoom the picture, he nudged the picture from left to right to study the prongs. Cesar was right. There were unique designs on each of the prongs, and the differences seemed distinctive enough to suggest the designs were intentional.

"Are the prong designs religious symbols?" he asked.

"That's what many think. Some consider it a trident, given it has a fork-like shape to it and the tips of the prongs look like barbs. They call it Viracocha's Trident."

"Viracocha? You're kidding."

"I thought the name might catch your attention," Cesar laughed. "The legends surrounding Viracocha mirror the 'fish-men' myths tied to the Munuorians. A god who arose in a time of darkness after a great flood, one who arrived by sea, one who exhibited special powers to lend assistance to survivors of the flood. And a god who eventually left the same way he came…by sea…never to return. It's been suggested that people built the monument as a beacon to Viracocha, should he one day return."

"Got it, sort of an ancient Batman floodlight."

"The only problem? The Candelabra was constructed sometime around the beginning of the common era. Yet, the Viracocha legend is an Incan myth, and the Incan empire didn't arise for over a millennium *after* the Candelabra was built."

"I could see how that would kill any connection between the Candelabra and Viracocha," Anlon said. "But, correct me if I'm wrong, the fish-men myths go much further back than the Incans. Couldn't the Candelabra still be connected to the same myths, even though the Paracas people might have had a different name for the god they were honoring?"

"Absolutely, and that's what proponents of the Viracocha theory hang their hats on. Only, there are other problems with this theory."

"Such as?"

"Well, first and foremost, the Paracas people were fine artisans, Anlon. In fact, they were one of the first in South America to craft gold jewelry. They also created beautiful textiles and terra-cotta sculptures. We can tell a lot about their daily lives and beliefs from these works of art. Yet, not one piece of pottery, not one gold medallion, or one tapestry depicts the Candelabra symbol."

"That is surprising. It's hard to imagine there wouldn't be other representations of the symbol if it was so important to the people that they built the monument of it."

"Exactly," Cesar said. "Go through artifacts of most cultures and you will find pervasive depictions of gods or important symbols everywhere you turn. Take the Egyptians, for example. Say...the eye of Ra. This symbol appears on temples, statues, murals, figurines, jewelry, you name it. You could say the same of certain icons from the Sumerians to the Maya to ancient Rome or the dynasties of China. But here...there is nothing... no connection whatsoever with the Candelabra in any Paracas art."

"That's bizarre."

"It is...and it's what's fed ancient alien theories."

"How so?"

"They label the Candelabra an out-of-place artifact, historically speaking, meaning it doesn't fit with other artifacts dated to the same time period," Cesar said. "They say the Candelabra is a depiction of a spacecraft or airplane, the prong designs representing exhaust spewed by its engines."

Anlon frowned and zoomed out the photograph on his phone. To his surprise, he could definitely visualize how one could envision the monument as a plane or rocket if one looked at it from a different perspective.

"This theory," Cesar said, "is of course bolstered in their minds by the mummies with the elongated heads found in the Paracas necropolis."

Ah, yes, thought Anlon, *Citali's rather prodigious noggin did have an otherworldly appearance to it.* He was about to ask Cesar about the mummies when he heard the archaeologist scoff. "Which is ridiculous. Thank God for DNA analysis."

"Oh? The mummies have been tested?"

"Yes. And, safe to say, their DNA is entirely human. Although, there is an oddity about the DNA, one that has puzzled my colleagues."

Cesar went on to say the genealogy of the DNA extracted from the elongated-skull mummies could be traced back to Eastern European ancestors. How was it, Cesar had posed, that a band of Anglos from Eastern Europe traveled all the way to Peru, settled among the indigenous population and interbred without some art memorializing their arrival or ascension into Paracas society?

"That is not to say there is an absence of Paracas art that depicts people among their population with the elongated skulls," Cesar said. "There is plenty of art showing such people. But there are many depictions of Paracas people with normal skulls too. Yet, the people with the deformed heads are the ones who received special burial treatment in the necropolis. They appeared to have been revered. For what reason remains unknown."

The longer Cesar talked about Paracas art, the Candelabra and the mummies, the more Anlon became convinced, once and for all, that Pebbles' visions were not dreams. They were memories of a real person, just as Pebbles had claimed after she had interacted with Citali at the oasis.

"Well, Cesar, you may be in luck. Pebbles might just be in a position to get you a definitive answer to that question...and others. Where are you now?"

"Guatemala. I'm helping excavate a recently discovered tomb at Nakum."

"Can you get away and meet us in Paracas?"

"I'm sure I can manage it, but I was thinking it might be better to meet up in Noumea on New Caledonia."

"Excuse me? Why New Caledonia?"

"You know the necklace in Pebbles' drawing? The one worn by Citali? There is one in Muran's collection that looks eerily similar."

Anlon hopped up from the bench. "What?"

"I'll text you a picture of it…hold on…there, it's on its way. I hope you don't mind, but I took the liberty of speaking with the curator of the collection, the New Caledonian Minister of Cultural Affairs. He's indicated a willingness to let me examine the piece…in exchange for an…uh… honorarium."

Anxious to receive Cesar's text, Anlon began to pace. "How much are we talking about?"

"We did not discuss a specific amount…though he indicated honoraria to examine other pieces in the collection have been in the range of fifty thousand US."

As Cesar spoke, the text arrived. Anlon clicked on the thumbnail image and examined the picture. The necklace was made of gold, just as Pebbles had recounted in her dream journal. However, unlike Pebbles' oasis sketch, each of the domino-shaped tiles that ringed the necklace were stamped with different symbols — details that were absent in her drawing.

"Anlon? Are you still there? If it is too much, I can try to negotiate."

"Sorry, Cesar. I was distracted by your text. The amount is fine. Will a check suffice?"

"Um…I believe an offshore wire transfer is preferred."

"How silly of me. Of course, it is." Redirecting the conversation back to the necklace, Anlon asked, "What do you make of the symbols?"

"They are unlike any Paracas or Nazca symbols I've ever seen. In fact, I'd have to say they don't look Mesoamerican at all. That's why I want to examine it more closely."

"Understood. Question — what about testing its composition? You know, is it pure gold or gold plating over tin or some other metallic substance? If we knew that, we could compare its composition with other gold Paracas or Nazca artifacts."

"It's certainly possible to test its composition, but I'm not sure the curator will allow us to take a sample. They've denied similar requests to test other pieces from what I hear. It's part of the reason it's taking so long to authenticate many of the artifacts in the collection."

"All right. In that case, will it be possible for you to get Pebbles in to see it in person? She might see something about it that gives us some insight."

"I'm way ahead of you, my friend. I told the curator that I would want to bring two experts with me to help authenticate the piece, Pebbles and Mereau."

Anlon halted. "Mereau? Why Mereau?"

"I thought there was a chance he might recognize the symbols."

Pulling the phone from his ear, Anlon sat back down on the bench and reopened the picture of the necklace. He had seen enough Munuorian symbols in the past to know the ones on the necklace were primitive by comparison. He mentioned as much to Cesar.

"I agree…for the most part. It may be the lighting in the picture, or the angle at which the necklace was photographed, but there are two symbols that strike me as possibly Munuorian. Front left at about seven o'clock, you'll see a tile with what looks like three wavy lines."

Anlon used his fingers to enlarge the photo and zero in on the one Cesar mentioned. He would not have called the lines wavy himself. They were curved, but not in the shape of waves to Anlon's eyes. He asked Cesar to point out the other tile.

"The one with the star. Back side of the necklace. Between one o'clock and two o'clock."

Shifting the image, Anlon studied the star symbol. It did not look like a Munuorian star, the one they used to depict their most powerful stone tool, the *Tuliskaera*, or the Flash Stone as Anlon's uncle used to call it. But…the symbol did look like a crude star.

"Are you suggesting the necklace is a Munuorian artifact? I thought Mereau went through the pictures of Muran's collection a while ago? It was my understanding he didn't find anything but a cache of *Lifintyls*."

"You are correct. But I wonder how closely he studied the necklace."

"Gotta be honest with you, Cesar. Seems like a stretch."

"All the same, I think it would be of value to have Mereau join us, especially in light of the possible connection with Muran's manifesto."

It took a few seconds before the implication of Cesar's comment registered in Anlon's brain. Along with the art collection Muran had amassed over her ten-thousand-year odyssey, she had penned a manifesto detailing the lives she had lived in the bodies of other women. "You found a mention of the necklace?"

"Possibly."

"Cripes, Cesar. Talk about burying the lead."

"Well, I didn't want to get you too excited before I consulted with Mereau. As you know, he and I have been working collaboratively to translate the full text and line up her personal histories with those of ancient cultures, to see if the manifesto offers new information of historical significance."

"Yeah, I'm aware."

"Well, if you recall, the manifesto is not entirely in English. Muran must have recopied it many times throughout the millennia, so the last iteration is a hodgepodge of English mixed with words, phrases and passages in other languages. Some of which remain indecipherable. Yet, despite the challenges the language mix has caused us, we have been able to pinpoint certain eras she lived in. One such period spans a several-hundred-year stretch around the beginning of the Common Era."

"The time you think Citali lived."

"Yes. It's clear from the text that Muran made her way into South America from Central America in the first century BCE and we know she fled Naranjo in Guatemala around 700 CE. The span in between, roughly six hundred years, encompasses three lives she memorialized in the manifesto."

Three lives over six hundred years. Thank the anti-aging, life-extending effects of the Munuorian elixir 'enjyia', Anlon thought.

Cesar continued. "Two of those lives don't appear to have been contiguous as there were abrupt ends to those histories, meaning she didn't describe her transitions from one body to another as she typically did in other sections of the text."

"I guess that's not all that surprising," said Anlon. "If she was run out of a village or city, she probably laid low for a while, took on an interim identity before plotting her next power grab."

"Precisely. That is what Mereau and I think too. She obviously liked being in charge. With her skill in wielding the Munuorian stones, she typically found it easy to rise to power. But, early on in the manifesto, she bemoans her challenges holding onto power. Whether confronted by revolts or foreign attacks or betrayals by those close to her, Muran frequently lost out and found herself on the run. But, over time, she developed a keener ability to sniff trouble brewing and stamp it out before it became a threat. Every now and then, however, she overreached and it cost her dearly."

Cesar paused, then said, "One such backfire occurred right around the dawn of the Common Era — a situation where Muran apparently became obsessed with a cult of mountain-dwelling oracles that held sway over a wide cross-section of tribes across northern South America. For a long stretch of time, she tolerated their existence, but at some point, she learned something about them that upset her terribly. She does not mention the catalyst for her change in attitude toward the oracles, but whatever it was, it riled her so much that she systematically hunted them down and killed them all."

"Are you saying you think Citali was one of the oracles?"

"Maybe. She is not named. None of the oracles are named in Muran's screed."

"Then what makes you think Citali was one of them?"

"Muran has a rather extensive rant about the lengths she had to go through to kill the last of the oracles, a three-month chase through the desert, over mountains and down rivers. Her chronicle of the chase ends with the slaughter of the oracle deep in a jungle."

"Hmm...does Muran refer to the last oracle as a woman?"

"No. But neither does she refer to the oracle as a man. She refers to them collectively as *signae*, which raises another possible link."

"How so?"

"There are scattered mentions in ancient Greek texts of a mysterious culture of nomads called the Sigynnae who roamed territory along the Danube in Central and Eastern Europe circa 500 BCE."

As Cesar spelled out the two variations of the similar-sounding words, Anlon considered the clues Cesar had found in Muran's manifesto. Earlier, the archaeologist had said the bones of the Paracas mummies, the ones with the elongated skulls, could be traced back to Eastern European ancestry. So, Cesar was thinking Muran's *signae*, the mountain-dwelling oracles, were descendants of the Sigynnae who emigrated to South America. It was a speculative theory based on a thin amount of circumstantial evidence but, Anlon had to admit, it seemed worth further exploration.

"What about the necklace? You said you found a possible mention."

"Yes. Muran was most explicit in her description of how she killed the last oracle. It's gruesome to read, as much of the manifesto is. Apparently, at one point during the lengthy torture, Muran tried to cut the *signae's* head off — a common form of execution in those times — but was stymied by the thickness of the *signae's* chain. A chain isn't necessarily a necklace, but it is suggestive of one."

"I guess. Seems iffy to me, but added to everything else you've presented, I can see how it stuck out to you." Anlon paused, then asked, "Cesar, I'm curious, you said going after the oracles backfired on Muran. How?"

"The expression 'cut off your nose to spite your face' comes to mind. You should read the account yourself. I will send it to you."

Anlon's and Pebbles' five-hour visit to the hospital ended with the doctor declaring Pebbles fit for release, telling them he found nothing of concern in her bloodwork or CT scan. "Given your test results, combined with the fact you haven't had seizures before and the one you had today was short, it's likely the seizure was anxiety-related. I'd recommend rest and increase in fluid intake."

As soon as the doctor left the room, Pebbles said, "Told you so."

"Don't get all high and mighty. It's better to be safe than sorry."

"Yada, yada." Pebbles hopped off the examining table. "Deal's a deal. On to Paracas."

"Uh…yeah…about that…"

Later that evening, over dinner, Anlon shared the details of his call with Cesar with the rest of the group. Pebbles, of course, was already on cloud nine, having been briefed by Anlon on the way back from the hospital.

Anlon had not been sure how Sanjay would react to the news. Traveling across the Pacific to New Caledonia and continuing on to Peru was a significant change in plans. But Sanjay had embraced the revised itinerary, saying he wanted to help Pebbles through both trips.

Sanjay raised a couple of sticking points, however. He told Anlon he needed to return to Sedona to retrieve his passport and make arrangements for someone to dog-sit Happy while he was away.

"Not a problem, Sanjay. We'll make the travel arrangements for you. We wouldn't have been able to leave tomorrow anyway. Too many logistics to sort out."

The latter issue was also resolved quickly when Griffin volunteered to stay behind and dog-sit Happy. He further suggested tagging along with Sanjay back to Sedona and staying with Happy at Sanjay's home.

"Happy will like it better and I'd rather be in open country than on a docked boat, especially if no one else is going to be around."

While Sanjay indicated the plan was acceptable to him, the red rising in Jennifer's face signaled she was unhappy with the arrangement. Before she could raise an objection, Griffin said, "It'll only be for a few days. A week tops. Right?"

"Yeah, I guess," she said.

"Plus, I'm not sure what I could add if I came along."

"Don't say that. You've got lots to offer, especially to me."

"I appreciate that, but I can be a bigger help to the cause by keeping tabs on old slobber-buddy here." Griffin scratched Happy's head. The dog barked his approval.

Jennifer relented and Anlon left to begin working on the travel plans.

CHAPTER 13

A LINK IN THE CHAIN

Three days later, Anlon, Pebbles, Jennifer and Sanjay landed in Noumea, the capital of New Caledonia. As they deplaned the chartered flight, Sanjay whispered to Anlon, "I am nervous about meeting Mereau."

"Why?"

"One does not meet a ten-thousand-year-old man every day."

"Don't worry, he's a good guy. A little intense sometimes, but you'll like him. You'll like both of them, Cesar and Mereau."

After clearing customs, they found the aforementioned men waiting for them at the security exit. Sanjay stood to the side at first and watched the friends greet each other. Then, Anlon introduced him to Mereau.

Sanjay smiled as Mereau said, "Hello, my friend, it is good to meet you."

Tanned and relaxed, the diminutive, middle-aged Mereau looked to Sanjay like the sort of man who spent his days lying on a hammock under swaying palm trees, but his voice sounded like a man used to barking orders and dispensing wisdom. It was a strange mix. Then Sanjay recalled there was a very good reason the voice did not match the image of the man standing before him.

"The pleasure is mine. I've heard many tales about you over the last few days. I'm excited to finally meet you." Mereau smiled and clasped Sanjay's shoulder. "We will do great things together for Pebbles. I know it."

The tenor of his voice and the glint in his eye made Sanjay want to salute and fall in line.

Next up was Cesar Perez. He was diminutive as well and appeared much older than Mereau…physically. Sanjay guessed him to be in his seventies. But his looks were also deceiving. Though he was sun-weathered and wiry, the man still sported a full head of black hair and the grip of a man twenty years his junior.

"Anlon tells me we have you to thank for helping Pebbles connect with Citali," said Cesar.

"My part was small compared to hers."

"Well, I thank you, nonetheless. Your assistance may not only bring peace to Pebbles but also help us solve some baffling ancient mysteries."

In the taxi van ride to the hotel, Sanjay reflected on Cesar's comment and prayed it would be possible to bring Pebbles peace.

CASBAH CAFÉ
NOUMEA, NEW CALEDONIA

There were moments during dinner when Pebbles forgot why they had all gathered in Noumea. It felt more like a reunion of old friends, the kind of get-together where smiles and laughter were as prevalent as the retelling of events that bonded the friendships. Mix in some side conversations where everyone shared updates about recent goings-on in their lives and moments when individual conversations silenced to tune into a fascinating tale shared by one person or another, and the gathering felt magical. Of course, the Casablanca aura of the Moroccan-styled café added to the effect, as did the freely flowing wine.

Ironically, to Pebbles, the person most responsible for the pleasant vibe of the evening was Sanjay. For many of the stories told by the others at the table were shared to welcome him into the fold. In that way, it reminded her of bringing a boyfriend to a family dinner for the first time, or a happy hour with a new co-worker and Pebbles was shocked to discover Sanjay was as gifted a storyteller as Mereau and Cesar.

Holding hands with Anlon under the table, surrounded by friends and the festive atmosphere, Pebbles felt as relaxed and happy as she'd been in a long time. Yet, every now and then throughout the evening, she would look around at other diners in the dimly lit restaurant, or at the softly crooning pianist in the corner, or the palm trees swaying in the ocean breeze outside, and she would remember why they were there.

She could not help but zone out in those moments. Her eyes would glaze over until everything was a blur of shapes and lights. The buzz of other diners, the crooner's voice, even the laughter at her own table, would fade into a distant din. The warmth of Anlon's hand would dissipate. Utterly alone, her thoughts would begin to drift toward Citali and the two possible outcomes that lay ahead. Their next steps would either sate Citali's spirit or the woman's memories and consciousness would forever reside in Pebbles' mind.

BANQUE CALEDONIENNE
NOUMEA, NEW CALEDONIA
SEPTEMBER 23

The next morning, Pebbles stepped out of the taxi under a blanket of gray above. Anlon came up beside her on the right and took hold of her hand. Jennifer took position on Pebbles' left. From a second taxi emerged Cesar, Mereau and Sanjay.

When the six were together on the curb, Cesar said to the group, "They are a suspicious lot. These New Caledonians. There will probably be armed guards with scowls on their faces that escort us everywhere. The minister, Garnier, he will act like the lord of the manor. The best approach is to play along, kill them with kindness."

Her heart thumping in her throat, Pebbles trembled. Anlon whispered to ask her if she was okay. She nodded, but it was not true. Slightly dizzy, mind foggy, she could feel something tugging at her, warning her to go no farther. Was it Citali trying to press her way into Pebbles' consciousness or the fear of the unknown? Like a zombie, she marched behind

Cesar, her hand clasping Anlon's, with Jennifer, Mereau and Sanjay following behind.

The entourage from the bank was waiting for them in the lobby. As Cesar had predicted, the contingent included a half-dozen security guards. With them were two besuited executive types. One of them introduced himself as the bank manager, Claude Fremont. The other was Jean Garnier, the curator of Aja Jones' art collection. As Cesar made return introductions, Pebbles could feel the beginnings of another seizure. Closing her eyes, she concentrated her thoughts. *Not now! Not now! This isn't the time. Oasis...oasis...oasis...*

She felt a tug on her hand. Anlon whispered. "Are you okay?"

Pebbles opened her eyes and nodded just as Garnier expressed his frustration at the size of their party. "Dr. Perez, we expected three, not six."

Cesar assured him there would only be three to examine the necklace. "Dr. Cully, Dr. Varma and Ms. Stevens are traveling with us. They are happy to wait here in the lobby, though we may wish to step out and consult with them during our examination. Perhaps an office or conference room could be arranged?"

While her dizziness continued, Pebbles listened to a brief side-conversation in French between Fremont and Garnier. Afterward, Garnier announced that Anlon, Sanjay and Jennifer would be situated in a conference room while Pebbles, Cesar and Mereau examined the necklace in a separate room. Escorted by the security guards, they began to walk toward an elevator. Pebbles stumbled but was steadied by Anlon. The bank manager inquired if there was a problem.

"She's feeling a little under the weather," Anlon said. Pebbles felt his arm wrap around her shoulder.

Fremont halted, bringing the full group to a stop as well. "Would *mademoiselle* care to sit? Perhaps a glass of water?"

"No. I'll be fine." Pebbles smiled, her trembling hands hidden behind her back.

"*Très bien.* Then if *mesdames et messieurs* will follow me, we shall *procéder.*"

The quivering inside Pebbles continued during the cramped and glacially slow elevator ride to the second floor. It worsened as they were led to the conference room where Anlon and the others would wait. Her body began to shake. She swooned and looked at Anlon. "I'm sorry. I tried. I can't stop it."

An image flashed into Pebbles' mind. It was the teenager kneeling before the bonfire, her eyes pleading with the burly man who gripped a spear. The smell of smoke was overwhelming. Pebbles began to cough. She felt Anlon's arm grip her tightly as he called for a chair and some water.

Trees exploded into splinters as the masked men pushed into the clearing. They hooted and hollered as they slayed the stragglers who had stayed behind to buy Citali time to escape.

From the cover of bushes beyond the clearing, Citali watched the evil bitch emerge from the smoke. Strutting like she was already victorious, her own mask shimmering in the bonfire's flames, she dispatched an old man with a flick of the jagged knife in her hand. Voices called to Citali.

"Run! Get away! You cannot save them!"

But her eyes were riveted on the sobbing teenager at the edge of the bonfire. She knelt with her head bowed, the weighty headdress lolling to one side of her head. As the conquering queen approached, knife poised, her army of savages advanced too. The burly man waved his spear back and forth, shouting at them.

Citali could not hear the words he spewed at them, but she understood the gist.

Come closer, and I will kill her!

In a flash of horror, Citali watched him wheel around, spear the teenaged girl in the chest and fling her flailing body into the bonfire.

"No!"

The words were out of Citali's mouth before any of her escorts could stop her. The evil bitch staggered momentarily, but her head snapped in Citali's direction when she heard her yell.

"Run, Keeper! Run!"

Citali clutched her necklace and screamed at the top of her lungs. *"You shall pay, demon! I will eat your heart!"*

With Pebbles yelling in a tongue that Anlon had never heard, he held out his arms to quell the itchy security guards standing around the conference table. "It's okay, it's okay. Just take it easy." Over his shoulder, he looked for Sanjay. "A little help, please."

But the psychologist was already kneeling beside Pebbles, his monotone voice repeating the word *oasis*.

"What in the devil is going on?" demanded Garnier.

Anlon was too focused on Pebbles to take the time to answer, but he need not have worried. Mereau stepped forward and spoke to the man in French.

An animated conversation between the two men ensued, during which Anlon held onto the railing Pebbles as tightly as he could. He joined Sanjay in chanting the word *oasis*, but to no effect.

Cesar joined the battle of words between Mereau and Garnier. Fremont entered the verbal fray as well. Anlon watched Garnier shake his head from side to side. *"Non! Non! Fini!"*

"S'il vous plaît, mon ami. Compassion," Mereau appealed.

"Non! Fini! Au revoir." Garnier turned away from Mereau and headed for the conference room exit. Fremont, standing beside Garnier, signaled for his guards to escort Anlon's party from the room.

Out of the corner of his eye, Anlon saw one of the guards move toward them and then he felt Jennifer push past. He looked up to see her bar the guard's way. With her hand pressing against the man's chest, she said, "Easy, tiger."

The guard pushed her hand away and grabbed her by the arm.

"Get off," she said, yanking her arm free.

Two other guards reached for their weapons. While Cesar protested, Anlon returned his attention to Pebbles, for she fought against his hold, spittle flying from her mouth as she screamed at an invisible adversary.

From behind, he heard Mereau boom, "Stop where you are, *messieurs*, and tell your men to do the same."

Anlon looked up to see Mereau rubbing his hands together, a glow of red emanating from between them. *Oh, shit!* Anlon vaulted up. "Mereau, don't!"

"I am sorry, my friend. I am not leaving until we have seen the necklace."

"What do you have in your hands? Is it a bomb?" Fremont's tone was frantic as he stepped back. The guards and Garnier stepped back as well.

"No," Mereau laughed.

"A weapon, then?"

"If I choose to use them in such a way, they can be."

"You brought a weapon into *my* bank?" Fremont was purple faced. "Surrender it at once or I shall have you arrested!"

Anlon moved in between Mereau and the guards. Turning to Mereau, he said, "There's no need for a confrontation."

"Tell that to the men with guns pointed at us," Mereau said.

"Leave at once! *Partir*!" shouted Fremont.

"Come now, Claude, be reasonable," said Cesar.

"*Raisonnable? Raisonnable?*" Fremont spat. "He has a weapon! He has threatened me! This woman…she is deranged."

"She's just having a vision," Sanjay said. "She means no harm."

Cesar echoed Sanjay's comment. "She is a clairvoyant. She feels the presence of the necklace. It is speaking to her. She's just answering back."

"*Excusez-moi?* You told me she was an archaeologist," said Garnier.

"No, I did not, *monsieur*. I told you she was an expert."

"You said she could help authenticate the necklace."

"Indeed, she can…if you will let her."

In the midst of the angry jawboning going back and forth, Anlon heard a thump. He turned to see Pebbles slumped on the floor, Sanjay holding her in his arms. Tears running down her face, she said, "She was just a child."

Seconds later, she passed out. The room silenced. Looking up once again, Anlon saw confused expressions from all the New Caledonians. He focused on the bank manager. "Please, just give us a little time to get her back on her feet. She'll be fine." Before Fremont could answer, Anlon instructed Mereau to surrender the glowing stones in his hands.

"When they put away their guns, I will—"

"Look, Mereau. I appreciate your gallantry, but it's hurting more than it's helping right now. Just give them the frickin' stones so we can try and talk this out." Anlon turned to Fremont. "I'd like to think calmer heads can prevail."

Though it took several more minutes of cajoling both parties, Anlon brokered a cessation of hostilities. Mereau gave up his *Dreylaeks*, the cookie-sized Munuorian stones capable of leveling the bank, and the bank manager ordered his guards to holster their weapons. Meanwhile, Cesar negotiated with Garnier to regain permission to examine the necklace.

Anlon was not thrilled with the compromise Cesar and Garnier agreed upon. Only Cesar and Mereau would examine the necklace. Pebbles would stay in the conference room with Anlon and the others. He appealed to Garnier. "If she recovers sufficiently before you finish with the necklace, I'd like to ask that you reconsider and allow her to join them."

The curator denied the request. "*Non!* Under no circumstances will she be allowed in the room with the necklace. If she has another fit, she could damage it. I will not take the risk."

As Anlon prepared a rebuttal, Mereau pulled him aside and whispered, "Trust me, my friend. If what I suspect about the necklace is true, she will get to see it. Just go along with the compromise for the time being."

The clasped necklace was laid out on a white cloth. Cesar flicked on the lights of his magnifier-eyeglasses and began his examination. Mereau stood on the opposite side of the table. Hands behind his back, he watched Cesar meticulously study the artifact from one end to the other, every so often looking up to smile at Garnier and two security guards standing behind Cesar. All three looked ready to pounce at the slightest hint of trouble.

"Tell me, monsieur, what is your view of the relic's origin?" Mereau asked.

The curator, shaken from his surveillance, blinked several times and cleared his throat before answering. "It is hard to say. It is obviously from antiquity, but we have not been able to classify it as belonging to any known culture. It is a problem we face with a number of pieces in the collection."

"I see. Then what is the basis of your claim that it is from antiquity?"

Garnier frowned. "It is not *my* claim. It is the claim of experts who have examined it."

"*Excusez-moi.*" Mereau bowed. "I did not mean to offend. I only meant to learn how it has been determined to be ancient."

With a dismissive snort, Garnier said, "You are suggesting it is modern? A forgery, perhaps?"

"I suggest nothing. I only ask. If it can't be tied to a specific culture, then how did you...your experts...arrive at the conclusion that it is of great age? It was not found *in situ.*"

"There are several indications. *Par exemple*, the markings on the tiles. From a historical perspective, they are unique."

"That does not make them old."

The curator flushed red. "They are crudely etched."

Cesar, still examining the necklace, interjected. "Yet the metalwork is quite sophisticated. The tiles are not plated; they are cast." He looked up at Mereau. "Come have a look. I think you will recognize the technology."

Mereau smiled. "No need, my friend. I already recognize it."

"Why did you not mention it before?" Cesar asked.

"I did not suspect it until we exited the elevator. But, now I have seen it, now that I am in its presence, I am sure."

The look on Garnier's face was a mix of anger and confusion. "What is this *absurdité*? You have barely looked at it. Yet, you speak of *la technologie*. Are you clairvoyant like *le femme hystérique*?"

"You should not mock her, monsieur. She is capable of telling you more about this piece's history than I."

"I do not mock her, monsieur. I mock *you!*"

"Then let me educate you." Mereau stepped forward. Pointing at the necklace, he said, "I'm sure the first puzzling attribute your experts faced was the strength of the piece's magnetism."

Garnier flinched. Mereau smiled. "I sensed its magnetism as soon as I exited the elevator. No doubt, Pebbles sensed it earlier than me. I'm certain it was the trigger for her derangement in the conference room."

"*Sacré bleu!* You are *voyant* too?"

"*Non, Monsieur.* Just sensitive to magnetic fields." Mereau turned to Cesar. "This would have puzzled the experts, would it not?"

Removing his magnifiers, Cesar said, "Possibly. It would have confirmed the necklace is made of a gold alloy instead of pure gold. Though, they would have surmised as much from its hardness, the scarcity of scratches and dents."

Mereau nodded. "I think you will find it is far more magnetic than any gold alloy ever examined by Monsieur Garnier's experts. Is that not so?"

Garnier did not respond.

"In fact," continued Mereau, "I would venture to guess they sampled the alloy, much like you hoped to do, Cesar, and discovered the gold content in the tiles was much higher than one would have expected given the intensity of its magnetism.

"Of course, even before they received the sample's test results, I'm sure the experts noticed the seams suggesting the tiles were cast. I suspect they first weighed the necklace to confirm their suspicions, and as they expected, the necklace weighed less than it should have if the tiles were made of solid gold or a solid alloy. Would these have been reasonable steps, Cesar?"

"Yes. And if they had already noticed its magnetism, they would have also ordered X-ray and CT scans to see through the tiles."

Mereau nodded and turned to face Garnier. "Those scans revealed dense metallic objects inside the tiles, didn't they, monsieur? Not as dense as gold, but not feather-light, either."

The curator deigned to answer with a tiny nod.

"So, it is Munuorian, then?" Cesar asked.

"No...the craftsmanship is too crude to be Munuorian," Mereau said, "but it was made by someone familiar with our techniques...right down to the magnetic clasps."

"Moon what?" Garnier asked.

"I imagine your experts are actually divided, Garnier. There must be some who question whether an ancient culture could have made such a piece of jewelry." Mereau turned to Cesar. "Did you find the slash mark?"

"I found *a* slash mark, yes. Whether it is *the* slash mark is another question."

"You talk in riddles!" Garnier's voice trembled. "What about the slash mark?"

"*Calmer, monsieur,*" Mereau said. "Señor Perez will explain. I will be back shortly."

"Where are you going?" Garnier said.

"To consult with *le femme hystérique.*"

"Why?"

"There are things I wish to know that only she can answer."

CHAPTER 14

UNMASKING THE ENEMY

BANQUE CALEDONIENNE
NOUMEA, NEW CALEDONIA
SEPTEMBER 23

The room was quiet when Mereau entered. Pebbles was awake and sipping on water. Seated with her at the table were Jennifer and Sanjay. Anlon was leaning against the wall, staring down at his shoes.

From the look on Pebbles' face when she turned toward him, Mereau could tell she was angry. He smiled at her but received no more than a tepid nod before she turned away and took another drink from the bottle. It was to be expected, he realized. Given the strength of the necklace's *gensae*, its magnetic field, he supposed she felt its presence more than he did.

"You have news?" Anlon asked.

"Yes, I do," Mereau said. "It is as we thought. The necklace is almost assuredly the one in Pebbles' drawing. What's more, I think I know why Citali wore it, and why Muran was hunting her. It was more than just a ceremonial piece."

"Whoop-de-do," Pebbles murmured. She turned Mereau's way again. "Am I gonna get to see it or not?"

As he sat down across the table from her, he said, "I think there is a strong possibility Monsieur Garnier will appear at any moment to request an audience with you."

From the change in her expression, the news appeared to come as a welcome surprise.

"Before he arrives, I have some questions for you…and for Sanjay."

"Okay. Shoot." Pebbles put aside the bottle and scooted her chair closer to the table.

"They may be painful to answer. I will try to ask them as delicately as I can."

"Nothing could be more painful than the headache I have right now."

"It is the *gensae* of the necklace. It is quite strong."

Anlon sat down next to Mereau. "*Gensae* as in, the necklace is Munuorian?"

"Not quite, but I believe it may have been made *for* a Munuorian. If not that, it was commissioned, or possibly designed, by a Munuorian." Mereau described the construction of the necklace, then said, "If I am not mistaken, the magnets inside the tiles were chipped from a meteorite — it would not surprise me to discover the meteorite was one of the thousands that showered the Earth during Munirvo's passing."

The most confused look at the table came from Sanjay. For his benefit, Mereau explained. As the asteroid passed, it flipped the planet upside down. In so doing, the asteroid disrupted Earth's magnetic field *and* the Munuorian race's unique ability to detect and interact with the field. The disruption, combined with the ravaging of the food sources that nourished that ability, Mereau told him, was responsible for the eventual extinction of his people…and Mereau's own death.

"We had lived our whole lives cognizant of magnetic currents in the air, land and sea. We sensed the magnetism of all living things. We relied on that sixth sense more than we did our eyes and ears. Overnight, everything we knew about the field changed. It was like going to sleep in a forest where you knew every tree, rock and hill…and then waking up in a desert of endless sand.

"And in that desert, there was no food. At least, no food with the nutrients necessary to maintain our *gensae*, our magnetic energy. It would be like, if today, the human race suddenly lost its immune system. In short order, disease would ravage the world's population. So it was with us…with me…"

Mereau found it hard to finish his sentence. Too many memories of Munirvo's aftermath flowed through his mind. He stared blindly at the surface of the table as visions of the bitter struggle to survive raced by. Thankfully, a question from Anlon cut short the nightmarish scenes.

"So, you think the necklace was made for one of your people, a Munirvo survivor, to help her — or him — interact with the magnetic field."

"I can see no other explanation for creating such a necklace," Mereau said. "It would have acted like a sonar of sorts, projecting magnetism that echoed back when it interacted with the field around the wearer. But the wearer would have had to possess some level of *gensae* already in order for the necklace to have been of value."

"How could Citali have stood it?" Pebbles asked. She aggressively rubbed her temples. "If you're right, and what's causing my headache is the necklace, I can't imagine having it around my neck all the time."

Mereau shrugged. "Perhaps she built up a tolerance over time. Or perhaps, she did not wear it all the time…which leads to the first of my questions. In your visions of Citali's memories, is she always wearing the necklace?"

"I don't know. There are some dreams, some memories, where she feels for it around her neck, and I do remember her putting it on when she got out of bed in the last replay of the temple dream," Pebbles said. She looked to Jennifer. "Do you recall other mentions of it in my journals?"

"Nope. Matter of fact, I'm pretty sure you've never mentioned her feeling for the necklace before, or about her putting it on." Jennifer turned from Pebbles to look at Mereau. "I want to make sure I get this straight. You're thinking Citali was a Munuorian?"

"In a way, yes. A descendent of one, however far removed." Mereau directed his attention back to Pebbles. "In your recitation of the temple dream, you said Citali was called *Seer* by some, *Keeper* by others. In Muran's manifesto, the passage we think is linked to Citali, she is referred to as an *oracle*."

Pebbles stared at him. "She could read the magnetic field. She could *see* it."

"A valuable skill to have where Paracas is situated," Anlon said. "Tropical depressions brewing near the coast, she would have detected them long before they turned into hurricanes. Same with tremblors ahead of earthquakes or volcanic eruptions."

Mereau nodded. "And she would have sensed the coming of the change in seasons, the approach of large forces, the presence of large herds or schools of fish. Any unusual ripple in the field would have caught the attention of her *gensae*. Unfortunately, it appears her *gensae* caught the attention of Muran."

There was a knock at the door. When it cracked open, the head of Garnier appeared. Mereau suppressed a smile when he saw the curator's eyes light up upon spotting Pebbles. Moments later, she was on her way to see the necklace. As Mereau stood to follow them, Sanjay said, "What about your other questions?"

"They will have to wait. I must be there when her visions begin."

With each step closer to the room with the necklace, the throbbing in Pebbles' head intensified. Spots began to dot her vision and she felt flush. As she squinted to shield her eyes from the brightness of the hallway lights, Mereau, walking beside her, took hold of her arm and said, "It's only a little farther."

"Are you feeling this too?"

"Yes, but it is not as strong to me. The *gensae* in old Foucault's body is not as potent as that which flows through you."

Garnier must have noticed her discomfort, for he asked if she was feeling ill again. Mereau interceded and explained she was feeling the effects of the necklace's magnetism. "She is very sensitive to strong magnetic fields."

Through the open door ahead, Pebbles spied Cesar speaking with the bank manager. There were smiles on their faces and their conversation appeared relaxed and cordial. The sight calmed Pebbles. She'd had enough of confrontations for one day.

When they reached the doorway, Mereau and Garnier stepped aside to let her enter the room first, but Cesar stepped out and asked to speak to Pebbles alone. "It will only take a moment."

While the other men entered the room, Cesar led Pebbles to a small nook of cubicles wedged between two offices. Dizzy and weak, Pebbles slid onto the first chair she spotted. Cesar pulled another alongside and sat facing her.

"How are you feeling?" Cesar asked, his face displaying concern.

"I'm a little woozy right now." She leaned close and whispered. "I'm also scared. What happens if I go into another trance?"

"Not to worry. I have told Garnier it is likely. He is at peace with the possibility."

"What's going on? Why's he suddenly so accommodating?"

"He sees profit in cooperating."

"I don't understand. What do you mean?"

"I showed him a picture of the oasis sketch."

"You did what?"

"The redacted version Anlon sent me. I wanted him to see the necklace and Citali's unusual head…and the Candelabra."

It had been important for two reasons, Cesar explained: to persuade Garnier of Pebbles' psychic abilities, and to show the curator how Cesar arrived at a possible link between Citali, the necklace and the Paracas culture.

"I would have shown him the passage from Muran's manifesto to buttress the link, but no one takes her journal seriously. To them, it is fiction. The ravings of a lunatic," Cesar said. "In any event, it was not necessary. Garnier was thrilled."

Pebbles frowned. "Why?"

"The necklace is a mystery piece. As much as he tries to pretend it is valuable, he has no proof it is ancient. Therefore, it is unlikely it would fetch a high price at auction. We have provided him with a possible history he can attach to the necklace. It is a weak history at the moment, and he knows it, but he now sees an incentive to help us learn more about the necklace. And I've told him, in no uncertain terms, that *you* are the key to discovering more about the piece."

"And he bought that?"

"Hook, line and sinker." Cesar smiled and patted her shoulder. "So, fear not, if a vision comes. Learn as much as you can."

"Did Mereau tell Garnier about the connection with the Munuorians?"

"Briefly, and not in much detail." Cesar looked up. "Ah, Garnier approaches. Come, it is time."

One foot into the room, the second she laid eyes on the necklace, visions began to flash through Pebbles' mind. They were snippets, no more than a few seconds each.

…she was floating down a river lit by torches on both sides, unseen people chanting…a woman kneeling before her in the temple, her head bowed…crawling through jungle vines to reach a hidden cave…standing at the prow of a ship as it cut through dark waters…a woman straddling her, knife poised to strike…

Pebbles gasped and staggered backward against the wall, her hands flailing to knock away the knife. Suddenly aware of her surroundings, she shot looks at Mereau and Cesar. "Holy shit!"

"You have had visions?" Garnier queried.

"A jumble of them."

"Take the necklace," Mereau said.

In unison, Pebbles and Garnier said, "What?"

"*Non*! There is to be no touching!" said Garnier.

"How else is she to put it on?" Mereau asked in a matter-of-fact tone.

More visions cycled through Pebbles' mind.

…arms raised above her head, something heavy in her hands. Before her, hundreds of people bowing…seated around a campfire among a circle of people, listening to a man talk — a man with an elongated head… pushing her hand against a rock wall, the wall trembling…the cackle of the woman slicing her neck…

Pebbles staggered forward and braced herself against the table. Face dripping with perspiration, she listened to Mereau shouting at Garnier.

"Tell me this, *monsieur*. Have you been able to unclasp the necklace?"

She looked over at Garnier. The red-faced man with the pinched lips said nothing.

"Yes, it is as I thought," Mereau said. "You have tried many ways, I expect. You and your experts. But none have worked. The magnetism is too strong, the locking mechanism beyond your or their comprehension. If nothing else, let *mademoiselle* unclasp it for you."

Pebbles gazed at Mereau. "What are you talking about? I don't know how to —"

"I will instruct you," said the curt Mereau. "What say you, Garnier?"

Her eyes traveled back to the necklace, now within hand's reach. Under the harsh glow of the room's fluorescent lights, it looked pale, faded, as if someone had sucked the life out of the gold. Yet her fingers prickled from its energy.

"What if she damages it?"

"She will not. You will be shocked at the ease with which she opens it."

As she stared at the symbols on the tiles, on came another rush of visions.

…a finger dipping in gold paint and then swirling a design on her cheek…sloshing in mud as hands ripped away her clothes…letting go of the bag in the river…her face shoved into the riverbank…clawing at the mud, desperate to breathe…

More gasping. Pebbles could taste the mud in her mouth. Through parched lips, she begged for water. Hands guided her onto a seat. A bottled water touched against her lips. She was aware now of Cesar's voice. "Sip it slowly…don't gulp."

Her eyes fluttered open as she sipped. The necklace was gone from the table. She darted her head around, dribbling water down the front of her shirt. "Where is it? Where did it go?"

It was still close by, for her head still throbbed, her fingers still prickled. Mereau moved into view. He sat on the edge of the table and outstretched a hand. The necklace dangled around it.

"You do not pull. To separate the two ends, you slide each end in opposite directions, one over the other. But, first, you must align the release. You cannot see it. You can only feel it. The ends will start to vibrate as you twist them. Do it slowly. Until your fingers are used to the sensations, you must move them slowly. The vibration will intensify as you get closer to lining up the release. There will be an unmistakable pulse when it releases. Then slide the two ends apart."

Mereau handed Pebbles the necklace. The rumbling in her chest started immediately. The sound of a woman cackling echoed in her ears. Pebbles looked up at Mereau, her eyes pleading forgiveness. "I'm sorry…I can't. It's Muran…she's coming."

In a lightning-quick motion, Mereau took up the necklace, separated the clasps and wrapped it around Pebbles' neck. When the clasps clicked closed again, he let go, allowing the necklace to drape around her neck. As Pebbles began to tremble, Mereau leaned forward and whispered, "Let her come. She cannot harm you now."

In the darkness, the sounds of the battle echoed in the clearing. Fire burned all around. Pinned to the ground by the masked woman, Citali grappled for control of the knife. Despite her size advantage over the woman, however, she was too weakened from the chase. The blade inched closer and closer to her neck. The masked woman growled. *"Last chance. Where are they? What have you done with them?"*

"You are too late…you will never have them."

The woman pushed harder on the knife, and Citali's strength failed. The blade plunged into her neck. Citali cried out and clawed at the hand, driving the knife deeper. The woman cackled. *"No matter. I will find them on my own…and I will parade your head through the ashes of your city."*

Citali felt a tug on her necklace. A surge of anger spiked inside. She balled her fists and pummeled the woman's mask, knocking it from her face.

Do not give up! Do not let her take it from you!

The snarling woman ripped out the knife. As she raised it to strike again, Citali felt around for the mask, snatched it up and swung it at the hand with the knife. A flash of light crossed Citali's vision and she felt the woman on top of her shudder. Looking up, she could not believe her eyes. A flaming arrow had pierced her attacker. The expression on the stricken woman's face showed she was just as stunned as Citali. They both paused their struggle and stared at the flaming shaft sticking out of the woman's abdomen. Citali broke out of the daze first, knocking the woman away with the aid of the mask and scrambling to her feet. Citali clasped a hand on the searing pain in her neck and started to dash toward the edge of the clearing.

Run! Go! Go! Go!

But she made it only a few steps before she was tackled to the ground once again. She could smell burning flesh as her attacker burrowed Citali's face into the soil. She felt the woman's knife glide under her chin, slashing. But the blade's stroke was thwarted by the necklace. Another arrow must have hit the woman, for Citali heard her groan and felt her body tremble.

Wasting no time, Citali squirmed from beneath the woman only to be stopped by a sharp, slicing pain in her back. Her yelp was brief, for she could not breathe. She flailed her arms and gasped for air. She felt the necklace jiggle and slide free. The weight atop her vanished. Her senses began to fade… the pain in her neck and back…the shouts of men urging retreat…the acrid smell of smoke…the taste of blood…the woman's cackle…they all dimmed until Citali teetered on the edge of dreamless oblivion.

It is over. I have failed.

Pebbles muttered two words and passed out.

"What did she say?" asked Garnier.

As Mereau reached to stop Pebbles from falling from the chair, he spoke to Cesar. "Go get Anlon, the others."

Garnier demanded answers. "What is happening? Is she ill?"

"She will be fine." Mereau eyed the security guard. "Help me get her out of the chair, lay her on the floor."

"Be careful! Do not damage the necklace," said Garnier.

As the two men gently lowered Pebbles to the floor, Mereau shouted, "To the depths with your cursed necklace."

The first of her senses to revive was her hearing. The first sound her ears registered was the chirping of birds. Among them was a familiar warble, more of a whistle than a chirp. Next came the aroma of burning incense. She breathed in deeply and exhaled slowly, letting the comforting scent linger as long as possible. Black turned to gray, lighter and lighter gray beginning to take on colors.

She became aware of someone touching her forehead. She heard whispering voices, tried to open her eyes wider but her lids would not cooperate. She tried to move but her limbs would not respond. The finger touching her head was wet. It swirled in a pattern and then was gone. A second later, she felt another swirl, this one on her cheek. By the time the finger began a third design on her chest, she knew where she was and what was happening.

"It is over?"

The whispering ceased. Only the birds could be heard. The finger lifted from her chest.

"Did she find them?"

A man's voice, gentle and deep, replied. *"No, Keeper. They are safe where they were hidden."*

The finger designs resumed. Wet streaked her abdomen and then her forearms.

"She has my necklace. She will find them."

"Rest your mind. She took many arrows. She will not live to find them."

More streaks painted her thighs. Through labored breaths, she asked, *"How can you be sure?"*

"We will keep them safe. Have no fear."

As the last of the swirls coated her feet, she felt tears leak from her eyes. *"I am scared."*

A hand tenderly wrapped around hers. *"Be at peace. They will be safe in our care."*

"Promise me...give them to no one unless they speak the words, unless they bear the emblems."

The hand squeezed. She felt a kiss on her forehead. *"It shall be as you instruct...as your father instructed before you...as his father before him and so on...all the way back to the day of darkness."*

"You comfort my ears."

The man lowered his voice to a whisper, his mouth touching her ear. *"May the stars light your way."*

Tears ran down Citali's cheek as she replied, *"Until we meet under the same sky."*

She squeezed his hand and exhaled her last breath.

CHAPTER 15

LIFE AFTER DEATH?

BANQUE CALEDONIENNE
NOUMEA, NEW CALEDONIA
SEPTEMBER 23

Pebbles awoke to find herself once again lying on a floor with her friends kneeling beside her and Anlon holding her hand. He smiled. "Hey there."

"Hey." She smiled back.

"You all right?"

"Yeah, I think so."

As she started to raise up, a cold pack slipped from her forehead. Jennifer caught it and helped Anlon prop Pebbles into a sitting position. Mereau rolled a chair over while Cesar handed her a bottle of water. Sanjay moved in close and examined her eyes. When he was finished, Pebbles looked around at her friends and said, "We *really* have to stop meeting like this."

There were smiles and light laughter from the others as they helped her into a chair. She noticed Garnier was absent and so was the security guard. Pebbles reached for her neck and discovered the necklace was gone.

"Mereau took it off," Anlon said. "Garnier took it back to the vault."

Pebbles rubbed her forehead. "Gotcha. Kinda glad. It was pretty intense, gave me a splitting headache. Seems mostly gone now."

"Are you up to talking about what happened?" Anlon asked.

"Yeah, sure. Guess we should while it's all fresh in my mind." Pebbles glanced over at Jennifer taking her pen and pad out of her tote bag. "I know you want me to start at the beginning, but I want to start with the stuff that confused me."

"Like what?" Jennifer asked.

"Muran didn't transfer Citali's mind to a memory stone. She stabbed her real bad, took the necklace and left her to die."

"Are you sure?" Anlon asked.

"I'm positive. *No one* transferred her mind. She died. I experienced her passing." Pebbles paused and looked around at each of her friends. "So how did her memories, her consciousness, get inside me?"

"Maybe someone revived her after she died," said Jennifer.

"I don't think so. When she was dying, she was saying goodbye to the person with her and it wasn't Muran. I couldn't see him, but the voice I heard definitely belonged to a man. And there was no mention of the stones, just a ceremony that struck me as being like last rites. He made no effort to treat her medically. And all Citali seemed to care about was making sure Muran didn't get her hands on whatever she had been trying to keep away from her."

"Is it possible to transfer a mind to one of your memory stones after death?" Sanjay asked Mereau.

"I recall of no instance in our history of a mind transfer involving the deceased," Mereau said, "but that does not mean it has never been tried."

"Sanjay, isn't it pretty well documented that the brain survives for a period of time after the heart stops?" Anlon asked.

"That is true, but only for ten, maybe fifteen minutes."

"Then maybe the man tending to Citali tried it right after she died. Maybe that's what the ceremony was about. Prepping her for the transfer."

Pebbles frowned. "I don't know, Anlon. It didn't seem that way to me."

"Well, if you think about it, an after-death transfer might explain why you only have snippets of Citali's memories," Anlon said. "And why those memories are all related to events near the end of her life. Events that are all pretty much intertwined. Maybe that's because that's all that made it through onto the stone before her brain shut down...the last of her memories."

"That is an excellent point you raise, Anlon," said Sanjay. "About Citali's memories being linked to events near the end of her life, nothing earlier. But I wonder if that might suggest a different explanation than an after-death transfer."

"Such as?" Pebbles asked.

"It is an idea I have been pondering since our conversation about amnesia. It should not be possible, there are no credible, documented cases among adults…but in children? Specifically, children under the age of six, there have been some remarkable case studies."

"Case studies of what?"

"Past life recall."

"You mean like your Pearl Harbor visions you told us about earlier?" Jennifer asked.

Sanjay shook his head. "No. Past life recall is very different. It is a phenomenon where children recall being a specific person. They can share specific memories of places, people and events connected to the person. Names, dates, jobs, friends. Cars they drove. Houses they lived in. They seem to know it all. And I have to tell you, their descriptions are sometimes so accurate, it defies explanation. What is most stunning about these children, however, is that the people they remember being in a past life all met violent deaths. And the children can recount the deaths in excruciating detail."

Sanjay described one case chronicled by a reputable university researcher who was asked by the parents of a child to meet with their son. According to the parents, the father had given the four-year-old a toy airplane. Within a short time of playing with it, the child smashed it on a coffee table. In the following days, the boy repeated the act, smashing other toys that he had pretended were airplanes. When questioned by his parents as to why he was destroying his toys, the boy told them, *"This is how I died."*

He told his parents what his name had been. He told them the name of the ship he had served on and the name of the pilot in the plane next to his when he crashed. When the researcher met with the child, the boy related other details of his past life. The names of his parents and siblings, the street address where he had grown up and other biographical information. He also described what had happened in his crash, how his plane had been shot up during a battle in the Pacific, that he'd tried to make it back but lost control and nosedived into the ocean within eyesight of his ship.

"The researcher took all that information and sought out corroboration. There was indeed a pilot with the name given by the child who did serve on the ship he named and who did crash returning to his aircraft carrier. There was a wingman who was on the same mission who safely returned. His name was just as the boy said. The most amazing thing? The researcher found a living relative of the pilot who crashed. The man's sister. He arranged a meeting between the boy and the now-elderly woman. Trust me, the researcher's report of the details shared back and forth between brother and sister during that meeting would make you shiver."

Pebbles didn't need to read the report. She had goose bumps all over just from listening to Sanjay. As she rubbed her forearms to make them go away, Sanjay finished up.

"No one knows what sparks the recall. It seems to be spontaneous, with onset occurring between the ages of four and six. And by the time they're eight, they begin to lose the memories. By the time they reach adulthood, the memories are gone altogether. That is one of several reasons why I did not raise the possibility before."

"But you've changed your mind? You think it's a possibility now?" Anlon asked.

"On the spectrum of possible supernatural explanations, it seems no less improbable than an after-death mind transfer," Sanjay said. "Though, there are problems with it. There is no connection between past-life recall and PTSD or brain damage, in children or adults. Plus, every study of adults who claim to have had similar experiences has concluded their experiences are bogus. And even in credible case studies of children, the lives they recall occurred within one or two prior generations, not eighteen hundred years ago."

"Sounds like you're talking yourself out of the possibility just as quickly as you raised it, Sanjay," said Jennifer.

As Pebbles watched him shrug his shoulders, seemingly agreeing with Jennifer's comment, she could not help but find herself drawn to Sanjay's alternative. "Before we throw the idea in the trash, let me ask you this —

if I am recalling a past life, what would have caused the recall to start a few months ago? I mean, if you're saying it has nothing to do with PTSD or the fact my brain was damaged, what could have triggered it to start?"

"I have no idea. I'd be totally speculating if I tried to come up with an explanation."

"Speculate anyway."

"Very well. I would have to say, in your case, your recall of Citali's memories is somehow related to the rewiring of connections in your temporal lobe that were damaged last fall. As we have discussed, your savant artistry began around the same time as Citali's memories started to appear in your dreams. So, the two seem to go hand-in-hand."

Jennifer raised her hand to interrupt. "So, are you saying Citali's memories have always been embedded in Pebbles' brain, and she just didn't know it until her brain *found* the memories when it was rewiring itself?"

"No. What you describe falls into the category of reincarnation, and I do not think that is what has happened here."

"Then you've lost me. How did the memories get into her brain?" Jennifer prodded.

"If you seek a rational explanation, I have none to offer. If you are willing to consider a *supernatural* explanation, there is a theory about what causes past-life recall in children that may be relevant." Sanjay directed his gaze at Pebbles. "The theory goes like this: when a person dies, they leave behind psychic energy — a combination of the person's memories and consciousness. Under unknown conditions, the developing brains of certain children come in contact with the psychic energy and absorb it."

"When you say, come in contact, you mean physically?" Pebbles asked.

"It sounds like a ghost story," Anlon said. "A restless spirit wandering around runs into a child and suddenly the child thinks he is a World War Two fighter pilot."

"As I said, it is a supernatural theory."

"But, supposing it's not BS," Jennifer said, "how would that work? The fighter pilot died in the Pacific. The kid wasn't in the Pacific, was he? He was in his house somewhere in America, when he started up with the recall. Right?"

"That is right," Sanjay said. "Perhaps psychic energy travels. Who knows? It is just a theory."

Pebbles observed the skeptical looks on Anlon's and Jennifer's faces. They were not buying Sanjay's explanation, but as she recalled the vision of Citali's fight with Muran, Pebbles found herself tilting toward his theory. "Question. Is it possible for psychic energy to reside in physical objects?"

"Your guess is as good as mine," Sanjay said.

"Where are you headed with that, Pebbles?" asked Anlon.

"Well, there's obviously a common connection between Citali and me — Muran. It would be a pretty amazing coincidence for me to run into the free-floating psychic energy of a person who also had a run-in with Muran, don't you think? I mean, we're separated by almost two thousand years but, somehow, Citali found her way into my head. I could *maybe* understand it if we'd been in the same place somewhere along the line. But I've never been to Peru. The closest I've been is probably Ecuador on one of our trips to the Galapagos. I doubt Citali was ever in America or other places I've traveled. *But* there are two objects I *know* we both came in direct physical contact with, possibly three."

"Oh, my God…the necklace," Jennifer said. "But wait, that was here in New Caledonia when you were with Muran in Mexico. That couldn't be it."

"Good point."

"The *Sinethal*," said Anlon. "Of course. Muran may not have successfully loaded Citali's mind on it, but it doesn't mean she didn't try. Citali's psychic energy may have latched onto the same stone Muran used to transfer your mind."

"Maybe," Pebbles said, "but like I said earlier, I've seen no vision of a memory stone, and as far as the visions show, no one tried to store Citali's mind."

"Muran, herself, then," Cesar said.

"Now you're getting warm," Pebbles said.

"Wait a minute. Hold on," Anlon said. "You said it yourself, you and Citali were separated by close to two thousand years. And Muran switched bodies multiple times over that span. Hell, she spent half of those years trapped in her own memory stone. You expect me to believe Citali's psychic energy stuck to Muran through all of that? No way. I don't buy it. It's gotta be the *Sinethal*."

Pebbles smiled…a big, *I know something you don't* kind of smile.

"Why are you looking at me like that?" Anlon demanded to know.

"Because I love it when I figure things out before you do. Though it's kinda unfair. I noticed something in Citali's fight with Muran I haven't told you about yet."

"The mask," Mereau said.

Mouth agape, Pebbles turned to him. "How did you know?"

"You said 'the mask' when you briefly came out of your trance."

"I did?"

Mereau nodded.

"What about the mask?" Anlon asked.

Pebbles explained. Muran had been wearing a mask when she attacked Citali. In fact, all of her soldiers wore masks too. During the struggle, Citali knocked it off Muran's face and used it to defend herself.

Pebbles watched Anlon's eyes dart back and forth as he studied her face. Then *his* face twitched.

"Ah. I see. When you told us about the strangling on *Sol Seaker*, you said Muran covered your face with a mask."

"Pebbles, are you saying it was the same mask Citali used to defend herself?" Jennifer asked.

"I don't know. I never saw the mask she put on my face. I just remember the wall of masks in the room. They all depicted animals…and the one Muran was wearing during the attack was an animal. A leopard, jaguar or something like that."

Jennifer rummaged through her tote bag and withdrew her cell phone.

"Who are you calling?" Pebbles asked.

"Helen Li at the FBI," Jennifer said. "The Mexican police seized the compound where Muran held you hostage. They would have collected evidence from the cabin where you were strangled. They may have the masks or pictures of them."

As Pebbles watched Jennifer leave the room, Cesar asked, "Pebbles, you said Muran's soldiers also wore masks. Were they the same as the mask Muran wore?"

She turned to see Cesar scanning his cell phone.

"Uh…not sure. Why?"

"There was a culture in northwestern South America that flourished around the same time as the Paracas culture. They are known today as La Tolita. We do not know what they called themselves. They are renowned for the jewelry and masks they created. Many of the latter were of animals, including jungle cats…such as this one."

He stood and handed his phone across the table to Pebbles.

"Oh, my God…that's it."

JOURNAL OF DR. SANJAY VARMA
SEPTEMBER 24

In flight once again, this time headed for Lima, Peru, after stopovers in Auckland and Santiago. Though I am physically tired, my mind is energized. The developments of the last twenty-four hours have taken this case in an entirely different direction than I first imagined. Could it be I am witnessing a bona fide instance of past-life recall in an adult? The evidence so far is compelling.

There are Pebbles' dream journals, her drawings, her oral recitations of visions. Their contents are supported by discoveries of connections with the necklace in Muran's art collection, Cesar's picture of the puma mask kept in Ecuador's Museo del Banco, which happens to bear a striking resemblance to a picture the FBI forwarded to Jennifer of one of the masks recovered from Muran's compound in Laguna Milagros. There are also the Paracas mummies and the Candelabra monument, both of which we are on our way to see in person.

Although Muran's manifesto would not hold up to scrutiny by serious scholars, according to Cesar, it contains further evidence pointing to a link between Muran's reign as the leader of an unnamed culture (presumably La Tolita) and the disappearance of the Paracas culture.

He has told us La Tolita's culture disappeared somewhere between 300 and 1000 CE, the same general timeframe as the Paracas people disap-

peared. Perez says archaeologists who have studied La Tolita believe the impetus for their disappearance was a natural disaster. According to these scholars, their settlement, situated at the mouth of the Santiago River, was destroyed by a sudden shift of the river. What caused the river shift is unknown, but sediments found among La Tolita artifacts in the region hint at a volcanic eruption, an event, Cesar says, that may coincide with a suspected eruption of the Chimborazo volcano between 300 and 1000 CE.

If Cesar's speculation is correct, that Muran was the ruler of La Tolita, he wonders if the volcanic eruption is what caused the sudden change in her attitude toward the oracles mentioned in her journal. Had they foreseen the eruption and not informed her? Had they informed other cultures in the region but not La Tolita? Had they been blind to it? Muran's journal is silent on the catalyst for her bloodlust hunt of the oracles, one can only speculate. So says Cesar.

But in the process of hunting them down, it is apparent she discovered a link to her own past. The oracles were descendants of Muran's own race, the Munuorians.

Or so it seems. Evidence backing this supposition is scant at this point, relying predominantly on Mereau's assessment of the unique qualities of the necklace in Muran's collection. However, Pebbles' recollection of Citali's passing has provided two other tantalizing clues; on her deathbed, Citali spoke of something she hid, something that had been passed down through many generations all the way back to the day of darkness.

Taken together with everything else, it appears Citali and her forebearers were entrusted with protecting something that belonged to the Munuorians. Something that Muran found out about. Something she wanted.

So now we are off to follow Citali's trail, in the hopes of discovering answers to the following: What did Citali hide? Where did she hide it? Why did Muran want it? Each of us has different reasons for wanting to know these answers. For Cesar, it is a matter of historical significance. To Mereau, it is a chance to learn more about what happened to his civilization after the passing of the asteroid he calls Munirvo. For Jennifer, it is a crime to solve.

In Anlon's case, I think he only cares to bring peace to Pebbles. He hopes that if the answers are found, it will satisfy Citali's restless spirit and she will depart Pebbles' consciousness. There is some merit to his hopes, I believe. In past-life recall cases among children, there does seem to be an undertone of a desire to seek resolution. The spirits that inhabit the children seem to seek closure, to know loved ones are okay, to tell loved ones they are okay. Perhaps that is what Citali seeks — to know whether the 'something' she was entrusted to protect indeed eluded Muran.

Whether that is what Citali wants or not, I am certain that is what Pebbles desires. Now that she knows what Citali was up against, Pebbles wants to know whether she succeeded or failed. Cesar has tried to temper her curiosity by noting that Muran's passage about the oracles ends with her extolling her triumph over the last oracle. The following passage in the journal discusses a new life, he says, one in which she called herself Wak Chan Ajaw. History records this name as belonging to a powerful Mayan ruler known alternatively as Lady Six Sky, a woman who rose to power a century or so after the Paracas civilization disappeared into the deserts of Nazca.

For myself, I seek to help Pebbles manage the turmoil inside her brain so that she may pursue this extraordinary investigation to its conclusion. I am also captivated by the possibility of proving to myself that psychic energy lives on after death. Many cultures throughout history have fervently averred as much, but it has never been proved. This is a chance to answer a basic question that humans have asked since the dawn of intelligent thoughts, one I often wonder about myself — what happens to our consciousness when our bodies die? Are our thoughts, personalities, hopes and dreams nothing more than chemical reactions inside our heads, or is the human body just a cocoon for our spirits to develop and mature before it is time for our psychic energy, our essence as individuals, to transform into something else?

One way or the other, the coming days should illuminate answers for all of us.

CHAPTER 16

KEEP YOUR HEAD

LA BAHÍA DE PARACAS
PARACAS, PERU
SEPTEMBER 26

Anlon had hoped for an up-close look at the Paracas Candelabra but Cesar told him the geoglyph's conservator refused to allow them to visit the site.

"He said there are no roads to the site and hiking to the Candelabra is prohibited," Cesar had relayed to the group.

So, Anlon and his traveling companions did the next best thing and hopped aboard a tour boat excursion. At first, Anlon had been apprehensive about the possibility of Pebbles experiencing a trance while on a boat filled with other life-jacketed tourists, but the fear proved unfounded.

When the boat slowed its engines to allow tourists to take photographs of the geoglyph, Anlon said to Pebbles, "It looks like it could just blow away in this wind."

"I know. It's crazy that it hasn't. I heard a couple of people chatting with the tour guide. Did you know they had an 8.0 earthquake here in 2007? It wiped out the whole town of Paracas, apparently, but didn't do diddly-squat to the Candelabra. Talk about built to last."

Jennifer, seated on the opposite side of Anlon, nudged against him in order to ask Pebbles a question without shouting over the wind, gaggling tourists and rumble of the idling engines. "Are you getting anything? Any tingles? Flashbacks?"

"Nope. Nothing."

"That's so strange. Then why do you think you added it to the oasis drawing?"

"Beats me. I don't remember drawing any of that picture."

"And you don't remember Citali making the design in the sand by the pond during your vision?"

Pebbles shook her head.

"Strange," Jennifer said, her voice trailing off. She leaned back, her bulky life jacket releasing its pressure on Anlon's.

The wind whipped up, almost blowing off Anlon's baseball cap as he turned to talk with Cesar, seated on the other side of the boat with Mereau and Sanjay. Leaning forward, he said, "It does look like it's intended to be a landmark for ships approaching the cove, doesn't it?"

"It does, but its placement puzzles me. The Candelabra is really only visible to ships close enough to the coastline to see the cove entrance."

"I agree," Mereau said, his voice rising as the boat driver increased power to the engines. "There are other more meaningful landmarks available to a sea captain seeking the cove, ones visible from open waters as well as from the coast."

Anlon nodded. It was true. During the drive from Lima to Paracas, Anlon had studied a map app on his cell phone. Just beyond the entrance of Paracas Bay was a small set of islands known as *Islas Ballestas*. Farther north, there was another small island chain, *Islas Chincha*. Directly west of the cove was a large island, *Isla Sangayan*. Seafarers approaching the cove from any direction would encounter these islands long before they ever saw the Candelabra.

"I see what you mean," Anlon said as the boat turned toward *Islas Ballestas*, Peru's version of the Galapagos Islands.

Mereau stood and stepped over to Anlon's side of the boat and slid into a gap between Anlon and Pebbles. "I find it meaningful that Citali lived so close to islands with rich sea life, both plant and animal. Her diet would have bolstered her *gensae*."

How true, thought Anlon. The abundance of cryptochrome-rich algae and plankton in the waters surrounding Paracas meant many of the fish, birds and other sea life up the food chain in the area had heavy cryptochrome concentrations, an essential nutrient found in animals that could detect and interact with the Earth's magnetic field.

This was meaningful to Mereau because the same type of habitat had once flourished in the waters surrounding Mereau's ancient island homeland, Munuoria, meaning Citali had been nourished with the same kinds of nutrients that had once fueled the Munuorians' *gensae*, their magnetic sixth sense. To Anlon, it was another data point that suggested a connection between Citali and Mereau's people.

Later, after the boat excursion docked in Paracas cove, Jennifer drove the group to the nearby *Museo Histórico Paracas*, where a number of the elongated skulls found at the various sites of the Paracas necropolis were displayed.

Here, too, Pebbles exhibited no reaction upon seeing the skulls. This surprised Anlon more than the lack of reaction when they passed by the Candelabra geoglyph, considering she had experienced a seizure and a vision when she viewed photographs of the Paracas mummies aboard *Sol Seaker*. Then again, walking by glass display cases of the skulls in the midst of a crowded museum was not the same as seeing photographs of the full mummies in the cemeteries where they were unearthed.

Anlon watched Pebbles closely. She seemed downcast, almost depressed, a disposition noticed by everyone in the group. Jennifer came up beside her and wrapped an arm around Pebbles' shoulder. "Don't get all bummed out. We've got lots more to look at."

"I know. It's just, I thought being here, seeing things, sniffing the air, feeling the breeze would stir something up from Citali," Pebbles said. "Paracas is so beautiful. The ocean, the cliffs, the beaches. I can't imagine Citali wouldn't have felt the same way."

"Maybe it's because there are no ruins left of Citali's city," Cesar said.

"Maybe. But I thought I'd stand on a spot, sort of like Sanjay did when he went to Pearl Harbor, look around and see something familiar, something I would remember…I mean…something Citali would remember."

"Well, let's keep moving," Anlon said. "Sooner or later, we're going to hit one of those spots. One of the necropolis sites, perhaps."

The first cemetery they visited was close to the museum, on the desert plain near the hillside where the Candelabra was carved. There, they met up with an archaeologist colleague of Cesar's who provided them a tour of the site.

Unfortunately, there was not much to see, just empty holes. According to the archaeologist, the mummies that had once been buried there had been removed from the site for preservation reasons. As the archaeologist launched into a broken-English description of the burial practices of the Paracas people, Anlon noticed Pebbles step away from the group. Thinking a trance was imminent, he came up beside her. He did not want her to fall into one of the holes. Pebbles turned to him and said, "This is a waste of time."

Anlon wrapped his arm around her waist. "Hang in there. We've got two more sites to go."

Their next stop was the ancient cemetery at *Oof Wari Kayán* on the slopes of the Cerro Colorado mountain overlooking Paracas Bay. As they walked around the perimeter of burial plots, Anlon detected a change in Pebbles' demeanor. She had been walking a few steps ahead of him, her hands tucked into the back pockets of her jeans. As she shifted her gaze from the cemetery to the surrounding landscape, her pace slowed, and her hands slipped from her pockets. Seconds later, she halted and let out a small gasp.

Standing at the tower window, Citali soaked in the sunshine. In the distance, the waters of the cove sparkled silver atop the canvas of deep blue beneath. She watched the boats of fishermen returning from their predawn expeditions pass by the vessels of the city's naval forces on their way out to sea.

In the city, the streets bustled with activity. Traders and their trains of carriers lugged provisions into the city from the northern trails. Waiting for them were merchants, haggling prices before the goods were even unloaded. In the opposite direction traveled tradesmen from the city on their way to meet waiting canoes along the riverbank. They would return at dusk, after making the rounds to sell their wares in the villages that lined the river.

Citali shifted her view to a group of women leading children for their morning lessons. They bowed as they passed, a few of the children touching their hands to their foreheads. She smiled and touched hers in response. Turning away from the window, Citali saw her attendant enter the chamber.

"You have a visitor, Seer. She has requested an audience."

"Who is she?"

"She did not give a name. She says she is acquainted with Seer Nonali."

"She knows my sister but does not give a name?" Citali turned to face the attendant. *"Where does she come from?"*

"The woman did not mention her city, but I can tell she is not of our people. She wears gold and silver in her hair, on her wrists and ankles. She dresses like our queen, but she is not our queen."

"Does she seek a blessing? A reading?"

"I do not think so, Seer. Her attitude is of one who comes to tell, not to ask."

Citali frowned. Most often when foreigners sought an audience, they came to ask her to bless their children or sailor men. Or to know whether clouds over the sea would bring rain to their crops or if it was safe to build homes in valleys below the rocky mountains.

"Lead her to the worship room. Offer her refreshment. Tell her I will be with her shortly."

With the attendant gone, Citali picked up her necklace from the table by the bed. She had not finished clasping it when a sharp pain sliced into her back. Wincing, Citali pulled the string of golden tiles away from her neck and the pain abated. She sat down on the edge of the haybed and once again raised the necklace. This time when she clasped it into place, there was no pain in her back, but her forehead began to throb, and her eyes blurred.

They were the kinds of sensations Citali felt when the Earth stirred beneath the mountains, but these were weak. They did not ripple like waves. This typically meant the disturbance was far away.

Perhaps this woman comes to tell me Nonali has sensed a disturbance too.

Citali rose from the bed and started for the tower stairs. As she descended them, her eyes blurred again, and she experienced a moment of dizziness. Stopping to steady herself against the wall encasing the circular staircase, Citali felt a new sensation sweep through her mind and body. Fear. She quickened the pace of her descent.

The woman has come to bring me other news. Nonali is in danger! Has the northern tyrant attacked her city?

The woman was kneeling when Citali entered the worship room. She wore a hooded cloak. With her head lowered, she said, *"Seer. Keeper. Sister. I bow before you and ask for your help."*

Despite the practiced formality of the greeting, the voice that delivered it was young. Citali judged the woman to be no more than fourteen.

"Stand and remove your hood."

The visitor did as instructed, revealing a woman of the river tribes in the far north, her skin redder than those of the south, her black hair shorn at ear length in an even line that circled her head; her face, hair and neck were adorned with a variety of gold and silver jewelry, elaborate finery for one so young.

"You have come a long way, child. What brings you so far south?"

"I come to deliver a message on behalf of Seer Nonali and to receive your answer."

The answer caused Citali to frown. Nonali's city was located more than a full cycle of the moon from the heart of the river tribe settlements, a strenuous journey whether one chose to follow the desert coastline or follow the river before crossing the mountains. And Nonali's city was nearly two cycles of the moon from Citali's. Unless, of course, one decided to shorten the trek by backtracking to the coast and sailing south. Still, it was an arduous journey under any circumstances, even for the toughest of men.

"What is your name?"

"I am Rashana."

"Tell me, Rashana, why would Seer Nonali choose to deliver a message to me through a foreigner?"

"She did not say, Seer Citali."

"Very well. What is the message?"

"The masked lady is coming."

So, the rumors were true. The tyrant was pushing south. Her eyes narrowed as she stared at Rashana.

"This message comes from Nonali or from the masked lady?"

"From both, Seer," Rashana said. *"There is more to the message. One part from Seer Nonali and one from the masked lady."*

"Speak."

"Seer Nonali says: the masked lady seeks that which was hidden. Give her what she asks for, show her the way. Take the river, lead her into the cave and she will honor the pledge."

Citali swooned. Her mind raced. Under no circumstances would Nonali have spoken such words to a messenger. Rashana lifted a bag from beneath her cloak. She held it out toward Citali.

"The masked lady says: listen to your sister."

She opened the bag and withdrew Nonali's head.

Pebbles' eyes flashed open. She was in the middle row of the van. Anlon was seated on one side of her, Sanjay on the other. Outside, she saw Cesar and Mereau talking with the necropolis archaeologist. Jennifer sat in the driver's seat, looking back at Pebbles.

"Effing *bitch*!" Pebbles punched the back of the driver's seat.

Jennifer recoiled. "Hey, what's that for?"

"Out of my way," Pebbles said. She crawled over Anlon and yanked the sliding door open.

"Where are you going?" asked Anlon.

She stumbled out of the van, her eyes focused on the city of Paracas below. Looking to the left and right, she paced back and forth, squinting through the reflection of the sun bouncing off the desert slope of the mountain.

"Which way did you go, Citali? Give me some help here?" Pebbles whispered.

She heard car doors slam and footsteps kicking up sand. A voice from behind, Cesar's voice, asked, "Is everything all right?"

Pebbles marched down the slope a little and peered north. "The closest river is that way, right? We crossed over it coming down from Lima. Near Pisco."

The archaeologist answered for Cesar. "*Si, senorita, Rio Pisco* is the closest."

Waving for the others to follow her, Pebbles said, "Come on, let's go."

As she stomped past Anlon on her way to the van, Anlon called to her. "Hold up."

Pebbles stopped and turned as Anlon ran up beside her and asked, "What's going on?"

Looking past him, she focused on Jennifer. "Is your tablet up front?"

"Uh, yeah. Driver's door. Why?"

Without answering, Pebbles walked around to the driver's door and pulled the tablet from the door pocket. She immediately realized it was too bright outside to see the screen and so Pebbles ducked her head inside the vehicle and laid the tablet on the driver's seat. She called out. "Password, please."

Jennifer rattled it off as she and the others gathered around Pebbles. They pelted her with questions, but Pebbles ignored them. She opened the map app, typed in *Paracas* and waited for the screen to fill in the map. It was slow going, as the map populated the screen in chunks, as if the tablet was completing a jigsaw puzzle. Pebbles turned and looked at the bewildered group around her.

"The city was here. Well, a bit down the slope from here. But this angle," Pebbles spun toward the cove and spread out her arms to form an alley, "was Citali's view from her window in the temple tower." Turning back to her audience, she continued. "I don't want to waste time explaining the vision, I'll tell you on the way."

"Way where?" Anlon asked.

"The river." Pebbles looked down at the tablet. The map had finished loading. Her eyes scanned the area surrounding Paracas. She spotted the river. "Good. There's a road that runs alongside of it. Come on, let's get going."

"Wait a minute." Anlon's hand rested on her shoulder. "Why?"

A pique of annoyance flowed through Pebbles. "To follow the river." She looked to Cesar and the necropolis curator. "Are there any archaeological sites in caves along the river?"

While the two men conferred in Spanish, Anlon appealed to Pebbles. "Hey, can we take a deep breath here? Before we go anywhere, I'd like to hear what you saw in the vision. I'm sure everyone else wants to hear it as well."

"Look. Do you want to find out what Citali was protecting or not?"

"Yes, of course."

"Then we follow the river and find the cave. It's that simple."

Cesar cleared his throat. Pebbles turned toward him. "There are many cave and cavern sites in Peru, but the closest of any historical significance is the Temple of the Moon. However, it is over eight hundred kilometers from here, at Huayna Picchu, next to the famous Machu Picchu site."

Pebbles picked up the tablet and typed in *Temple of the Moon* in the search box of the map app. When the pin marking its location appeared on the screen, Pebbles zoomed out and studied its position relative to Paracas. It was just a bit north of due east from the mouth of the Pisco River, and the squiggly road that abutted the river as it snaked into the Andes, Route 28A, linked up with another squiggly road, Route 28B, that led to Huayna Picchu. Pebbles pointed at the two roads and asked the curator, "These roads are through mountain passes, correct?"

"*Si, senorita.*"

"They both look like they run along rivers for long stretches."

"The *rios* are mostly dry now, but, *si*, you are correct. It was easier to build roads along the contours of the *rios* rather than go over the mountains."

"All right. Then the Temple of the Moon is where we're headed."

"Pardon me, Pebbles, but I must point out — the Temple of the Moon is an Incan site," Cesar said. "It was almost assuredly built a thousand years *after* the end of the Paracas civilization."

"Aren't a lot of ruins built on top of older ruins?" Pebbles asked.

"Yes, that is often the case."

"So, couldn't that be true of the Temple of the Moon?"

"Yes, but there is no physical evidence to suggest—"

"No physical evidence, *yet*, you mean," Pebbles interjected.

"I don't mean to be combative, Pebbles, but there are likely tens of thousands of caves in the Andes between here and the Temple of the Moon," said Cesar. "Do you really believe Citali bypassed all of these and walked *eight hundred kilometers* through the mountains to hide her relics at Huayna Picchu?"

"I don't know, but weren't you the one who told us Muran's manifesto said she hunted the last of the oracles for *three months*? If she kept close to the river, she could have covered eight hundred kilometers in ninety days. That's less than ten K per day. That should have been manageable, even with elevation changes, don't you think?"

Anlon joined the debate. "We don't know how much of the three months she spent in the mountains, Pebbles. The manifesto said Muran followed the oracle *through the desert, over the mountains and down rivers* before she caught up to her in the jungle."

The vision of Rashana dangling Nonali's head flashed through Pebbles' mind. She gritted her teeth and glared at Anlon. "Look. If you don't trust me, just take me into town and I'll get my own car. I'm going up that river. I'm going to the Temple of the Moon. If I spot something on the way that takes me in a different direction, I'll call you and let you know where I've gone, but I'm done arguing about it. Jen, give me the keys."

She pushed Anlon aside and held out her hand toward Jennifer. Anlon stepped in between the two women and glared back at Pebbles. "We go together, or we don't go at all."

"Fine, then everybody get in the van and let's get going. We're wasting daylight."

"Not until we agree on the game plan."

"I've told you the game plan. Follow the river, just like Citali did, and—"

"Think about it, Pebbles. Citali didn't follow the river. At least not initially. She went into the desert first," Anlon said.

"You don't know that."

"Actually, I think I do. Hear me out." Anlon grabbed Jennifer's tablet from the driver's seat. Pebbles watched him reposition the center of the map app over Paracas and tap an icon that toggled the screen to show a satellite view of the area. Pointing at the screen, he said, "Mereau, I'll defer to you on military tactics, so correct me if I'm wrong." Anlon turned to Pebbles. "In your temple vision, the one where she fights off the intruders, you said the soldiers from the city went north to confront Muran's forces, and that most of the people from the city fled south. Why would Citali have fled north to the Pisco River, right into Muran's forces?

"Further, even though we don't know the order of your visions, doesn't it seem more likely the desert one precedes the mountain, river or jungle visions? I mean, look at the map. Once you get into the Andes, there's no desert unless Citali backtracked out of the mountains and went due south. Doesn't it make more sense she fled south into the desert from the get-go, and then curled back north toward the Pisco River later on? Like here, through this pass where Route 1S heads into the mountains. And look…" Anlon zoomed in on the road. "There's a river right next to Route 1S too. *Rio Ica.* Who's to say that's not the river she followed? Am I wrong, Mereau? Isn't that a more logical escape route?"

"In light of what we know, it does seem the more prudent route for Citali to have taken."

"Excuse me for disagreeing," Sanjay said, "but do we know how close Muran's forces were? Maybe she had enough time to reach *Rio Pisco* before Muran's army arrived."

"You forget Citali was assaulted in her own temple," Mereau said. "Muran's spies were already in the city. Some, no doubt, stayed hidden outside the temple. It would have been an easy matter to follow her. In fact, from Pebbles' visions, we know Citali was pursued at every turn throughout her escape. Better to not give away your intended destination, better to hope to lose your pursuers by taking an unexpected route."

It was hard for Pebbles to quell the urge to fish the keys from Jen's pocket, tell them all to go to hell and take off in the van. But the longer she listened to Anlon and Mereau, the more she realized she was wrong, and they were right, albeit for an entirely different reason. The message delivered by Rashana encouraged Citali to follow the river and lead Muran to the cave or end up like Nonali.

The visit had been a set up. Though the vision had not lasted long enough for Pebbles to see Citali reach the same conclusion, she obviously realized it at some point. It came down to this: if Nonali had fully revealed how to find the relics, why would Muran have needed Citali to lead her to them?

Muran must have hoped the content of the message, combined with the shock value of seeing Nonali's severed head, would have caused Citali to panic and act to protect the relics, which meant Muran likely had spies in the city long before the failed kidnapping, waiting around so they could track Citali when she left the city.

"So, that's why she stayed so long," Pebbles whispered. "She felt trapped."

CHAPTER 17

FOLLOW THE RIVER

They returned to Paracas to eat lunch, gather provisions and gas up the van. During lunch, Pebbles had shared the full vision of Rashana's visit. She was still being peppered with questions as they started out of Paracas on Route 1S. Concerned she would miss a clue as to the route Citali had followed, she cut off the conversation and kept her eyes peeled on the surrounding landscape.

There was desert, lots of desert, in every direction. As they angled away from the coast and drove inland, vineyards began to appear by the roadside. Pebbles looked past them, her eyes focused on the Andes drawing closer with each mile. It was probably why she did not see the road sign until Jennifer blurted, "Holy crap, look at that!"

When Pebbles turned to look where Jennifer was pointing, her mouth fell open. The two-line sign was printed in Spanish above and English below. It read: *HUACACHINA 10km. Visit South America's only desert oasis.*

Pebbles felt dizzy. An image flashed into her mind. She was crawling up a dune like a lizard, her body inches above the sand. When she reached the top, she peeked over the edge. There, in the valley of sand below, was a glistening pond surrounded by lush bushes and palm trees. Citali's thoughts echoed in Pebbles' mind.

They think me a fool. Do they not notice their own footprints in the sand? Or are they too thirsty to care?

Citali backed down the dune and turned her gaze toward the mountains.

Others wait for me in the pass, I am sure of it.

Pulling the hood over her head, Citali looked around for the nearest dune casting a shadow. As she began to walk toward it, she devised her plan.

I will wait until nightfall and go deeper into the desert. They will not dare to follow. Then I will sneak into the mountains.

The vision faded. Pebbles looked up to see Anlon staring at her from the front passenger seat. "You want to go see it or head up into the mountains? Junction is coming up."

He handed her Jennifer's tablet showing their approach to the town of Ica. On the right, the Huacachina oasis was highlighted as a point of interest. On the left, she could see Route 1S leading into the mountains.

"Neither. Go through Ica. Keep going south."

Anlon took back the tablet and gazed at the map. "Are you sure?"

"Positive. Citali did come this way, but Muran's goons were waiting for her. She went farther south, out into that big-ass desert."

Sixty miles of desolate terrain later, Anlon queried Pebbles once again. "Are you sure about this? We're coming up on a sizeable river, the Rio Grande, but the road that runs alongside it looks as if it dead-ends halfway into the Andes."

"I'm sure. Just keep going."

Inside, however, Pebbles was not sure at all. She closed her eyes and willed guidance from Citali. She replayed what she could recall of the scene of ascending the mountain trail. There had been a village below the mountain. She remembered that from the dots of light coming from torches and firepits. Thinking back, Citali had seemed neither tired, thirsty nor hungry. Had she stopped to rest, had someone given her aid?

A vision flickered into view in her mind. It was a banquet. There were others with heads elongated like Citali's. The banquet was outside, under the stars, with cauldrons of fire surrounding the courtyard where they ate. It was not a festive occasion. The people who sat in a circle around Citali wore somber expressions.

Pebbles was aware of a hand clasping hers. She opened her eyes and looked down. Mereau was seated next to her but he was asleep, his hands folded across his chest, his head leaning against the window.

She felt a squeeze. A voice said, *"Fear not, sister. We will stop them here."*

Even with her eyes open, Pebbles saw his face. The man smiled, his neck adorned with a necklace similar to Citali's. Similar, but not exact. A wind pressed through the courtyard and nearly extinguished the cauldrons. Pebbles shivered. Something heavy covered her shoulders. She looked down and saw a fur. Lifting her eyes, she could see the outline of cacti beyond the walls of the courtyard. Beyond that, a large tree. She heard herself speak. *"You cannot stop her, brother. She comes to take. She comes to kill."*

"She may come to kill, but she will never take. For twenty-eight of our fathers, we have protected what was hidden. Our family has survived droughts, famine, wars, the trembles of the Earth, the fires it belches from underneath. This tyrant from the north is but a flea compared to that which we've endured."

"But she has killed our sister, she has burned my city."

"It is true. But the people believe in us. They know what we have done for them, what our fathers did for their fathers back to the day of darkness. They will die to protect us until the new ones are of age."

Pebbles' eyes shot open. "Pull over! Stop the van!"

A series of images sped through her mind. A sprawling city on a mountaintop surrounded by wildflowers and cacti…creeping through the darkness underneath a ledge, the black maws of three caves ahead…entering the cave, a hand covering her mouth…standing at the prow of a boat, the riverbanks lined with torches…the teenaged girl crying as she knelt by the fire…

Pebbles became aware of the van slowing. Its brakes squeaked as it came to a stop. A semi coming from the opposite direction passed by, throwing up a cloud of sand that coated the windows. The sound of sand grains pelting the vehicle sounded like rain.

"What's the matter?" Anlon asked.

"Not only does Citali have a sister, she has a brother. And there are children. Citali's brother called them new ones. The girl who was speared and thrown into the fire. I think she was one of them."

She turned around to look back at Cesar and Sanjay, who occupied the third row. Her first question was to Cesar. "There was a stone city on a mountaintop. It was big, but it wasn't Machu Pichu. I know what that looks like, and this wasn't it. It was more square, flatter terrain. The valley below was green, you know, not just a rocky landscape. And it was weird because there were lots of cactus around the…"

A shiver suddenly raced up her spine as another vision came into focus…cacti arranged around a tall tree with snaking roots…buildings painted red, gold and white…a wall with embedded seashells…people in white tunics trimmed with crimson and gold…

Pebbles turned to Mereau. "They had a replica of the Seybalrosa monument. No wonder Citali was so confused to see the ocean." She gripped his arm. "And they had mosaics of seashells, just like the terrace on the cliff. It was just like a mini Munuoria. Only the buildings were not as ornate, more stone-block-looking than polished marble. And they were painted instead of their natural colors."

"Painted, you say?" Cesar asked.

"Yes." Pebbles redirected her attention to Cesar. "Does any of this ring any bells? Is there a site like this in the Andes?"

"Were the buildings red, by any chance?"

"Yes! Not all, but some. Others were white, a few gold. Do you know it? Do you know where it is?"

Cesar nodded. "You may have just solved a long-wondered mystery. The site is near a modern city called Ayacucho. The site is known as Wari, or Huari. It was a massive city, the largest settlement of ancient Peru. Some say as many as sixty thousand people lived there at its peak. As I recall, it flourished between 600 and 1000 CE, but the first buildings are believed to have been built earlier in the common era."

Pebbles looked around at Anlon. He was tapping the screen of Jennifer's tablet. "Have you found it?"

"Working on it."

"What is the mystery surrounding the city?" Sanjay asked Cesar.

"It was home to a number of civilizations, each building onto the creations of earlier occupiers, but no one knows which culture was the first to build, or why they abandoned it. However, archaeologists do know one thing about them. They loved oysters. Oysters with colorful red and white shells."

"Found it," Anlon said. "Looks like the best way to get there is turn around, head back to Ica and start up into the Andes from there. It's going to be a long drive, though. From where we are now, app says it's an eight-hour drive to Ayacucho. Add a stop or two along the way and we probably won't get there until close to midnight."

Cesar laughed. "Don't believe it, Anlon. If the app says eight hours, count on twelve. May I see the map?"

Pebbles relayed the tablet to Cesar, who studied the map for a few minutes, the frown on his face deepening with each passing second.

"What's the matter, Cesar?" Pebbles asked.

"I'm afraid you will not like what I have to say."

As a practical matter, he explained, the best route to Ayacucho started in Pisco, the original path into the Andes that Pebbles had wanted to take. The other nearby route options into the mountains, he told them, were treacherous. "While I have never been to the Wari ruins, I have traveled to many other sites in the Andes. Most of these roads on the map are not paved and they are very narrow. There are hairpin turns next to precipitous drops, few towns and one encounters wild vicuñas crossing the roads when least expected."

While there were still uncomfortable twists and turns on Route 28 from Pisco, he told them, it was a major road, paved all the way, with a number of towns along its course. "If we have mechanical trouble, or need more fuel, we do not want to be stuck on a dirt road, in the middle of the night with no cell signal, no Wi-Fi, in the Andes. Truthfully, even on Route 28, we are better served by waiting until dawn tomorrow and making the full trip in daylight. It will still be slow, and we will undoubtedly be stuck behind buses and trucks at various points, but it will be a safer journey."

Lastly, there was also the change in altitude to consider. They would ascend nearly twelve thousand feet before they descended into the valley where the city of Ayacucho and the Wari ruins were situated. It was wise, Cesar said, to stop periodically and acclimate to the thinner air. "I do not mean to make the trip sound like Hannibal crossing the Alps, but it is not, as you Americans say, a Sunday drive, either."

WARI RUINS
AYACUCHO VALLEY, PERU
SEPTEMBER 27

As frustrating as it had been to Pebbles to drive three hours back to Pisco, stay the night and start for the Wari ruins at dawn the next day, Cesar's advice proved sound. The supposed six-hour drive according to the map app took ten. But despite its length, the trip was more enjoyable than she expected. The scenery was breathtaking, the towns quaint and making the trip in daylight allowed Pebbles the chance to scan for landmarks that might evoke other visions.

None occurred, leading Pebbles to conclude Citali had not followed the Pisco River. So, even though she had felt vindicated that her original choice of road into the Andes was the one they ultimately chose, she realized she might not have had the vision of Wari if they had not followed Citali's path into the desert.

The absence of other visions suggested another conclusion to Pebbles. Citali had gone to Wari before she went to the caves, a point she made to Anlon as they pulled into the ruins' parking lot.

"You're probably right," Anlon said. "I know if I were being chased, I'd be thinking about finding a safe place to hole up. But, damn, she sure went a *long* way to find a sanctuary."

"Was her choice of destination about finding sanctuary, or did she come here to warn her brother?" Mereau asked.

As they piled out of the van, Anlon said, "You know, I thought about that a lot on the way up here. Don't you think she would have sent out a messenger as soon as Rashana flashed Nonali's head? To warn her brother?"

"I would venture a guess and say she did send a messenger, probably multiple messengers, but they never made it." Mereau yawned and stretched his arms above his head. "Though we do not know the time gap between Rashana's visit and the vision of the city preparing for war, I find it hard to believe Muran sent Rashana to the city alone. I'm sure there were confederates who watched the comings and goings to and from the temple. They likely would have followed and killed any messengers. After all, Citali received no warning of her sister's death before Rashana arrived. Correct?"

Mereau turned toward Pebbles. She nodded. "That's how I read the vision. Citali was totally shocked to see Nonali's head, although she seemed to be aware of rumors about Muran threatening to attack Nonali's city."

The discussion continued as they walked toward the admissions office to pay their entrance fees. At one point, Jennifer turned back toward the parking lot and remarked she was surprised to see only one other car parked there. "It's midafternoon, shouldn't this place be crawling with tourists?"

"I would imagine most people come here by bus, on tours. We may have arrived between tour stops," Cesar said. "We should count ourselves fortunate."

"I can't believe how warm it is given how high up we are," Sanjay said. "And how green it is. It looks nothing like what we passed through to get here."

"The weather is very pleasant, isn't it?" Cesar said. "Again, we should count ourselves fortunate. The valley is sheltered from the harsher climate in the surrounding mountains."

With admissions paid, they walked through the short maze of administrative buildings and came upon the cross-section of paths leading to different sections of the ruins, many of which appeared to be protected from the elements by open-air, steel-roof structures erected over the top of the various excavations.

"Geez, this place is huge," Jennifer said.

"It is indeed," Cesar said. "As I mentioned yesterday, upward of sixty thousand people lived here at one time. What you see is only a fraction of what once stood here. Much of the city remains buried."

"Where should we start?" Pebbles asked.

He smiled. "I was just getting ready to ask the same of you."

They had not traveled far through the excavations when Cesar stopped to show them proof of what he had said earlier about various cultures having built and occupied the city. "Notice the different stonework. How some buildings were constructed with small stones and mortar. And how others, like these, have much larger slabs, custom-fitted against one another with no mortar. Much like the stonework one sees at Machu Pichu, there is a question as to who cut and moved these large stones. Their edges are precise, as if sliced by a laser, yet there are no tooling marks."

Pebbles watched Cesar's eyes drift toward Mereau. The ancient Munuorian smiled. "These do have a familiar craftmanship to them. Crude, but familiar all the same."

"The strange thing, of course, is the more technologically advanced structures here are believed to pre-date the latter structures," said Cesar. "It is a similar phenomenon to that observed about Egyptian pyramids. The earliest were significantly better constructed than later ones. One would think as their civilization expanded, their construction methods would have improved, but they did not. They worsened. We see evidence of the same here."

As the historical conversation continued, Pebbles' eyes drifted to the sloping terrain and stony remains of the city littering the fields below. She searched for evidence of a courtyard, an area where a great tree might have stood. In the distance, above a stone wall, she could see the top of a solitary tree that stood out among others. It was too small to be the tree from her vision and from where she was positioned, she could see no cacti surrounding it. The wall blocked her view of the terrain surrounding the tree. Pebbles grabbed Anlon by the arm. "Come on, follow me."

They racewalked toward the tree. To reach the plateau on which the tree stood, they had to scamper up a rise in the trail. As soon as they crested it, Pebbles' heart began to race. The dusty plateau was square, bounded by walls. On the far end from where they entered, in an opening below the plateau was a horseshoe-shaped enclosure, a courtyard.

"Oh, my God. Look at that."

She turned back and looked at the tree, and then once again at the courtyard. Nothing looked right. The tree was too short, the plateau devoid of cacti, the shape of the courtyard was wrong and the stones that made up its walls were nothing like the slabs she recalled.

But that did not stop the vision from coming. Pebbles sat down, her legs dangling over the side of the plateau, and stared at the courtyard until it faded from her view.

At the sounds of the drums, Citali exited into the courtyard. She could see smoke rising from the mountain pass above the city. Soldiers dashed across her view. A voice called to her. She turned to see her brother, Marleau.

"Come, it is time. You must go. Her army approaches."

"No! I will run no more."

"Don't be foolish. You must fetch the new ones. You must take them to the dwellers. Take also that which was given. Go now, while there is still time."

"I will not leave you alone to face her. I will not see your head on a spike."

"And I will not see both of ours on spikes. You are the Keeper. You must go. Even if she defeats us, she will never find you in the jungle. The dwellers will not let her pass. Now, go!"

Marleau kissed her cheek and ran after another group of soldiers. Citali watched him disappear around a corner of a building before she returned inside the temple to gather her things. With the necklace clasped around her neck, she pulled on the poncho over her tunic, grabbed her bag and left. She stopped long enough at the armory to gather supplies and then exited the city toward the valley.

Pebbles snapped out of the vision to find Anlon and Sanjay holding onto her arms. Her torso was dangling over the gap between the plateau and the courtyard. Anlon smiled at her. "You almost did a header."

"Help me up." With assistance from Mereau and Jennifer standing behind, they lifted Pebbles to a standing position. She turned around in a circle, looking at the horizon. Her eyes came to rest on the curve of a mountain shaping the way farther into the valley. "She went that-a-way. Come on, let's go ask the museum people if there are caves around here."

The others followed her back to the museum where Cesar helped translate Pebbles' request. The middle-aged man behind the desk nodded enthusiastically and led them outside to the parking lot. Turning toward the mountain whose shadow loomed over the Wari ruins, he pointed at its lower slope. "*Cueva de Pikimachay.*"

CUEVA DE PIKIMACHAY
AYACUCHO VALLEY, PERU

Jennifer sat beside Pebbles at the mouth of the Pikimachay cave. The last remnant of sunlight had passed below the horizon behind them, leaving only a gray dusk over the valley. Anlon and the others had already walked back down the slope and waited for them at the van.

Even before they had all hiked up to the cave, Jennifer had a strong suspicion it was not the cave from Pebbles' visions. First of all, Pebbles had described three cave entrances, not one. Further, she had told them the three entrances were situated on a shallow landing beneath a ledge. There was no ledge at Pikimachay and no landing. It was just a gap in the slope of the mountain.

Pebbles had scrambled up the scrubland and loose rock, anyway, deflecting Jennifer's observations about the obvious differences. "Maybe there was an earthquake that knocked the ledge away. Maybe there was always one cave, and the earthquake knocked down the walls between the entrances. It's been almost two thousand years since Citali came here, you know."

Once they arrived at the cave, they discovered the entrance was huge but the cave inside was very shallow. While there were gaps in a few places along the back wall, they did not appear to be tunnels. According to another tourist they had met at the entrance, the cave had been used for shelter by humans as far back as fifteen thousand years ago.

Owing to the man's apparent knowledge of the cave, Pebbles had asked him if there were others in the area. He swept his hand over the landscape and said, "Are you kidding? There are caves everywhere in these mountains."

She had then described the caves from her vision. The man shook his head and told her he didn't know of any such site. When he left, Pebbles sat down on a slab-like formation next to the entrance and stared blindly down at the valley as sunset rapidly approached. She had been sitting there ever since, waiting for it to get dark enough to see the lights emanating from communities in the valley below.

Jennifer balanced a flashlight on her knee and said, "We should probably get going."

"Yeah, I know." Pebbles kicked at a stone near her foot.

"I'm sorry this didn't turn out to be *the one*."

"Me too, but I'm kinda glad it isn't. From what that guy said, this cave's seen a lot of use. If it had been *the one*, it probably would have been picked clean of any clues a long time ago."

"Good point," Jennifer said. She stood and brushed dust off her rear. "I wouldn't sweat it. Tomorrow's another day. Cesar said he'll call around to some of his colleagues, see if they know of any good prospects off the beaten path. And we can always go back to Wari. You might have another vision that points us in the right direction."

She turned to see Pebbles standing beside her, taking one last look at the valley. "Maybe. I just wish there was a way I could summon Citali and ask her. I keep trying Sanjay's trick, imagining a sanctuary kind of place like the oasis, but it's not working. I can't seem to reconnect with her."

Jennifer flicked on the flashlight and pointed it down the slope. "Like I said, tomorrow's another day. Now, come on. I'm starving. I'm sure the guys are too."

About halfway down the slope, Pebbles said from behind. "Well, at least this wasn't a total loss."

"Yeah? How so?" Jennifer said.

"The lights, down in the valley. You see them?"

"Uh huh. Can't miss 'em."

"The angle's way too shallow. Whatever cave Citali went into, it was higher above the valley."

CHAPTER 18

DIVIDE AND CONQUER

Sanjay ordered a second cup of after-dinner coffee, not because he particularly wanted another jolt of caffeine, but because Pebbles had asked to speak with him alone as the group readied to leave the restaurant.

In some ways, the request did not surprise him. Despite the breakthroughs of the past two days, she had become increasingly withdrawn and her frustration was plain for all to see. The latter had been the subject of much conversation over dinner, as the group took turns trying to cheer her up. They were right to do so in Sanjay's eyes. She was zeroing in on the final stages of the mystery. But Pebbles did not see it that way. To her, with each breakthrough, the answers she sought seemed to be moving farther away, a point she revisited as soon as the others had left.

"I don't understand. For a while, things seemed to be speeding up, the visions happening more frequently, but now they're tailing off. I'm not having dreams at night anymore, and inside I feel like I'm losing touch with Citali, like she's fading away. Why do you think that is?"

"There could be many reasons," Sanjay said as the coffee arrived. He thanked the waiter and returned his attention to Pebbles. "When you say you feel like you are losing touch with her, what do you mean? How do you sense it?"

"Well, I feel kind of numb now. It's not like it was when the nightmares first began. I felt a lot of emotion then. Fear, panic, desperation. I mean,

I still get mad when I see what Muran did to her and stuff like that, but I don't feel Citali's emotions as much. And I don't understand why the visions keep getting shorter, and why some of them are so jumbled up. I thought the opposite would happen. I thought the closer we got to finding out who she was, what she was running from, what she was trying to hide, what she was protecting, the visions would fill in, give me a full picture of what happened."

Sanjay stirred cream into his coffee and nodded while he listened. When she finished speaking, he asked, "Do you think it is possible you may be expecting too much from Citali? From yourself?"

Pebbles stared at her own coffee, apparently weighing Sanjay's question. Without looking up, she said, "Could be. I do feel like I'm trying real hard to connect with her."

"If Citali were to fade from your memory, bit by bit, until you did not think of her or her memories at all, how would you feel about that?"

"Kinda pissed, actually." Pebbles lifted her gaze. Sanjay saw a tinge of red rise in her face.

"You fear that is what is happening."

She nodded.

"And that angers you because you want closure."

Another nod. "I feel like, if I could talk to her again, like at the oasis, I could ask her straight up. Get the answers I need. Put this whole thing to bed."

Sanjay sipped his coffee and contemplated his next comments. When he looked back at Pebbles, he could see her eyes searching for answers in his. Putting the cup down, he said, "I remember speaking to Anlon about PTSD when we first met. One of the things he was frustrated about was that you struggled with nightmares soon after you came out of your coma, then they went away for a while, only to come back. He wanted my help to *make* the nightmares go away once and for all. I told him at the time that it is not uncommon for symptoms to fade and resurface. I said to him — PTSD proceeds at its own pace *and* at its own rhythm. One cannot force symptoms to be over. They end when they end."

"But this isn't about PTSD." The red in her face flushed darker. "This has nothing to do with what happened to me."

"I am not talking about you."

For a moment, she seemed flustered, her expression turning to one closer to confusion than anger. Then the frown on her face relaxed and she edged back in her seat. Sanjay continued. "As I said earlier, there could be many reasons why the visions feel different now than they did at one time. It goes without saying we are treading through uncharted territory as far as the capabilities of the human mind are concerned. But even so, I doubt human nature has really changed that much over two thousand years. People loved and hated back then. They love and hate now. Ancient people feared and felt joy. We still do today. So, if Citali's consciousness is inside you, why would her emotions be any different than yours or mine?"

Pebbles' head lowered. "They wouldn't be."

"You have good reasons for wanting closure. The same can be said of Anlon, Jennifer, Cesar and Mereau when it comes to their desire for closure for you. It is why they are all here with you, why I am here too. But none of us, me included, can force closure. Not for you. Not for Citali."

Wiping away a tear, she nodded. "I hear you. She's shutting down because I'm pushing her to deal with what happened."

"It is one possibility. A strong one, I think."

"What can I do to show her I'm backing off?"

"Clear your mind. Do not put pressure on yourself to find the cave."

"I'm not sure I can do that. It's not the kind of person I am."

"There is no harm in trying, is there?"

"I guess not. But what if it doesn't work?"

"Ah…but what if it does?"

ROOM 216
SANTA ROSA HOTEL
AYACUCHO, PERU
SEPTEMBER 28

After departing the restaurant, Sanjay walked Pebbles to the lobby of their hotel and wished her a good night. Too wired to go to sleep, he decided to go for a stroll around *Plaza de Armas*, a park-like square near the hotel. The stroll turned into several laps as he replayed the coffee conversation with Pebbles. While he walked, he pondered the dilemma Pebbles faced. In the midst of her own recovery from trauma, she was experiencing the first-person stress of someone else's trauma. When he returned to his room, it was after midnight. Sanjay powered up his laptop and crystallized his thoughts in his journal before climbing into bed.

Given everything I have learned about Citali, I am convinced she suffers from PTSD, but I confess I am at a loss to figure out how to treat her. I cannot reach her directly. Pebbles, herself, has difficulty reaching her. While it might be possible to connect with Citali's consciousness directly by hypnotizing Pebbles, essentially treating Citali as a separate personality within Pebbles, there is no guarantee I could summon Citali, and I am reluctant to try, for fear of stirring a hornet's nest within Pebbles' mind. It is a frustrating circumstance, for if I could engage Citali in a direct dialogue, I believe I could help her. But, for now, the best I can do is to suggest strategies to Pebbles and leave it to her consciousness to find a way to connect with Citali.

ROOM 302
SANTA ROSA HOTEL
AYACUCHO, PERU

It was just after five thirty when Anlon gave up on trying to fall asleep. With too many thoughts cycling through his mind, he snuck out of bed, careful to avoid waking Pebbles. Aided by the dimmed glow of his cell phone screen, he dressed, loaded his laptop into his backpack and left the room. After descending one floor to the hotel lobby, he went in search of coffee.

To his dismay, the sign outside the hotel restaurant indicated it would not open for another two hours, so Anlon went to the reception desk to inquire whether there were any nearby coffee shops open at this hour. He learned there was a shop that opened at six on the other side of *Plaza de Armas.*

He originally expected to buy a to-go cup and return to the hotel lobby, but when he saw the small coffee shop had Wi-Fi, he occupied one of the three tables in the establishment and powered on his laptop. Sipping coffee while he waited for the operating system to load, Anlon contemplated the words that had rattled inside his mind all night long. Rashana's message to Citali.

Take the river, lead her into the cave…

What river? What cave?

There was little to go on to find the answers. Pebbles' cave-dream visions had all occurred at night and, as such, provided no landmarks to guide them. Further, while Pebbles' vision of Citali departing Wari seemed to suggest Citali had visited the city before heading for the cave, Pebbles had seen nothing definitive in that vision, or any other vision, to confirm it.

The only information at their disposal was Pebbles' description of Citali's approach to the cave. She had ascended a series of switchbacks up a rocky slope until she reached the pinnacle. Then she had descended the back side of the slope to reach another switchback trail until she came to a spot where the trail diverged. One path led farther down the back side of the mountain, the other veered along the side of the mountain to reach a ledge over a chasm.

Pebbles had supplemented this description at dinner the previous evening by sharing her observation about the angle of the sight line between Pikimachay and the lights in the valley. This suggested Citali had hiked a steeper slope than the one leading to Pikimachay, or the village she had seen below the cave had been closer to the mountain, or possibly both.

But unless Pebbles discovered more information in new visions, finding the cave would require making some assumptions. The first one Anlon made was to trust Pebbles' intuition — Citali visited the cave after leaving Wari. Next, he chose to assume the instructions delivered by Rashana still held true — that from Wari, Citali followed a river to find the cave. Third, Pebbles' perception of the direction in which Citali traveled after leaving Wari was accurate — she headed toward Pikimachay Cave.

With his laptop now ready, Anlon opened the web browser and searched for a topographical map application. Finding one, he typed in

Ayacucho to begin his search. Moving around the map, he found Wari and, to the northwest of the ruins, the Pikimachay Cave. Zooming out, he looked for northwest routes leading to rivers from Pikimachay.

One leapt out immediately. There was a river that ran along the backside of the mountain where Pikimachay was situated. Once it passed the mountain, the river curled north into the largest valley in the area. At the end of the valley, the river, called Rio Warpa, joined the much larger Mantaro River.

Toggling the map to show a satellite view of the valley, Anlon zoomed in on a plateau on the north side of the junction of the two rivers. The plateau had everything he would have expected to find. Easy access from the junction of the rivers, prominent visual landmarks that anyone approaching from the valley could spot, switchback trails up the sides of the arid-looking mountain ringing the plateau, ledges along sections of the mountaintop and three small towns at the base of the mountain.

A quick revisit of the topography map showed Anlon the elevation rise from plateau to peak was twice that of the area surrounding Pikimachay. He could also see several viable routes on the backside of the mountain that one could take to escape into the jungles east of the Andes, including riding the Mantaro or taking a shortcut and hiking down one of several nearby mountain passes. And the distance between Wari and the plateau was approximately thirty miles. Depending on the route Citali took and how hotly she was pursued, thirty miles was certainly a manageable distance for Citali to have trekked in a day or two.

But were there any caves? On the satellite image, Anlon had seen numerous dark spots that might be caves, but realized the vast majority were likely just shadows. Still, given the assumptions Anlon had staked, it looked to be a credible area to search for Citali's cave.

Could his assumptions be wrong? Absolutely. Citali might have ducked into a cave on the way from Paracas to Wari. She might have turned in a different direction after leaving Wari. But in either case, Anlon could see no viable way of narrowing the search radius without new insights from Pebbles. It was folly to traipse through the Andes and peek through every cave they came across.

And that is really what had kept Anlon awake, he now admitted to himself — the fear that they had reached a dead-end. For without knowing where Citali headed after leaving Wari, cave or no, they could not go forward or backward with any confidence.

Nope, he thought. *There are only two choices that make sense. Head for the plateau and hope the visual sparks a new vision or return to Wari and hope for the same.*

Resolved to present the two options to Pebbles and the others when they awoke, Anlon revisited the map application for directions to the plateau. As luck would have it, there was a road that led from Ayacucho to the heart of the plateau, running right beside Rio Warpa for most of the trip. Anlon downed the last of his coffee, shut his laptop and headed back to the hotel, Rashana's message echoing in his mind.

Take the river, lead her into the cave…

With the full group assembled in the hotel restaurant for breakfast, they discussed their plan for the day. Anlon led the conversation by sharing the findings of his early morning research and proposing a trip to the plateau.

Jennifer, however, proposed returning to Wari. Much like Anlon, she said she had been up most of the night contemplating their next steps. "We know Pebbles has already had one vision there. I think there's a good chance she has another one if we go back. Especially because we only saw a small part of the ruins before we left for Pikimachay."

"I agree," Cesar said. "While the plateau is an intriguing possibility, we don't know if Citali traveled there. On the other hand, we *know* she visited Wari. Before we venture too far from Ayacucho, we owe it to ourselves to revisit Wari and provide Pebbles the time to fully explore the grounds."

Mereau added his voice in support of the Wari option and then turned to Pebbles. "What is your view?"

"I dunno." Pebbles shrugged and turned to Anlon. "You feel strongly about the plateau?"

"I do, but I can't argue with the points raised. Going there *is* speculative, and it will be a full-day affair to drive there, hike up the mountain and search for caves."

"Yeah," she said. "That's true. But at least it would feel like we're making progress."

"So, you favor the plateau, then?" Cesar asked.

"I don't know what I favor." She darted a look at Sanjay. "If you guys think we should go back to Wari today, I'll go along with it. If you want to go the plateau, that works for me too. Just don't expect any miracles at either place."

Sanjay cleared his throat and said, "Perhaps we should split up. Two of us go with Pebbles to Wari. The other two go with Anlon to the plateau."

Anlon frowned. "I'm not sure going to the plateau without Pebbles makes a whole lot of sense."

"Maybe, maybe not," Sanjay said. "But it would allow Pebbles the space to explore the grounds without five of us hovering around, give her the chance to tour the ruins at her own pace, at her own rhythm, if you know what I mean."

"Actually, that's not a bad idea," Jennifer said. "I'll go with you, Anlon. We can take a bunch of pictures to show to Pebbles when we get back. Who knows? Maybe we'll stumble across something of interest."

Pebbles and the others rallied around Sanjay's suggestion and quickly divided into two teams — Sanjay and Cesar would accompany Pebbles to Wari, while Anlon would explore the plateau with Jennifer and Mereau. A short while later, both teams were on their way, the Wari team in a taxi, the plateau team in the van they had rented in Lima.

WARI RUINS
AYACUCHO VALLEY, PERU

The museum was not yet open when the Wari team arrived at the ruins, so they chatted with the taxi driver while they waited, asking him about caves in the area. The driver, content to keep the fare running, told them of some lesser caves near Pikimachay and other, more well-known caves within a day's drive. But when Pebbles asked him about the area Anlon had gone to investigate, the driver said he knew of no caves there. He seemed more interested, Pebbles thought, in telling them about other attractions near Ayacucho, no doubt motivated by a desire to garner more business.

He told them of *Bosque de Piedras*, a great stone forest with unusual formations. Some people, he said, claimed the stones were carved by an ancient race of master stonemasons, while others claimed the wind atop the mountain had been the instrument that shaped the stones. Pebbles wished Mereau had been there to hear the driver's description. She was sure he would be interested in visiting the site.

Next, he regaled them with a tourist-guide-worthy description of *Las Piscinas Naturales de Millpu*, where one could see natural pools of turquoise water. He advised against swimming in them, however, as the water, he told them, was very cold.

As he switched gears to describe *Catarata Batán*, an impressive waterfall on the way to the *Millpu* pools, Pebbles tuned out. With her head resting against the taxi window, she stared at the clouds floating over the museum. She thought of Sanjay describing his recurring dream of Pearl Harbor, how the visions had first been stimulated by the view of clouds over Fiji.

Did you see this sky, Citali? Does it look familiar to you? Where did you go from here? If you won't show me the way, show me the sky.

Her thoughts were interrupted by the sound of a truck pulling into the parking lot. She turned to look out the back window. It was a small shuttle bus painted with the logo of a local tour company. Shortly afterward, a group of tourists marched past the taxi on their way to the museum, their feet crunching the parking lot's gravel as they walked. Pebbles noticed the taxi driver grumbled something in Spanish as he looked in the rearview mirror. She turned and looked again at the tour van and understood why. Along with the tour company's logo, there were painted callouts highlighting other tours they offered, including Pikimachay and the three attractions the driver had just finished describing.

"Looks like it's about to open," Cesar said. "Should we go?"

"Yeah, let's get a move on," Pebbles said.

As Sanjay and Pebbles exited the taxi, Cesar held an extended conversation in Spanish with the driver as he paid the fare. Pebbles watched the driver smile broadly and vigorously shake Cesar's hand. When Cesar joined them on the museum steps, she asked, "What was that all about?"

"I asked him to stay. Told him we had need of his services for the day... just in case we hear of a development from Anlon or discover something here."

"Uh...then why is he leaving?" she asked.

"Lunch."

"Lunch? It is ten a.m.," said Sanjay. "Is lunch that early here?"

"It's not for him, it's for us. He insisted on going back into town to put together a picnic lunch for us. He said he'd be back by noon."

"Aw, that's kind of sweet," Pebbles said.

Cesar laughed. "Wait until you see the bill. Now, come, let us roam the grounds at leisure."

After waiting their turn at the admissions ticket office, they walked to-gether to the junction where the paths to different sections of the ruins diverged. They each chose a different path. Before separating, Sanjay said to Pebbles, "Do not feel compelled to examine every nook and cranny. Relax. Enjoy the stroll. Find a comfortable place to sit here and there. Take in the scenery. Or close your eyes and listen to the sounds. Breathe in the aromas. Use all your senses, not just your eyes."

"Sounds heavenly." Jokingly, she asked, "What if I fall asleep?"

"Do not worry," Sanjay said. "We will find you when lunch arrives."

EN ROUTE TO JUNCTION OF RIO WARPA
AND THE MANTARO RIVER
AYACUCHO VALLEY, PERU

The early part of the drive was just as Anlon expected, a twisting but grad-ual descent from Ayacucho into the valley. Citali, if she had followed a similar path along the contours of the landscape, would have been able to escape Wari at a pretty aggressive clip. While there would not have been any paved roads for her to follow, the terrain was mostly made up of sparse scrubland. In many ways, the scenery reminded Anlon of the drive from his home on the north shore of Lake Tahoe down into the Washoe Valley where Carson City and Reno were located. She would have had good sight lines, and she would not have been impeded by rocky terrain.

When he shared these observations with his van-mates, Mereau had said, "True, but she would also have been easy to spot, easy to follow."

"Good point, I hadn't thought of it that way. Are you thinking she kept to the mountains?"

"No, based on what we know transpired afterward, I think haste was probably the most important consideration to her after leaving Wari. She may have become stealthier when she neared her destination, but early on, I think your instincts are right. She took the easiest, quickest path available."

Once they passed the midpoint of the valley at a city called Huanta, their route turned toward Rio Warpa. Here was where they first stopped to take cell phone photographs of the river and the mountains ahead. At the junction with the Mantaro River, they pulled over and took several more pictures of the mountains that ringed behind the plateau.

As they began to climb out of the valley and drew closer to the plateau, switchbacks became visible. Not switchbacks for foot traffic, but dirt roads that zig-zagged up the mountains. Pulling over yet again in the town at the foot of the switchback that most interested Anlon, they photographed the steep slope.

He retrieved his laptop and showed Mereau and Jennifer a screenshot he had taken of the satellite image looking down on the switchback. "Look how it crests at the top and divides in two directions. One along the ride, and the other that begins a new switchback down the backside of the mountain. That's where I think we should start."

"Gosh, it really does look like it fits Pebbles' description," Jennifer said. "Town right below it, two trails at the top. There's even a step-down to what looks like a ledge above a chasm right there." Jennifer directed her eyes up at the mountain. "But holy crap, that road looks crazy dangerous."

"It does look pretty scary," said Anlon. "Even if we had four-wheel drive, it would still look scary, but in our van? No way."

"Agreed. Let's grab our backpacks and get moving. If we want any daylight for the walk back down, we need to start now. It'll take four or five hours to hike to the top."

As Jennifer turned toward the van, Anlon said, "Wait a sec. I've got a different idea." He held up the laptop to show her the satellite image. When Jennifer returned to his side, he pointed to an area to the left of the switchback road on the map. "See how the main road we took from Ayacucho continues on up the mountain? It crests at this town, right there. Churcampa. I know it's out of the way of the area we want to search by a good six miles, but it looks like we could walk along the ridgeline from Churcampa and avoid having to hike up a two-thousand-foot slope. See how the top of the mountain flattens out for a good stretch of the walk."

Jennifer nodded. "That does look like a better alternative. Even though it'll be a longer hike, mile-wise, it'll go a lot faster and be a heckuva lot less strenuous than trying to go up the switchback."

"Agreed. What do you say, Mereau? Sound like a good plan to you?"

Anlon turned to find Mereau looking away from them, his gaze focused on the narrow pass through which they had traveled to reach the plateau. He then spun around slowly, taking in the arena-like bowl formed by the mountains and said, "This is not a plateau. It is the bottom of a crater...how clever of them."

CHAPTER 19

PECKING THROUGH THE RUINS

WARI RUINS
AYACUCHO VALLEY, PERU
SEPTEMBER 28

The solitary stroll through the ruins had been medicinal for Pebbles, though it had been difficult for her to relax at first. Early in her walk, she had stopped to scrutinize fallen structures and imagined how they might have looked once upon a time. She would close her eyes and try to fit the imagined structures into the layout of the city she recalled from Citali's visions. But the exercise proved fruitless, which should not have surprised Pebbles. The ruins were a conglomeration of original structures, renovations and new buildings erected by successive occupiers of Wari. But she had given the exercise a shot anyway because the renovated courtyard and replacement tree had stimulated a vision yesterday.

Once she dispensed with the idea of recreating the layout of the city, she followed Sanjay's advice. She found a patch of ground that looked down upon a field of strewn ruins and sat down, letting the mild springtime temperature, budding greenery and soft breeze relax her mind. She watched puffy white clouds move slowly across the blue sky until they, combined with the warmth of the sun, lulled her eyes to close.

Breathing in deeply, Pebbles gathered the fragrant scents of the flowering bushes in the field of ruins. She listened to leaves fluttering and birds chirping. She could hear distant conversations and laughing from other tourists walking the grounds as well as the occasional vehicle passing on the road behind the ancient walls that marked the borders of the city.

Just as it seemed she might fall asleep, a sound cut through the background noise. It was a bird call, a high-pitched staccato. Pebbles' eyes flashed open. On a rock within a stone's throw was a yellowish bird. She recognized it immediately — an Andean flicker.

The bird called again, and the vision began.

Stay low! Do not let them see you!

Crouching down behind bushes, she watched them trudge along the bank of the river. Most of them looked exhausted, some wearing bandages covering wounds that still seeped blood. At the vanguard, one of them stood on a boulder and scanned the area.

You will not see my footsteps, you fool! I know better than to walk in soft soil.

The man on the boulder scolded the others for walking too slowly. He exhorted them to speed up, but they seemed to ignore him.

What a strange collection of men.

Most were fat and old. The few young ones were skinny, their steps weak. Yet, the one on the boulder and the one bringing up the rear looked like hardened men, warriors. Citali smiled.

The battle goes ill for the masked bitch. She sends only two good men to track me.

While those two men were obviously shrewd — they had tracked her this far despite her best efforts to mask her trail — the others slowed them down too much. Lifting her gaze, she looked down the line of the river to the mountains in the distance. If she quickened her pace, she could go around them and lose them in the mountains, but she would have to wait until nightfall. There was too little cover to attempt to bypass them now.

Citali watched them until the man on the boulder climbed down and joined the others. Edging from the cover of the bush, she slinked forward. On her third step, she heard a bush rustle and a bird's panicked flapping. Rapid shrills followed. Citali froze and dove to the ground, cursing herself. Looking up, she saw the birds shoot from their holes in the rocks as they sounded their alarms.

No! You fool! How did you not see the nests! Get up! Get up and run!

As shouts from the men tracking her echoed in the valley, she scrambled up the sandy rocks, kicking up a cloud of dust the men would surely see. Citali cursed but it was too late to think about masking her escape.

Go! Go! Into the mountains! Quickly! Do not look back!

As soon as the vision ended, Pebbles found the flicker had hopped its way closer to her. It was now just a few feet away. It pecked at the grass around a rock and then looked up at her, puffing out the yellow feathers on its chest as it eyed her suspiciously.

Pebbles reached in the pocket of her hoodie and pulled out her cell phone. The bird, frightened by the quick motion, flew away deeper into the ruins. Rising to her feet, she texted Sanjay and Cesar, asking them to meet her at the ticket office. Then she sent off a message to Anlon. "Any pictures yet?"

She was halfway back to the entrance when her phone buzzed. It was a reply from Cesar. "Be there shortly."

Neither was there when she arrived at the ticket office. She ducked her head around the corner to look in the parking lot. They were not there either. Just another tourist van with a waterfall painted on its side.

A wave of dizziness swept over Pebbles. She staggered and reached out to steady herself against the museum wall as a flurry of images sped through her mind.

…a massive waterfall…wading through water…a hand reaching down…other hands pulling her out of the water…a bonfire…a stick streaking gold paint on her arm…standing on the prow of a boat, arms raised, holding something heavy…torches all around…people chanting… ducking down by the waterfall…pushing through the thicket…disappearing into blackness, her feet deep in mud…reaching into her bag…a glint of light…diving into the water…the swipe of blade across her throat…the roar of the waterfall…

MOUNTAINTOP
CHURCAMPA DISTRICT, PERU

The drive to Churcampa was not without drama. While the main road looked less treacherous than the switchback they had forgone, it still had its fair share of hairpin turns as it climbed up the mountain. As such, Anlon avoided making conversation with Mereau so as not to distract Jennifer. Inside, however, he was burning to question him.

During the earlier, less dicey, part of the drive, Mereau told them his *gensae*, his magnetic sixth sense, detected incredibly strong magnetism in the ground beneath their feet and in the walls of the mountain ringing the plateau. This led him to suspect a meteor had blasted a crater into the terrain, scattering its magnetic debris throughout the area.

"If you examine the plateau closely, you will see there is an unnatural gap in the walls of the mountain through which we drove up from the river," Mereau had said. "You will also notice a significant amount of water erosion on the remaining crater walls. At some point since the crater was formed, I believe it became a lake. Water drained down from the top into the lake, until something caused the wall near the river to give way and drain into the river valley. An earthquake, perhaps."

He also explained his "how clever of them" comment.

"Even with Citali's necklace, Muran would never have found the cave," Mereau had said. "She would never have detected the beacon. There was too much competing magnetism."

"Beacon? What beacon?" Anlon asked.

"I do not know for certain, but I suspect the cave was marked with a magnetic beacon similar to those we used to mark our Maerlifs."

A Maerlif, Anlon recalled, was a Munuorian burial chamber. Most often, they were burrowed into the sides of a volcano, a symbolic gesture that returned the souls of dead Munuorians back to the source from which they believed all life sprung. In these crypts, they laid to rest their most honored dead…along with the dead's private supply of the Munu-orians' special stones. It was in such a Maerlif on the slope of the Mount Pelée volcano on the Caribbean island of Martinique where Jacques Foucault had discovered the crypt of Mereau and his memory stone over four hundred years ago.

But the Munuorians had also hastily created other Maerlifs to cache supplies of their stones along their trade routes prior to the destruction caused by the asteroid close encounter ten thousand years ago.

Believing there was no way to protect their island homeland from the devastation, they divvied up their inventory of stones and stored them in newly constructed Maerlifs across the western hemisphere. Some were built into hillsides near shorelines or major rivers, others into mountain slopes near prominent landmarks known to the Munuorians.

Their logic had been simple. If any Munuorians survived the asteroid, they would need their special stone tools to rebuild. By storing them in multiple locations, they increased the odds that some of the tools would also survive.

As soon as the road straightened out, Jennifer, apparently also curious to question Mereau, asked, "If this whole area is super-magnetic, what good would a beacon have served?"

The answer was one that Anlon knew and one Jennifer would have recalled if she had been able to devote her full concentration to the question. Anlon, Pebbles, Jennifer and Cesar had discovered one of the Maerlifs in a jungle of eastern Nicaragua the previous year.

"Remember the Maerlif we found in Nicaragua," Anlon said. "The beacon did more than just mark the general location of the crypt; it told us which of the rocks in the Maerlif wall was the entryway."

"Ah, that's right. If we had picked the wrong rock to move, the Maerlif would have caved in." She glanced up at the rearview mirror, presumably to look at Mereau. "So, you think there's a Maerlif inside the cave?"

"It may not be a Maerlif in the classic sense, but, yes, now I see this place, now that I know of its magnetism, I do think we are likely to find a structure inside the cave that served a purpose similar to a Maerlif.

"Remember also what Pebbles told us of the conversation between Citali and her brother. Marleau told Citali to take that *which was given* to the dwellers. And then we have Rashana's message to Citali. She said Muran sought that *which was hidden.*"

Anlon's mind once again thought of Rashana's message. *Take the river, lead her into the cave.* "Now the part about leading her into the cave makes sense. That's all Muran needed. She would have been able to find the beacon on her own once she was inside the cave, but not until then."

"Yes, now you see why it was so clever to mask the Maerlif's location inside a highly magnetic environment. It is curious, though, why the builders wanted to hide its location. I get the sense, based on what Pebbles has shared with us, that whatever was hidden inside the cave, presumably some of our *Tyls*, was put there a long time ago, long before Muran's path brought her to this part of the world. What led survivors among my people to climb so high into the mountains and stash their stones here?"

As they neared the outskirts of Churcampa, Anlon disappeared into thought. There was something that just did not fit with Mereau's theory. If Citali, Nonali and her brother had access to a stash of Munuorian stones, why would she have taken them to the dwellers, whoever they were? Why wouldn't Citali or her brother or others of their people have used the stones to defend themselves against Muran and her army?

The longer he pondered the questions, the more an answer began to form. Citali was called the Keeper. Pebbles had indicated Marleau said they had *protected* what was hidden. Perhaps Citali, her brother, and the generations of their people before them who had protected what was hidden, who *kept* what was hidden, had *not* been Munuorians. But they had *known* Munuorian survivors of the day of darkness. And for some reason, the Munuorians had entrusted Citali's people with their stones. Anlon shared these thoughts with Mereau and Jennifer.

"It could very well be as you say," Mereau replied. "But, remember, Citali was also called Seer. She wore the necklace. She was revered as a priestess. These bits we know about her suggest she had some mystic power. To me, knowing how intense the magnetism of the necklace was, it suggests to me she had *gensae*. That leads me to believe she was a descendant."

The van slowed and stopped at an intersection. Jennifer turned and looked at Anlon and Mereau. "What about the elongated heads? Maybe there was something biologically different about Citali and her people that gave them an ability to sense the magnetic field that had nothing to do with Munuorians."

Anlon nodded. The thought had occurred to him as well. Cesar had said the DNA from elongated skulls discovered at the Paracas necropolis were genetically linked to people of Eastern European origin, people who lived far from where the Munuorian homeland was located. Anlon did not recall whether Cesar had mentioned if the Paracas mummies' DNA showed a genetic mutation that produced the elongated skulls but if there was a mutation, it likely meant their brains would have been shaped differently and been larger than brains of humans with normal-shaped skulls. Was it possible certain regions of their brains had been oversized as a result? Specifically, could the structures that control sensory perception have been more prominent features of their brains, heightening their abilities to interact with the world around them, including an ability to detect the Earth's magnetic field?

"I think you're on to something there, Jen. I'll have to remember to ask Cesar if the Paracas mummies' brains have been scanned. Their bodies are supposedly well-preserved, but I'm not sure whether that applies to their brain tissues."

The conversation continued as they passed through Churcampa. As they neared the last buildings of the small town, Jennifer looked for a place to park the van. Soon after, the backpack-laden hikers set off along the mountain ridge.

Anlon was surprised at the temperate climate. At almost eleven thousand feet above sea level, some two thousand feet higher than the valley below, he expected it to be significantly cooler. But much like Ayacucho and the Wari ruins, it was pleasant despite constant gusts of wind. He guessed it was somewhere in the high 50s or low 60s. Anlon mentioned his surprise to the others.

"Yeah, it's another check mark next to Pebbles' vision about the mountain," Jennifer said. "I remember asking her if it was cold. You know, figuring it was night, it was windy and Citali was on top of a mountain. Pebbles said the only time she remembered Citali being cold was when she crouched down to cover her bare legs and feet underneath her poncho.

Who goes hiking up a mountain in bare feet and bare legs if they know they're going somewhere really cold?"

The first stretch of the ridgeline they were able to traverse was along the main road leaving Churcampa, and Anlon was glad they had decided to leave the van back in town. The road hugged a narrow strip that abutted a steep cliff and there were several hairpin turns that would have made for some very uncomfortable moments of driving.

Their good fortune continued once the ridgeline flattened onto another plateau, for the road continued on for the next two miles, making for an easy walk past a number of cultivated fields on both sides of the road.

"Who grows crops on the top of a mountain?" Anlon had asked at one point.

"Uh…people who don't want to walk or drive all the way down in the valley for food," Jennifer had replied. "Given how warm it is, they probably grow all kinds of crops up here."

When they reached the point where the road began to descend back into the valley via switchbacks, they stopped and Anlon retrieved his laptop again. Pulling up the screenshot of the satellite image of the mountaintop, he pointed to the spot where he estimated they were standing, and then dragged his finger along a two-mile swathe of roadless ridgeline.

"This is the area where I think we should search. We'll have to work our way over the crest, and it looks like there's a fairly steep decline, but it looks walkable."

"Yeah, we'll have to serpentine down, create our own switchbacks, but we should stay a good distance back from the edge."

"Agreed." Anlon pointed toward the end of the two-mile swathe. "That area, right there, is where I'm betting the cave is. Look at the shadows in those crevices." He looked up at Mereau. "Do you think you can detect the beacon if we get close enough to it?"

Mereau pulled off his backpack, unzipped the center pocket and withdrew a bowl-shaped stone, the Munuorian *Tyl* known as a *Breylofte* to Mereau and a Sound Stone to Anlon. Holding the tool up, Mereau said, "If there is a beacon up here, this will find it."

WARI RUINS
AYACUCHO VALLEY, PERU

Propped up against the museum wall, Pebbles looked at the concerned faces of Sanjay and Cesar. A crowd of tourists stood behind them, bottles of water held forth in their hands.

"Are you all right?" Cesar asked.

She nodded.

"You had a vision?"

She nodded again and held up two fingers. "The taxi. Is it here yet?"

"It is."

"Have you heard from Anlon?"

She watched as Cesar looked to Sanjay, who shook his head to say no. Cesar said, "Not yet. Why?"

Pebbles slid her cell phone from the hoodie pocket. No notifications. "Can you help me up?"

"Of course."

Reaching out her arms, she pushed her butt off the ground while the two men tugged her arms until she stood. "Where's the taxi?"

Sanjay pointed to the left. Pebbles looked at Cesar. "What do you know about waterfalls around here? Not the one the taxi driver was talking about. Not that one." She pointed at the picture of *Catarata Batán* on the tourist van. "I'm talking huge. Crazy long. Like a waterfall from the top of a mountain. Only it's in a jungle."

Cesar stared at her for a few seconds, a frown on his face, then shook his head. "I don't know."

"Come on, let's go. Maybe the driver will know."

Pebbles started for the parking lot. As the three of them approached the taxi, the driver stepped out, a smile on his face and a large bag in his hand. He raised it and said something in Spanish, presumably announcing lunch had arrived. She turned to Cesar. "Ask him about the waterfall."

Cesar engaged the driver in a short back-and-forth conversation. The man nodded enthusiastically and said, *"Catarata las Tres Hermanas."*

"Trey what?" Sanjay asked.

"*Tres Hermanas*," Cesar repeated. "The three sisters. He says it is the third tallest waterfall in the world."

"Spell it," Pebbles said, pulling out her cell phone. As Cesar recited the spelling, Pebbles entered the name in her web browser. As soon as the first picture populated her screen, she looked back up at Cesar. "Where is it? How far?"

Cesar conversed again with the driver. This time, the dialogue included expansive hand gestures on the parts of both men. When they finished, Cesar said, "It is located in Otishi National Park, according to our friend here. It is about two hundred fifty kilometers from here, but...he says it is not accessible by road. Only by boat. And he says it is dangerous. The waterfall sits at the edge of the jungle. He says it is home to an indigenous tribe that isn't very friendly to outsiders."

As Cesar's last words bounced around Pebbles' mind, she whispered, "The dwellers."

As fate would have it, from the Wari ruins, there were two roads that led down the mountain to the inland Peruvian jungles. The very road that they had traveled from Ayacucho to Wari, and the road Anlon and the others had taken to explore for caves at the far end of the valley.

While it would have been more expedient to head directly for Otishi National Park, Pebbles, Sanjay and Cesar agreed it made more sense to link up with Anlon and the others and then drive to Otishi together.

The plan was welcomed by the taxi driver, who, according to Cesar, preferred to drop them off two hours away rather than an eight-hour trip to ferry them to the end of the road leading into the jungle. So, they piled into the taxi and began the journey, consuming lunch on the way.

Pebbles and her co-passengers tried several times to call all three of their cave-exploring colleagues, but without success. In between bites of her empanada, Pebbles said, "Either there's no cell signal on top of the mountain or they've found a cave."

CHAPTER 20

TRAPDOOR

The slope they intended to serpentine down came with an unexpected surprise. The resolution of the image Anlon had captured on his computer did not show it, but there were crisscrossing, well-worn walking trails all over the plateau. While this made for easier access to the area they wanted to search, it also suggested people had traversed the area extensively. To Anlon, that meant the possibility the cave, if one existed, had already been explored. And if there had been booty in it, it was probably long gone.

"Not necessarily," Mereau had said when Anlon voiced his concern. "Look at all the ledges and crevices. Many are covered with bushes and trees. Gaps in the rock, whether they look like caves or not, may have escaped others' notice."

"Yeah, but there weren't trees or bushes in Pebbles' mountain-chase vision. She said it was barren."

"Is it not possible that as people settled on the mountaintop, and began to grow crops, they brought with them plants that have spread?" Mereau asked. "It has been eighteen hundred years since Citali's time."

"True." Jennifer said. "Okay, then. How do we want to do this? Stay together? Split up? Grid search?"

"I say we go together," said Anlon. "We'll start here, go trail by trail as we move across the ridge from left to right, with Mereau at the point, humming on the Sound Stone. If he feels a vibration from the beacon or we spot anything that might be a cave or gap on either side of the trail, we leave the trail to investigate. Otherwise, we move on to the next trail."

And so that was what they did. For an hour, they hunted for signs of a cave. While they did not find one, they did come across another unexpected surprise. At a junction of two trails, they came across a small set of ruins. Stone ruins. They were the remains of two or three small buildings that overlooked a chasm where the Mantaro River flowed around the back side of the mountain.

"From its size, its position, it looks like it was a sentinel post aimed at watching the river," Mereau said. "See the small village below at the bend of the river? There was likely a similar settlement in the past. With mountains on both sides, and how the river twists, the village would have had little warning if set upon by attackers who came by river. By posting men up here, where they could observe the river and mountains for many miles in each direction, they could warn the village with smoke signals if they saw trouble approaching."

Anlon pulled his cell phone from his backpack to photograph the structures and noticed his screen filled with call and message notifications. "Huh, that's strange. I don't remember hearing my phone ring. I didn't even think we had a signal. In fact, I don't."

Jennifer and Mereau retrieved their phones as well and discovered the same rash of messages and no cell signal.

"We must have walked through a pocket where we had a signal," Jennifer said.

They opened and read their text messages, receiving a very brief summary of the two visions Pebbles had experienced and learning the three members of the Wari team were headed their way.

"I should let them know where we are," Anlon said. "I'll head closer to the ridge, see if I can pick up a signal from the valley or Churcampa. You guys keep searching."

Anlon headed away from the trail, angling to get as close to the cliff's edge as he could without invoking vertigo or risking slipping on loose rocks and tumbling down two thousand feet. The wind intensified as he neared the edge, whipping against his jacket and jeans. Holding out his cell phone, he turned in all directions. A one-bar signal appeared in the direction of Churcampa. Was it strong enough to place a call? Only one way to find out.

He pressed the icon for Pebbles' number and cupped his hand over his other ear to cut down on the sound of the wind and gushing water. It took several seconds, but then he heard the warble of Pebbles' phone ringing. The sound faded in and out, and so he missed when Pebbles answered the call.

"...lon? Anlon? Are you there?"

"Hey there, yes I can barely hear you," Anlon shouted into the phone. "Signal sucks. Lots of wind up here."

"Okay. That better?"

"Yes, much."

"Where are you?"

"We made it to the top. We're looking around for a cave. Nothing yet, though."

Pebbles said something but again the wind and water interfered with Anlon's hearing. "Can you repeat? I missed what you said."

"We're about an hour away from the plateau. Where did you park?"

"Oh, you'll have to come up—"

Anlon stopped in mid-sentence. Water? Why am I hearing gushing water up here? He looked around. There were dry cuts in the terrain that looked like places where water drained after a rain, but he saw no running water.

"Anlon? Are you still there? Did I lose you?"

"Uh. Yeah. I'm here." Afraid to move for fear of losing the call, Anlon tried to peek over the cliff. He didn't remember seeing a waterfall on the satellite image or when they looked up at the mountain from the plateau. But it damn sure sounded like a waterfall. "Hey. Can I call you back in a couple of minutes?"

"No. Don't hang up yet. Tell me where you parked. Tell me where we can meet you."

Anlon gave her quick directions and ended the call. Unwilling to step any closer to the edge, he dropped to the ground and crawled until he could poke his head over the ridge. To his left, there were several waterfalls. One big, the others small. None of them descended very far down the sheer mountain wall before they disappeared from view.

"Son of a gun. No wonder we didn't see them from the plateau."

The waterfalls were tucked into a mini chasm that did not appear visible from where they had initially parked. The water was seeping from gaps in the rock, which meant there was a stream inside the mountain… which meant there were cavities in the rocks that allowed the water to flow. And where there were cavities…

He squinted to focus on the gaps where water poured out. There was a thin ledge that ran along the vegetation-covered mountain wall. The water appeared to be exiting from spots along it. Anlon edged his head a little further out. That was when he saw the caves. There was no ledge above them like in Citali's vision and they did not look accessible without rappelling down the side, but they were the reason the water disappeared. The waterfalls slid back inside the mountain through the mouths of three caves.

Anlon frowned. *Could it be? No. It's on the wrong side of the mountain. Or is it?* He thought of the stone ruins and Mereau's comment about sentinels warning the village below. Anlon pushed back from the edge and stood. Retracing his steps to the ruins, he spied switchback trails leading down to the village. Had Citali come up the back side instead of from the plateau? It was certainly more barren than the plateau side. But how could she have reached those caves? And where was the ledge?

Another of Mereau's comments popped into his head. He had described the crater as having formed a lake for water running down the mountain until erosion or an earthquake caused a break in the crater wall that resulted in the lake emptying into the river valley. Had similar erosion from the waterfalls eaten away the overhang above the ledge until it broke free and fell into the valley? Had water, wind and vegetation then chipped away at the unprotected ledge? He recalled Pebbles said Citali had first had to descend step-like rocks to reach the ledge.

Returning to the edge, Anlon once again lay down and peeked over. In the corner of the mini-chasm, there was a runnel that indeed had a step-like appearance. It was very steep and looked slippery and worn, but eighteen hundred years ago, had it looked the same? Perhaps the over-hang had protected the steps from the flow of water at that time.

He pulled back from the edge and went in search of Mereau and Jen-nifer. Fifteen minutes later, all three lay with their heads over the edge peering down at the waterfalls and the caves below.

"Anlon, my friend," said Mereau, patting Anlon's back. "You have blessed us with an answer, but you have cursed us to find a way into the caves."

In turn, Jennifer patted Mereau on the back. "I know a way. Where's that Sound Stone of yours?"

They made it back to the van in time to meet the taxi carrying Pebbles, Cesar and Sanjay. The reunion was brief. Anlon grabbed hold of Pebbles' hand and began to race-walk toward the cliff above the waterfalls. On the way, he explained what he had found and how it seemed to fit what she had seen in the visions. Their pace quickened to a jog as Pebbles relayed more details about her visions from Wari, including a discussion of the Three Sisters waterfall. Before lying down to look over the side of the cliff, Anlon showed Pebbles the switchback road descending the back side of the mountain and the small village it led to at the bend of the Mantaro.

"I know your visions of the mountain happen at night, but does any of this look or feel familiar?" Anlon asked.

"Not really. But I do know Citali had to leave the river while she was in the valley to avoid the men tracking her, so hiking up this side of the mountain makes more sense to me. She would have been much more ex-posed if she came up from the plateau side. And the slope down to the river looks very steep. I'd have to see lights from that village down there at night to be sure, but the angle looks better than what I saw at Pikimachay."

"What about the terrain? It's not entirely barren but it's pretty spartan compared to the plateau side."

"I dunno. I just remember lots of small rocks by the trail."

The others caught up with them as Pebbles finished speaking. Together, they went to examine the small set of ruins before returning to the cliff to gaze down at the caves. Cesar took several photographs of the decayed structures and vowed to check with local archaeologists to learn more about the ruins' suspected heritage.

Then it was time to view the caves. It would have looked bizarre to anyone walking on the trail behind them. There they were, six adults, lying on the ground at the edge of a two-thousand-foot drop, staring over the side and discussing options for reaching the caves.

Concerned about the prospect of Pebbles having a seizure or a vision in which she became agitated, Jennifer and Sanjay held onto her shoulders as she edged her head over the side. She was quiet as Anlon pointed out the ledge, runnel and caves.

"I know the overhang's gone and the ledge looks too narrow, but—"

"And the cave openings are way too big," Pebbles interrupted, the tone of her voice expressing disappointment.

"All of that could be explained by erosion," Anlon said. He turned to Cesar. "Wouldn't you agree?"

"Over eighteen centuries? Yes, it's certainly plausible, especially considering the prevalence of earthquakes in these mountains. Eroded, unstable features could easily break free."

"But I don't remember any waterfalls," Pebbles said.

"Maybe the stream inside the mountain hadn't cut its way through yet," Jennifer suggested.

"Or maybe it channeled in a different direction at that time," said Mereau.

All eyes were on Pebbles as she scanned the area below. After a short interval of silence, she said, "So, how do we get down there to check out the caves?"

Jennifer pointed to the runnel in the corner nook of the mini chasm. "Looks like the runnel goes all the way down to the plateau. I'd suggest hiking up the runnel from the plateau to get as close as possible to the caves and then have Mereau use his Sound Stone to lift Pebbles the rest of the way."

"Use the stone to do what?" Sanjay said.

"Oops, sorry about that," Jennifer said. "Sometimes, I forget you're not familiar with everything the stones can do."

The Sound Stone, she told him, projected sound waves capable of lifting heavy objects and moving them through the air.

"It's true," Pebbles said to the unbelieving Sanjay. "I've seen it. I've done it."

"What do you say, Mereau? Is it doable?" Jennifer asked.

"Projecting her from the ground to the caves is an easy matter, getting her down from the caves is not."

He explained the sound waves projected by the stone were most concentrated, most powerful, when the object being moved was in close proximity. The farther away the object, the more the sound waves would dissipate, making it more difficult to lift and move distant objects.

"There are two additional problems with that plan," Anlon said. "First, I don't think it's a great idea for Pebbles to go into the caves alone. Second, Mereau's the best choice to go with her, but none of the rest of us is experienced enough with the Sound Stone to lift him up there."

"Why Mereau? Can't one of us go in his place?" asked Sanjay.

Anlon described Mereau's theory about the cave housing a beacon marked Maerlif. He finished by saying, "Since Mereau's the most experienced with the Sound Stone, he'll have the best chance of finding the beacon."

"I don't need Mereau. I can find the beacon," Pebbles said. "I've done it twice before, the Maerlif in Nicaragua and Malinyah's tomb on Isabela Island. I can do it again."

"I know you can, but you're missing the point," Anlon said. "How do we get you *and* the Sound Stone to the cave?"

Pebbles turned to Mereau. "You only have one Sound Stone with you?"

"Unfortunately, yes."

"And you still need someone else to go with you, Pebbles, even if it's not Mereau," said Anlon. "We have no idea what's inside the caves. You could get stuck or fall. Rocks could fall on you. And the whole purpose of sending you in there is to stimulate your memory, stimulate a vision, right? What happens if that works and you have a seizure? We'd have no way of knowing something bad had happened and no way to reach you. To do this right, to do this safely, we need a well-thought-out plan."

RESTAURANTE NINO
CHURCAMPA, PERU

The group devoted another hour to debating alternatives before it became clear that a quick solution was not at hand. With the afternoon sun beginning to fade in the west, they decided to find a place for dinner in Churcampa before heading back to Ayacucho. It was a bittersweet way to end an eventful day, but the practical realities associated with exploring the caves could not be ignored.

An hour later, over a family-style dinner comprised of fried chicken, rice and sautéed vegetables, a plan began to take shape. It would require climbing gear, walkie-talkies and orchestrating some speculative engineering to make it work, but the napkin-sketched plan, first envisioned and diagramed by Anlon and subsequently modified by Jennifer and Mereau, appeared feasible.

As soon as the plan was agreed upon, Cesar pulled out the business card of the Ayacucho taxi driver and called him to solicit his help in rounding up the necessary supplies. The walkie-talkies would be easy to procure, the driver told him. The climbing gear, not so much. He told Cesar he would check around and call back.

Though it was a modest first step toward enacting the plan, Cesar was excited enough to suggest a celebratory toast of bottled waters. All but Sanjay and Pebbles raised their bottles. Sanjay was too absorbed watching Pebbles. She had taken the pencil used to sketch the plan and was in the midst of drawing something on another napkin.

The table quieted as Pebbles continued to draw. When she finished, she dropped the pencil and stared blankly at the wall. Anlon picked up the napkin and let out a low whistle. Handing it to Sanjay, he mumbled, "Take a look at that."

The picture showed the three, smiling, bare-chested children from the waist up. A girl surrounded by two boys. They stood arm-in-arm in front of a waterfall. The hair on their elongated heads appeared to be wet, as if they had just emerged from playing in the waterfall. Around their necks, they wore thin necklaces adorned with identical pendants…pendants bearing the same symbol shaped into the shoreline sand of Paracas.

A hand covered her mouth and pulled her into the darkness. A voice whispered in her ear. *"Be still and listen. There is little time. You must take what was given and go immediately."*

Citali pushed away the hand covering her mouth and whispered back. *"Are you mad? Can you not see the glow of their torches? There is one way out, one way down to the river. If I leave now, they will capture me. We will wait until they are gone and go together."*

"You cannot wait. Take what was given, Keeper, and go. Those that followed you will not prevent your escape. My men will see to that."

Shouts and screams from outside the cave could be heard through the entrance.

"What about the new ones? Take me to them."

"They have been sent ahead."

"What? Why?"

"Other lights, many lights, are in the valley. They are headed this way. Fires burn behind them. You must go now, Keeper, before it is too late. Some of my men will go with you. Others await you at the river. They will guide you to our village. Hurry. Fill your bag and go."

"I cannot find my way in the dark."

Amid more screams pouring into the darkened space, Citali heard the echo of rocks hitting together and saw a trail of sparks. A pungent odor filled her nose. More sparks leapt up and then a flame ignited. It quickly spread along a soaked cloth wrapped around a stick, illuminating a man whose body was covered with designs painted in gold. He handed her the torch.

"Go!"

Crouching down, Citali entered a tunnel at the back of the cave. As she moved deeper into the mountain, the sounds of the skirmish outside the cave began to fade. Ahead, she could see the spot where the tunnel began to widen into a sculpted chamber with an arched ceiling.

Even at a distance, she could see the painted murals that filled the left wall of the shrine and the seashell mosaic that graced the wall to the right. But her eyes soon focused on the stone blocks at the rear of the chamber. The skin beneath her necklace began to warm and prickle.

She passed into the shrine and slotted the torch into a holder just inside the entrance. She bowed before the mosaic, her hands touching the sacred symbol formed by the seashells. In a whisper, she recited the pledge and then stood to face the wall of blocks. The tiles of the necklace began to vibrate as she approached.

A panicked voice echoed down the tunnel. *"Quickly! We must go! Others have started up the trail. They do not walk. They run."*

Her heart sank as she listened to his words. She stared at the wall and sighed.

It is too late, then. May the fathers forgive me.

Citali slipped a Sound Stone from her bag. Moving closer to the neatly cut and placed blocks, she raised the bottom of the bowl-shaped stone to her lips and began to hum.

Dust filled the chamber as stone blocks shattered and the ceiling gave way. The tumbling of rock shook the floor with the force of an earthquake. Through the deafening sounds, Citali heard the man's voice again.

"Keeper! What has happened? Are you—"

"Stay back," she called out.

What was left of the chamber descended into a brief darkness. Then a dim light flickered through clouds of dust. Citali turned and spied the sputtering torch lying on rubble. Retrieving it, she wedged it into a mound of rock and then scrambled atop the fallen blocks.

Averting her eyes from looking into the dark hole beyond the debris, Citali hummed on the Sound Stone. Sweeping it to and fro over the debris …

…moments later, Citali emerged from the tunnel. Her body caked with dirt, she coughed, wiped her eyes clear of grit and handed the torch to the man. His face displayed a petrified expression.

"What has happened, Keeper? Where are the given—"

"They are safe. Now, go. I will follow."

Citali watched him exit the cave and then turned toward the tunnel. Out came the Sound Stone again. She touched it to her lips and began to hum. Shortly after, down went the entrance to the tunnel. The man returned to protest, his eyes horror-filled.

"Keeper, what have you done?"

"Honored the pledge."

Pushing past him she exited the cave and dashed along the ledge. Bodies of fallen attackers and defenders littered her way. Citali reached the gap and climbed the step-like stones to reach the trail. Seconds later, the gold-painted man scrambled up the gap and came to halt beside her. *"Why do you pause? We must go."*

"Start down the mountain. Do not look back." Citali pointed at a small group of men crouching at the junction where the path to the cave met the switchback trail. *"Tell them the same. No matter what you hear, no matter how bright the sky lights up, do not look back. Do you understand me? It is forbidden."*

"But, Keeper—"

Turning to face the overhang protecting the ledge, Citali commanded the man to leave. As she dipped her hands into the bag again, she heard the pounding of his feet on the trail and his shouts to the men at the junction.

She looked down at the two stones in her hands, one that was cone-shaped, the other a small cylinder. After whispering another plea for forgiveness, she began to grind the bottom of the cone against the other stone. They began to glow. Citali intensified her grinding until the heat from the stones burned her palms.

Yanking them away from each other, she pointed the tip of the cone at the overhang and smashed the cylinder against the bottom of the cone. A bolt of light shot forth, lighting up the chasm. The ground trembled. Rocks at the receiving end of the beam chunked loose from the overhang. A large crack formed. She pulled the stones apart and smashed them together again, this time grinding them with all her might as a new bolt leapt at the crack.

The flash of light that followed lit up the waters in the lake below. The boom accompanying the disintegration of the overhang rattled the mountainside. She lifted her eyes and stared at the lights in the valley and the small dots lining the trail beside the lake.

"You will never take what was hidden!" Citali screamed. *"Never!"*

One last time, she slammed the glowing stones. This time, she aimed the beam at the small channel where the lake fed into the river. The ground rumbled again. She ground the stones together until she heard the channel begin to break apart.

Dropping the throbbing stones over the side of the mountain, she listened with satisfaction as the channel gave way and water gushed through the widened gap. Gazing through the darkness toward the valley in the distance, she saw thousands of lights scatter in all directions. Many would perish beneath the inescapable torrent of water. She prayed the evil bitch would be among them.

No matter. Whether she dies or lives, she will never touch what was hidden. Not now.

Citali smiled as she turned and headed for the switchback, her singed hand sliding inside the bag to touch each of the orbs. The smile vanished as a wave of disgust churned her stomach. She dropped to her knees and began to retch.

CHAPTER 21

SLEEPLESS IN AYACUCHO

RESTAURANTE NINO
CHURCAMPA, PERU
SEPTEMBER 28

It took several seconds before Pebbles could see through her watery eyes. It took a few more to remember where she was and recall the names of the people with worried stares seated around her, two of whom propped her up in her chair.

Well, at least I'm not on the floor this time.

As Pebbles endured a flurry of questions about her wellbeing, Anlon handed her a bottled water. After downing half of the bottle, Pebbles placed the container on the table. Her eyes drifted to the napkin spread out in front of Mereau.

"What the heck is that?" she asked.

Mereau pushed it across the table. "You don't recognize it? You drew it."

"I did?" She lifted the napkin and studied the drawing.

"We presume it shows the children, the *new ones*, mentioned in your previous visions."

Pebbles pointed at the necklaces. "Those are the same symbols on the Candelabra."

"It appears so," Mereau said.

"The same symbols on the wall of seashells in the cave…" Pebbles' voice trailed off as the memory of Citali kneeling before the mosaic came back into her consciousness.

"You've seen a vision of the cave?" Anlon asked.

She nodded, her mind still half focused on the mosaic memory. As it faded into the recesses of her mind, Pebbles turned to Anlon. "There's no point in exploring the cave. Citali destroyed it...well, made it impassable. Even if we can get into it, it would take months to clear a path to what's left of the Maerlif."

"So, there was a Maerlif!" Anlon turned to Mereau. "You were right."

"Pebbles, you said she destroyed it? How?" Jennifer asked.

"She had a Sound Stone in her bag...and a Flash Stone." Pebbles stared off in the distance. "She purposely caved in the Maerlif wall and tunnel leading to it with the Sound Stone. Blew up the overhang and ledge with the Flash Stone." Pebbles paused and then focused her gaze on Jennifer. "And then frickin' used it to empty the lake into the valley."

Jennifer frowned. "I thought you said she didn't have any of the Munuorian stones."

"I know. Apparently, I was wrong."

Pebbles provided them with a full description of the vision ending with the part where Citali fell to the path and vomited. "I think she was grossed out by what she had done. She kept begging for forgiveness."

"It's an understandable reaction," said Anlon. "She was charged to protect what was in the Maerlif, and instead she destroyed it."

"That's what's confusing," Pebbles said. "She knocked down the Maerlif wall, but I don't think she actually destroyed what was inside. I remember seeing a black space behind the rubble of the wall, but the weird part is she never went in it."

"Didn't you say she took some pieces from the rubble?" Cesar said.

"Uh huh. I didn't see them in the vision, but I could tell she was using the Sound Stone to search for something in the rubble. Then, after she left the cave, I felt them when she reached into her bag. They were kind of oblong. Smooth, orb shapes about the size of big pinecones."

"Aha!" Mereau said. "That's it! Now I understand her purpose. Citali was as clever as her forebearers." He paused. Pebbles watched a smile spread across his face. "She didn't destroy the Maerlif. She knocked down the wall to take the beacons...to prevent Muran from finding the crypt. And then for good measure, she sealed the tunnel and rendered it inaccessible by destroying the only way she could reach the cave."

As he spoke, Pebbles replayed what she recalled of the vision. Mereau was right. Citali had used the Sound Stone to search for the beacons in the rubble. But, if that was the case, why had she been so remorseful? Why had she begged forgiveness? Pebbles posed these questions to her friends.

"I think I have an explanation," Sanjay said. "I feel badly I did not think of the possibility earlier but, as Mereau has observed, Citali was clever. She has deceived us. She has deceived you."

"What?"

"She has manipulated us to feel sympathetic toward her. She has used her visions to justify her actions. It is a common defense mechanism used when we feel guilty about our actions."

"I don't understand what you're saying," Pebbles said. "Guilty about what?"

"Citali let loose the lake. While she no doubt rejoiced in killing her adversaries who got caught up in the deluge, she also likely killed hundreds of innocent people in villages in the valley and others along the course of the river.

"My guess is, as she started down the switchback, she noticed the lights in the village, the ones she had seen during her hike up, were no longer visible. I imagine it only took her a few more seconds to realize the full scope of implications."

Sanjay lifted up the napkin drawing. When Pebbles grasped the meaning of his gesture, she shot from her seat and ran outside. Dropping to her knees, she bent over and vomited on the sidewalk.

How could you! What were you thinking?

The new ones, the children who were to be the next generation of Seers, had been sent ahead. That was what the gold-painted man had said. They would have been too little to trudge through the mountains. They would have gone by boat.

EN ROUTE BACK TO SANTA ROSA HOTEL
AYACUCHO VALLEY, PERU

It was a quiet ride back to Ayacucho. Pebbles slept most of the way, her head resting against Anlon's shoulder. Cesar sat up front with Jennifer, switching places as driver about halfway through the valley. Sanjay and Mereau occupied the third row, whispering back and forth so as not to wake Pebbles.

Anlon spent most of the trip looking out the window but he could not remember a single thing he had seen. During the ride, his mind had cycled question after question. Some for Pebbles, others for Sanjay and yet more for Mereau and Cesar.

It would have been easy to shut his mind off, endure a sleepless night and rise early to check the flight schedule from Ayacucho to Lima. But there were questions that still needed answers, the most important of which was: how do we get Citali's memories out of Pebbles' mind?

He had hoped that by chasing the clues to find out what had happened to the items Citali had been charged to protect, the answers might have soothed her restless spirit and her psychic energy would have passed away. Such an outcome, he now realized, was more wishful thinking than anything else.

But what the hell good would it do now to go any farther? He doubted Sanjay would recommend a confrontation between Pebbles and Citali, and chasing any more clues was a waste of time. All they would be doing is playing into the hands of Citali's guilty conscience.

From a historical preservation perspective, Anlon was sure Cesar and Mereau would ultimately want to return to the mountain and excavate the cave, find the Maerlif and see what Citali and her family had promised to protect. But the exercise would take months. And there was no guarantee they would find anything. The waterfalls or the stream inside the mountain might have washed away all the artifacts centuries ago.

Even if they did discover some archaeological evidence of importance, how was it going to help Pebbles? Citali's memories would continue to haunt her unless Sanjay could find a way to expunge her from Pebbles' mind. And Anlon knew Sanjay would say such a feat was impossible. If you cannot force a living human mind to come to grips with trauma, how could anyone hope to force the same from psychic remains of a mind that died eighteen hundred years ago?

ROOM 302
SANTA ROSA HOTEL
AYACUCHO, PERU
WEE HOURS OF SEPTEMBER 29

Just as Anlon had predicted, his mind refused to sleep. Trying desperately to sneak out of bed without waking Pebbles, he moved in slow motion. All that did, however, was accentuate the length of the time the bed creaked.

As he pulled on his clothes in the dark, he heard Pebbles' voice. "Where are you going?"

"Can't sleep. Didn't want to disturb you."

"Don't worry, I can't sleep either. Come back to bed."

"You sure?"

"Uh huh."

Anlon dropped his pants and slid back under the covers. Pebbles curled up to him and said, "Pretty much a FUBAR situation, huh?"

He wrapped his arms around her. "Yeah. I'm sorry."

"I can't believe she wasn't honest with me. I mean, we're sharing the same brain, for cripe's sake."

"I guess if you can't be honest with yourself, you can't be honest with someone else."

She took hold of his hand and kissed it. "That's very prophetic. Sounds like it ought to be on a greeting card."

Anlon laughed. So did Pebbles.

For several minutes, they cuddled together in silence. Finally, Pebbles pulled away and hopped out of bed. "I could use a stiff drink. How about you?"

"More like a stiff bottle."

"That works too. Come on, let's go see what we can scare up."

After throwing on their rumpled clothes, they crept down to the lobby. It was just after two a.m. They were both surprised to see the lights in the hotel restaurant still on. Their surprise jumped up a notch when they found Sanjay, Cesar, Mereau and Jennifer seated at a table with shot glasses, a half-empty bottle of Tequila and the stack of Pebbles' dream journals and sketch pads. Jennifer looked up and said, "Pull up a chair. Join the 'Sleepless in Ayacucho' party."

Anlon looked around the empty restaurant. "How long have you been down here?"

"Since we got back," Jennifer said.

"They kept the restaurant open for you?"

"Yeah. Cesar sweet-talked them into it. We're supposed to let the front desk know when we leave so they can lock up." Jennifer rose from her seat. "You guys want a drink?"

"Make mine a double," said Pebbles.

Jennifer snagged two more shot glasses from behind the restaurant bar and returned to the table. As she poured drinks all around, Sanjay asked Pebbles how she was feeling.

"Numb. Lost. Angry. Embarrassed."

"Why embarrassed?" Jennifer asked.

"Because I got suckered. Because I pulled you all into a wild goose chase."

"No one pulled us, Pebbles," said Cesar. "We came because we wanted to come."

"Yeah, well, I appreciate that. You've all been super supportive. I'm just sorry it ended up the way it did."

"Ended?" Mereau said. "You do not wish to continue on? See inside the cave? Visit the Three Sisters waterfall?"

"Why would I want to do that at this point?" Pebbles said. "More importantly, why would *you* want to do that?"

"We've spent the better part of the night discussing the reasons…and we see many. For you and for us," Cesar said.

"Yes," Sanjay said. "We all seek closure of one kind or another…including Citali."

"Citali? Why should anyone care about closure for her?"

"She carries a heavy burden, Pebbles. One that was powerful enough to allow her spirit to find its way into your mind. We have the opportunity to ease that burden."

"Why should we ease her burden? She lied to me. Everything in the dreams, the visions, everything she showed me was all about protecting what was in her damn bag. It was just a sick kind of spin to hide what she did."

"There is no arguing the fact that she was manipulative," said Sanjay. "But I believe she deserves our compassion. It cannot be an easy task for a mother who killed her own children to readily confess her sin to a stranger."

Pain sliced through Pebbles' chest. She stared at Sanjay, her lips opening to speak. Finding it impossible to form words, she shook her head.

"I know it comes as a shock," Sanjay said, "and I may be wrong, but we have spent the better part of the night debating Citali's visions, and we are in agreement. It seems the most likely explanation."

Pebbles looked around at the others. All but Anlon nodded. His expression showed he was as stunned as she felt.

"You're wrong," she said. "She never showed me she had any children. Not once."

"Yes, I know. Well, she did show you one, but she was not honest about what really happened to her. The girl at the bonfire. Then again, I do not think it was actually a memory she showed you. I think it was a nightmare. In fact, in retrospect, I think a number of the visions you experienced were really nightmares...Citali's, not yours.

"I am angry at myself for not considering the possibility earlier. From Anlon's first description of your visions, I believed they were dreams. *Your* dreams. The symbolism in many of them was too apparent to think otherwise. But sprinkled among those dreams were true memories and that threw me off. Once you started to identify real objects, real places, it became impossible to ignore the possibility that all the visions were Citali's memories. Until tonight, I never stopped to consider the possibility the visions included nightmares...Citali's nightmares."

Pebbles felt heat rising throughout her body. "You don't know what you're talking about. The bonfire was as real as it gets."

"Nightmares often feel that way. But if you pause to consider the vision closely, there are a few aspects that are confusing. For example, what purpose did the burly man serve in sacrificing the young girl? If she was, as you suspect, one of the *new ones*, why would anyone charged to protect them so willingly sacrifice her? Why didn't the burly man urge Citali to take her? And if it was a memory instead of a dream, where were the two boys? The answers become clearer if we view the vision as a dream and the contents as symbolism.

"Citali stands in the bushes and watches a girl speared and cast into the fire. Citali screams at the masked lady emerging from the jungle, vowing to cut her heart out, then flees. Before the deed occurs, the girl and Citali change clothes. Do you see what I mean?"

"Uh, no."

"Very well. Let us take them one by one, starting with the changing of clothes. This appears to be a futile ruse, does it not? Why would the burly man have wasted time to have the two women change clothes? Would not it have made more sense for him to compel both Citali and the girl to flee for the river before the invaders arrived in the village? If he believed that was not a viable option, say, because the younger girl was too small to outrun the invaders, it still does not explain the changing of clothes."

"Forgive me for interrupting, Sanjay," said Anlon, "Desperate people do stupid stuff all the time. Just because it was a futile ruse doesn't mean the vision was a dream."

"True, but ruse or no, I do not think the bonfire event ever happened. Instead, I think it was a dream that expressed Citali's despair at causing the loss of her children, particularly of her daughter. Not that she did not care about the boys, but the loss of the daughter hurt her especially.

"In that light, the changing of the clothes strikes me as symbolism that tells us the girl was a reflection of Citali...a daughter. The masked lady emerging from the jungle? I think this is also symbolism. The masked lady in this scene is *Citali*, not Muran. Citali yells at herself, in a sense, for killing the daughter. When she screams she will cut out her heart, I believe she is really saying she cut out her own heart when she killed the children."

"Now you're just talking crazy," Pebbles said. "The flood killed the new ones, not a bonfire."

"Not true," Cesar said. "The flood was a consequence of the fire she created to destroy the lake wall. The fire was the actual instrument of their deaths."

Pebbles' head swooned. They were wrong, she was sure of it. She replayed the scene in her mind. The girl on her knees before the fire, crying. Citali protesting the exchange of clothes, being told to run. Hiding behind the bushes, watching the girl die. People around her urging her to escape.

The more she considered the scene, the more Pebbles began to see the manipulative nature of it. *It wasn't my fault. There was nothing I could do to save her. I was told to run. I had to go. I had to protect what was given…*

"The bag." Pebbles shot a look at Sanjay. "You told me when I woke up from the bonfire vision, I said Citali forgot the bag. But she didn't forget it, did she? It was gone. Because what it held was gone. The bag was a symbol too."

"Yes, a bag slung around the *hip*…a womb…protecting precious objects inside," Sanjay said. "We have Jennifer to thank for that insight."

Pebbles turned toward Jennifer, who tapped the dream journals and said, "I didn't believe Sanjay either, at first. I'm like, there's no way the visions were dreams. But I started going through the journals and noticed that in some of your entries, Citali carries the bag on her back. In other ones, it's slung by her hip. We think that distinction points out which of the entries are her memories and which are dreams. It explains why it was so hard for you to tell what was in the bag in some cases and not in others.

"All the entries where you said Citali reached in the bag to feel things, but you couldn't make out what she was touching, were all entries where your journal said Citali reached into the bag by her hip. But the ones where she pulled out items like the torch in the mountain vision, or when she put her belongings in the bag at the temple, you wrote that she slung it over her back."

Pebbles' mind drifted to the aftermath of destroying the lake wall. Citali had started down the trail and slid her hand in the bag by her hip; she touched three orbs before she fell to the ground and started barfing. Three orbs…three eggs…three children.

"She didn't take anything from the Maerlif," Pebbles said. "When she smiled when she put her hand in the bag after destroying everything, it was her way of saying she'd done what she set out to do…protect her children…and that's when it hit her!"

"We think you are mostly right," Mereau said. "We think she did indeed take a beacon…as well as the Flash Stone and Port Stone, to use your vernacular for the stones. In your recital of the cave vision, you said she prayed before she broke open the Maerlif, begging for forgiveness. She asked for forgiveness again before she used the Sound Stone and once more before she knocked down the overhang and ledge with the Flash Stone. Remember also, she told the gold-painted man not to look back. She told him it was *forbidden*."

As Mereau spoke, Pebbles recalled that among Munuorians, only a subset was taught to use their magnetic tools. Not because there was an elitism, but because of how the opposing polarities of the stones interacted with their users. It took time and training to teach users how to balance their emotions when using the stones. Use them when you were angry, and your internal rage could unleash tremendous destructive power. Use them when you were serene, and you could build monuments of grandeur…or help survivors of catastrophes.

Viewed in this light, Mereau's commentary suggested Citali had begged for forgiveness not because she was about to destroy the Maerlif and the way to reach it, but because she had been forbidden to use the stones. She was the *Keeper* of what was given, not a trained user of what was given. Oh, she knew how to use the stones, all right, that much was obvious to Pebbles from the cave vision. But she was not supposed to use them. Pebbles stirred from her thoughts to find the others staring at her.

"Another vision?" Anlon asked.

"Uh…no. Just thinking." She turned to Sanjay. "Okay. You sold me. So, what now? You said we should show her compassion. How?"

"Go to Three Sisters. Let the rest of the timeline of her memories play out. Summon her if you can. I will help you create mental imagery of a waterfall sanctuary to attract her consciousness, similar to what we did to create the oasis."

"Okay, then what?"

"Let her mourn. Offer her forgiveness."

"Excuse me?"

"I see what he means, Pebbles," said Anlon. "Citali died without properly mourning her loss. Muran chased her into the jungle and mortally wounded her, probably before she could even bury her children, presuming they were found before she died."

"I get that. But offer her forgiveness?"

"You want her inside your head for the rest of your life?" Anlon asked.

"No, I don't." Pebbles turned to Sanjay. "You think if I forgive her, she'll leave me?"

"I think it is possible," Sanjay said. "Admitting guilt, confessing sins, asking and receiving forgiveness all provide us with inner peace. It is why the concepts of atonement and forgiveness exist in many theologies, past and present. We cannot offer Citali a deity's forgiveness, but we can offer her our understanding. She made a terrible mistake in judgment that resulted in horrendous consequences. Citali knows that better than anyone else. She has lived with her remorse for eighteen hundred years. What is to be gained by letting her remorse linger? For her or for you?"

Even though Pebbles was still angry that Citali had plied her with deceitful visions for months, she understood that harboring anger toward Citali was unlikely to stop the visions. But what if offering forgiveness did not work? Pebbles was about to pose this question to Sanjay when his earlier advice came to mind.

Ah, but what if it does?

CHAPTER 22

MUDDY WATERS

SANTA ROSA HOTEL
AYACUCHO, PERU
SEPTEMBER 29

T he late-night gathering broke up soon afterward. After grabbing a few hours of sleep, they reconvened in the lobby later in the morning to plan their trip to Three Sisters…and quickly discovered it would not be an easy or short journey.

To begin, the three-tiered waterfall was located approximately two-hundred-fifty kilometers from Ayacucho. Second, the remote site was inaccessible to automobiles. The closest road came to a dead end twenty miles short of the falls.

From the end of the road, one had two options to reach the falls. Either hike twenty miles through a dense, mountainous jungle forest or rent boats and go by river. The latter still involved a mile hike along the stream fed by the falls.

"Sounds like something out of an adventure movie," said Jennifer.

"No kidding," Anlon said.

"I vote for renting boats," Pebbles said. "If we go by river, the scenery might stimulate more visions."

"That assumes Citali traveled by river," Sanjay said.

"I'm convinced she did. I've seen flashes of her in a boat on a river."

"True," said Mereau, "but you also have had visions of people chasing her through a forest."

"Yeah, I know, but the river feels right to me. I can't explain why. It just does."

"Well, it is certainly more practical," Cesar said.

"And faster," Jennifer added. The others agreed.

Anlon stood. "Okay, that settles it. We go by river. I'll go talk to the hotel concierge and see if she can find us a place where we can rent boats."

When he returned from the consultation, he said, "Good news, bad news. The concierge hooked us up with an exotic travel group based in a town called Pichari. It's about two hundred kilometers from here. They can take us to the falls by kayak, but they are booked for today. So, that means we'll meet up with them tomorrow."

"If we have to drive two hundred kilometers, that's just as well," Jennifer said. "We won't get there until after dark tonight anyway."

"We won't be driving," Anlon said. "Concierge said helicopter's the best way to go. She's working on booking us a charter right now. She said the trip's about an hour. We'll leave first thing tomorrow morning."

Anlon told the group the exotic travel company would take care of everything from kayaks to camping gear to guides. "They'll set up camp for us near the falls, prepare meals, the whole megillah. I booked them for three nights."

"Anlon, that sounds wonderful. Just one caution," Cesar said. "The taxi driver told us the waterfall abuts the territory of an unfriendly indigenous tribe. While I supposed the tribe is probably used to adventure tourists stopping at the site to snap pictures or take a dip in its waters, I do wonder if they will tolerate multi-night campers."

Mereau assured Cesar and the others that he could protect the group with his backpack collection of Munuorian *Tyls* if they were confronted. To boot, he reminded the archaeologist that Jennifer and Pebbles were experienced in wielding the ancient stones, so they had three potential defenders if the tribe appeared.

"I do not doubt your prowess with the stones," Cesar said, "but these tribes know the territory far better than we do. And you must keep in mind, many indigenous tribes in the Amazon valley are fed up with encroachment on their native lands. They sometimes attack without warning, meaning they might strike us all down before we have a chance to defend ourselves."

"It's probably not of any comfort," Anlon said, "but the guides coming with us carry side arms, not just because of the tribe. Apparently, river piracy can be an issue too."

"Peachy," said Pebbles.

"Hey, if any of you have got a better idea, I'm all ears," said Anlon. "Whether we go by river or hike through the jungle, there are risks. I'm personally comfortable with the risks, but I don't want to speak for you guys."

Everyone first focused their attention on Pebbles. Without hesitation, she said, "I'm in if you guys are in."

A quick show of hands showed everyone was willing to go, so Anlon returned to the concierge desk and finalized the travel plans. When he rejoined the group, he said, "We're all set. As an FYI, I asked the concierge to find out whether it would be possible to have the pilots take a detour into the jungle for a fly-over of the waterfall on our way to Pichari. I think it's worth the diversion to get a lay of the land. Assuming the pilots agree, any objections?"

No objections were expressed and so the group split up to begin packing for the trip. Later in the afternoon, Sanjay and Pebbles met up to rehearse a mental image of a waterfall sanctuary in the hopes that Pebbles could lure Citali for a direct conversation once they were near Three Sisters. The full group reconvened for dinner and then retired early.

IN FLIGHT OVER OTISHI NATIONAL PARK
AMAZON JUNGLE, PERU
SEPTEMBER 30

At eight the next morning, they boarded the chartered helicopter and flew toward Three Sisters Falls. As the terrain began to transition from mountain to jungle, Anlon peered out of his porthole window and marveled at the Amazon valley in the distance. It looked as vast as an ocean. Directly below, however, the jungle was marked by mountain ranges.

In one of these mountain ranges, they came upon the Three Sisters, so named for the three tiers of the waterfall as it flowed down the mountainside. Given the staggering height of the falls from top to bottom — three thousand feet — Anlon had expected to easily spot it when the pilot told them they were coming up on it. But amid the tree-covered mountains surrounding it, Anlon found it very hard to pick out the waterfall until they swooped into Cutivireni Canyon, the gap where Three Sisters was situated, and only then because Pebbles pointed it out.

He positioned the microphone of his headset in front of his lips and said to Pebbles, "The third tier looks like it drops into an abyss."

"It's deceiving, isn't it? The pool at the bottom of the second tier looks like the end of the waterfall. But it spills over the edge and the third tier seems to disappear behind trees."

"Does it look familiar?" Jennifer asked Pebbles.

"Not from this angle, but damn, how are we going to get to that? I don't see any river. I don't even see the stream at the bottom of the falls. There are too many trees. They're too tall."

Cesar asked the pilot whether he could circle around and give them a better look at the lower tier and stream. When the copter hovered above the area for a closer look, Anlon said, "I don't see a pool at its base. It looks like the third tier goes directly into the stream."

Mereau pointed out his window. "Yes but look at the streambed. Most of it is dry. Maybe there is a pool that forms there during heavy rains, or perhaps the flow of the falls was heavier during Citali's time."

"Good point," Anlon said. "I have to keep in mind I should be looking at everything through the lens of eighteen centuries ago. I'll tell you one thing, though, I'm sure glad we decided not to try to come here on our own."

"No kidding," said Jennifer. "I wouldn't want to get lost in the jungle down there. Looks spooky."

Sanjay and Pebbles used their cell phones to take many pictures of the falls and the surrounding area before the pilot veered away and flew toward the Cutivireni River to give them a look at the waters they would kayak.

Flying downriver, Anlon looked at the series of winding twists. From above, they looked like the curves of a slithering snake bordered by jungle on both sides. Despite its menacing appearance from the helicopter, however, the river flow seemed relatively placid. Anlon could see no evidence of rapids or smaller waterfalls.

As they neared the point at which the Cutivireni met up with the larger river it fed, the Ene, the constitution of both rivers changed quite a bit. The twists became more pronounced given the presence of small islands and sand bars that randomly interrupted their flows.

For the second time in less than an hour, Anlon was thankful they were part of a guided expedition. None but Jennifer and Cesar were experienced kayakers, and though Anlon was well accustomed to navigating boats on lakes and on the ocean, he was not accustomed to navigating jungle rivers. A wrong turn here or there around a sandbar or island might take them down unintended side streams. As it was, it appeared there might be spots where they might be forced to drag their kayaks over sand bars. Better to leave it to experts who knew the intricacies of traveling both rivers.

They traveled a lot farther down the Ene River than Anlon anticipated. When he mentioned this to Cesar, the archaeologist reminded him they would not be kayaking the full distance.

"We will be landing in Pichari and the travel company will drive us back close to the merge of the Ene and Cutivireni. We will put our kayaks into the Ene there. We will only be kayaking about twenty miles. I say that as if it will be an easy task, but the man from the company I spoke to before we left Ayacucho says it could take us up to twelve hours if we go the full distance to Three Sisters today. He advised against that, knowing we'd then have to backtrack to set up camp."

Anlon heard Sanjay ask Cesar how far upriver their campsite would be.

"That has yet to be negotiated," Cesar said. "The spot where they normally set up is about halfway to the falls. I am hopeful we can prevail upon them for something closer."

"Are there any ruins in the area?" Pebbles asked.

"I do not know, and I did not ask the man from the company," Cesar said, "but I would be surprised if there weren't. Many ancient cultures settled by riversides for obvious reasons and we know there are indigenous tribes still living in the surrounding jungles."

When they finally landed in Pichari, Anlon was impressed to see the eight-man tour company team ready and waiting for their arrival. With them, they brought two full-sized vans, one hitched to a trailer laden with kayaks while the other hauled two river rafts.

The head guide, a wiry man with a bushy beard and mustache, introduced himself as Pablo in perfect English. Joint introductions followed and without any further preamble, they loaded into the vans and drove off.

In Anlon's van, Pablo sat in the front passenger seat with one of the other crewmembers at the wheel. Joining Anlon in the back were Pebbles and Jennifer.

"How far is the drive?" Anlon asked.

"Just under forty miles," said Pablo. "It will take us about two hours. There are many bends in the road, so we have to go slow. We don't want to tip the trailers."

During the early part of the drive, the road tracked close to the Ene, providing Anlon, Pebbles and Jennifer glimpses of the river. About a third of the way, however, the road turned inland and for most of the rest of the way, the scenery on both sides of the road alternated between jungle forests, open patches of farmland and the occasional small community.

Near the end of the drive, they stopped briefly in the town of *Los Ángeles de Primavera*. There, they had lunch and received kayak safety instructions delivered by Pablo and one other English-speaking member of the team, a college-aged young man whose name was Alejandro. Afterward, sunscreen and bug sprays were applied, and they loaded back into the vans for the final mile drive to the jetty.

Once they arrived, Anlon and his group stood aside to don life vests while Pablo and the crew unloaded boats, oars and supplies. While they waited, Alejandro doled out dry bags to Anlon and the others, which they used to stow their backpacks. The dry bags were then loaded into one of the river rafts along with other gear and supplies. The rest of the gear went into the other raft. Afterward, Pablo asked them to divide into two-person kayak teams.

"I think I should go with Sanjay," Pebbles said. "If I start to have a vision, I'd like him close by."

"Makes sense," Anlon said. "Jen, why don't you go with Mereau and I'll pair up with Cesar."

"Sounds good," Jennifer said. As they walked down the ramp to the waiting kayaks, Jennifer posed a question to Anlon. "Um, I know it's late in the game to bring this up, but should we mention anything to Pablo about the possibility of Pebbles going into a trance?"

"No! Don't do that!" Pebbles whispered. "Pablo seems like a by-the-book kind of guy. He might make me sit the trip out."

"Yeah, but what happens if you pass out and fall overboard?" Jennifer asked.

"Look, I'll be fine," Pebbles said. "If I start to feel like I'm going to pass out, I'll give Sanjay a heads up. Just tell Pablo I'm dehydrated or overtired. I'm sure it happens all the time. They'll probably just load me in one of the rafts and keep on going."

Before they could finish the conversation, Pablo called them to gather around. Anlon noticed Pablo and his crew now wore gun belts with holstered pistols. Pablo addressed the wardrobe additions right off the top.

"You may have noticed we are all carrying handguns. It is not something we like to do but your safety is our number one concern. However, I do not want to unduly alarm you. In the six years we have operated tours in these waters, we have only run into pirates twice. They were looking for easy pickings, not a gun fight, so they just turned away and left our group alone. I know there are also many rumors about the natives who live in the jungle, but the only tribesmen we ever encounter along the riverbanks run back into the jungle as soon as they spot us. Still, we would be irresponsible if we did not have a means to protect you if they, or pirates, took a greater interest in us.

"Now, I know you are on this trip to have a good time, see some of our beautiful nature and relax. We will do our very best to ensure you have a wonderful experience but please help us by observing some basic precautions. While we are on the river, keep to the middle as much as possible. If something attracts your interest on either riverbank, please do not go off on your own to investigate. Alert one of my crew and we will all go together. The same goes if you become tired and want to pull over to rest.

"Finally, when we are ashore, whether to set up camp or rest, please do not wander off into the jungle alone. If you need privacy to relieve yourselves, go in pairs or ask one of my crew to accompany you. Always make sure to tell me or Alejandro the direction you intend to go and please make sure the river and our group are always within eyesight. All clear? Everyone understand? Good. Now let's go have a fun and safe adventure."

Anlon raised his eyes to the sky. *Amen to that, brother.*

ENE RIVER
EDGE OF AMAZON JUNGLE, PERU

The first two miles went by quickly, thanks to the assistance of the Ene River's current. Pebbles, seated in the front of her kayak, scanned the environment as they glided along, hoping to spot something she had seen in a vision.

Thus far, the only features that seemed familiar were the muddy banks and density of trees on both sides of the river. *At least it's something,* thought Pebbles. It had been a day-and-a-half since her last vision, the longest gap she had experienced over the last several weeks. She did not want to admit it to the others, but the sudden drop-off concerned her.

Was it a sign that Citali was withdrawing again? Had she sensed Pebbles' disgust? Her anger? Or had sharing what happened at the cave been a catharsis for her?

"Sanjay, let me ask you something. Do you think it's possible Citali's spirit doesn't want forgiveness? That maybe all she cared about was coming clean about killing the new ones?"

"It would surprise me if that was the case."

"Why?"

"She has shown you several visions of events that appear to have happened after destroying the cave. The ones that happen here in the jungle."

"Couldn't those just be additional attempts by Citali to justify what she did? You know, showing me how hard she fought against Muran, how she was so concerned on her deathbed about honoring her ancestors?"

"Maybe. There is clearly denial involved in those visions. There is also evidence of bargaining."

"Bargaining? What do you mean?"

"Rationalizing, justifying, her actions."

"Oh, right. Like I said."

The conversation was interrupted by shouts from Pablo. He was up ahead in one of the river rafts. Apparently, they were about to turn into the headwaters of the Cutivireni River. He instructed the kayakers to line up in single file. Up ahead, Pebbles could see the Ene bending to the left as they neared a gap in the jungle trees on the right. She saw the lead kayak, steered by Alejandro, turn sharply to the right.

Alejandro beached his kayak onto a sandbar, then hopped out. He pulled it further onto the sand and then dashed into the water until he was knee deep. With exaggerated arm movements, he urged the next kayak, the one piloted by Anlon and Cesar, to head toward him.

"What's he doing?" Pebbles asked one of Pablo's crew.

The man stopped paddling long enough to motion for her and Sanjay to head in Alejandro's direction. As they complied, she watched Anlon and Cesar paddling frantically to turn their kayak but the current of Ene took hold of them and spun them around backward. Alejandro waded up to his waist and grabbed a cord on the nose of the kayak, pulling the paddlers toward the sandbar.

"Ah. Now I see," Pebbles said.

On the other side of the sandbar was the Cutivireni. As it added its muddy water to the Ene, the flow of the Ene picked up speed, making it difficult to turn into the Cutivireni without getting swept up in the increased downriver flow of the Ene. Therefore, instead of trying to paddle against the Ene to enter the mouth of the Cutivireni, it appeared they would beach their watercraft and carry them over the sandbar until they found a more suitable place to enter the Cutivireni.

When it came Pebbles' and Sanjay's turn, she found herself laughing at their inability to coordinate the turn. Suddenly, it felt as if they were on a spinning amusement park ride until two of Pablo's men corralled them and pulled them onto the sand. As she got out of the kayak, Pebbles continued to laugh. "That was fun!"

She looked back toward the Ene and saw Jennifer and Mereau waving off Pablo's men. The experienced kayakers dug their paddles into the river as if they were Olympic medalists and swung into the Cutivireni with no problem. Pebbles cupped her hands around her mouth and shouted, "Show-offs!"

As Jennifer and Mereau passed by, she admonished Pebbles and the others to quit loafing and get back in the water. Pebbles raised her hands to shout a retort but froze in place. On the far side of the mouth of the Cutivireni, at the spot where the Ene finished its left-hand turn, was a jumble of debris that had washed onto another sandbar. She staggered backward and plopped down onto the sand as a myriad of images cycled in her mind.

...the shattered shell of a boat...bodies half buried in mud...trees, stripped of their foliage and coated with muck, felled by the side of the river...urgent shouts...splashing through the water...a group of men kneeling...the mud-caked arm of a child sticking out from a pile of debris...

No! Fathers! No!

Citali stumbled and fell beneath the water. Pushing up against the slick bottom, she resurfaced. Wiping brackish goo from her eyes, she waded to reach the group of men. Under her breath, she cursed.

It is the end! I have done the evil bitch's work for her!

Two of the men turned toward her as she climbed up the gooey bank. Their expressions were grave. Citali fell to her knees and began to scream at the gray skies above.

No! It cannot be!

A third man turned. In his arms, he cradled the limp body of a child. A little boy covered in mud from head to toe. The man carried him to Citali and knelt down before her. She lowered her head and sobbed. She could not bring herself to look at the boy.

The man spoke. His voice barely above a whisper.

"He is alive, Keeper. He breathes. I can feel his warmth."

CHAPTER 23

SPEAK THE WORDS

CUTIVIRENI RIVER
OTISHI NATIONAL PARK, PERU
SEPTEMBER 30

"What is the matter?" Pablo asked. "Why does she shake?"

Anlon held out his arm to push Pablo away. "Stop. Don't touch her."

"Answer me! What is wrong with her?"

"Nothing…she's having a nightmare, that's all."

"In the middle of the day?" Pablo challenged.

As Anlon knelt down beside Pebbles, she began to growl. Without warning, she leapt up and charged through the circle of onlookers. Anlon was too slow to grab hold of her as were Sanjay and Pablo's men. Swinging her arms wildly, she burst between them and sped toward the Cutivireni.

"Jen! Mereau!" Anlon shouted. The two kayakers heard him and turned his way. He pointed toward Pebbles as she ran into the water. "Get her! Quick! She's in a vision!"

Anlon heard Pablo issue an urgent order in a flurry of Spanish. All his crew dashed after Pebbles, kicking up big clumps of sand on their way. Anlon, Cesar and Sanjay joined the chase. Pebbles' head disappeared briefly beneath the water before her life vest pulled her back up. In the swift current, the vest seemed to make Pebbles weightless. She drifted away as easily as a leaf upon the water.

"Shit! Shit! Shit!" Anlon yelled. "Hurry!"

The young bucks among Pablo's crew were first into the water. Two of them waded in while the third, Alejandro, shed his life vest and dove into the river. Pebbles' arms flailed and Anlon heard her call out for help.

"Hold on, Pebbles!" Anlon shouted. "Help is on the way!"

By the time Anlon reached the spot where Alejandro had gone in, Pebbles was fifty yards beyond and nearing the junction of the two rivers. Anlon was about to jump in when he heard the sound of an engine starting. Anlon wheeled around to see Pablo in one of the river rafts. He was in the Ene, his hand on the controls of a portable motor at the stern. The boat sped off, the whining engine spouting smoke into the air.

Sanjay and Cesar ran up beside Anlon just as Alejandro caught up to Pebbles. Shortly thereafter, the swift-paddling Jennifer and Mereau came alongside the two swimmers. Alejandro grasped the craft with one hand while he held Pebbles in the crook of his other arm. The kayak crested a small rapid and entered the Ene.

Speechless, Anlon watched Jennifer and Mereau coordinate their oar strokes to angle the kayak toward the closest bank. A hundred yards up the Ene, Pablo finally caught up with them. Alejandro let go of the kayak and grabbed hold of the safety line ringing the raft. As the raft disappeared behind the bending Ene, Anlon saw Pablo pull Pebbles into the boat.

"Thank God," he whispered.

Behind him, he heard Pablo's voice through the walkie-talkie of one of the crew still ashore. The man answered back and then Anlon heard the sound of spraying sand. He turned to see the crewman running for the second raft. Moments later, after affixing another portable motor, the raft went off in pursuit of the others.

Twenty minutes later, the rafts came back into view. In one, Anlon could see Jennifer and Mereau, their empty kayak being towed alongside. In the other were the stern-faced Pablo, Alejandro and Pebbles.

Pebbles was wrapped in a blanket. For some reason, she was smiling from ear to ear.

As the nose of the raft pushed onto the sand, Pebbles hopped out of the raft and ran toward Anlon, Cesar and Sanjay. Pablo angrily yelled at her to stop but she ignored him and shouted, "One of them didn't die! One of the boys! He made it! He survived!"

It took a half hour for Anlon and Cesar to convince Pablo to resume the trip. In the end, the goal was accomplished through a combination of creative prevarications on Cesar's part and Anlon's promise of additional compensation to win the tour guide's agreement.

However, Pablo did extract two additional concessions. For the remainder of the trip, Pebbles would ride in the raft with Pablo. And if she ran off again, whether into the river or jungle, the tour would be cancelled.

Out of earshot of the others, Pablo leaned toward the two men and whispered, "I did not want to alarm you earlier, but the natives watch all who enter the Cutivireni. You cannot see them; they hide in the jungle. But we see the bushes move, sometimes see their footprints on the riverbanks. They occasionally show themselves. I do not know their reaction to your friend's outburst, but I do know they will follow us until we return to the Ene. If she has another outburst, I will not hesitate to turn and leave. I am not risking your people or my men to those savages."

The look on Pablo's face told Anlon the man was deadly serious. "They're that bad?"

"If they feel the slightest bit threatened, they will attack. Not with arrows and spears, but with machetes and machine guns."

"Machine guns?"

"Yes. Favors bestowed by those who grow coca in the jungle in exchange for safe passage."

Anlon and Cesar convened with the other members of their party, sharing the deal reached and the risk associated with continuing on. "As always, we only go forward if we're all in agreement."

Hands on her hips, Pebbles sighed. "Then we're screwed. My skin is tingling. I can feel more coming, A.C. Like, any minute. You guys should head back, but I can't."

"Uh, that's not happening," Anlon said. "If you're staying, I'm staying."

"Me as well," Jennifer said.

Anlon looked to Cesar, Sanjay and Mereau. "Gentlemen? No hard feelings if you want to go back."

Cesar laughed. "I've met my fair share of rebels and machete-wielding natives. These can be no worse than others. I'm staying. Especially if Mereau is willing to aid in our defense."

"You may count on it, my friend." Mereau patted Cesar's shoulder then turned and smiled at Jennifer and Anlon. "We will prevail as we did at Calakmul."

Anlon looked to Sanjay. Despite the doubt evident in the psychologist's eyes, he said, "Do not even think it, Anlon. I am staying here with my patients."

"Patients with an 's'?" Jennifer asked.

"That's right. Pebbles *and* Citali. One cannot find peace without the other."

Mereau turned and walked away. Anlon called to him. "Where are you going?"

"To fetch my backpack. My *Lifintyls*."

"Ah. Gotcha."

Pebbles tugged on Anlon's sleeve. "A.C.?"

"Yeah?"

"You need to tell Pablo what's going to go down. Like right now."

She covered her mouth and backed away. Her eyes rolled back, and she collapsed on the sand.

The man painted in gold looked into Citali's eyes, his brow furrowed, his eyes blinking. *"But, Keeper, I do not understand. The child lives. This is worthy of rejoicing."*

"No! They must not know. No one must know he is alive."

"But some already know."

"Those that know must swear their silence or be silenced. Do you hear me? It is the only way."

"Yes, Keeper."

"The fathers will watch you to make sure you keep your word. They will strike you down and all whom you love if you betray me."

"Yes, Keeper."

"Now, go! Make ready the preparations. Send forth your messenger. Make sure he tells the evil bitch where to find me. The man in gold bowed and ran off. As she watched him go, she whispered, *"She will not leave the jungle alive…and neither will I."*

The villagers gathered around, bowing as Citali walked among them. She kept her eyes on the young girls. Some were too young, others too old.

Will the bitch notice in the dark? No, she will thirst for revenge.

Citali took the burly man by the hand and led him away from the villagers. *"The one with the golden hair. Paint her with the emblems."*

"I will do as you say, Keeper, but please do not ask me to take my own daughter's life."

"If you cannot do it, I will find someone who can."

"Is there no other way? She is young. She is innocent."

Citali squeezed the man's wrist. *"How many generations of your people have enjoyed the blessings of life because of the sacrifice of the fathers?"*

The burly man bowed his head. *"I am sorry, Keeper. I think of my daughter, of myself. Instead, I should think of our people. Of your people. Of those who have come before, and those that will come."*

"It will be quick. She will not suffer."

"No, Keeper. I am her father. I will do it. We will die together."

Anlon tried to calm Pablo. "Look, she's not going anywhere. We've got her. If she tries to run, we're ready this time. She won't cause problems. We just need to wait until she comes out of it. Then, everything will be good."

The tour guide was sweating profusely. He kept turning to look at the opposite side of the river, then back at Pebbles writhing on the ground. "She is upsetting them, I know it. We must go. We must go now."

One of Pablo's men cried out. Anlon and Pablo turned in his direction. The man pointed across the river. There was a clearing fifty yards or so farther down the Citivireni. Anlon saw several men dashing away across the field.

If they were natives, they were the most modern natives Anlon had ever seen. Dressed in oversized T-shirts and long shorts, the six barefoot men had rifles or machine guns slung by straps over their shoulders.

"They go to tell the others," Pablo said. "They will be back with more men. We must go."

"Sorry, Pablo. No can do. If you don't want to stay, take the kayaks but leave us the rafts and the supplies. I'll make sure you're compensated for any loss."

"How can you compensate me if you die?"

"No one will die," Mereau said. "Some might be frightened, but no one will die."

Anlon saw a Sound Stone in Mereau's hands. He raised it to his mouth. The bowl-shaped *Tyl* was pointed at the stand of trees directly across from them.

"What are you going to do, Mereau?" Anlon asked.

He turned and smiled. "Send a message. There are more men still in the bushes."

Before Anlon could stop him, Mereau hummed on the bottom of the bowl. The water in the river roiled. The ground on the far riverbank trembled. The trees shook. Mereau paused, inhaled and blasted a sharp, audible hum against the stone. Trees splintered, their foliage ripped apart as if fed into a wood chipper. The hum lasted for less than five seconds. When Mereau pulled the stone from his lips, what was left of the stand of trees looked like a pile of fallen matchsticks. Out of the corner of his eye, Anlon saw two men scurrying across the field, screaming and waving as they sprinted for cover in the jungle beyond the clearing.

Anlon was afraid to look back at Pablo. He winced and turned to see the wiry man tugging on his bushy beard. Mouth open, he said something inaudible.

Mereau's voice, fierce and demanding, called out. "What did you say?"

Pablo stepped backward and repeated the phrase.

"How do you know these words?" Mereau stomped toward Pablo. "Speak or I shall blow you across the Ene!"

Anlon chased after Mereau. "What's going on? What's the matter?"

Pablo cowered and repeated the words. "May the stars light your way."

The exasperated Mereau turned to Anlon. "He utters a salutation of my people."

From behind, Anlon heard Pebbles' voice. "Until we meet under the same sky."

Spinning around, Anlon saw Pebbles was no longer lying on the sand. Eyes clear, she had awoken from the vision and sat looking at Mereau. Anlon threw his hands up. "Would someone please tell me what the hell is going on?"

"Though they say the words in English, they speak a Munuorian greeting. Well, more of a farewell," Mereau said. He pointed to Pablo. "He says: *may the stars light your way*. Pebbles answers: *until we meet under the same sky*. It was spoken when setting off on a journey to wish a traveler a safe return."

Pebbles stood and said, "It's not just that. It's the exchange Citali had with the man who painted her body before she died. It was sweet, sort of like they were saying goodbye to each other. You know, kind of like, I'll miss you, Keeper. I'll miss you too, gold man."

"Keeper?" Pablo said. "You talk as if it were real. But it is just a fairy tale. Nothing more. Like Ali Baba."

"What is Ali Baba?" Mereau asked.

"It is an ancient folk tale. Ali Baba and the Forty Thieves," Cesar said. "It's about a man who opens a cave with treasure inside by speaking a password. It is a sordid tale, full of deceit and treachery. I can see why Pablo associates it with what we know of Citali's travails."

"How many know the tale of the Keeper?" Mereau asked Pablo.

"Every man, woman and child who has grown up in this valley."

"Tell it to us."

"You seem to know it already."

"In your own words. If you please."

Pablo shrugged. To Anlon, it seemed the man was going to blow off Mereau's request, but instead he sat down on the frame of one of the river rafts and provided a robust description of the legend.

There was a goddess with divine gifts. She used them to ward off evil spirits. The people loved her for it, for the gifts protected the people from harm, protected them from hunger. One day, an evil spirit grew jealous of the love the people showed the goddess and the spirit tried to take the divine gifts. The goddess escaped and hid the gifts, casting a spell over the hiding place. She returned to confront the spirit, but the spirit snuck up from behind and struck her down. The spirit was so pleased to bring despair to the people, she forgot about the divine gifts. When she realized her error, she went back but found the goddess dead.

Before the goddess died, however, she confided in one of the people, telling him where the gifts were hidden and how to break the spell. She implored him to keep the secrets safe until a new goddess came to replace her. The man despaired.

"How will I recognize the new goddess? How can I be sure she is not the evil spirit in disguise?"

"The new one will bear the same emblems as I do."

"But, goddess," the Keeper of Secrets replied, "the spirit has seen you. She knows the emblems you bear."

"Yes, but the spirit does not know the spell. The new one will. You need only speak the first words. If she completes the spell, take her along the river and lead her to the hiding place. She will retrieve that which was hidden, restore blessings upon the people and vanquish the evil spirit."

The man was heartened by the goddess' answer and thanked her. The goddess replied, "Repeat the spell, Keeper, so that I know you hold them in your mind. Say the words, comfort my ears."

"Yes, goddess. I will say to her: may the stars light your way. She will answer: until we meet under the same sky."

The goddess smiled and passed away.

"The Keeper waited but the new one never came," Pablo said. "The people still wait for her. It is said the evil spirit still lurks in the valley, searching for the hiding place of the divine gifts, waiting to intercept the coming of the new one."

"Holy Moly!" said Pebbles. "If that doesn't give you the heebie jeebies, I don't know what will."

Anlon gazed at Cesar. "Have you heard this folktale before?"

"I have not. But that should not surprise you. There are thousands of oral traditions throughout the continent and many more lost to time."

"The men who hide in the jungle, they know the tale too?" Mereau asked.

Pablo nodded. "The old people in the valley, they say the Keeper of Secrets is one of the tribe. They say the hiding place is known to them. They guard it."

"Excuse me?" said Jennifer. "The tribe guards the hiding place? How? It's two hundred fifty kilometers from here."

"What?" Pablo laughed. He motioned his hands toward the tree line. "No. It is somewhere here in the jungle."

"I'm confused," Jennifer said. She turned to Pebbles.

"Don't look at me. I'm confused too," Pebbles said.

"Perhaps there are two different Maerlifs," said Sanjay. "If I recall the journal entry about Citali's deathbed vision correctly, the man with Citali told her that they would keep safe what she had hidden. So, whatever Citali took from the mountaintop, she hid with the dwellers."

"That makes sense," Pebbles said. "It would clear up something that's been gnawing at me."

"What's that?" asked Anlon.

"Well, in the visions, sometimes Citali talks about what was given, and other times she talks about what was hidden. For a while I'd thought they were interchangeable ways of referring to the same stuff, but maybe not. Maybe the *Tyls* were what was given, but what was hidden was something else." Anlon turned to Pablo. "I don't understand something. If the hiding place is here, and the legend includes the spell, why hasn't anyone—" Anlon paused briefly, then said, "Never mind. I answered my own question. The people in the valley know the spell but not the emblems."

"More cleverness." Mereau chuckled and looked at Pebbles. "Remarkable. They have kept the promise. For eighteen hundred years, the jungle dwellers, their descendants, have waited for the one who speaks the words and bears the emblems."

"But, surely, the legend goes back further than that," Cesar said. "Pablo said the goddess told the Keeper of Secrets to take the new one along the river, lead her to the hiding place. Muran knew this phrase when she sent Rashana to visit Citali, which means the goddess and spirit in the tradition are not Citali and Muran."

"Ah, there we disagree, my friend. I suspect Muran was indeed the evil spirit in the legend, even though there was another goddess who predated Citali."

Anlon nodded. "I think Mereau may be right, Cesar. It better explains Muran's sudden shift in attitude toward the oracles in her manifesto. She probably had no idea Citali and her people were descendants of Munuorians that she had tussled with sometime in her past. But someone told her the legend and it opened an old wound."

"Excuse me, gentlemen. May I interrupt?" Sanjay said. "The historical implications are very fascinating, I am sure. But I wonder if further discussion might wait until after Pebbles tells us what she has seen in her latest vision? Especially given Pablo's revelation about a hiding place here in the jungle."

Pebbles bowed. "Thank you, Sanjay. I had two visions, actually. Back to back. And you're not going to believe what Citali did."

"Hold up, Pebbles," Jennifer said. "Question — does either of the visions help us find where Citali hid what was given?"

"Uh, no. They kind of clear up stuff we've already talked about."

"Then the visions can wait until later, too. Sun's getting low in the sky. We need to get moving again and set up camp before it gets dark."

"One moment, please," Mereau said. He turned to Pablo. "Can you and your men go upriver to set up camp for us and then come back with the river rafts to pick us up when all is ready?"

"I don't understand. You wish to stay here? Alone?"

"Just until your men come back with the rafts. With your motors, I would think you could set up camp and return in less time than it would take us slowpokes to paddle upstream."

"It is not a good idea to split up. The tribesmen may come back."

Anlon watched Mereau break into a smile. "I'm counting on it. By the way, do you know their language? Can you communicate with them?"

"Yes."

"Good. That will come in handy."

"What's up your sleeve, Mereau?" asked Anlon.

"I will tell you in a moment." Mereau turned his attention back to Pablo. "Actually, I do need one man to stay behind and go back into town for some paint."

"Paint?" Pablo asked. "Why?"

"The tribesmen expect to see emblems, do they not?"

"Now hold on, Mereau," Anlon said. "What's the deal? What are you concocting?"

"When we go up the river, I think we should send another message. The one who wears the emblems is coming for what was given. It is my hope the dwellers will show us the way."

CHAPTER 24

RETURN OF THE NEW ONES

CUTIVIRENI RIVER
OTISHI NATIONAL PARK, PERU
SEPTEMBER 30

Once the rafts disappeared from view and Alejandro left to procure paint, Pebbles raised her hand. "Uh…point of interest…I don't know the symbols for the emblems."

She had felt the designs being painted on Citali's body in her visions and she recalled glimpses of the symbols painted on the girl at the bonfire, but not full images. Pebbles told the others she assumed the emblems were some of the symbols etched into Citali's necklace, but she did not know which symbols or where they were supposed to be painted on her body.

"I wouldn't be so sure about a connection with the necklace," Anlon said. "The emblems could be related to the Paracas Candelabra. We know from the napkin drawing that the children wore medallions with the symbol. You told us the cave had a mosaic of it outside the Maerlif. You added it to the oasis drawing while you were in a trance. It's obviously an important symbol, even though we don't understand why or what it symbolizes."

"I have to side with Pebbles," said Jennifer. "You guys probably don't remember, but in one of Pebbles' journal entries she wrote that Citali believed she would need the necklace to convince the dwellers of her identity. She was concerned the emblems would not be enough to satisfy them. That suggests to me that the emblems are the symbols from the necklace. By having the original source of the designs with her, Citali thought the dwellers would be less likely to challenge the designs painted on her body."

"It is likely the emblems include both the symbols from the Candelabra as well as those from the necklace," Mereau said.

"Yeah, well, even if that's true, I still don't know which ones were chosen and where they go," Pebbles said. "I know one was painted on Citali's forehead, two on her cheeks, another two on her arms, one on her chest, a couple on her thighs. Kinda, sorta remember one being painted on Citali's tummy when she was on her deathbed, but I might be wrong about that. Point is — there are twelve tiles on the necklace, right? Plus the Candelabra symbol. That makes a total of thirteen symbols. I just don't think there were that many painted on her."

"Cesar, you took a bunch of pictures of the necklace, didn't you?" Anlon asked.

"I did."

"Let's take a look at them and see if any stand out as good candidates."

While Cesar retrieved his cell phone, Pebbles watched Jennifer begin pacing along the riverbank. She looked annoyed. Pebbles called out to her, "Hey, you're gonna dig a new channel if you keep going back and forth. What gives?"

Jennifer paused and turned toward Pebbles. "I don't like this whole idea. It's too risky."

"You mean, guessing about the emblems?"

"Yeah. That, and the fact we're pushing an interaction with the tribe before we know what happened in the rest of Citali's visions." Jennifer looked over at Sanjay. "I'm surprised you haven't said anything. It's gotta be bugging you too."

"I do have some concerns, but I can see Mereau's aim. He hopes to stimulate more visions by going upriver as Citali did."

"See, that's the part that troubles me," said Jennifer. "What happens if we guess the wrong symbols, or Pebbles goes into a trance at the wrong time? Like right in the middle of saying her part of the password. If those dudes are armed and they don't like what they see, it could get ugly quick."

"I will ensure it doesn't get ugly," Mereau said.

"And how do you plan to do that? Another manhood demonstration with the stones?" Jennifer crossed her arms and began tapping her foot. *Oh, boy,* Pebbles thought. *She's about to blow.*

"If need be, yes."

Jennifer shook her head and mumbled something inaudible. Pebbles had seen her like this before. She was not one who liked going into a potentially dangerous situation without a well-thought-out plan *and* a backup. But Mereau's idea was not like that. It was more of a 'let's throw shit against the wall and see what sticks' kind of plan.

"Is no one else but me bothered by the fact Pebbles hasn't seen a single vision of this part of Citali's timeline?" Jennifer said.

"She's seen flashes," said Anlon.

"Yeah, but come on, Anlon. There's a crap ton of important stuff missing from the flashes. All we know from them is Citali was standing up in a boat, holding something heavy above her head. All Pebbles has seen is torchlights on both sides of the river and she said she heard chanting. That's it.

"She hasn't seen Citali speak the words. We don't know if she was alone in the boat or if she was with other people. We don't know what she was holding. Was it the boy who lived? One of the children who died? Was it part of what was given? Was there some sort of ceremony before the greeting was exchanged? Without knowing more, we're really putting Pebbles…and ourselves…at risk."

"What do you suggest then, Jen?" Pebbles asked.

"That we don't try the reenactment until we've been to the waterfall. Somewhere between here and there, you might have more visions that fill in some of the remaining gaps."

"Um…thinking it might be a little late for that," Anlon said. "Look!"

Pebbles turned and looked in the direction where Anlon pointed. Across the river, in the clearing between the stand of trees Mereau had destroyed and the next section of jungle, a large group of men was running toward them waving machine guns and machetes.

"Great. Just great," Jennifer said. She walked up to Mereau. "Looks like we're going to need to defend ourselves. What do you have in your bag of tricks?"

As Mereau opened his mouth to respond, two sounds echoed down the river. The whine of a motor and the rat-tat-tat of gunfire. Pebbles turned to see a river raft come into view. Pablo was in the front, wildly waving at them to flee. With each gunshot, he and the other men in the boat ducked lower and lower.

Pebbles felt a tug on her arm. It was Anlon. He pulled her from the riverbank and said, "Uh…Mereau, this would be a pretty good time for that manhood demonstration."

"I was thinking the same."

Mereau strode to his backpack with Jennifer following close behind. The rest of the group backed away and ducked down. Pebbles saw him pull out the Sound Stone again. Jennifer reached for it but Mereau pulled it away from her and motioned for her to join the rest of the group. Jennifer stood her ground and snapped back at him. He clenched his jaw and dug his hand inside the pack again. He pulled out two cookie-shaped stones, the *Dreylaeks*, and slapped them in Jennifer's hands. Once more, he motioned for her to join Pebbles and the others.

Jennifer ran up to the group and ducked down with them. She stared back toward Mereau and said, "He's effing crazy."

"What's he going to do?" Sanjay asked.

"Watch."

Pebbles saw Mereau break into a sprint toward the riverbank, waving at Pablo to drive his raft past him. Pablo appeared to welcome the request. He revved the motor and sped by, his wake splattering Mereau's jeans and boots. Mereau turned and ran back toward his backpack. For a moment, Pebbles thought he had changed his mind about using the Sound Stone and was going back for something else. But then he turned and dashed for the riverbank again. On the far side of the riverbank, the men running across the clearing began firing their guns. Jennifer splayed onto the sand.

"Get down. Lie flat," she said.

No one debated the command. From her prone position, Pebbles kept her head up, still watching Mereau. Raising the Sound Stone to his lips, he puffed out his cheeks and angled his head toward the sand. A second later, the sand around his feet sprayed in all directions, the ground underneath Pebbles rumbled, Mereau soared over the river.

"What the hell?" mumbled Sanjay.

Pebbles thought he would crash into the pile of fallen trees on the other side, but he raised his lips to the stone again and his flight slowed. The sand on the other bank swirled up. Mereau disappeared from view. When the sand cleared, Mereau stood at the edge of the clearing.

Once again, he raised the bowl-shaped stone to his lips. Into the air flew one of the tribesmen, then another. The area around Pebbles shook with the force of a distant tremblor. A tree on the edge of the clearing was ripped from the ground and rose into the air. It hovered above the clearing for a few seconds and then plummeted from view. There was a loud thud and shards of the tree twirled through the air. When they, too, disappeared from view, all was quiet save for the river's gurgling. No guns. No shouts. No birds chirping. Nothing.

Mereau stood in front of the stunned collection of tribesmen. He lowered the Sound Stone below his chin and said, "Drop your weapons."

Some of the men stepped back. Others flinched. Mereau pulled the stone back against his lips and hummed sharply. The machete in one man's hand trembled and ripped from his grip. Mereau aimed at another but the first disarming did the trick. The others cast down their weapons. Lowering the Sound Stone to his side, he said, "That's better."

Several of the men exchanged glances with each other. A few more edged back. Mereau said, "Any of you speak English?"

They looked at him with a mix of puzzlement and fear. Mereau contemplated uttering the ancient farewell in his native tongue but decided on a different way to communicate with them. He waved his hands to signal the men to step back. The gesture was understood, and the tribesmen retreated. He urged them to retreat some more and then signaled them to stop.

Mereau lowered his head, raised the stone to his lips, and hummed. A strip of Earth ripped up, leaving a dirt line where grass had been. He hummed again and formed another dirt line. As he furrowed other lines, the tribesmen began to chatter amongst themselves. The chatter grew louder as Mereau moved about, adding to the design.

Lost in the process of etching the Candelabra into the soil, Mereau was unaware the men had dropped to their knees until he finished the last flourish of the design. Looking at his handiwork and then at the stunned men, Mereau smiled. "Excellent, gentlemen. Now that's a more appropriate welcome for the one who comes to speak the words."

His smile and tone of voice must have struck the tribesmen as friendly. They smiled back, some of them uttering nervous laughs. Mereau motioned for them to stay put and he backed away. Craning his neck, he shouted across the river.

"Anlon? Pebbles? Anyone?"

A shout came back. It was Anlon. "I'm here. You okay?"

"Yes. All is well. Come across. Everyone. Bring Pablo too."

While he waited for their arrival, Mereau gathered up the strewn weapons and stacked them away from the tribesmen. When the work was finished, he looked toward the jungle, thinking of a plan of action. His eyes drifted to the mountain farther upriver.

There was a rustling of leaves from the direction of the river. Mereau turned to see his wet comrades walking toward him. He smiled and waved. All but Pablo returned the gesture. He looked as if he was heading to his doom.

Mereau watched them take in the scene — the piled weapons, the shattered remains of the tree, the crater formed when Mereau slammed it into the ground, the kneeling tribesmen and the land carving of the Candelabra. Jennifer was the first to speak.

"You are batshit crazy, Mereau."

He laughed. "Is that a compliment?"

"Uh, no."

Sanjay stared at him. "You flew across the river. You tossed men and trees like they were toys."

"Nice artwork," said Pebbles. "Did your new friends do it, or you?"

"It is my creation. They watched. As you can see, it is familiar to them." Mereau turned to Pablo. "Come forward, please. I need your translation assistance."

Pablo glared at Mereau before leveling his angry eyes at the tribesmen. His hand was on the butt of his pistol.

"Hand me your gun, Pablo. This will be a friendly chat."

"They shot at me. They damaged one of my rafts, injured two of my men."

"I am sorry. It is my fault, not theirs. I should have taken your concern about their return more seriously. Now hand me the gun."

"No. They are bloodthirsty. They know only one way."

"I'd do what he says, Pablo," Jennifer said. "You don't want to end up like the tree."

The tour guide grumbled and passed Mereau the gun. He, in turn, handed it to Jennifer. She added it to the weapon pile as Mereau conferred with Pablo. "You said you know their language. Please ask who among them is in charge."

Pablo posed the question and a man on the far right answered. Mereau motioned for him to stand. He was a middle-aged man, paunchy around the middle but otherwise muscular. He eyed Mereau warily as he approached. Mereau turned and invited Pebbles into the small group.

"Ask him his name," Mereau said to Pablo.

After an exchange of words, Pablo said, "Tuka."

Mereau said his own name and bowed. He then placed his hand on Pebbles' shoulder and said to Pablo, "Tell Tuka this woman is the one who speaks the words. The one who has come to claim what was hidden. Tell him her name is Citali."

The mention of the name Citali caused the man's face to twitch, even before Pablo relayed Mereau's message. *As I expected*, thought Mereau. *The tribe even remembers the name of the last true Keeper.* When Pablo finished the translation, Tuka took a step back and bowed to Pebbles. There was a momentary buzz among the other tribesmen. Mereau whispered to Pebbles. "Bow."

She took a step back just as Tuka had done and mimicked his bow. Mereau handed her the Sound Stone. "You are skilled with this, are you not?"

"It's been a while, but, yeah."

"Scatter the weapon pile. Just a brief demonstration to provide Tuka your credentials."

"Okay."

Pebbles turned, crouched slightly and huffed a tone against the base of the bowl-shaped stone. The stack of guns and machetes spiraled away in a chaotic jumble of flying objects that landed fifty yards away. The tribesmen chattered. Tuka bowed again.

Mereau asked, "Can you lift an object? Say, a tree stump?"

"Got an idea better than that." Pebbles smiled and crooked a finger at Jennifer. "Front and center."

"Uh…"

"Come on. Don't be bashful. After all, I *am* the one who speaks the words and we *do* need to convince our friends here to help us." Pebbles smiled at Tuka.

Jennifer sighed and walked up. "When do I get to be the priestess?"

"Next time there's a restless spirit around looking for someone's mind to invade. Now, hush and stand still. I haven't done this in over a year."

"Yeah, I know. That's what I'm worried about." Jennifer closed her eyes and widened her stance. "Remember, *Citali*, focus on my center of gravity. Just in case you don't remember, it's down here near my belly button, not up near my boobs."

Pebbles laughed. "Look, I apologized for that, like twenty times already."

"Uh huh, that's because you missed twenty times."

"Shh…I need to concentrate."

Mereau stood behind Pebbles and watched her aim the bowl at Jennifer's abdomen. She began to hum, low and steady. Jennifer's shirt and cargo pants rippled. Pebbles increased the power of her hum and Jennifer's feet lifted off the ground. She circled her arms as if trying to balance on an invisible ledge. Pebbles blew harder and Jennifer rose above the heads of those standing. Pebbles moved to the left while holding Jennifer captive in the sound waves from the *Tyl*. Jennifer moved left in the air as well. Her face turning red, Pebbles reduced the intensity of her humming and Jennifer drifted back down. When she stumbled onto the ground, Pebbles pulled the stone from her mouth and turned back to Tuka. The tribesman, mouth agape, bowed once more, retreated two additional steps and knelt.

Mereau put an arm around Jennifer. "As a reward for your courage, I will defer to your earlier instincts."

"Meaning what?"

He stepped away and addressed Pablo. "Tell Tuka the one who speaks the words, the stone blower, the one who comes to claim what was hidden, will visit the waterfall upriver. Tell Tuka we will camp near the falls. None in our group should be harassed in any way."

The translation yielded brisk head nods and a one-word reply from Tuka.

"He agrees," said Pablo.

"Excellent. Later tonight, after the one who speaks the words visits the waterfall, she will go to see the Keeper. Ask Tuka to light her way."

Outside the tent, Pebbles could hear Pablo's men conversing while they ate their dinner. Even though she did not understand their words, she could tell from the slow-paced speech and occasional dramatic inflections that they were sharing stories by the campfire. No doubt one of the stories was about Mereau's earlier theatrics and possibly another was about Pebbles' levitation of Jennifer.

The main event, however, seemed to be a retelling of the legend Pablo had shared earlier. She guessed this because the man speaking alternated between male and female voices and he spoke at a low volume, as if trying to avoid arousing the attention of others outside of their group.

She wondered if the purpose of the retelling was to prepare the men for what was to come. Pebbles stared up at the tent ceiling and murmured, "How about preparing me too?"

Would she be able to summon Citali? If Citali did appear, would she show Pebbles the emblems? If she did not appear, were there more visions in store? And would they reveal more deceptions on Citali's part?

Pebbles still had not shared the details of her last two visions with anyone. Partly because other events had overshadowed the need to discuss them, but partly because Pebbles struggled to come to grips with what Citali had shown her.

Sanjay had been so adamant about his belief that the bonfire vision was a dream instead of a memory. He had argued the dream's symbolism indicated Citali's mind was trying to cope with the knowledge she had killed her own children. Pebbles had found it hard to deny Sanjay's instincts, especially when she stopped to consider how odd many of the visions had seemed.

The latest visions, however, showed Pebbles that Sanjay was only partially right. He was correct that the bonfire vision was definitely an attempt on Citali's part to rationalize her actions. But he was wrong about it being a dream. It was not. It was a memory in which Citali changed the facts of what really happened to hide her culpability. She had painted herself as a well-meaning victim rather than a calculating puppet master whose grand plan had backfired.

That realization had caused Pebbles to retreat to her own tent instead of joining Anlon and the others in the dining tent. It caused her to now lie on the cot, close her eyes and reevaluate the rest of Citali's visions while asking herself a question. Were the visions a mix of memories and symbolic dreams as the others supposed, or were they *all* memories laden with lies?

A voice penetrated her thoughts. Anlon's voice. Pebbles' eyes opened and she looked around. She saw Anlon peering at her through the entrance flap of the tent.

"Sorry to wake you," he said.

"No problem. I wasn't sleeping. Just thinking with my eyes closed." She shook her head to clear her mind and became aware of a commotion outside the tent. "What's going on out there?"

"Tuka just showed up."

Pebbles sat up. "Really? Why?"

"I'm not sure. He's brought a bunch of his people. Mereau's with him now." Anlon reached out his hand. "Come on, let's find out what's going on."

"No. Not yet." Pebbles patted her hand on the cot. "Sit with me. I need to talk with you about the visions I had earlier today."

As Anlon lowered onto the cot, he said, "I guess we did kinda skip over them. Sorry about that."

"It's all right. There was a lot going on," Pebbles said. "And I didn't know what to make of the visions when they first happened anyway. But now that I've had a chance to think about them, I'm starting to get a *real* bad feeling about Citali."

"More deceptions?"

"Bingo. A *lot* more." Pebbles described her latest visions in detail and then said, "Citali wasn't a helpless bystander at the bonfire. That was BS. She's the one who pulled all the strings. So, it got me thinking about all the other visions. And the more I've thought about them, the more convinced I am that a lot of the stuff that happened in the other visions was BS too. The question I've been struggling with is whether the BS was intentional or not. I'm trying to give Citali the benefit of the doubt, but it's hard to believe the deceptions are innocent."

"What do you mean? Give me an example."

Pebbles massaged her wrists as she answered. "Let's start with the children. Citali never talked about them or showed them in any of the early visions I had. That's kinda weird, don't you think? I mean, I'm not a mom, but, if I was, and I felt my kids were at risk, they'd be on my mind all the time."

"Absolutely," said Anlon. "But is it really true they weren't on her mind? Couldn't the amorphous objects in her bag have been proxies for her children? If Sanjay were here, he would probably say Citali was in so much pain about their deaths, she turned them into inanimate objects in her visions."

"Yeah, I guess. But the thing is, as I was thinking back through all the visions, I realized she *did* show them to me, but I missed it. It was in the Rashana vision. Before Rashana arrived, Citali had been looking out the window as a group of women with children walked by. A few of the kids — not all of them — made a gesture to Citali, touching their hands to their heads. Citali smiled and touched her head in return. Sort of blowing kisses to each other. I'm not a hundred percent certain, but I think her kids might have been the ones who touched their heads."

"Hmm…why is that significant?" Anlon asked.

"I don't know that it is," Pebbles said, "only it seems Citali went out of her way to hide the fact she had kids in other visions and now that part of the Rashana vision comes across like a slip-up. Just like the whole *new ones* thing. I'd always assumed it meant the children were the new generation of oracles."

Anlon nodded. "But then Pablo used the same term to describe the new goddess in the legend. *The new one will bear the emblems...*"

Pebbles halted her wrist-rubbing and gripped Anlon's knee. "Exactly. It could be coincidental, but if it's not, it kinda implies Citali believed her children had a right to claim what was hidden, ergo..."

She watched a frown form on Anlon's face. She waited for him to say, "Ergo, what?" But then the frown began to fade and Anlon said, "Ergo, Citali believed *she* had a right to claim what was hidden."

Tapping her hands on the wood frame of the cot, Pebbles said, "Exactly. Where did she get the Sound Stone, A.C.? The one she used to open the Maerlif? It wasn't in her bag when she left Wari. I saw what she put in the bag. And how did she know how to use the Sound Stone? Same with the Flash Stone. They're not the kinds of weapons you can just pick up and use the way she used them."

Anlon shrugged. "Maybe it was like you said earlier — the *Tyls* were what was given. Maybe the *Tyls* were passed from Keeper to Keeper or shared among the Seers."

"But why not show me that? Why hide it?"

"Maybe she didn't trust you earlier, but now she does. Remember how you said she called you a sorceress at the oasis? And didn't she say she thought you were Muran's agent?"

"She did, but I don't think it is as innocent as that."

Pebbles stood and walked toward the tent flap.

"Hey, where are you going?" asked Anlon.

"To find Sanjay. I want to talk to him about amnesia."

Outside the tent, Pebbles saw a large group of people at the far end of the campsite. Among the mix of Tuka's tribespeople and Pablo's men, she spotted Mereau gesturing to Tuka with Pablo acting as interpreter. Off to the side, Jennifer, Sanjay and Cesar watched the proceedings.

As Pebbles headed toward Sanjay, Anlon came up beside her. "Amnesia? You think Citali hid the stones from you because she had amnesia?"

Picking up the pace of her strides, Pebbles kept her eyes on Sanjay. "No."

"Then, I don't understand."

When Pebbles and Anlon were within ten feet of the group, heads began to turn their way. The tribespeople began to chatter, several of them bowed toward Pebbles. Jennifer intercepted Pebbles and pulled her aside.

"Good timing," Jennifer said. "They're just about ready to start."

"Start what?" Pebbles asked as Anlon joined them.

"Tuka's come to show you the way to the hiding place."

"What? Tonight?" Anlon said. "I thought Mereau told Tuka we were going to visit the waterfall first and then come see him later. Later as in tomorrow."

Jennifer shrugged. "I guess Tuka misinterpreted what Pablo relayed from Mereau."

"But I'm not ready. I don't know what emblems to wear," Pebbles said.

"Apparently, that won't be a problem," Jennifer said.

Pebbles frowned. "What's that supposed to mean?"

Jennifer reached out her hand. "You'll see. Come on, let's go chat with Mereau. He'll fill you in."

"No. Not right now. I have to chat with Sanjay first. I'll catch up with you guys in a few minutes." Pebbles pushed past Jennifer and walked up to Sanjay. Taking him by the hand, she said, "Come with me. We need to talk."

Moments later, Pebbles and Sanjay were standing alone by the river. In the distance, she could see torchlights illuminating a path up the dark slope of the mountain beyond the campsite.

"Sanjay, do you remember our conversation back on *Sol Seaker*, about amnesia?"

"Yes."

"You said my visions could be memories I don't recall because the original pathways to the memories might have been disrupted due to my coma. You gave the example about forgetting a birthday party because the pathway to the memory of a favorite gift was lost. Do you remember that?"

"Yes. Why?"

"The visions I had earlier today were a lot like the one I had in Churcampa about Citali destroying the lake. They weren't replays of my recurring visions. They were new visions that contradicted things Citali had shown me before." Pebbles described the scene with the gold-painted man about the messenger and the scene that appeared to be a prelude to the bonfire vision, then said, "If Citali's memories found their way to a damaged part of my brain, I'm wondering if the reason I'm seeing contradictions now is because my brain is making new connections to Citali's memories."

"Sort of like your example about the birthday party. You said a damaged brain might eventually connect new pathways to the birthday party memory by using different cues related to the memory other than the favorite gift — kids singing happy birthday, tasting a birthday cake. Well, I've had a whole bunch of new cues since Jen made the connection between my flicker sketch and the bird carving."

Head lowered, Sanjay massaged his neck. "You are thinking Citali's original visions were influenced by your amnesia."

"Not just my amnesia. Citali's too."

Sanjay frowned. "I am not sure what you mean. I can see how amnesia on your part might have influenced the visions. It may, in fact, explain why the visions started out as nightmares. Your mind could not make sense of the bits and pieces of Citali's memories it encountered as it rewired around the damaged areas of your brain and modified the memories into dreams that made sense to your unconscious mind. But I have a harder time imagining how amnesia in Citali is—"

Pebbles interrupted. "Sanjay, the details in the visions I'm tapping into now are outright contradictions to details in the original visions, and *all* of the contradictions seem to be about things Citali said or did, and they *all* seem to show an ugly side of Citali."

For a short stretch, Sanjay did not answer. He just stared into the blackness across the river. Finally, he said, "You think Citali's original visions were selective memories."

"That's what it seems like to me," Pebbles said. "She was covering her tracks, mentally, to hide unseemly details she didn't want to think about, things she didn't want to remember. But in the process of my brain rewiring around damaged areas, it's found new pathways to Citali's real memories."

"Because your mind has encountered new memory cues."

"Exactly."

Sanjay turned to look at Pebbles. "Very interesting…You may be right. What you describe about Citali is analogous to pathological lying behavior. It does happen in some PTSD sufferers. They cannot cope with memories of their trauma, so they literally concoct fake memories out of whole cloth.

"I recall a patient of mine who crashed his car in a moment of road rage. His family was in the car with him and they all died in the accident. He refused to accept what had happened. He told everyone his family was alive and well, just away on vacation. He made up grand stories of where they were, the activities they were enjoying. He would pull out family albums showing pictures of old vacations to prove his stories. For years and years, the lies went on, growing more and more elaborate over time."

Sanjay paused and looked away from Pebbles. She watched his eyes move back and forth as if searching for answers in the night sky. While maintaining his gaze into the heavens, he said, "You know, it may explain why the visions diminished for a period of time, and why you see only flashes of others. Citali realized at some point she could not control what you saw in the visions. It may be why you have had difficulty summoning her to a sanctuary like the oasis since we left *Sol Seaker*."

Pebbles had not considered that possibility, but now Sanjay had mentioned it, there did seem to be a correlation to Citali's withdrawal and the spate of recent contradictory memories. Pebbles mumbled, "She's afraid I might discover the truth."

Moments later, Anlon walked up. "Hey, Tuka and his people are getting restless. I think you need to come over and pay your respects."

"Oh, okay. Sorry. We're pretty much finished anyway," Pebbles said. She turned to Sanjay. "Thank you. That was super helpful."

When the three of them rejoined the group, Tuka and Mereau were standing in front of the contingent of torch-bearing tribesmen and tribeswomen. Both the men and women were bare-chested, wearing only ceremonial skirts around their waists. Tuka was painted with gold symbols.

Pebbles felt Anlon's hand on her shoulder, then his whispered voice in her ear. "Looks like Tuka's the Keeper."

"Kinda figured that from the paint," she whispered back. "What do we do? Just paint the same designs on me?"

"No. You don't wear any paint," Mereau said.

"But the legend says the new one has to wear the emblems and speak the words," said Pebbles.

"Mistranslation," Mereau said. "The new one has to *bear* emblems... present them...which apparently you and I did during our Sound Stone demonstrations...though *you* have to do it again for real during the ritual."

"Ritual? You mean when I speak the words?"

"It's a bit more elaborate than that," Jennifer said. "I don't think you're going to be fired up about it."

Jennifer leaned closer and began to whisper the details of the ritual in her ear. Pebbles' eyes widened. She pulled away and turned to face her. "I have to do what?"

CHAPTER 25

RAGING SOUL

CATARATAS LAS TRES HERMANAS (THREE SISTERS FALLS)
OTISHI NATIONAL PARK, PERU
SEPTEMBER 30

The tribespeople lining the way chanted in unison, repeating the same mantra over and over again as Tuka escorted Pebbles up the mountain beside the Three Sisters Falls. During the first leg of the hike, Anlon and the others had been allowed to walk with her, and it was then that Pablo had translated the pledge for them:

New ones will come by water. They will bear the emblems. Say the words to them. If they answer true, light their way to the place of hiding. Return to them what is theirs and they will honor the people, filling their bowls, protecting them from evil and teaching them anew.

But once they reached the spot where the last of the three falls splashed into the stream that fed into the Cutivireni, only Pebbles was allowed to go forward with Tuka.

The trail was steep and slippery, and Pebbles had to stop several times to catch her breath. The spry Tuka, he of the generous belly, showed no sign of weariness. Each time she stopped, he patiently waited and joined in with the chanting.

Pebbles longed to ask how much farther they had to hike, but she doubted Tuka would have understood her question. In any event, she could now tell for herself. Up above, call it a hundred yards away, the torchlit trail ended. Pebbles girded herself for the baptism-like ritual and wondered if seeing the pool up close would trigger new visions.

Would Citali finally come clean or would there be more deceptions? Pebbles thought of the vision where Citali discovered the wreckage of the boat that had carried her children. The limp, mud-caked boy the man brought to Citali had not looked alive to Pebbles. Was the sudden revelation the child was alive an instance of wishful thinking on Citali's part? A white lie to lessen her sense of guilt? Or had Citali planted the idea of the surviving child to justify to Pebbles her plot to trap and kill Muran? As Pebbles trudged up the mountain, she became convinced it was the latter.

Citali had wanted Pebbles to believe she had a noble motive to sacrifice the villagers — to protect her son, the last of the Munuorian blood line — so she fabricated his survival. But her real motives were about vengeance and desperation more than anything noble.

This realization helped Pebbles to finally arrange the jungle visions in an order that made sense. And the laced-together visions gave Pebbles a clear picture of Citali's plan after discovering the boat wreckage.

Once she knew for sure her children were dead, Citali sent a messenger to Muran. While Pebbles did not know the content of the message, she inferred from the conversation between Citali and the gold-painted man that it told Muran all the children were dead, and that the distraught Citali was hiding in the jungle village.

There, Citali had laid a trap. She selected a girl from the village who, in the glow of the bonfire, she hoped Muran would believe was Citali. Sobbing, on her knees, the girl had played her part beautifully.

Pebbles imagined Muran must have been stunned to see the burly man spear the girl and chuck her into the fire. Pebbles also imagined Muran must have realized at that moment she had been hoodwinked. Enter Citali with her shout from the edge of the forest.

"I will eat your heart out."

Oh, that must have really popped some veins in Muran's neck, Pebbles thought. Seething at Citali's deception, Muran and her soldiers charged after Citali, chasing her through the woods until they caught up with Citali at the riverbank. Pebbles did not know how much of the vision of the attack on Citali at the riverbank was real or fabricated, but somehow Citali escaped and made it across the river and into a clearing…the same clearing, Pebbles suspected, where Mereau had confronted the tribesmen earlier in the day…the same clearing where Muran took Citali's life.

Someone lit the forest surrounding the clearing, trapping Muran, her soldiers, Citali and some of the villagers inside. Pebbles assumed it must have been part of Citali's trap, given the flaming arrows that pierced Muran later in the vision. Citali had known going in that she was going to die; she had said so in the vision after sending off the message to Muran. But Citali had expected Muran to die with her. Only the trap had not played out as she planned. And Citali never knew what happened to Muran after the evil bitch stabbed her in the back and swiped her necklace. She never knew what happened to the relics she had been charged to protect…

Before Pebbles knew it, she and Tuka crested the small plateau where the water from the second falls collected in a pool. Torches had been set around the perimeter of the small pond, making it easy for Pebbles to spot the notch where water emptied and formed the third section of the waterfall. She reminded herself to stay clear of that area so as not to go over the edge.

Looking up at the falls above and then back down at the pool by her feet, Pebbles thought of the mountaintop waterfall near Churcampa and the waterless crater below it. Pebbles closed her eyes and tried to summon Citali.

I'm here. I've come all this way.

But inside, she felt no dizziness, no tingling and no memories flickered in her mind. Pebbles knelt down and listened to the sound of the waterfall. She inhaled the aromas of the surrounding foliage and dipped her fingers into the icy pond.

No more hiding. No more trickery. No more lies. Show yourself.

Still nothing. So, Pebbles stood and faced Tuka. She took a deep breath and unslung her backpack. Placing it on the ground by the pond, she unzipped her jacket and then untied her boots. Next to come off was her shirt. Followed by her pants.

When she removed the last of her underclothes, she dipped her toe in the pond. The image of the napkin drawing filled her head. *Was it as cold,* she wondered, *when you brought the children here?*

Did you have them practice drawing the Candelabra in the dirt too? Were their squiggles better than the ones you added to my oasis drawing? Did they know what you were going to do, Citali? Or did you lie to them like you lied to me?

Pebbles slipped into the pond. Shivering, she disappeared under the surface, her hands sliding down the curved surface of the bowl-shaped wall. Images flashed through her mind.

…standing on the prow of a boat…a torchlit river…chanting…something heavy lifted above her head…looking up…the limp body of a mud-covered child…

Don't try that with me, Citali. You're not the victim. You caused it all to happen. You tried to lure the evil bitch into a confrontation. It was a fight you never had a chance of winning.

Other images raced by…Rashana holding Nonali's head…smoke in the air near Wari…struggling for the knife…knocking Muran's mask off…

All on you, Citali, and you know it.

Cold invaded deep into Pebbles' bones. Her body began to spasm as she sank into darkness. She heard the water ripple. A warm hand wrapped around her wrist.

Is that you, Citali? Are you going to save me? Or hold me under?

The hand squeezed and then pulled. Pebbles, almost completely numb, felt her body rise. When she broke the surface, she looked up to see Tuka's concerned face. He wrapped his arms underneath hers and pulled her from the pond — a symbolization of a new one arising from the water.

Tuka held her against his warm body. He spoke to her as if comforting a child. He cleared water from her eyes and covered her in a cloth.

This is how it should have happened, Citali. But it didn't happen this way, did it? Your son didn't survive. You made it up. You killed them all. My friend, Sanjay, says I shouldn't force you to own up to what you did, but I'm tired of you toying with my mind. So, own it, coward.

Pebbles tucked her body into a ball. Tuka squeezed her tight. Though her vision was blurry, she could make out the dark blob that was her backpack. Reaching her arm out from beneath the cloth cover, she tried to grab the bag. On her third try, with Tuka's help, she succeeded.

Her hand shook so badly she could not find the open pocket. She felt fingers tenderly wrap around her wrist and guide her hand inside the pack. Her fingers brushed up against the scratchy surface of the bowl. Pebbles tried to pinch the Sound Stone in her hand, but it slipped free. She started to cry. Though her body was frozen, it burned like it was on fire.

A hand smoothed her hair. Tuka spoke softly in her ear. Pebbles tried to reply but her jaw wouldn't move. She clenched her hand inside the pack and cursed Citali.

Coward! Murderer! Own it!

She opened her hand and grasped hold of the *Tyl*. Her arm cramped as she tried to pull the stone from the pack. With a muffled groan, she hoisted it free. It slipped from her grip and clattered on the edge of the pond. She saw Tuka's hand catch hold of it before it fell into the water. He guided it to Pebbles' chest and closed her arms around it.

Suddenly, the weight and warmth of his body was gone. Pebbles fell over, the Sound Stone clutched to her chest. She looked up to see Tuka raising his hands to the black sky, acting out his part of the spell.

May the stars light your way.

Crawling onto her knees, Pebbles held up the Sound Stone toward Tuka to perform her parts of the ceremony — presenting the emblem, the Sound Stone, and speaking her part of the spell. Without the strength to stand, she tried to speak the words. Nothing would come. Tuka smiled and pulled her up. He wrapped his arms around her and held her body against his, Tuka's way of helping Pebbles act out the word she was supposed to speak.

Until we meet under the same sky.

It was not until that moment that Pebbles understood the purpose of the ritual. When Jennifer had whispered it to her at the campsite, she had thought it was simply a primitive reenactment of the instructions given to the Keeper in the goddess-evil-spirit legend. But Pebbles now realized it went back further than that. All the way to the day of darkness. It was intended to be a visceral reminder to the new one of the suffering of the people who survived the passing of the asteroid, and the solemn obligation of the new one to lend aid, to comfort the weak and weary.

That's where you went wrong, Citali. You saw yourself as the new goddess instead of the Keeper. And you decided to kill the evil spirit instead of protecting the weak. But, instead, you led the weak to their deaths.

Dizziness overtook Pebbles and all went dark.

Thunder and lightning. Pounding rain. Through the deluge, Pebbles saw Citali. She was atop a masked figure, snarling as she squeezed the figure's neck.

Don't try that, Citali. I know what she did to me. I get how evil she was. It doesn't make what you did right.

Citali pulled her hands from the figure's neck and slapped the mask from her face. Pebbles felt the blow and looked up to see Citali straddling her, knife in hand. Snarling again, Citali yelled, *"Do you? Do you know what she did to my people? I will show you."*

She plunged the knife into Pebbles, over and over again. Each strike felt like a laser piercing clear through her body. Pebbles flailed her arms to knock the knife away, but she was too slow. Blood spattered her eyes. Citali screamed uncontrollably as she stabbed and stabbed. Citali paused the onslaught and grabbed Pebbles' head with her bloody hands. Leaning close to Pebbles' ears, she railed.

"She cut the head off my sister. She burned my city. My brother's too. She was evil. She had to die."

Pebbles yanked Citali's hands away. She wiped the blood from her eyes and pushed Citali off. Rising to her feet, Pebbles looked down at her body. There were no wounds. Citali, however, was a blood-soaked mess. Pebbles spoke to her.

"What did you do to anger her, Citali? Was it the volcano? Did you or your sister know it was going to blow? Did you purposely not warn her?"

"You know nothing."

"I know enough. No matter how many ways you tried to hide the truth, some squeaked through. And the more I've thought about the visions you've shown me, the more truth…and lies…I've noticed. For example, there were no invaders at the temple. You killed the girl who warmed your bed your-

self and blamed it on imaginary assassins. You needed a reason to justify leaving the city before it was overrun."

"Lies."

"Don't think so. You know how I know? You showed me the items you put into your bag before you left your bedchamber, Citali. There was no knife. But, suddenly, there you are in the dark hall near the dead body of the girl and you pull a knife from your bag to defend yourself. That's not the only lie in that vision, Citali. There are others. I should have noticed them right away, but I never stopped to consider the possibility you were intentionally deceiving me. Want another example?"

Pebbles conjured the image of the Flash Stone.

"Where did you learn to use the Tuliskaera, Citali? No one could have done what you did to the lake without a helluva lot of practice. Which means you had the stone long before you used it on the lake. You didn't pluck it from the rubble of the Maerlif right before using it."

A fresh cycle of images flashed through Pebbles' mind…standing on the mountain in the dark…a beam shooting down toward the lake… more beams, one strafing dunes in the desert, another slicing furrows into a hillside, a third cutting across the path of a river…

"That was a no-no, Citali. You were the Keeper. You were supposed to guard what was given and what was hidden until new ones arrived. You weren't supposed to use the Tyls yourself. I'm right, aren't I? The Tyls were what was given. You were supposed to turn them over to someone who knew how to use them."

"Bah. What do you know of it? The evil bitch had Tyls. She used them to take many lands, kill many people. She used a Tuliskaera to crack open the volcano to intimidate Nonali's city into submission."

"So, you were just defending yourself, is that it?"

"What else was I to do?"

The revelation about Muran stimulating a volcanic eruption puzzled Pebbles. If they were both talking about the same eruption, it was the one that wiped out the settlements of La Tolita, the culture Cesar believed Muran had ruled during the time period when Citali lived in Paracas. Who would wipe out their own city to intimidate another city?

Then she remembered. La Tolita had not been destroyed by the volcano directly. Cesar had said the lava flow had changed the course of a river and the resulting flood leveled the settlement. The image of a beam cutting across a river filled Pebbles' mind again.

"So that's what started this string of tragedies. You moved the river. You destroyed her city to send a message. Back off from Nonali's city. Did Nonali know what you did?"

Defiance etched on her face, Citali said nothing.

"I'll take that as a no. You didn't count on the masked lady surviving the flood, did you? Actually, I'll take that back. You didn't care. You'd decimated her population, her army, with the flood. You figured she would be too weak to defeat Nonali's city. But she did. She sacked it and cut off Nonali's head."

Another realization pinged Pebbles' brain. Muran had not known about the connection between the oracles and the Munuorians until she saw the cuts in the ground that changed the river's course. As soon as she saw them, she knew the flood had not been a natural disaster...it had been sabotage. And Muran knew exactly what weapon had raked the cuts.

"No wonder you were so stunned by Rashana's message. Not just seeing Nonali's head, but also hearing Rashana reference the legend."

Rashana's message told Citali that Nonali had been compelled, likely in a very unpleasant way, to reveal Citali was the one who had access to the *Tyls*. From that information, Muran would have surmised Citali had been the one who moved the river. With that conclusion reached, Muran headed Citali's way, not only to exact revenge on Citali and her city, but also to take possession of the *Tyls*.

Pebbles recalled Mereau and Cesar discussing the goddess-evil-spirit legend, how it appeared to pre-date Citali but not Muran. She then thought of Citali's anger-filled comments from earlier in their conversation. *Do you know what she did to my people?* Citali was not talking about the people of her own city or those of her siblings; she was talking about her ancestors.

"When she forced your sister to talk, and Nonali told her the legend, the masked lady recognized it, didn't she?"

Citali seethed, bloody fists clenched by her sides.

The three Seers must have known for some time that the masked lady of La Tolita was the re-embodiment of the evil spirit that had killed the goddess in the legend — their ancestor — but they did not act against her. Pebbles could understand why. They were no match for Muran. They were not a collection of bloodthirsty warriors. They were mystics, guardians of a secret. So, they kept quiet, kept their distance and turned a blind eye toward Muran's conquests...until Muran directed her attention to Nonali's city.

Pebbles felt a pang of sympathy for the Seers' predicament. If they did nothing, Muran was sure to eventually overrun their cities. Even if they fought back using conventional means, they knew they were outmatched and knew their cities would fall. And usually, conquerors were not keen on letting deposed leaders stick around...especially beloved leaders with mystical powers. No, those kinds of leaders ended up with their heads on spikes at the city gates.

So, really, what Citali had done was hasten what she had viewed as an unavoidable conflict. And in making that choice, she had decided to even the odds by turning from Keeper to wielder of what was given...a new goddess. But Pebbles did not think it was a choice Citali made in the moment. She had made her decision to fight Muran long before Muran harassed Nonali's city.

"Your brother and sister rejected the idea of taking the fight to the evil spirit, didn't they?"

"More lies!"

"They wanted you to honor the pledge. They wanted you to protect what was given and what was hidden. But you couldn't do it."

As Citali trembled, a pool of blood spread around her feet.

"Come on, Citali. There's no point in trying to hide the truth any longer. I know what happened. I've seen through your lies."

The blood coating Citali's body began to turn black. Pebbles saw a burst of new visions...the entry stone of a Maerlif...a chamber filled with relics...a catacomb-like crypt...skeletons draped with cloaks of crimson and gold...hands opening a chest of *Lifintyls*...a trail of switchbacks... walking along a ledge...slipping into a cave, a torch lighting the way down a dark tunnel...a hand placing a bulging bag in a cranny of rock...

"You weren't a helpless observer at the bonfire, Citali. You set the whole thing up. You tried to trap the masked lady, but it didn't work. By the time

you came upon your dead children — yes, Citali, don't look surprised, I know none of them survived — by the time you found their bodies, you knew the masked lady had survived your second attempt to drown her.

"*So, you sent one of your men to be captured. You fed him the words he was to say. You told him to tell her where you were hiding. You knew she had to be incredibly angry, mad enough that she would come after you.*"

Citali's body began to fade into a mist. Pebbles rushed forward and grabbed her arm.

"*Nice try. You're here to the end. You're going to listen to me and face up to what you did.*"

Pebbles felt Citali try to pull away.

"*You stood in the bushes and watched her butcher the dwellers. You watched a man devoted to you kill his own daughter before he died himself. And then you yelled at the masked lady and ran. In your vision, you make it seem like you were afraid as you ran through the forest. Men with torches bearing down upon you. But I don't think you were afraid at all. You knew what was waiting in the jungle on the other side of the river.*

"*You let them catch you, tear your clothes off. You knew they wouldn't kill you. That was reserved for the masked lady. She's the one who tried to suffocate you in the mud. And then the arrows let loose, and the men you had in hiding lit the jungle in front and behind. You'd trapped her. In the confusion, you slipped away but you didn't make it far.*"

Citali's tugging waned. Through the mist, she saw Citali bow her head.

"*She caught up to you, took your necklace and killed you with her knife. You died with her mask in your hand. There was no ride down a torchlit river. You were not comforted on your deathbed. You received no promises that what was hidden was safe.*

Pebbles could feel Citali's body jerk as she sobbed.

"*You died not knowing if the evil bitch found the Maerlif, without knowing whether your children were laid to rest properly. Worst of all, you died without a chance to say to your children and the other people you hurt — your brother and sister, the people of your and their cities, the people who lived along the rivers who lost their lives in the flood, the dwellers and the ancestors you sought to avenge — 'I'm sorry, I didn't mean for things to work out this way.'*"

The hand slid from Pebbles' grip. Citali's body spread out into a pool of black.

"I can't forgive you, Citali. It's not my place. But I can help you learn whether the Maerlif is intact and whether your children lie among the long line of past Keepers buried inside."

The inky pool faded into mist.

Through the mist, Pebbles heard the distant sound of cascading water. As the sound grew louder, she detected the scent of flowers and felt a warm breeze pass over her body. Colors invaded the mist, shapes formed and soon Pebbles looked upon the pool at the base of the waterfall. The sun was shining bright and a symphony of bird calls echoed in the surrounding trees. Sitting on a rock by the pool was a gray-haired man dressed in a crimson tunic trimmed with gold. His eyes focused on a young, bare-shouldered woman in the water. He spoke to her.

"In accepting this responsibility, child, you will face many temptations, but you must never give in to them. The Tyls can bring you power and riches, but they can also eat your heart. They can fell mountainsides and part waters, but they can blacken your soul. They can right many injustices and protect, but they can defile and usurp with equal ease."

"Yes, father of fathers, I will honor the pledge."

"Your voice is strong, young Citali, but I do not feel the same conviction in your gensae. Your mind and voice should speak as one."

Citali lowered her head and sighed.

"Unburden your mind, child. Tell me what troubles you."

Citali looked up at the man and said, *"Many Keepers have passed, and still no new ones like you have come. Meanwhile, people starve. They labor to survive. They suffer from the lash of oppressors. The Tyls could do much to ease these difficulties, but instead they gather dust in this dark hole. Your wisdom and the wisdom of your brothers and sisters could bring relief and hope, but your minds stay hidden in stone, resting atop lifeless bones."*

The man replied softly. *"Yet, for all of our wisdom, all of our Tyls, we could not overcome the Betrayer, the taker of souls. Our gensae was too weak. And the gensae of our line has steadily weakened over the long march of time.*" He paused and smiled at Citali. "*But one day, my child, a new one will arrive with gensae strong enough to defeat the most evil of spirits.*"

"*But, first father, what if they never come? What if the taker of souls rises again? What then?*"

"*You must keep this place a secret at all costs, just as the Keepers who preceded you pledged to me. Even if it means your death. If the Betrayer finds this place, she will destroy all that is in it. Then there will be nothing left to aid new ones that come, and no one left who can stop her. The suffering of the people will know no end. Do you understand?*"

Citali nodded.

"*Then arise from the water, Citali, Keeper of Secrets, and accept that which is given to you as a reminder of your oath.*"

In his hand, he held out a necklace.

The scene began to fade from Pebbles' mind until there was only a faint glow in the darkness. In the dim light, Pebbles saw Citali return a *Sinethal* to the chest of a skeleton draped in crimson and gold. From his palm of bones, she picked up a necklace, clasped it around her neck and once again disappeared into the mist.

CHAPTER 26

UNDER THE SAME SKY

CATARATAS LAS TRES HERMANAS (THREE SISTERS FALLS)
OTISHI NATIONAL PARK, PERU
SEPTEMBER 30

When the mist inside her mind cleared, Pebbles was once again being held. This time, by Anlon. She looked around and saw the rest of her friends, including Pablo and her new friend, Tuka. Anlon squeezed tighter. "Hey there. You okay? You're shivering like crazy."

She nodded. "What are you doing here? I thought you weren't allowed?"

"Tuka sent for us once the ritual was over."

"Oh. That was nice of him." Pebbles noticed she was still wrapped in a blanket-like cloth. "Where are my clothes?"

"Got 'em right here," Jennifer said. "Let's get you dressed."

While the men turned away, Jennifer held up the blanket while Pebbles redressed.

"What happened during your vision?" Anlon asked.

"Had a heart-to-heart with Citali."

"So, she talked with you. Did you learn anything new?"

"Yeah. Ironically, though, I did most of the talking."

Pebbles emerged from behind the blanket. As she zipped her jacket up, she said, "I'll fill you in on it later. Right now, I want to find the Maerlif. Where's the Sound Stone?"

"Right here," Mereau said. Pebbles turned to see him holding it out toward her. "Tuka says he will show us the hiding place. The honor of finding the beacon, opening it to see what Citali hid should be yours."

"Citali didn't hide anything in it. She took some things, but she never made it back here to replace what she took. You should be the one to open it. It's your people who are buried inside."

"My people?"

"Uh huh. There was no Maerlif in the cave on the mountain. Complete fabrication on Citali's part. One of many. There has only ever been one Maerlif guarded by the generations of Keepers. And it's *here*, where descendants of your people who survived the day of darkness built it after they fled into the jungle to escape Muran…long before Citali was born. I just hope it is intact. I hope Muran didn't find it and desecrate it."

They climbed up farther on the mountain, guided by Tuka and the light provided by torches they took from their places around the pool. Along the way, Pebbles was peppered with questions about her vision. She deferred all answers, saying she would address them later.

Finally, Tuka disappeared behind a thicket of vines. Pebbles and the others followed. They walked along a thin ledge. Overhead, a prominence of the mountain formed an overhang. Where the ledge ended, there was a cave. Inside there were three tunnels. Holding his torch ahead of him, Tuka started down one of them. Pebbles' heart raced. The tunnel looked exactly like the one from Citali's vision on the mountaintop at Churcampa. And just like what Citali had shown Pebbles, the tunnel eventually widened out into a chamber with an arched ceiling.

There was the seashell mosaic of the symbol that looked similar to, though not exactly like, the Paracas Candelabra. On the opposing wall, there were painted scenes. Pebbles had not seen them clearly in Citali's earlier vision of the cave, but it did not take her long to understand their purpose now. Nor did it take long for Cesar to reach the same conclusion.

"No wonder the Keepers have been able to carry the memory of the legend throughout time," he said.

The painted scenes were faded in spots, flaked away in others, but enough remained to decipher the images. They depicted a step-by-step storyline of the goddess and evil spirit legend. Mereau and Cesar studied them with fascination. Pebbles turned to see Anlon examining the seashell mosaic. Tuka stood beside him.

"Pablo," Anlon said, "ask Tuka if he knows what this symbol is. What it's supposed to represent."

After the two men conversed in Tuka's tongue, Pablo said, "It is a torch. A beacon to light the way for the new ones."

"Of course," Anlon said. "The new ones will come by water...light their way."

An image flashed through Pebbles' mind...a beam of light carving a furrow into a hillside. "Citali's last act before fleeing Paracas."

"Excuse me? What's that you say, Pebbles?" Anlon asked.

"The Candelabra. Citali showed me a snippet of her using the Flash Stone to carve it."

"That sure would explain the petrified sand, wouldn't it?" Jennifer said.

"I guess so. It's sad, though," Pebbles said.

"I don't get you. How so?"

"Well, I think she knew she wasn't coming back. I think she knew Muran was going to destroy her city. I'm sure she hoped her children would carry on the legacy, return and rebuild the city. If only she had known they wouldn't survive."

"Wait a minute. You said one of them lived."

"Nah. Just another lie from Citali. They all died, but she wouldn't have known they were going to die when she carved it." Pebbles reached out to touch one of the seashells. "So, in the end, the Candelabra was a symbol that a new one coming by sea wouldn't have understood, even if they had seen it. Only the Keeper knew the meaning. It was a reminder to light the way." She turned to Cesar. "You said the symbol doesn't appear in any other art from Paracas, right?"

"That is correct. It appears nowhere else in all of Mesoamerican art."

Pebbles sighed and turned to Pablo. "I need you and Tuka to come with me."

"Where are you going?" Mereau asked. "The Maerlif. I was going to open it."

"You go ahead, I've got something else I need to do first." Pebbles turned back to Pablo. "Could you ask Tuka to take me to where Citali and her children are buried? I'd like to pay my respects. Tell him, I'd like to pay my respects to Tuka's people too."

"Tuka's people?" Pablo asked.

"Uh huh. The ones who've served as Keepers since Citali died. If you don't want to come, that's cool. I understand it's spooky. Just ask him to show me the way and give me your torch."

Sanjay and Jennifer accompanied Pebbles and Tuka to visit the tomb of the Keepers, while Anlon remained behind with Mereau, Cesar and Pablo at the Maerlif. The speed and skill with which Mereau used the Sound Stone to push open the Maerlif's entry was astounding.

Out of deference to Mereau, Anlon waited in the tunnel chamber to allow the Munuorian to enter the crypt and visit the remains of his descendants. There would be time later to see what was inside. Cesar followed Anlon's lead and joined him at the Candelabra mosaic.

"It's remarkable. Now I know what it is, the symbol makes sense to me," Anlon said. He pointed to the man-like figure on the left of the design. "This looks like it is supposed to represent a new one. The middle prong is the torch. The far right strikes me as a torchlit path. Light the way, show the new ones to the hiding place."

"I see it in a similar way," said Cesar, "though the design on the right might also be a depiction of the Three Sisters. Either way, the intent of the symbolism is the same. Right down to including a mountain, and line from the torch descending into a tunnel below."

From behind, Anlon heard Mereau's voice emanating from the Maerlif entry. "Gentlemen, come see what was hidden. You will not be disappointed."

The tunnel leading to the catacomb of the Keepers terminated in a cavernous space, an open area punctuated with stalagmites protruding from the floor and stalactites extending down from the ceiling. In the center of the space, another mosaic of the Candelabra was inset into the floor. Around the circumference of the space were holes that had been chiseled into the walls. There were two tiers of the spaces. Inside each, the remains of past Keepers rested, wrapped in ceremonial garb.

Pebbles counted a total of eighty-six occupied holes and one empty one. Fifty-six in the bottom tier, thirty on the top. From what Pebbles could judge, there was room for another five to six berths on the second tier and space to go up at least another three tiers, though each tier would have successively fewer berths given the chamber narrowed as it went higher.

Tuka led Pebbles, Sanjay and Jennifer to the empty berth and touched his chest. It was the thirtieth berth of the second tier. He pointed to the first tier below and walked forward nine berths. There, Pebbles saw an elongated skull. The next three chambers held the remains of skeletons with smaller elongated skulls.

Over her shoulder, she heard Jennifer doing the math out loud. "Eighteen hundred years, forty-four Keepers after Citali's last child. That's around forty years per Keeper that followed. So, if we go backward from Citali's berth at thirty-nine, and we assume the average tenure was about the same, the first of the Keepers buried in here is about three thousand years old."

"I wouldn't count on that, Jen," said Pebbles. "I'll bet when Cesar tests the bones, we'll find the oldest are twice that. Depends on how long they imbibed *enjyia* before the art was lost."

"Good point."

"Look at the earlier skulls," Sanjay said. "They are of normal shapes and sizes. It's not until, what, the eleventh, that the shape starts to elongate. Then, of course, after Citali's last child, the skulls return to normal dimensions."

"I wonder what caused the mutation?" Jennifer asked.

"I have given that considerable thought," Sanjay said. "I see one of two explanations. It is either the result of multiple generations of inbreeding… or the introduction of a foreigner into the genetic chain. It would be easy enough to answer through DNA testing, but it would not surprise me if Tuka and his people consider the remains sacred."

"A discussion for another day," Pebbles said. She sat down in front of Citali's tomb and closed her eyes.

"I am here, Citali. I am with you. Your children are beside both of us. They rest in honor. So do you."

A mist arose in Pebbles' mind. She waited for it to clear and for Citali to appear but neither happened. Yet, she could feel Citali's presence. Pebbles heard a thin voice ask, *"What was hidden? Are they safe?"*

"The Maerlif is safe. What was hidden is safe. The Keepers who followed after you honored the pledge. The evil spirit did not find the sacred gifts."

Citali's voice grew stronger. *"The people will rejoice. A new one has come."*

"May the stars light your way, Citali. Rest in peace."

When Pebbles, Jennifer, Sanjay and Tuka returned to the Maerlif entrance, Mereau was standing outside, his eyes red and wet. Standing nearby was Pablo. Mereau spoke to him, "Tell Tuka he may enter and see what was hidden."

Pablo translated the message and Tuka backed away. Pablo relayed the message again and this time received an angry reply. Pablo turned to Mereau. "He says it is forbidden. He is the Keeper. He is not allowed to see what was hidden."

"Very well," Mereau said. "Tell the Keeper the new ones will honor the pledge. The people will have their bowls filled, no evil spirit will haunt them and I, one of the new ones, will teach them anew. Tell him to go share the good news with the people."

After Mereau's proclamation was delivered, Tuka bowed and left the cave, his own eyes red and wet.

Just then, Anlon and Cesar emerged from inside the Maerlif. Anlon looked at Pebbles and said, "Wow."

"It's that amazing?" Pebbles asked.

Anlon stepped aside. "Go see."

Pebbles entered the torchlit Maerlif behind Mereau, so she did not see anything inside the crypt until he moved to the side. When he cleared out of the way, Pebbles could not believe her eyes. The cavern was enormous. Its walls had been shaped into arches that created the impression of a cathedral. Though there were many objects set around the cavern, Pebbles' eyes were drawn to the center of the room where a tree towered toward the ceiling, its roots snaking over the floor. Some of the tree's bark was still white. There remained some pink on its leaves.

"It's not real, is it?" Pebbles asked.

"It is very real…but made of stone. Carved by a master craftswoman." Mereau pointed to a nook to his right. "You may notice some of her other works over there."

Pebbles turned and mumbled, "Oh, my God."

The nook was filled with other stone sculptures. Many of them Pebbles recognized from her sketch pads. Especially the array of flickers. It was further proof that Citali had entered the crypt. The sculptures surrounded a slab bearing the skeletal remains of a woman dressed in crimson and gold. On her chest rested a *Sinethal*.

"There is more," Mereau said.

He guided her to another nook holding the remains of a man. He was surrounded by a vast array of gold jewelry and odd-looking devices. Pebbles felt a headache coming on as they neared the collection. Pebbles noticed he wore a necklace like Citali's and he, too, had a *Sinethal* on his chest. An empty palm of bones rested at his side.

Pebbles turned in a circle and saw a score of other nooks around the cavern. All were occupied by remains, each surrounded by relics. Pebbles recognized some of the relics as *Tyls* but other relics were foreign to her. Many of the slabs holding the remains were painted with emblems and Munuorian inscriptions. All had *Sinethals*.

"What do the inscriptions say, Mereau?"

"They tell of each person laid to rest here and list their ancestors back to the day of darkness." Mereau swept his arm in an arc around the room. "These are all descendants of Munirvo survivors, and I shall get to know them all and learn their stories. They were artisans, craftspeople, farmers, builders. There are even a couple of mariners like me. They are my brothers and sisters. At last their journey is over." Mereau wrapped his arm around Pebbles. "You and I, we meet them under the same sky."

EPILOGUE

Happy was the first to hear them coming. The dog cocked his head from side to side, sniffed the air and then bolted off the patio chair. Sanjay smiled as he watched him round the corner of the house at full speed.

Rising from his own chair, Sanjay ambled from the patio toward the driveway, following the dust trail left behind in Happy's wake. In the distance, he could see Anlon and Pebbles walking down the dirt road, hand in hand. Anlon appeared to be carrying a large shopping bag in his free hand.

At the end of the driveway, Sanjay caught up to Happy, who now raced in circles as he barked at the approaching guests. Sanjay spoke to the dog in a soothing tone. "They will be here soon."

The assurance did little to calm the dog. Sanjay looked left and right down the road. Seeing it was all clear, he said, "Okay, go say hello. Watch the slobber."

Happy took off in a flash, his chubby butt bouncing with each stride. Sanjay waved to Anlon and Pebbles and shouted, "Brace yourselves!"

The dog went for Pebbles first. An understandable choice. She had been a frequent visitor the last few weeks and the two had developed a strong bond. Sanjay wondered how Happy would react once he figured out she would not be visiting regularly anymore.

Sanjay laughed when Happy shifted his affection to Anlon. He began his greeting with a brisk shake of the head, slinging a glob of saliva across his shirt. Anlon turned his body to protect the bag and ignored the liquid greeting.

"Hello, hello!" Pebbles said as she approached Sanjay with open arms.

"Namaste," said the bowing Sanjay.

"Forty-eight days," she said. "Can you believe it?"

"I am happy for you, Pebbles. Your hard work is rewarded."

It had been almost four months since she ascended Three Sisters Falls and brought to an end the nightmares of a restless spirit. But soon after they returned to the States, new dreams had surfaced. Dreams about the brutality she had suffered the year before. Tired of suppressing her emotions and thoughts, she reached out to Sanjay and together they had spent many hours over the past few months talking through her anger and pain. The payoff? It had been forty-eight days since her last nightmare.

"I owe it all to you." She kissed him on the cheek.

"No, you owe it all to yourself." Sanjay turned and shook Anlon's hand. "Good to see you. All ready for your trip around the world?"

"Yes, indeed. It's been a long time coming." Anlon wiped his shirt.

"I understand," Sanjay said. "Come, let us go inside and chat. I am anxious to hear the latest developments about Mereau and the dwellers, Cesar and the Paracas mystery, not to mention what has become of Jennifer and Griffin."

Over a plate of curried chicken sandwiches and a pitcher of iced tea, they talked for over two hours while Happy slept at Sanjay's feet. During that time, Sanjay learned that Mereau had been true to his word to Tuka. Together, the two men had rid the jungle of drug trafficking within a hundred miles of Tuka's village. This had been largely accomplished, Anlon told him, through Mereau's steely negotiations with the drug lords and a few well-placed displays of his manhood.

At first, many in Tuka's community had taken exception to Mereau for disrupting the status quo — after all, the drug lords had been generous to Tuka's tribe — but once Mereau showed them alternative ways of extracting valuable commodities from the jungle, the doubters fell in line.

"It's crazy," Pebbles had said, "but Jennifer was the one who helped Mereau win them over. Well, Cesar helped too."

She explained that Jennifer had remembered an incident from an earlier adventure she had shared with Anlon and Pebbles and had passed her recollection to Mereau.

"The woman who murdered Anlon's uncle, a woman named Margaret Corchran, went on the run after the killing. We probably would never have found her except she ended up getting stabbed in the Amazon jungle in Brazil. An indigenous tribe there, a tribe called the Cinta-Larga, found her, triaged her wounds and brought her to a fishing lodge."

Anlon picked up the tale. "That's right. What we had forgotten, what Jennifer remembered, was that when the Cinta-Larga brought Margaret to the fishing lodge, they performed a ceremony before turning her over to the lodge staff. They bathed her, covered her in a gold cloak and painted a gold emblem on her forehead, the Munuorian symbol for the Sound Stone."

"What?" Sanjay had said. "Why would they have done that?"

"You know, that's funny. That's the same question Mereau asked Jennifer," said Pebbles. "When the Cinta-Larga found Margaret, she apparently had a Sound Stone with her. In their little ceremony at the lodge, the Cinta-Larga cupped her hands around the stone after they dressed her in the golden cloak. Sound familiar?"

"Familiar? It sounds like a near duplicate of the ritual at Three Sisters," Sanjay said.

"Exactly," said Pebbles. "Apparently, the influence of Citali's ancestors stretched pretty deep into the Amazon jungle. Anyway, Jennifer passed her suspicions on to Cesar, and he remembered an ancient legend about a supposedly fictional place in Cinta-Larga territory called the Waterfall of Jewels. The legend said a man wielding a strange device had turned a rocky riverbed into a place where the legend said 'diamonds flowed like water.'"

Anlon finished the story. "The device in the legend was described as a serpent's tooth, a triangular object with a sharp point."

"The Flash Stone," Sanjay said.

"Right," said Pebbles. "So, Jen and Cesar told all this to Mereau, and he decided to use the Flash Stone on a section of the Cutivireni upstream from the Three Sisters. He apparently spewed mud everywhere, but when the river started flowing again, Tuka's people found a whole bunch of diamonds. Now they don't have to rely on drug runners for money to buy stuff the tribe needs."

Sanjay sat back and shook his head. "Incredible."

After a few minutes of quiet reflection, Sanjay asked about Cesar and his work to prove a link between the necklace held by the New Caledonians, the Munuorian Maerlif at Three Sisters and the Paracas Candelabra.

"It's slow going," Anlon said. "The fact that Cesar was able to produce a similar necklace from the Maerlif helps validate the origin of the necklace the New Caledonians have, but the archaeology community has been resistant to accept Cesar's theory about the Candelabra."

Sanjay frowned. "But the Candelabra mosaic outside the Maerlif, the inset in the floor of the catacomb of the Keepers, the mummies inside the catacomb. How can anyone dispute the connection with the Paracas Candelabra or the Paracas mummies?"

Anlon laughed. "You don't know much about the stubbornness of archaeologists, do you? Right now, they view Cesar as a whack-job heretic. But he's not worried. He's been down this path before. In fact, he enjoys proving his pompous colleagues are wrong. Cesar's a lot like my uncle Devlin in that way. As soon as the DNA tests are back on the mummies in the catacomb, he'll have the last laugh."

The conversation then turned to Jennifer and Griffin. Sanjay said, "When last I heard, she was going on tour with the Ice Zombies."

"Yep, that's the plan," Pebbles said, "but she's going to join us for parts of our trip. As much as she's into Griffin, she's not real keen on the roadie-groupie dynamic. Plus, she said she needs some space to figure out her next steps."

"How do you two feel about her joining you?" Sanjay asked. "I imagine you would like some time alone to figure out your next steps too."

Pebbles reached out and gripped Anlon's hand. "That's the thing about the three of us, Sanjay. We kinda like to figure things out together."

Sanjay smiled. "I can see why. You make a good team...apart and together."

"What about you, Sanjay?" Anlon asked. "What's next for you? Pebbles said you were contemplating heading in a new direction."

At that moment, Happy awoke and stared up at Sanjay. "You are spot on, Anlon. I have spent a great deal of time thinking about our adventure, about the implications of psychic energy living on past death, and it has inspired me to take a harder look at reports of past-life recall — my own Pearl Harbor experience and recall experiences of others."

"Sounds exciting," said Anlon.

They talked about Sanjay's plans for another hour before the visit ended. As they stepped outside Sanjay's house, Anlon said, "We're gonna miss coming out to see you, Sanjay."

"We shall miss you both too. Won't we, Happy?"

Happy barked and pawed at Sanjay's legs. As Sanjay bent down to pet the dog's head, he asked Anlon, "How long will you be gone?"

"If all goes according to plan, about a year."

"Good, good. Well, I hope you both have a wonderful time."

"Thank you, Sanjay." Pebbles hugged him. "Thank you for everything."

"It has been my pleasure." Sanjay hugged both of them and then urged Happy to say goodbye.

As Pebbles knelt to kiss Happy on the head, the dog looked up at Sanjay. To all of them, Happy seemed confused.

Sanjay knelt down and scratched Happy's back. "It is okay. I am sure they will come for a visit when they get back."

"Count on it," said Pebbles. "Until then, I made a little something for you. To say thank you, to let you know how much I appreciate everything you did for me, for Citali, for all of us."

Pebbles took hold of the bag Anlon had been carrying and handed it to Sanjay. He reached into the bag and pulled out a large picture frame. In it was one of Pebbles' savant sketches depicting the ritual at the Three Sisters Falls. In a pool at the base of a waterfall, a bare-shouldered woman reached up to take hold of the hand of a man bending over at the water's edge. As Sanjay studied the picture more closely, he noticed there was a reflection of the man's face in the water. But it was not Tuka's face he saw; it was his own.

Sanjay smiled when he realized the meaning behind the gift. During a break in one of her therapy sessions, Pebbles had told him she believed the ceremony had been more than just a symbolic re-enactment of the Keeper welcoming a new one.

"I think it was also intended to symbolize the arrival of the Munuorians after the day of darkness," Pebbles had said. "The new one in the water became one of the asteroid survivors, someone in need of help. The Keeper on shore became one of the Munuorians, someone offering aid."

"A role reversal," Sanjay recalled saying.

"Exactly. The person who conceived the ritual wanted to make sure both parties remembered they had an obligation to help each other, even when their roles were reversed."

Inserting Sanjay into the picture as the Keeper was Pebbles' way of telling Sanjay that he had been there to help her when she needed it, just like the Munuorians had helped the traumatized survivors of the day of darkness. Sanjay looked up at Pebbles and said, "I will treasure this always. As a reminder of the journey we shared *and* of the people who sacrificed so much for so long to make sure we remembered the most important of memories."

ABOARD *SOL SEAKER*
EN ROUTE TO THE GALAPAGOS ISLANDS
JANUARY 18

Anlon stood in the background as Pebbles addressed the crew. She wore jeans cut off at the knees, and a blouse two sizes too big. She was barefoot and wore a patch over one eye. Strutting back and forth in front of the crew as if she was a military commander reviewing her troops, she said, "From this moment forward, ye shall refer to me as Pebbles or you'll be walking the plank. Understood?"

Confused looks abounded on all the crew's faces except for Popeye. He grinned and said, "Aye, milady."

She wheeled around and stepped up within inches of Popeye's face. "It's Pebbles, Popeye. Not milady."

"Aye, me Pebbles."

"Better." She slapped him on the shoulder. Turning her attention back to the rest of the crew, she said, "There's gonna be some more changes around here too. Cap'n Hansen?"

Anlon fought back a smile as the captain first looked at him before answering Pebbles. "Yes, miss, uh, me Pebbles."

"The proper response is *aye*," Pebbles said, lifting the patch to glare at Hansen with both eyes.

"Aye, me Pebbles."

Pebbles turned and winked at Anlon before returning her attention to Hansen. "When we are at sea, we'll be flying the skull and crossbones. There will be no bowing. Only high-fives and fist-bumps are permitted. And under no circumstances are the crew to button the top buttons of their shirts. Is that understood?"

"Aye," Hansen answered, his face turning crimson.

"What about the rest of you salty dogs?"

There was a smattering of tepid *ayes*. Pebbles shook her head and said, "What kind of pirates be ye? Give me a hearty *argh*."

Nervous looks drifted Anlon's way. He shouted *argh* and motioned for the crew to join him. Popeye laughed and slapped Hansen on the back. Then he stood in front of the crew like a symphony conductor and coaxed a boisterous *argh* from all but the captain.

"That's more like it," Pebbles said.

Moments later, she dismissed the crew and turned to face Anlon.

"That was epic," he said. "Feel better?"

"Argh, matey."

GLOSSARY OF MUNUORIAN TERMS

Enjyia – (n-gee-yah) – a drink produced from flowers of plants, the seeds of which are altered by a *Terusael* (described below). *Enjyia's* taste is similar to sweetened herbal tea and it has a translucent, pinkish appearance. Munuorians who consistently imbibed *enjyia* were able to live for up to five hundred years.

Gensae – (jen-say) – the Munuorians' magnetic sixth sense.

Lifintyls – (liff-in-tills) – Munuorian translation: survival tools. The set of six Munuorian tools/stones depicted on the etching carved into a *Sinethal*. The *Lifintyls* were magnetized devices forged by the Munuorian civilization. Except for *Sulataers* (described below), the composition of each *Tyl* (tool) was a combination of three magnetic stone types: olivine basalt, kimberlite and pure diamond. The *Tyls'* different powers were dictated by the relative concentration of the three magnetic stone types and their unique shaping. The six *Tyls* are described below:

Aromaegh – (air-uh-may) – Munuorian translation: teacher, helper. A square or rectangular tile that houses virtual-reality-like recordings (sights, sounds, aromas, touch and taste). A *Sinethal* is one type of *Aromaegh*. *Aromaeghs* were created to store the collective memories, skills and accomplishments of the Munuorian civilization. They were used

302 Priestess of Paracas

to transfer knowledge from one generation to the next, to teach specific skills and to retain important cultural events and memories.

≈ **Breylofte** – (bray-loft) – Munuorian translation: air mover. A bowl-shaped stone that amplifies sound waves to levitate and move objects. Devised as a building tool, *Breyloftes* helped Munuorians place or remove large, heavy objects. They are also used as medium-range weapons to blast or throw opponents and objects.

👌🖐 **Dreylaek** – (dray-lock) – Munuorian translation: healer, defender. A cookie-shaped and -sized stone. Two of them are needed to create their desired effects. When two *Dreylaeks* are rubbed together or slapped one against the other, different powers are generated. If slapped with no grinding, *Dreylaeks* can generate a close-quarters blast of air. If slapped together after grinding, *Dreylaeks* emit a thin laserlike beam that can be used to treat injuries (e.g., cauterize wounds, conduct surgery) or as deadly short-range weapons.

▶🐟 **Sulataer** – (soo-la-tare) – Munuorian translation: stone melter. A token/coin made of pure, 24-karat gold. *Sulataers* are embossed with a fish symbol on each side. The coins were used by the Munuorians to trade with foreign nations/tribes, and they also served as electricity conductors during *overtae*, the mind-transfer process, regulating the flow of electricity generated by a *Tuliskaera* into a *Taellin*.

🐦 **Terusael** – (tare-uh-sail) – Munuorian translation: the refresher. An egg-shaped stone, used in conjunction with a *Breylofte*, to alter the chemistry of the seeds from poisonous flowers into seeds that produce life-extending flowers. The altered flowers are crushed into a tincture called *enjyia*. The enzymes in *enjyia* attack diseased cells in the body, which slows the aging process, thereby extending life.

✳ **Tuliskaera** – (tool-uh-scare-uh) – Munuorian translation: fire cutter. A cone-shaped stone that produces a powerful laser when used in conjunction with a *Naetir* (described below). *Tuliskaeras* were used by the Munuorians to cut and shape objects (mostly stone objects). *Tuliskaeras* can also be used as long-range weapons against structures and people, and they provide the jolt of electricity needed to facilitate the transfer of a Munuorian's memories and consciousness into a *Sinethal*.

Maerlif – (mare-liff) – the vaults/chambers where the *Lifintyls* were stored prior to the Munirvo catastrophe. Maerlifs were also used as burial tombs of Andaers and prominent Munuorian citizens.

Munirvo – (moon-ear-voh) – the passing asteroid that nearly wiped out all life on Earth ten thousand years ago. The name means "star washer."

Munuoria – (moon-war-E-uh) – the Munuorian homeland.

Munuorians – (moon-war-E-uns) – the lost civilization. The name means "star watchers."

Naetir – (neigh-teer) – Munuorian translation: spark. A hockey-puck-shaped stone that served as a catalyst to operate *Tuliskaeras*, *Dreylaeks* and *Aromaeghs* (including the *Sinethal*).

Seybalrosa – (say-ball-rose-uh) – a Munuorian cliffside shrine that features a massive ceiba tree surrounded by a garden of saguaro cacti.

Sinethal – (sin-uh-thawl) – Munuorian translation: mind keeper. A specific type of *Aromaegh* that houses the memories and partial consciousness of select Munuorians, including Malinyah. Unlike other *Aromaeghs* (which contain static presentations or tutorials), *Sinethals* are interactive. A user can ask questions of, and receive answers from, the Munuorian whose memories and consciousness are stored on a *Sinethal*. Not only does a *Sinethal* interactively share sensory experiences (sights, sounds, aromas, touch and taste), but it also shares emotions associated with memories.

ABOUT THE AUTHOR

Kevin Patrick Donoghue is the author of the mystery thriller series the Anlon Cully Chronicles and the science-fiction thriller series the Rorschach Explorer Missions. He lives in the northern Virginia suburbs of Washington, D.C., with his wife and two sons. His books include:

THE ANLON CULLY CHRONICLES:

Book 1: *Shadows of the Stone Benders*
Book 2: *Race for the Flash Stone*
Book 3: *Curse of the Painted Lady*
Book 4: *Priestess of Paracas*

THE RORSCHACH EXPLORER MISSIONS:

Prequel: *UMO* (novella)
Book 1: *Skywave*
Book 2: *Magwave*

WAYS TO STAY IN TOUCH WITH THE AUTHOR:

Follow K. Patrick Donoghue — Novelist on Facebook
Join the author's email subscriber list by visiting
kpatrickdonoghue.com and clicking on the
"Join Email List" link on the top menu bar.

Made in the USA
Monee, IL
29 June 2020

35344528R00185